VESUVIUS

Published by Peachtree Teen
An imprint of PEACHTREE PUBLISHING COMPANY INC.
1700 Chattahoochee Avenue
Atlanta, Georgia 30318-2112
PeachtreeBooks.com

Text © 2025 by Cassidy Biehn
Jacket and interior illustrations © 2025 by Chris Sack

All rights reserved. No part of this publication may be reproduced, stored in a retrieval system, or transmitted in any form or by any means—electronic, mechanical, photocopy, recording, or any other—except for brief quotations in printed reviews, without the prior permission of the publisher.

Design and composition by Lily Steele
Edited by Zoie Konneker

Content Advisory: This narrative contains mentions of sexual assault, emotional and physical abuse, mental illness, suicidal ideation, homophobia, violence, death, and physical injury.

Printed and bound in April 2025 at Sheridan, Chelsea, MI, USA.
10 9 8 7 6 5 4 3 2 1
First Edition
ISBN: 978-1-68263-732-6

Library of Congress Cataloging-in-Publication Data

Names: Biehn, Cass, author.
Title: Vesuvius / Cass Biehn.
Description: First edition. | Atlanta, Georgia : Peachtree Teen, 2025. | Audience term: Teenagers | Audience: Ages 14 and up. | Audience: Grades 10-12. | Summary: "In the final days of Pompeii, two boys—Felix and Loren—must grapple with closely-guarded secrets and untangle myth, magic, and memory to escape the burning city alive"— Provided by publisher.
Identifiers: LCCN 2024044776 | ISBN 9781682637326 (hardcover) | ISBN 9781682637999 (ebook)
Subjects: CYAC: Vesuvius (Italy)—Eruption, 79—Fiction. | Pompeii (Extinct city)—Fiction. | Secrets—Fiction. | Memory—Fiction. | LGBTQ+ people—Fiction. | Fantasy. | LCGFT: Historical fiction. | Fantasy fiction. | Romance fiction. | Queer fiction. | Novels.
Classification: LCC PZ7.1.B533525 Ve 2025 | DDC [Fic]—dc23
LC record available at https://lccn.loc.gov/2024044776

EU Authorized Representative: HackettFlynn Ltd., 36 Cloch Choirneal, Balrothery, Co. Dublin, K32 C942, Ireland. EU@walkerpublishinggroup.com

VESUVIUS

CASS BIEHN

PEACHTREE *Teen*

I loved you, so I wrote you into
my mythology—

the creation and breaking
and revision of me.

AUTHOR'S NOTE

Vesuvius was born in the summer of 2020, when the world had shut down, but suffering had escalated. I was angry, I was isolated, and I was scared. So I did what I'd always done, what my blood and bones know to do: I wrote what I needed to read.

I needed a book about two queer kids changing their fate. I needed a book to show that while trauma molds us, it does not define us. I needed a book about facing down the end of the world—a swallowing dark wave—and saying *no*.

Though heavily researched, I'm the first to admit that *Vesuvius* takes some creative liberties with history. But one thing will forever be true: Queer people existed in ancient times as they exist today. Young people like Felix and Loren lived and loved then as they do now—and my hope is that you, the reader, can see yourself or a friend in their story.

At the time *Vesuvius* goes to print, we're on the precipice of great global change. From a rise in banned books to politicians challenging our right to exist and to love and to have autonomy over our own bodies, it's probable that scary times are ahead, especially for those most vulnerable in our communities. But I think now more than ever, it's heartening to look back at how queer people have always existed throughout history, even in the face of insurmountable odds. Queerness is beautiful, diverse, and—most importantly—resilient. When we stick together and find community, our stories will never be lost.

Just like Felix and Loren in *Vesuvius*, we're here, we're facing down the dark wave, and we're saying *no*.

—cass

CHAPTER I
FELIX

Felix robbed the Temple of Apollo just before dawn.

Temples were embarrassingly easy. Bolts of fine fabrics, sacks of coins, baskets of cherries left to rot—any thief worth his salt knew it was fair game. Nothing fun about it. So unchallenging, in fact, that the afternoon prior, following a quick scout, Felix almost looked the other way. Moved on.

Until he spotted Apollo's treasure: a shiny silver helmet unguarded on a plinth and begging to wear Felix's fingerprints all over it. A feeling far stronger than want sparked in his gut, a magnetic pull to an item that'd buy him a damn palace if he rolled his dice right.

No question about it. Felix would own the helmet.

At a tavern, he challenged the temple's guard to a drinking game until the man slipped into a wine-thick slumber. After, edging daybreak, Felix crept into the temple, snagged the helmet, and strolled out. Too easy.

In retrospect, he should have realized much sooner that he was being followed.

Two streets from the Forum, muffled footsteps fell in sync with his. Fine. Felix could shake them. He picked up the pace. When the soft *schnick* of a gladius drawn from its sheath split the night air, he moved a little faster.

Felix had spent less than a day in Pompeii, but like any good Roman town, it was laid out in a grid. It didn't matter if he took two detours or ten, the side streets would spit him out onto the main road eventually. His sandals slapped against uneven cobblestones. Novice move. Every thief knew the best work was accomplished barefoot, in silence. But this was supposed to be an easy job. In, out, on the road. Let the city lament its stolen treasure when Felix was already halfway to Herculaneum.

Screw it. Ducking into an alley, Felix spared half a second to kick off his sandals. His only pair, but not worth more than his hands. Or his neck. Once he sold the silver, he'd replace them. That was the elegance of rejecting sentimentality. If you never got attached, losing things was just that. Simple.

Cradling the helmet under his arm, Felix set off again, footfalls whisper-quiet.

His plan should have worked. He'd pulled off trickier heists with far more to lose. Like the other week, when he stole half a dozen bottles of top-shelf wine from the Lassius vineyard south of the city. Felix had made a decent profit hawking them in Salernum's market before guards ran him from town. Really, it wasn't fair. Reselling wasn't a crime per se.

Speaking of wine—Felix made another detour to grab his satchel, stashed in an alcove. Salernum's guards may have taken his earnings, but he still had one bottle left, and he intended to cash in on it.

Then he dashed for the city wall. A giddy, hushed laugh bubbled in his chest, a burgeoning high from the thrill of the game. Damn, he was good at this.

Right then, bare feet flying over stone in a backwater city he never had to see again, Felix had no past. He had no future.

He had that moment. It was exactly enough.

But all the luck Felix's name promised him ran out at the gate.

Like he'd read Felix's mind, a bulky man waited under the archway leading out of Pompeii, a scarlet cape dripping from his shoulders. Not a city guard. The officer Felix had drunk with wore muted brown. This was some patrician's private guard, the type desperate to do their master's dirty work, even when it broke the law.

Hoping against hope the guard hadn't seen him, Felix turned and picked a different path. Time for a new plan. He was good at that, shifting strategies as easily as slipping coins from a pocket. If he ever took an apprentice—perish the thought, children made him uncomfortable— Felix would teach the core rules the way his da' had taught him. Rule one, of course, was: Don't love anything you can't stand to lose.

Rule two: Know when to quit the chase.

Felix wouldn't make it out of Pompeii this morning. But he could stash the helmet for now, reclaim it when a sword-wielding guard wasn't dogging his heels. A trio of crates sat tucked down an alley. He pried the lid off one and found it full of milled grain. But when he settled the helmet inside, he hesitated. Grain spilled between the twin metal wings framing a sharp nose plate and hollow eyes. An uncanny sensation of recognition washed over him. Like those eyes had stared him down before, but he couldn't place where. When.

Felix shook the feeling off and focused on his real connection to the helmet—what it could buy. His hands had never held value like this. The helmet was his ticket to the next ten towns, and that meant staying alive another few months. It meant bread in his belly that he bought instead of snuck, or a bed of his own where he didn't feel the discomfort of another's body so near. Watching wheat swallowing silver swooped his stomach the same way dropping from a height did.

If only his father could see Felix now, mourning what he'd only held for just a moment.

"I'll be back," Felix swore.

The helmet, buried in grain, offered no reply.

Replacing the cover and brushing off his hands, he strolled back onto the main road.

He only made it two blocks before the point of a sword met the nape of his neck.

"To your knees."

When Felix didn't obey, the guard swiped his blade across the back of Felix's calves, the pain so startling he collapsed. Blood trickled from the twin cuts, sluicing through the dust on his legs in slick, sticky rivers. A half-formed thought crossed his mind—that he should crawl away—but he wouldn't make it a foot before the guard's blade found a different place to slice.

A large hand wrapped around Felix's throat from behind and tightened.

"How did you take the helmet?" the guard demanded.

Felix struggled. Seemed the wrong question to ask. Wouldn't a more productive one be—

"*Where* is the helmet?"

"Don't know what you mean," Felix wheezed. The grip constricted. He clawed any skin he could reach, aimed an elbow and missed spectacularly. Useless. White spots, then—

Freedom. Felix slumped, palms pressed to the cobblestones, chest heaving.

"You'll come with me," the guard said.

He didn't leave Felix with a choice. He dragged him up by his tunic. Breath hot in Felix's ear, the guard muttered, "Make noise and I'll gut you. Leave your body to stink in the streets."

Felix swallowed hard, dread coiling his nerves. The guard pushed and prodded him to a different section of the city. Cobblestones changed color, worn gray shifting to modern red. The villas here were newer, gated and walled, a sure sign this was the wealthy part of town. Only society's richest could afford this degree of privacy, walls clean of graffiti, no vulgar anatomical artwork to be seen. They halted before one of the larger houses, but the guard didn't usher Felix through the front gate. Instead, he was marched down a side street to the servants' entrance.

Candlelight illuminated the small chamber Felix was shoved into. An alcove in the wall held a pair of carved ivory statues, a dancer and a jester. They must be the household gods. Lares, symbols of the owner's values, home protectors, and other things Felix didn't waste his breath or coin on. He didn't know which minor deities this pair represented. In the dim light, the jester's grin stretched into a leer, and the dancer's limbs were pulled too long, like misshapen dough. Felix shivered away.

"Drop your bag, thief," the guard said.

Felix's lip curled. "I didn't take anything. But if this is how you handle petty theft, I'd hate to see you deal with a real criminal."

His satchel was ripped off his shoulder and upended. Cherries and coins—so what if he dipped into the stash when he scouted the temple that afternoon?—scattered across tile. Felix's last bottle of wine rolled out like an accusation.

Felix stifled a wince. "All mine. Mine before."

Brow raised, the guard picked a ring of skeleton keys from the mess. *Jupiter*.

"I apprentice with a locksmith."

"Right." The keys clanked as the guard tossed them to the side. "Now explain the wine."

"Plan on interrogating me over everything in my bag? You're in for a long night."

"Not an interrogation," a cool voice said. "Thank you, Darius. I will take it from here."

A figure leaned against the wall, his arrival so sudden and silent he might have materialized from shadow. For such an early hour, he was immaculately dressed, tunic pressed, tall boots laced. Leather gloves encased his hands. A badge glinted at his shoulder, a crest of a swooping hawk. Some kind of statesman, a politician or patrician.

"So this is the thief," the statesman said. "Have a seat."

"Not a thief," Felix muttered. But the statesman merely smiled, impassive. Felix's skin crawled, the hair on his arms standing on end. This was the sort of man who looked as though he'd never held a strong opinion in his life. Those men, in Felix's experience, were the most dangerous. No commitment to any one cause, they'd change their mind on a whim if the outcome suited them better.

Darius the guard retreated to the door, stance casual but sword still drawn.

Felix sat on the edge of a wicker chair and chanced a glance around. He'd have to brave Darius to slip outside, and diving through the other door would only suck him deeper into a strange house. He wouldn't get out of this by force, at least not yet.

For the first time, Felix noticed the painting dominating the back wall: a conical mountain with steep slopes and Bacchus, god of wine, blessing the fertile soil. Below writhed a snake. He recognized the mountain as the one north of the city: Vesuvius. But he wondered what—or who—the snake was meant to represent.

The statesman held up the bottle. "Expensive taste. This isn't your everyday drink."

Felix knew. That was the point.

His back facing Felix, the statesman popped the cork, and Felix glowered as ruby liquid poured into a pair of silver cups. Sealed, that bottle could have bought him new sandals. When the statesman turned, he passed one cup to Felix. On instinct, Felix brought it to his nose. Sugar, mostly. Then—an undercurrent of acrid.

"You dosed this." Felix sniffed again. "Poppy sap. Lassius wine is sickly sweet. This stinks of bitter."

"Well-versed in poison?"

"No." Felix set his cup firmly on the tiled floor. "I just drink too much."

"Clever." Wicker and wood creaked as the statesman settled into the chair opposite. In the flickering candlelight, his eyes seemed drained of color. Reflecting orange flame, but otherwise empty. "I'll admit, the wine was a test. You passed."

"I'm not your student."

"Too clever for games, I see."

Felix had the distinct impression he was being mocked. *Don't rise to it.* Still, whatever his expression betrayed must've been satisfactory. Amusement tugged the statesman's lips.

"Tell me, boy. Do you believe in magic?"

Felix snorted. "No. Horseshit."

The statesman ran his gloved index finger around the rim of his own cup. Round and around. Unease grew as Felix tracked the movement. Nails bit into the meat of his palms. He hadn't realized how tightly he was clenching his fists until the sting reminded him to stay in the moment. He made his trade in details, the cataloging of them, the weaponizing. Being a thief was about spotting the right details and not letting a stranger distract him with others.

"Interesting position to take," the statesman continued. "For you, anyway. Tell me who you studied under. A priest? Which temple?"

"Couldn't tell you."

"Don't you remember?"

Felix shifted. The comment teased wounds where the only memories left were scars. Normally it suited him fine, lacking the ability to remember. Dwelling on history, fixating on the future—neither pastime kept him alive. But something about the statesman's question prodded Felix the same way wicker bands jabbed his sliced calves.

Rich people had the worst furniture.

"I consider myself a collector," the statesman continued. With an arrogant flip of his wrist, he held his cup to the side. Wordlessly, Darius came forward to whisk it away. "Land. Items. People, when it suits me. I have a specialized interest."

"What does this have to do with me?"

"Because I saw you in the Forum earlier, casing the temple. Subtle, but I recognized how hungrily you watched the helmet. As if you would die for it. Or worse." The statesman's smile widened. "Do you realize how precious that helmet is? Some call it divine, and Pompeiians are a superstitious bunch. They take everything as an omen, and they won't take news of its disappearance easily, nor exercise clemency when they catch its thief. But you and I have more in common than you know. Two wanderers who lost our homes, trying to find a way back to them. The helmet can help us both get there."

Sweat beaded on the nape of Felix's neck. He itched to demand how a helmet could help reclaim home. How the statesman knew Felix didn't *have* a home, not since he fled Rome six years ago, but asking questions would betray he knew about the helmet, an admission he couldn't afford.

Besides, this man already had everything, a house and guards and silver cups. The statesman could buy twenty helmets. He could have stolen this helmet himself, then staged its triumphant recovery, if that was what he wanted. Somehow, Felix didn't think that was the statesman's goal.

He repeated, "Horseshit."

"At least entertain my offer before baiting me toward anger, as I've humored you."

But thieves weren't humored. It was a kill-first, question-later lifestyle.

"Afraid I can't help you." Felix rose, sizing up Darius blocking the exit. "My father is waiting for me."

The statesman allowed Felix to make it halfway to the door. Then he said, voice the drawl of a lazy predator, "Your father is dead."

Felix stiffened, vision flashing red as bloodied pavement. "What would you know about my father?"

His sudden rage distracted him. Seizing the opportunity, Darius lunged and slammed Felix to the ground. He wrenched Felix's wrists behind his back, shoving his chest against the floor.

"A fortunate guess." The statesman paced to Felix's front, peering down his nose. "You could say I know how to inspire reaction. Where is the helmet?"

"I don't know," Felix snarled, wriggling pointlessly.

"You will bring it to me. Bring it to me, and you may leave the city with a full purse. I'll even give you a horse. Wouldn't that be a treat."

"Liar." Felix spat. It landed an inch from the statesman's leather boot.

The statesman sighed. "A different approach, then. Let's see if my technique works. Once you remember what was taken from you, you'll be as keen for revenge on Rome as I am."

Darius hauled Felix to his knees by his tunic for a second time. By sunrise—if he survived that long—his knees would be a blue, battered mess. Felix felt less than human, teeth bared and chest heaving, but the statesman appeared unconcerned as he knelt before him. Distantly, he was aware of the statesman peeling off his leather gloves, but he couldn't tear his eyes from the colorless gaze locking him in place.

"We'll be partners," said the statesman wistfully. "Collaborators. Cassius and Brutus of a new age."

He cupped Felix's jaw in his bare hands, and Felix slumped into a dim nothing.

Or not nothing.

VESUVIUS

He had the strange sensation of . . . falling. Dragged by a weight, bricks tied to his ankles, he plummeted backward. Blood pounded in his ears. Scenes teased him, memories of the night he'd had, told in reverse: cool cobblestones underfoot, smooth silver in his hand. Earlier, the sour tang of cheap wine while a drunk guard slumped across a table.

Earlier. An open road, stolen wine clinking in his bag.

Earlier, still. Salernum's city stench. The Lassius vineyard by moonlight.

A thumb prodded Felix's memory, flipping through scenes of his near past like sifting through a stack of papyrus. Searching. The sensation was uncomfortable, invasive, a foul mix of foreign and familiar. It churned his stomach, made him ache to flinch. He didn't tolerate touch well on a good day, and this was far from a good day.

Further back. To the time Felix had spent in the south of the empire, considering catching a ferry across the sea to Alexandria before learning the cost outweighed his pockets. He traced his path north in reverse, sleepless nights and heart-pounding chases and scattered roof tiles.

Until, at last, it landed on the road from Rome. There the thumb paused. Contemplated.

But nothing existed beyond that gate, Felix knew. He had lingered in that memory-space enough times to have lost hope of remembering what once dwelt there.

Except—in flashes—twin snakes curling up his father's forearm. A statue on a dais, pointing to the heavens, hollow eyed, a man in long robes shuffling near—

The clatter of silver on stone struck the memory down, and Felix opened his eyes. The statesman's hand had fallen away. Felix sucked in a breath so full it tore his lungs. His mind spun. At his side, wine spread across tile, his abandoned cup having tipped over unprompted. The statesman, too, looked shaken.

Then the ground lurched beneath Felix's knees, and he realized it was the world that was shaking.

Darius's grip loosened, and Felix scrambled away. Another grab. He was quicker.

He had no idea what was happening, how the statesman had made him lose consciousness, why the world was cracking apart, any of it, but he wasn't about to waste this chance. He catapulted through the door, into the alley, and sprinted.

Running over angry ground was treacherous. Cobblestones jumped to bite his ankles. Tiles crashed from roofs, shattering in deadly shards. Felix was dimly aware of shouting as the city received this violent awakening, but all that faded to background noise.

Because Darius still chased him, like not even the end of the damn world would shake him off Felix's tail.

Think. *Think*. Gods, his legs ached.

Felix had passed a temple on his way into the city yesterday, and he riffled through his mind, trying to pick out the street it stood on. If he could reach it, he could claim sanctuary. Time spent in any temple had never served his goals before—had compromised them, most often—but the attendants inside would be bound by ancient laws to honor that claim. All he had to do was survive long enough to get there.

Up ahead, a heavy wooden door beckoned Felix forward. He leaped up the few short stairs, slammed through the unlocked door, and prayed for the first time in years that someone was inside.

He found himself in an open-air courtyard, surrounded by a portico of marble columns and painted frescoes. An altar, bowl absent, jutted from packed dirt, and the temple's inner chamber, the cella, loomed in the center.

Empty. *Jupiter.*

Barefoot and bloody, his pulse thrummed. He trained his eyes on the door, waiting for Darius to barrel through. He envisioned iron arcing through air, a deadly downward crescent. One step back. Two.

Light spilled in a crisp, golden streak. A sharp intake of breath from behind.

Felix wasn't alone as he'd thought.

He turned. At the top of the cella's steps, a tall figure had frozen, half silhouetted in the glow of the open door. A veil obscured the lower part of their face. Felix's eyes fell onto long, elegant fingers clutching a bronze bowl. He tottered. For a brief, bleary second, he was certain he was in the company of a god. But no. Impossible. Felix rejected the thought as soon as it passed, for the same reason he refused to dwell on what the statesman had done to his mind.

Both broke Felix's most vital rule of all: *Magic isn't worth the cost of belief.*

Still, Felix stared, transfixed, as the figure descended the stairs, each footfall a sharp echo in the silent courtyard. He hardly dared breathe lest it shatter the spell.

The stranger whispered, "Not you."

Then the bronze bowl crashed against the side of Felix's head.

CHAPTER II
LOREN

Loren's life was easier before he started dreaming of the copper-haired ghost.

Months of jolting from sleep in a cold sweat, the ghost's name lingering on the tip of his tongue, out of reach, and now he was here to haunt Loren in person.

Except ghosts surely didn't crumple after being struck with an altar bowl.

This was a boy, flesh and blood, and Loren had killed him. Just like that.

By pure luck, Loren reacted in time to catch him before he hit the floor. They sank to the ground together, the boy's curls splayed over his lap.

"I'm so sorry," Loren said. "So, *so* sorry."

He didn't stir.

In all fairness, the subject of Loren's worst nightmares showing up blood splattered and wild-eyed at his job was more than a little unsettling. Especially after the night he'd had, tossing and turning and shouting awake, then the quake . . . But dear Isis, he hadn't meant to commit murder. Fear and guilt swirled in his stomach. Clumsy fingers searched for a pulse, but his hands shook so badly he doubted he'd found the right point.

Raised voices and pounding feet at the temple's entrance knocked Loren from his reverie.

"This is sacred ground," barked Camilia, another temple attendant. "Sheathe your sword."

She tried to block a man in leather armor from charging into the courtyard. Loren had to give her credit. Short but fierce, Camilia threw orders like a legionnaire captain, all while dressed in a sleeping tunic, cropped hair tangled as a bird's nest. Privately, Loren marveled at the speed with which she'd got here following the quake. Camilia lived across town, but nothing, not even distance, could stand between her and the temple during a crisis.

"You harbor a criminal," the guard said. "By order of my master—"

"I don't care if your master is Emperor Titus himself. You will not come in here. We have no criminals."

Camilia didn't know, Loren realized. She hadn't seen him yet. Hooking his arms around the body, Loren attempted to edge them both behind the altar. The boy's head lolled sickeningly. Camilia's back faced them, but the guard spotted the movement. He gestured with his gladius.

"Explain that."

Camilia turned.

Sometimes Loren wished his mystical gift was less prophetic in nature and more like the thought-sharing sort he read about in stories. At least that would be useful, something he could control. Particularly in times like these, when Camilia glared him down, eyes unreadable. Loren found himself the recipient of this look far too often lately.

I'll tell you everything. Every detail. Loren thought it as hard as he could at her. *Just get rid of him.*

Camilia's jaw clenched.

"Goddess Isis is a friend to the downtrodden," she said at last. "We provide sanctuary to all."

The guard sneered. "The thief didn't come here for sanctuary."

"Thief or not, you can't touch him under our protection. Surely your master is familiar with Roman law?"

Loren's heart raced. Camilia's boldness toed a line. Temple grounds or not, women didn't have the option of being bold when it came to dealings with sword-wielding men.

The guard's eyes slid past Loren and lingered on the collapsed body. After an excruciating pause, he sheathed his sword.

"I will report what transpired here." He nodded, reeking of condescension, before striding from the temple.

Camilia stayed stiff until the door stopped swinging, then exhaled. "That should keep him from our hair for now."

"For now," Loren echoed dully.

She hurried to Loren's side, brushing the boy's curls back for a better look at his blood-drained face. He couldn't be much older than Loren's age, sixteen. "Gods, Loren, what did you do to him? Is he alive?"

"It was an *accident*." Loren yanked off his smothering veil. "Well, I hit him, but only because he frightened me."

"He attacked you?"

Loren laughed, a choked little noise. There was another point in his defense: Anyone who witnessed the brutality he endured nightly would have reacted the same, bowl and all. But Camilia didn't believe his dreams. She had already made that clear.

She checked the boy's pulse. "Still beating. Good. I don't know what we'd do if we had to hide a body."

Too late, Loren caught her teasing tone. But the joke didn't hit. He was too overwhelmed by the confirmation that he hadn't, in fact, killed someone. He scrapped his defense tally—no murder, no murder trial.

Together they lugged the thief, as the guard called him, into the private quarters. No sooner had they settled him on a chaise than he stirred, lashes fluttering and lips parting. Camilia frowned. From her tunic pocket, she withdrew a vial. Uncorking it, she dripped liquid into his open mouth.

"Diluted poppy sap," she explained. "Should keep him quiet for a few hours until we figure out what to do with him."

"You carry that in your nightclothes?"

"Helps me sleep. Must be careful, though. It's potent." She tucked the vial away. "He's handsome, isn't he? Look at that clever jaw."

Despite their circumstances, Loren's cheeks burned, and he pretended for the world that the thief had no jaw at all, let alone a clever one. *Gods*. "I thought you weren't attracted to boys. Men."

"I still have eyes." She left Loren kneeling by the couch to fix a toppled stool. "How did the building fare?"

Loren blinked. The thief's arrival had caught him so off guard he'd nearly forgotten the quake. "No major damage, I think, but I didn't inspect. Castor and Pollux bolted. I don't know when we'll see them again."

He tore his eyes from the rise and fall of the boy's chest and scooted back. Distance eased his rattled nerves. Pulling his hair over his shoulder, he picked apart his sleep-mussed braid and started over. It wasn't until he reached the end that he realized his hands were still trembling.

"Loren?"

He jumped when Camilia touched his shoulder. Craning his neck, he offered a half smile.

She met it with a frown. "Are you all right?"

"The quake put me on edge."

"You were here early."

"Thought I'd start the chores."

"Well-timed that you were here, with the quake." Her eyes narrowed. "Well-timed that the altar flame had already been put out. That the bowl wasn't on the altar at all."

So she had noticed. Loren gnawed his lip.

"Tell me you weren't trying to scry again," Camilia snapped. "Tell me you aren't possibly that—"

Loren didn't have the patience to rehash this same argument after a night of no sleep. He knew it wasn't his place to scry. He knew he upset the divine order of Olympus by being a "non-ordained oracle with a penchant for meddling," or however Camilia phrased it. The last thing he needed was to be reminded of his own delusion. Again.

"We should return to the courtyard," Loren said tersely. "If the quake woke you, it's only a matter of time before the Priest arrives."

Camilia leveled him with one final glare before sweeping from the room.

The thief shifted, but lost in the deep pool of poppy sap, he didn't stir other than a brief furrow of his brow, as if he too saw unpleasantries in his sleep. Loren could've laughed if the situation at all warranted it. Instead, he felt ill.

If the thief woke, would he reach for a knife? Would he become the lifeless, cruel ghost Loren was all too intimate with? Burn the city, the way he did in Loren's dreams? Which of his friends would the thief cut down?

How long until the thief collapsed Pompeii's sky, with all of them trapped beneath?

Loren came to Pompeii with hopes of using his gift to help. To prove his value beyond his family name. But his visions only showed hurt, with no way he could fathom to stop it.

"Why you?" Loren whispered, ragged. "Why now?"

No answer. There never was.

Loren lingered by the thief's side a moment more, staring at anything *but* him, wondering if there was a way he could turn back time. Wondering if it would make a difference.

By the time Loren quelled his shaking fingers by rebraiding his hair thrice, sunrise was upon them, and the others trudged in.

They were an odd assortment, this cult of Isis. For one, they had the Priest, a man older than stone, who spent most of his days inhaling fumes wafting off the altar. Then there were the twins, Sera and Shani, two middle-aged women who never seemed to enjoy being around each other, or anyone else for that matter. Camilia, of course, and Loren.

And Celsi, the previous errand boy, but they didn't mention him anymore.

Sera's voice hit Loren's ears first, louder and more sinister than her sister's. He cringed as he edged back into the courtyard.

"—another quake," she was saying. "Three in as many months. If I didn't know better, I would think the gods were angry."

"You do think the gods are angry," Shani replied mildly. "You said so just last night."

The sisters supported a hobbled figure, the Priest, still half asleep. As Sera and Shani bickered, Loren crept to join Camilia. In his absence, she had tamed her hair, pulled on attendant robes, and returned the bowl-turned-weapon to the altar. Now she coaxed a small fire to burn higher.

"Have you thought what we should tell them?" he whispered.

"Is that my problem?" Camilia placed a bundle of incense in the crackling flames. Blue smoke curled into the early sky.

The Priest finally roused, and he pointed to Loren. "You, child," he said, and Loren felt the warm glow of acknowledgment for a heartbeat before the old man continued, "fetch a stool."

Loren held back a sigh. *Errand boy.* Retrieving the spindly stool, he placed it beside the altar, and Shani helped the Priest settle onto it. He inhaled the burning herbs, eyes glazing over.

"Mm, that is nice. Camilia, dear, what are these fumes?"

Camilia frowned. "Purchased from the hemp shop."

The Priest smacked his lips. "Divine. Now, where were we?"

"Earthquakes," said Shani.

"The gods' wrath," offered Sera.

"Perhaps a bit of both," the Priest said. "It does make one wonder. Back in my day, the earth shaking called for great appeasement. Greater than burning a bit of hemp, at any rate."

"Back in our day," Sera said, "the gods listened."

Shani scoffed. "Oh, don't let her start. Harping about the old days like the crone remembers last week."

Sera's nostrils flared, but Camilia stepped between them. "Save it for the Forum. Or the tavern."

Loren let himself huff properly this time, pulling away to slump on the stairs of the cella. Another day of pointless bickering, no different from his past four years here, where everyone had a voice but him and nothing was accomplished. He suspected if he told them about the thief's starring role in his nightmares, they might turn an ear. But only long enough to laugh. Or grow angry with him, the way Camilia had, for meddling where he shouldn't. Sometimes Loren feared he bore the curse of Cassandra, the Greek prophetess: cursed to speak truths, doomed to be painted a liar.

All Loren needed was a chance.

"A boy sleeps in the back," he blurted, ears burning hot when four shocked pairs of eyes turned on him. "He claimed sanctuary this morning. We don't know his name, but—"

"Is he handsome?" Sera asked at the same time Shani cooed, "Poor dear."

Camilia's mouth twitched down, but Loren met her glare. Likely, despite her snark otherwise, she'd been concocting some grand revelation of the thief's presence to prove to the Priest what a good temple trainee she was. Loren didn't feel the least bit guilty for snatching her opportunity.

"A thief, not a boy," she corrected. "That's what the guard who chased him here called him."

The Priest, still clouded in smoke, scratched his chin. "A thief. Perhaps..."

"Perhaps," said Sera and Shani together.

"Perhaps?" said Camilia.

The four exchanged a glance, and Loren ached at the way he sat apart.

For the second time that morning, the Priest pointed at Loren. "Child, fetch water. Return quickly. Time is wasting."

Loren scrambled up. "What are we doing?"

"Don't speak unless spoken to," Sera added, waving him off. "Gods, youths are so mouthy these days."

Loren didn't fetch water. At least, not right away.

Frustration followed him from the temple to the market street. Even hopping across the series of knee-high stones to the other side of the road did nothing to improve his temper, although it was an activity that once charmed him as a new arrival to the bustling city, four years prior.

Part of growing older, he'd found, was that everything lost its shine. For a dreamer, that realization didn't bode well.

Only Nonna calling his name from farther up the street jolted him from his sour mood, though Loren mostly credited that to the sweet roll she slipped him. Honey melted on his tongue, chasing away bitter anxiety.

"My sweet Loren," Nonna said when he kissed her brown, dough-soft cheek. "What have I told you about wearing a scowl so deep? Those lines follow you to your deathbed."

Grandmother to the city in all but blood, Nonna kept her collection of strays well-fed. She gave so much away, Loren didn't understand how she kept her bakery afloat. But he ran errands for her, so he figured that made them even.

He swiped another roll for his pocket. "Are you all right after the quake?"

She flapped a dismissive hand and returned to scoring lines on dough. "I only pray it rattled sense into the council. Taxes here, taxes there, and more to come, I fear, though it is never the council who pays the price."

"They voted down the proposal to raise rates last week. Umbrius said—"

Nonna scoffed. "Umbrius is a man of many words and little substance. Gods only know why you wish to join him. Chew with your mouth closed, sparrow, and go. Nonna's turn to be busy."

Easy as that, his storm clouds returned. Loren knew her words carried no heat, but her jab at his political ambitions stung worse than usual. Why should the council welcome Loren when he wasn't privy to his own temple's plans? Even when he knew more about the thief than anyone? *Errand boy.*

For good measure, he crammed a third roll in his mouth, fleeing before her scolding could catch him. Hoisting the water jug on his hip, he set off up the Via Stabiana in search of a functioning spout.

Red and yellow awnings hung vibrant in the sun. Merchants displayed their wares. plates and spoons, sandals and boots, silks and linens. Mountains of autumn pomegranates teetered, piles of fresh sardines sweated. Fragrant spiced nuts simmered in a wine-filled vat, and the seller hawked out prices that changed by the moment. A donkey-drawn cart trundled past, wheels creaking in cobblestone grooves.

Even the quake hadn't managed to do more than shake the surface. At her core, the city was built to carry on.

Familiar sounds and smells enveloped Loren, but he couldn't relax into them. Not when the catalyst for his city's destruction lay unconscious by his own hand.

He passed two fountains, but a quake that summer had knocked one dry, and the other had a line around the block. Sighing, he pressed on until the hum of the merchant district quieted and the hush made him itch. At the far end of the Via Stabiana, by the city's northernmost gate, he could've been the only soul awake. A water tower gurgled away in the shade of the city wall. Cool water thundered into the clay jug, splattering Loren's temple robes, but he paid the mess no mind. His gaze had snared on the open gate and the countryside beyond.

Pompeii was everything. Pompeii held all Loren's desires his parents spent his childhood stomping out. Pompeii was opportunity. Freedom. Ambition.

So why did Loren feel so trapped?

Corking the jug, Loren propped it against the spout, then—just to prove he could—strode through the gate and into the long shadow of Vesuvius.

The mountain dominated the horizon, sharp and steep as the fang of some wild animal, but it wasn't half so vicious. It stood watch over the city, an old sentry. The road snaked toward it through low hills. Herculaneum, Pompeii's sister town, lay beyond. Farther northwest was their capital, Rome. But breathing didn't come easier out here.

Anyone else—anyone smarter, more selfish—would have left Pompeii after the first dream of its destruction. After Loren woke, gasping for breath, with the truth buzzing in his head: that the city was doomed. Cleaner to cut one's losses, escape before it became clear no one would ever take his visions seriously.

His parents had words for him: Delusional. Stubborn. Filled with hubris, the same pride that dogged Odysseus and Icarus and all other heroes of misfortune.

Loren called it hope. He had to believe fate could be changed. He had to believe that the bloodied boy who stumbled into the temple—the living counterpart of the nightmarish ghost who caused the destruction—was Loren's answer to stopping Pompeii's calamity.

"There are closer fountains in town," said a girl's voice from behind with a dismissive sniff. "I passed four."

"Half of which are dry." Loren didn't turn. "Last time I petitioned the council to fund repairs, I was escorted out. And asked not to return."

Fabric rustled against stone as Aurelia slipped from her perch on one of the hundreds of aboveground tombs lining the road. She picked a late-season poppy as she crunched closer. Circles hung low under her eyes, far too dark for a girl of only twelve. Aurelia was the same age Loren had been when he fled his family's villa, but she always struck him as older. Mature wasn't the right word for it. Removed from her time, more like. At least, when she wasn't throwing pebbles at him or picking fights with those twice her size.

"Couldn't sleep?" Loren asked, dreading the answer.

"I came to visit Pappa. He never liked hearing about my nightmares, but he listens now." Aurelia's nose wrinkled. "Besides, I knew to find you here."

"What do you mean?"

"Saw it."

His stomach sank. "Aurelia."

"Not like that. I saw you leave the temple, then stop with Nonna. I raced you." She grinned, a wild thing, showing off her missing front tooth. "I won."

"You can't win against someone who didn't know they were playing."

"Spoken like the loser of a race. What's the real reason you're out here?"

Loren closed his eyes against the glaring sun cresting over Vesuvius's flank, schooling his features. The champion of half-truths, he said, "I needed fresh air."

"Something else is the matter." She flopped into the grass, stripping her poppy of its petals. Dark curls curtained her face. "But fine. Don't tell me. I'll figure it out. I always do."

He couldn't help the fond tug of his mouth. It died quickly.

A familiar ache panged his gut. Often he wished he could lay their dreams side by side, examine them, see where they matched and where they differed. He didn't know which would be worse—confirmation they saw the same end, or that her horrors were ones he hadn't yet seen.

Aurelia knew of their shared plight. It was what drew them together, close as brother and sister. But it was his responsibility not to worsen her burden by telling her what he saw. Not when most visions involved her death. Not until he found a solution.

Loren knew it shouldn't be this way. Visions were meant to be tools of change, and the stories he read proved ill fates befell those who didn't heed oracles. But in the eyes of society, he and Aurelia were children. Nobody believed children. Especially not children who were right. The unfairness stung like a wet slap. The thief's arrival brought Loren the closest he'd come to figuring out his dreams, yet he felt farther behind than ever.

Black wave. Copper streak.

At the center of the storm, the ghost.

Abstract, burning visions that gained clarity with each passing night. The clearer his dreams became, the closer the danger loomed. When the final details distilled, would the end begin?

A bee landed on the back of Aurelia's hand, and she giggled. The sound bruised Loren's heart, and the dregs of his frustration flamed. He'd figure this mystery out for her. He would save Pompeii. He would make these nightmares mean something, and he wouldn't let the ghost scare him from the answers.

But first—

"Scoot over." Loren nudged her to make space in the grass. "I'll braid your hair."

Aurelia lit up. "Do the twisty thing. Mamma thinks it's pretty."

One last moment before all turned to ruin. He could braid Aurelia's hair to match his own, and she could chatter about nothing and everything. Back at the temple, the others could wonder why he took so long, and the copper-haired ghost—the clever-jawed thief—could wait in exchange for haunting Loren all these years. The mountain could cast shadows against the daylight, and for a moment, he could forget about his dreams.

For now, Loren had this.

CHAPTER III

FELIX

Felix woke to a sharp headache, an acrid tongue, and a weight on his chest.

He knew the reason for the first, and he smacked his lips a few times to place the taste of the second. The third took his throbbing skull a moment, but he found the answer inches from his nose, where two yellow eyes glinted back.

"Piss off, cat," Felix said. Tried to say. He wriggled, but the cat stayed put. Damn thing was heavier than a cat had any right to be. Gods, his head hurt.

He took stock of his situation. Horizontal, as expected. On a soft chaise, less expected. The room was silent and dim, but his vision adjusted quickly. The style of bricks suggested the building was much older than the statesman's house, meaning Felix hadn't been given back to Darius post-howl attack. Somehow, that didn't make him feel better. He suspected he wouldn't feel anything but uncomfortable until he was far from Pompeii's gates.

Too much had happened here. Too many people acted like they knew him.

A low rumble broke the quiet, and for a bleary moment, Felix wondered if the earth was shaking again. But it was only the cat, calm and content and shaped like a bread loaf, blinking slow. Felix was at a loss.

He blinked back.

A door creaked.

"You've met Castor," a familiar voice said. Too familiar, given that he'd only spoken two words before snuffing Felix's lights out. "The Egyptians believed cats see what humans can't. Is it a good sign he's taken to you so readily?"

"Here to finish me off? Seeing how the bowl and the"—Felix smacked his lips once more to be certain—"poison didn't do the job?"

The boy moved into the orange glow of a sconce, casting his olive skin warm. Tall and thin with half his face still veiled, he was unmistakably the lunatic from the cella steps, though he'd lost the scarf swathing his head. Long dark hair lay braided over his shoulder. He wore the garments of a low-ranking temple worker and held a covered basket.

"Poppy sap can't kill you."

"You would be surprised," Felix said darkly. Twice in a matter of hours it'd been used against him in Pompeii. Maybe everybody in this backwater town lacked creativity.

The boy sighed and shut the door softly, closing them in. Felix repressed twisting unease. Being trapped with a stranger, in a temple no less, went against everything he'd ever learned. He brushed his hand down Castor's back, eyeing the boy, who took a steadying breath, then tiptoed to crouch by the chaise. It took all Felix's resolve not to cringe at the closeness.

At a cluck of the boy's tongue, Castor leaped off Felix's chest and slunk from sight.

Whatever. Felix didn't miss the weight.

"We don't have much time before the others realize you're awake," the boy said, half-muffled by his veil. From his basket, he withdrew a dish of fat purple grapes, glistening damp. "I brought you these, and bandages for your legs."

Felix's mouth watered. He hadn't eaten in ages, and he had a fondness for grapes besides, regardless of their stage of fermentation. Still, he hesitated. This boy had bashed in Felix's head, yet now tempted him with niceties. It didn't add up.

Kindness came with limits. If not a limit, a price. Who knew what the boy might demand in exchange for a handful of grapes?

"Not hungry," Felix lied. "Can I go?"

The boy set the dish at the foot of the chaise. "I can tend your wounds, if you want."

"I don't," Felix said, the truth this time. "Can I go?"

With another huff, the boy scrutinized Felix's face. His searching expression, like trying to solve a puzzle, made Felix's tongue stick to the roof of his mouth. It reminded him of how guards judged him on sight alone, wanting to pin him with any number of crimes if only because of his threadbare tunic and shifty disposition.

Whatever the boy looked for, he didn't seem pleased with what he found.

"Question for question," he declared. "To answer yours, no. You can't leave. Not until we're finished with you. But I'll let you ask another."

How generous. Body aching, Felix sat up. It was worth the pain to not be prone under a stranger's gaze. "Fine. Do you have a name?"

The boy blinked. "That's what you most want to know?"

"Is that your question?"

"No." Above his veil, across the bridge of his freckled nose, spilled a deep red flush. "My name is Loren."

Satisfaction spread through Felix's chest. He didn't care much for rules besides his own. Following rules didn't mean anything when you were bleeding out in an alley. But he did hold tight to something his father drilled into him when he was small: *Learn the names of those you deal with. Know whose name to thank.*

More importantly, whose name to curse. Cursing Loren would taste especially delicious when Felix escaped.

"Your turn." Only the slightest bit smug, Felix began wrapping the gashes on his legs.

Loren cast him an icy look at odds with the lingering fluster still on his face. "I want to be in this situation even less than you, believe it or not—"

"Not."

"—but the only way out is through." Loren seemed to be reassuring himself more than Felix. He tugged off his veil to reveal a wary indent at the corner of his bow-shaped mouth. "You didn't stumble into the temple by accident. What drew you here?"

Felix paused tying the bandages to stare in disbelief. "I don't know where *here* is. Tell me that much, and maybe we can figure out the rest."

"You ran in. I assumed you knew."

"Humor me."

"This is the Temple of Isis."

Felix swore.

He traveled a lot. It was part of the game, how he stayed alive. He'd been in cities with a dozen temples, villages with a single shrine, towns in between. The world was vast and full of gods and ways to worship. But one thing remained consistent in all his travels: Folks who followed Isis were always south of normal.

Loren sniffed. "I don't want to know what you mean by that."

"The followers of Isis are cannibals."

"Yes, that's why I brought you bandages. We like our dinner unspoiled." He glared. "We're not cannibals, but you are part of a ritual. The others didn't explain it. To me, at least. Something about virgin blood—"

"I'm not a virgin," Felix cut in.

Watching Loren blush without his veil was even more satisfying, an all-consuming reaction, spreading down his thin face and painting the long column of his neck. But for Felix, satisfaction came with a twinge of irritation. Who *was* this boy? Every thought, every feeling that crossed Loren's mind, he seemed to share with the world, intentionally or not.

Felix marveled at it. Hated it. Envied it.

"Not in *that* way," Loren said. "Virgin as in your blood has never been part of a ritual for Isis before."

"That's not what it means."

"Is too. Look." He flopped onto the chaise, jostling the bowl of grapes in a way that gave Felix the shape of an escape plan. Loren extended his arm, pointing to the pale X of a scar in the crease of his elbow. "That's why they can't use me this time."

"Are you a virgin, then? The other kind." Felix plastered on his best shit-eating grin, and the rest panned out perfectly.

Loren jolted back, like he'd only just realized how close they were sitting. The sudden action sent the bowl flying. The dish clattered and cracked against the tile, and grapes scattered across the room, rolling in every direction. Loren, apologizing to no one, dove to clean the mess, and Felix took the distraction as his cue.

Castor, surveying from atop a wobbly stool, shot Felix a look that said, *Nice going, ass.*

Felix hissed. Castor zipped away.

Standing was a clumsy gamble, but Felix only needed to stay upright until he reclaimed the helmet and escaped the city. He might risk recovering his sandals, but screw going back to the statesman's house for his satchel. Whatever happened there, whatever fit the statesman sent him into before the quake struck . . . Felix didn't want to think about that. Thinking broke *all* his rules.

Freedom would feel damned good. Holding the helmet again would feel even better.

Grapes squishing underfoot, Felix staggered to the door and burst outside.

"Wait!" Loren cried, but Felix wasn't stopping for anything, let alone some naive, indignant temple boy. He lurched toward the temple's courtyard, dizziness forcing him to brace against the wall, breathing shallow.

"Mm, this is not happening," a woman's voice said from behind. Felix jumped, but before he could bolt, she slammed him to his knees.

Not for the first time that day. Humiliating.

Felix glanced back at his latest attacker. Shorter and a few years older than he was, she had an upturned nose and hair cropped in an awkward bob. Her veil hung below her chin. In the doorway stood Loren, stunned betrayal casting him even more naive and indignant than Felix thought possible. With Loren's hair so long and hers so short, they looked a pair of fools. Felix wondered who they were trying to impress, or if the conditions for joining the Temple of Isis included a bad haircut.

"Loren, bind him," she said, and a moment passed before Loren stepped forward, dropping handfuls of loose grapes. Soft fabric wrapped around Felix's wrists. "Why didn't you say he was awake?"

The pinch of Loren's mouth tightened.

"Because it only just happened," he said, masking his fluster with ease. "He jolted to his feet and made a dash for it."

An utter lie. Loren didn't strike Felix as the lying type. His feelings were too loud for that. But here with this girl, he acted plenty well-practiced in keeping secrets. Felix puzzled at the contradiction. Where it stemmed from.

What else Loren might be hiding.

"Loren—" started the woman, suspicion thick.

"Camilia," Loren countered. "Shall I fetch the Priest?"

Camilia eyed him a beat too long. "Go on. Let's get this over with."

If one word could send Felix over the edge, it was *priest*.

In the taverns and gambling dens Felix frequented, drunk men often played the game of association. You'd throw out a word, then the table spat out whatever term first came to mind. So even something innocent, like *bed*, turned out an answer like *tits*. Usually crass. Rarely clever, but the men roared with laughter regardless.

Felix wasn't laughing now.

His deepest instincts associated *priest* with *pain*, two things he tried his best to avoid. Two things he'd found in abundance in Pompeii.

The Priest of Isis, waiting on a stool by the altar, didn't seem thrilled to meet Felix either. Almost as if even he knew this ritual, whatever it served, wouldn't make an inch of difference to the gods. Camilia led Felix over, still bound. Curling, sweet smoke soothed his headache.

"What's your name?" asked the Priest. Felix wondered if he cared about the answer or if this was his way of being polite. Felix didn't do polite.

"Fuck," he said.

The Priest frowned. "That is not a proper name, son."

"I'm not a proper person."

Someone stifled a nervous laugh. Loren, maybe.

The Priest scratched his chin before grumbling under his breath. A grouchy woman passed him a bone-handled knife. The bindings around Felix's wrists slid free, but Camilia gripped his shoulders. No chance of fleeing. She wrestled his arm onto the altar, tender palm exposed.

"Not the hand," Felix snapped, curling his fist. His hands were his source of income. Scarred tissue was less dexterous. Deadly for a thief.

Camilia glared, but she repositioned his forearm to the center of the altar. Then she produced a clay cup of floral wine—Eumachius, not

Lassius, so at least someone here had decent taste—and poured it over Felix's skin, staining it red.

"Goddess Isis," the Priest intoned. "We call upon you to grant us clemency. Accept this offering."

The grouchy twins knelt, hands to the sky. A beat later, Loren followed. Felix's attention snagged on the turn of his thin wrists, his fine-boned fingers. Silly, inconsequential details to notice. Distractions.

The Priest plunged the knife in a silver flash.

The blade pierced Felix's vein, inky blood pooling, and he stifled a cry. It stung worse than the cuts on his calves, somehow. Maybe because Felix had anticipated it.

Or maybe because it put him at the mercy of another priest.

"Guide us through death—"

Felix hissed as the knife slid deeper, then crossed an X in the bend of his arm.

"—and the afterlife—"

Legs buckling, Felix collapsed against the altar. Blood chased wine, running in rivulets down white marble to pool on uneven tile.

"—back to the world of the living," the Priest continued, gaze cast up. "Protect our city from the earth's turmoil. See our sacrifice, and know it is in your honor."

The blood made Felix's head spin. He stared, dumbstruck, as smoke from the altar bowl took shape, took flight, the splay of wings. Up, up.

Nothing.

And then—everything.

Orange streaked across the courtyard, a cat bolting for cover, and the ground beneath Felix's feet shuddered. Panic gripped him, that same water-sick instability he'd felt in the statesman's house.

The rattling intensified, stone chattering. Camilia released Felix, lunging to steady the Priest before the old man's knees gave out. Felix slid to the ground, back against the altar, cradling his wrist, pulsing hot and sticky. From this angle, he couldn't see where Loren stumbled off to.

This was Felix's chance. The animal part of his brain took over, and he scrambled on slick hands and bruised knees toward the door.

"No!"

A weight barreled into Felix, Loren tackling him off course. They rolled in a swirl of temple robes, grappling while the world continued to shake. Loren moved with the same decisiveness Felix had noted the instant before the bowl crashed down, eyes flashing with inexplicable, horrified recognition.

As if to say—*I know you.*

It ended, as all things had that day, with Felix dizzy and disoriented and smeared in his own blood. Loren took advantage of Felix's weakness and pinned him flat, didn't relent even as the rumbling quieted. Loren's chest heaved, and Felix's skin crawled. He was too close. Too close.

"Stop," Felix begged, desperation trembling like he'd swallowed the quake. "Let me *go.*"

At first, Loren merely blinked, and Felix's frustration heightened, not knowing how to convey he wasn't trying to run, not this time. All thoughts of escape had fled. What he needed was space, any amount of it, before he vomited bile over them both, but he had no hope Loren would grant him that. That he'd understand, without words, what Felix asked.

But after a long, sticky pause, Loren surprised him. He pulled back, grip loosening. With a final twist, Felix broke the hold and scooted away. He'd offer his other arm to be sliced if it meant strange hands would stop touching him.

A moment of suffocating silence passed before Felix realized all eyes were on him. Because *his* blood cooled on the altar. Because it was so easy for others to draw conclusions about him when they didn't even know his name.

"An aftershock," Camilia suggested, though she didn't sound convinced. "From the quake earlier."

The Priest hummed, rubbing his chin. The stare he directed at Felix cut him to the bone. He might as well have been on display at a school of medicine. Not a person, but an oddity. Something to ogle. "Curious."

"I propose," said one twin, "we read his entrails for a sign."

"Sera," scolded the other. "We would need to pay an augur for that. It's not in the budget. Though, given the circumstances, Umbrius might make an exception."

"With Umbrius in charge, the council ignores anything remotely resembling bad news," said Camilia. "Anything that threatens peace. Or the economy, rather. Why stir panic when he can pretend trouble doesn't exist?"

Sera muttered something about where this Umbrius character ought to stick the economy.

The Priest hefted onto the stool with a world-weary sigh. "We have not had funds for augury since I was a boy, and Umbrius shows little interest in omens besides. Though if we don't kill the boy, it begs the question of what, exactly, we do now."

"Let him go," Camilia said. "If we have no further use for him."

Sera cackled. "For free? You said that soldier wanted him. Demand a fee in exchange, and we can all eat well tonight."

"If I may," Loren said, still crouched an arm's length from Felix.

Felix couldn't help but focus on him. Loren thumbed a frayed cord around his neck, back and forth, an unsure gesture. The frantic drive he'd shown tackling Felix had fizzled away.

"You think he'd pay? More likely his master would cut off our heads before handing over the reward," Camilia said. "Clearly the thief is poor luck. Pompeii has enough of that already."

"If I may," Loren tried again.

"He seems sweet," Shani said. "We could keep him around. A pet."

Sera scoffed. "We have Castor and Pollux. How many more mouths must we feed?"

"I'll take responsibility," Loren blurted.

The room's attention fell on him.

"You?" said Sera.

"You," said the Priest, "with what authority?"

Loren's hands twisted in his lap. "I don't have much power in the city. But as a free citizen and temple attendant, I can offer him some protection from the council and guards, at least until we know if he's tied to the quakes. And what Camilia said, about bad luck—I fear setting him loose, without knowing what he's capable of, would do more harm than good."

Irony simmered low in Felix's gut, and it felt a lot like vomit. Loren bemoaned his lack of power in the city, yet in the same breath staked claim on another's freedom. Last night, Felix had been on top of the world, flying through empty streets, nothing on his mind but treasure and the next town. Now to sit there, helpless and bloody, while strangers blamed him for wreckage and debated his fate?

This was lower than low. Felix was a thief. What *capabilities* did Loren think he had?

The Priest returned to rubbing his chin. "An interesting proposition. If the gods are upset, and this boy is connected, perhaps it would be wise to keep watch on him. At least until I receive a clearer sign about his fate. But understand, if you vouch for his honor now, any further trouble he causes will land on your shoulders."

Loren hesitated. Slowly, he nodded.

All the while, he never spared a glance for Felix. That rankled him the most.

Another hum from the Priest. "Do something about that arm, won't you? Before he bleeds out in my courtyard."

Felix caught Camilia and Loren exchanging a look. Reading people had never come easy to him, but he got the sense she was asking if Loren knew what he was getting himself into. And Felix wanted to respond for him: No. Here was a boy willing to bash a stranger's skull on first sight, then hope he survived long enough to question later. Who, when doing the questioning, snuck around behind his fellow temple attendants, like he alone needed the information. Who clearly didn't trust Felix, not one bit, yet wanted him on a tight leash.

I know you.

Loren was unpredictable. Impulsive, not instinctive. And he seemed to know something Felix didn't.

That made him the most dangerous person in the room.

So, no. Loren had no idea the trouble he was in now that he and Felix were tied together.

CHAPTER IV
LOREN

"I refuse," said Loren, pulling a needle through the pinched skin of the thief's arm, "to believe you told the Priest the truth when he asked your name."

The thief's brow twitched up. "What tipped you off?"

They had retreated to the private quarters again, away from Camilia's scrutiny and the Priest's frown. Loren hoped the privacy might inspire the thief to talk, but he was as shifty here as he'd been at the altar.

Loren tried to make his words teasing, but even before they left his mouth, he knew his joke was doomed to fall flat. "No self-respecting parent would name their son something so crass."

"Who said anything about self-respecting?" He considered Loren across the table. With his free hand, he sifted through the grapes scooped from the floor. The thief selected one, inspected it for dirt, then popped it in his mouth. Chewed slow. "It's Felix."

Loren dragged his gaze from Felix's swallow, letting the name sink in. How odd to finally put a name to the face that had haunted him for so long. If he closed his eyes now, he could see it clear as day, Felix's copper curls tangled behind his eyelids. But even that wasn't right. The faded, cruel ghost that lurked in his dreams had nothing on how absurdly golden Felix was in reality.

Exactly Loren's luck that this was the closest he'd been to a boy in years, and here he was, putting stitches in his skin while Felix, manifestation of his nightmares, snacked on floor-grapes.

Pinch. Pull. Tight, even passes, as Camilia taught him. "No family name?"

"Just Felix."

"And what brings you to Pompeii?"

Felix flashed his teeth. "Shit luck."

Another draw of the needle, and Loren tied the cord. He dabbed blood with a damp rag before winding linen around the wound. Felix's arm looked less garish this way. Less brutal.

"Are you finished? I can't stand all this handling." Felix's mouth flattened. He'd worn the same expression when Loren stopped his escape during the aftershock.

If that *was* what the quake had been, as Camilia insisted. Loren wasn't convinced.

He pulled his hands away. "Poppy sap might ease the pain. Just a drop."

"I've had enough for one life, thanks." Felix cradled his injured arm and fished for grapes with his other. "Tell me what you want from me."

Rolling his surgical tools, Loren ruminated on how to approach the topic. Their question-for-question game earlier had got him nowhere, so perhaps it was time to be blunt. But asking *What are you?* seemed impolite. So did saying *I've seen the destruction you plan to cause.* And *Sorry for claiming responsibility for you without permission, but I can't let you leave until I learn why you haunt me. Truce?* was off the table.

"The man who chased you here . . ." Loren paused. Changed tactics. "Petty theft isn't unusual in Pompeii."

"What's your question?"

"Most guards wouldn't expend that much effort."

"For the right price, guards will do anything," Felix said. "I took something. Someone else wanted what I took."

"Who?"

"Some statesman. I was too busy running for my life to catch his name." His tone was dry, but he radiated discomfort. He sat strangely, perched on the edge of his chair, ready to take flight. He wouldn't get far. The Priest was holding session in the courtyard. Isis didn't attract many outside their small attendant circle, but Felix still wouldn't make it halfway without being seen.

"I don't have an issue with thieves," said Loren. "Most take what they need to survive. I respect that. But whatever you stole must be valuable. What was it?"

"What difference does it make?"

Loren locked eyes with him. Felix's were gray as rain-heavy clouds and twice as threatening. "Because I saved your life. Because Sera would sell you back to that soldier, or Camilia would turn you onto the streets to be caught anyway. Because your blood made the ground shake—"

"Did not."

"—and I'm protecting you now, *Just Felix*, yet you won't offer the courtesy of your full name, let alone your business in my city."

"I didn't ask for that." Lithe and slippery, Felix leaped to his feet. "If I have a family name, I don't remember. And I don't want your protection. If you're looking for gratitude, consider this your thank-you."

"If you leave alone, I won't be able to shield you."

"I suppose I'll risk it." Felix left.

Loren gave him a two-second head start. Then he followed, head pounding at the dull familiarity of watching Felix hightail it into the hall. This time he didn't have the advantage of Camilia's brute strength. Maybe he wouldn't need it.

He stopped short at the scene in the courtyard. The noise hit him first, dozens of murmuring voices that hadn't reached the private quarters. A crowd swarmed, far more people than the Priest's sessions typically attracted, and nervous agitation buzzed. Lingering fear from the quakes, perhaps, prompting folks to seek comfort in faith. But there must be more to it than that. Loren had experienced a dozen quakes since arriving in Pompeii, and none had caused such a stir.

Felix froze beneath the shelter of the portico, half hidden behind a column, tracking the gathering. Calculating his next move.

"Something else must have happened." Loren sidled beside Felix. "This is strange for Isis."

Felix's mouth tightened. "Is that the only exit?"

"You won't make it out unnoticed if that's your concern. Even if you did, the city is teeming with guards this week, extra security for the festival. You can't leave without me." Loren pulled off his veil. "But I'll let you borrow this. A disguise might help."

"Tell me what you want from me."

"Tell me what you stole."

Felix considered him for a long moment, face calculating, then let out a mirthless laugh. "Fine. Maybe you can explain what all the fuss is about."

In the end, they both wore veils, but Loren left his braid free and recognizable. He may not have much influence in the city, but if being known as "that strange boy from the strange temple" kept a gladius from skewering Felix, he'd take the side-eyes as they came.

Felix had to be more careful. His hair was too distinctive, shining copper in the midafternoon sun. Even swathed in a headscarf, he still stuck out in his blood-stained clothes.

"Remind me to take you tunic shopping later," Loren muttered as they stepped into the alley. "You look like a gladiator who fought a bear, and the bear triumphed."

It won a scowl from Felix, which Loren accepted as the best he'd get.

"I don't see your friend," he said once they reached the road. "Hopefully that means he can't see us either. Where to?"

Felix scanned the buildings with tight eyes, orienting himself to their surroundings. For a moment, Loren thought he might make a break for it, but a pair of city guards strode past, and Felix melted closer to Loren's side.

"Take me to the Forum," Felix said. "We can start there."

The street teemed with Pompeiians running errands in the autumn sun. Loren and Felix stepped into the flow of traffic bustling toward the Forum. Some eyed their veils with suspicion, but Loren paid them no mind. Isis was always being observed. Part of being in a foreign cult, a ragtag group of outcasts, refugees and former slaves, prostitutes and ex-politicos, and anyone else who didn't fit in. Even the fact that men and women interacted so closely raised alarm. They were an unconventional bunch, and in a Roman colony, that was distasteful.

The Forum was as busy as ever. The center for three temples and Pompeii's council, it only quieted well after dark. Here, beggars begged, merchants sold trinkets, and children chased dogs. Loren reveled in the happy hum.

"Don't they remember the earth shaking only hours ago?" Felix asked, eyes wide.

"You acclimate to it. Pompeii presses on."

"Mad. All of you." Felix pointed across the way, through the series of archways lining the Forum. "There's Apollo."

"Right. In the center is Jupiter, and over there—"

But Felix didn't wait for a lesson on layout. Peeling from Loren's side, he made for Apollo's temple, weaving through the crowd. Loren stumbled over his feet keeping up, stopping only to shout an apology to a group of children whose marbles game he trod through.

Closer to the temple, the mood took a sharp shift. A tight knot stood clustered outside the entrance. Unusual. Apollo's following was even smaller than Isis's, and the city only maintained the temple to not offend the sun god. Loren strained to see over the crowd, not realizing Felix stopped until he smacked into him.

"Jupiter," Felix cursed.

Loren quickly realized why.

A man knelt, stripped to his waist, guard leathers piled on the stones beside him. His head was bowed. Air whistled. Leather snapped his bare back. A cry tore from his chest.

A guard's voice called out a number—"Six!"—and the process repeated.

A handful of councilmen chattered idly nearby, looking bothered at the inconvenience of overseeing the punishment but otherwise unperturbed by the breaking of a man five paces away. Umbrius, head of the council, was not present.

"Despicable," Loren muttered, blood rushing cold. "Only brutes dole punishment with the whip."

"Seven!"

Felix's skin had drained of color.

"No one deserves this. I'll outlaw it when I'm on the council. It's inhumane. And to do it publicly—"

"Are you running for office?" Felix's question carried an edge, not quite mocking.

Loren's ears burned. He hadn't meant to admit it out loud, not to Felix. Everything he'd gathered about Felix so far pointed to little love for rule makers. As a thief, it made sense. But that didn't stop his tone from stinging.

"I'm not," Loren said. "I can't."

"Eight!"

"Not freeborn?"

"I am. But." Explaining meant confessing secrets. His family. His visions. That Loren wasn't who he claimed to be. Instead, he ignored Felix's heavy gaze and watched flayed flesh. "Can we go? Before I do something foolish, like intervene."

"Nine!" Another crack. The crowd tittered, disgusted and amused by the spectacle.

Felix made Loren wait in the moment a beat longer. Then, "Follow me."

In an alley a few streets up, a pair of old sandals sat abandoned. Felix laughed triumphantly upon discovering them, as if he'd found a pile of coins, and strapped them on his bloodstained feet.

"Is that . . ." Loren's question seemed too silly to finish. Still, Felix rolled his eyes.

"Yes, this is what he nearly killed me over. Don't you know? These shoes are magic."

"Piss off." Loren was suddenly glad for the veils. He couldn't stomach watching Felix's mouth curl into a smirk.

Felix led him across the city, zigzagging streets, until they wound up behind a row of shops in the heart of the city, a dingy place populated by barrels and stacked crates.

"Stay here." Felix ducked away. Moments later, he emerged, clutching a bundle wrapped in his headscarf.

"Your hair." Loren glanced around, as if a soldier might be squatting behind a crate.

"Rather they see that than this. Do you have somewhere we can go? Not the temple. Somewhere private."

Loren cringed. He figured Felix would learn sooner or later where he lived. But he'd rather banked on later. Still, he nodded. "I have a place."

Hand against peeling wood, Loren hesitated. They stood at the back of a building he knew all too well. He sensed Felix would recognize the type, too, the moment they stepped inside.

"You can't laugh," Loren warned.

"Is it funny?"

"Not to me."

"Then I won't," Felix promised.

Regardless, Loren took a deep breath before pushing open the door.

It swung to reveal a dim corridor, and Loren beckoned in Felix, who paused, scanning the place. Cubicles sectioned by curtains, explicit paintings above the booths, and the pervasive smell of musk and sweat—Loren knew what Felix must be piecing together in his head.

"Upstairs." Loren beelined for the staircase.

Too late. One of the curtains rustled open, and Elias slunk out. Hooded eyes half closed, he blinked at Felix sleepily, his oversized tunic dipping off one shoulder.

Elias broke into a grin. "Hello there. Can I call you fox? You look like one."

Felix met him with a frown.

"Wanting something in particular?" Elias yawned. Then he noticed Loren, and his mouth slid into a pout. "Oh. He yours?"

"No," Loren insisted. "He's a friend."

"I'm insulted." The pout deepened. Elias stretched his arms high, tunic riding up his thighs, and propped a hip against the doorframe of his cubicle. "Here I thought I was your only friend."

Hardly. These days, Loren didn't know what he and Elias were. Once upon a time, watching his skin stretch would've made Loren blush. It was only natural. The two were near the same age, living in proximity, and Elias had been so sweet that Loren dared hope . . . But Elias caught on and wasted no time constructing boundaries: He was off-limits. Until the day came when Elias bought his freedom, he would grow no roots in Pompeii.

Cut off from the source, Loren's feelings had died an abrupt, pitiful death.

The awkwardness, however, lingered.

"Elias, this is Felix. He's staying for . . . a while." Loren forced his voice to loosen. "I'm keeping him out of trouble."

From the way Felix's arms tensed around his cloth-covered bundle, Loren guessed his phrasing was bad, but he had no time to correct himself before Elias smirked.

"Keeping him," Elias repeated, dripping with implication. "Then I'll do my best not to *be* the trouble."

Loren's face flamed.

This time, he succeeded in ushering Felix away. They rushed upstairs, pausing only long enough for Loren to shove Felix through his door and shut it behind them.

Felix snickered. "You live in a lupanar."

"You promised not to laugh."

"I'm not laughing." His grin widened. "Virgin in a brothel."

Loren grabbed the nearest object, a leather shoe, and chucked it. Felix ducked easily, and it thudded against the wall.

"It's *cheap*. And they've been kind to me, Elias and the women." The landlord was a different story, but Loren rarely saw him around. "It isn't like I work downstairs. It's only a room."

Felix sobered. "Barely. More like a closet."

He wasn't wrong. Long and narrow, it barely held a bed, storage trunk, and washbasin. If not for the window, Loren would call it a closet, too. Speaking of which—Loren latched the shutters, then sat cross-legged on his bed.

"All right," he said. "Show me."

Felix fiddled with the wrapping. "Your turn not to laugh."

He didn't give Loren a chance to promise. He pulled the cloth away, and any laughter Loren might have felt was punched from his chest.

In his hand, like it meant nothing, Felix held the helmet of Mercury.

Loren's world plummeted, the bottom of his stomach dropping out.

Felix flipped it, knocked his knuckles on the dome. "Silly thing, isn't it?"

"Felix." Cold slipped down Loren's throat.

"Right there for the taking. If the statesman wanted it so badly, anyone could have grabbed it for him."

"Stop." Loren pressed a hand to his mouth, squeezing his eyes tight against a wave of nausea. *Gods alive*—He stumbled to his feet, dizzy. "You need to put that thing back. Tonight. Now. It can't stay here. I don't know how you took it, but—"

Felix offered it out. "It's a helmet."

"It," Loren said, stepping back, "is cursed."

That insufferable smile returned. "This old thing? Should I try it on?"

Felix bowed his head to duck into the crown.

Loren's vision flashed white. He teetered forward. Collapsed.

Black wave. Copper streak.

The ghost splitting a stormy sky.

Swirling gaze. A stinging strike.

White wings splayed.

Then—oblivion.

He gasped and found himself kneeling, palms to the floor. Ratty over-mended sandals and gore-splattered feet occupied his line of sight. Loren tracked up. Felix's gray eyes were wide. He gripped the helmet in one hand.

"Don't," Loren said. Blood washed across his mouth, salty and sharp. He must've bitten his tongue. "Never put it on."

"What happened?" Felix bent, but it brought the helmet too close. The hair on Loren's arms stood on end. He scrambled back until he hit the wall. Felix paused, then retreated, putting a closet's worth of distance between them.

"Isis." Loren slumped, pushing the heels of his hands against his cheekbones. If he'd thought their situation unstable before, they now navigated treacherous ground. Fear pulsed thin and choppy in his veins. "That's why the crowd at the Priest's session was so nervous. That's why the guard got whipped outside Apollo's temple. The helmet is one of Pompeii's most valuable treasures. It's been on display for centuries, the Romans stole it from the Corinthians ages ago, then gifted it to us. No one's been able to move it since. It should have burned you to the bone."

"It's a helmet."

Loren shook his head slowly. "Felix, you stole a relic belonging to a god. That's Mercury's helmet."

"Mercury?" Felix's fingers tightened. He looked at what he held.

Loren followed his gaze. For something claiming to be Mercury's, it was of unusual design. Most depictions of the god of money and merchants, travel and thieves, showed him wearing a wide-brimmed hat, the kind fieldworkers wore in vineyards. Aside from the crested wings framing the face, the similarities ended there. This was a soldier's helm, with a steep nose plate and angled eyes to strike fear in battle. This was a helmet for Mercury at war.

Whatever power it housed was angry.

"You took a helmet that no one else can touch, and the ground shook." Loren's stomach churned. "Your blood hit the altar, and it shook again."

"Coincidence," Felix insisted, even as he swallowed.

"I don't believe in those."

"Start. It makes life easier." He planted the helmet on Loren's bed. The dark hollows of its eyes stretched for eternity, delving to Tartarus.

"Mercury means nothing to me. I don't worship him. Neither do you. What does it matter?"

"It matters because—because this is bad. Mercury is sacred to traders, especially in a merchant town like Pompeii. The Etruscans worshipped him too, and before them, the Greeks named him Hermes. You disrespected a very old, very powerful god." Loren's thoughts tripped over each other, faster than he could keep pace with. "The divine energy that helmet holds should not be in the hands of a human."

"It's a *helmet*," Felix said, as if repeating it a third time would make it true.

"It's a weapon for someone with the wrong intentions. We need a plan. The statesman you mentioned, who is he? Why does he want it?"

"It would look pretty on his shelf. Why else do rich people own shiny things? He offered to bargain, to pay me to bring it to him, and—" Felix shook his head. "He'd sooner kill me to keep me quiet. So I ran."

Loren wondered what Felix wasn't telling him. But extracting answers from Felix was like pulling a soured tooth from a snarling dog. Impossible to do without getting bit. He set the statesman aside for now, returning to the bigger issue.

"This is *bad*. Why you? Why now?" Questions bubbled and spilled over, always Loren's same inquiries, but Felix pressed his back to the door, his defenses creeping higher. Loren examined him again, head to bloody hem. "Who are you?"

It seemed to throw Felix. His brow furrowed, but before Loren could make sense of his expression, he said, tone flippant, "I told you. Just Felix."

If he meant it as a joke, it didn't land. Loren stared, struck, until shock morphed into indignation. After years haunted by this boy, Felix finally stood before him, and Loren was still no closer to an answer. Hot tears pricked his eyes. He clenched his fists, knuckles blanching.

"Are you capable of taking this seriously," Loren said around the lump in his throat, "or is everything a laughing matter? Mock me if you want, but I will not let you endanger my city with your greed. Put it back."

Felix's smirk dropped. "No. Not now. You saw the Forum, it was swarming. I won't risk my skin to return a helmet."

"You're the only one who can touch it, and it can't stay with me."

"Then I'll take it when I leave. Sell it. Bury it."

"Do you want to be caught? *You* have to stay with me."

Felix snarled. "I'm not a dog."

"I would like you more if you were." Loren used the window ledge to hoist himself up. His knees still shook from his fit, but he managed to toss his laundry bag to Felix. Then he unlatched his trunk, shoving aside scraps and trinkets and other old temple offerings to form a helmet-size hiding spot. Felix didn't utter a word as he cinched the bag tight and nestled the helmet inside. Loren could only pray Mercury wouldn't take offense at being housed next to old linens.

"Stay till week's end," Loren said, latching the lid, a temporary tomb. "Four days. The city has twice as many eyes on it than usual. We need hope of catching the thief to wane and the festival to end. If I haven't figured out what the helmet means for you—and the city—by then, you can return it and go. In the meantime, I'll keep you out of the statesman's hands—and anyone else who wants a piece of you. I'm offering safety. Will you take it?"

"You? Protect me?" Felix said in disbelief.

"Unless you want to risk it on your own in a city that would do far worse than whip you," said Loren hotly. "You say you don't care what the helmet means? Fine. But I know you came here for a reason. I know we were supposed to meet. I intend to find out why."

"You're mad."

"Swear it. Four days."

Felix's mouth curled with brewing argument, but something akin to a shadow flitted across his face, and his jaw tightened. Stiff-necked, he gave a sharp, unwilling nod. "Is that all?"

The sneer in his voice crept under Loren's skin and burrowed deep. Was that all?

Black wave. Copper streak. Details spiraling clearer.

For the first time, Loren wished he was mad. He wished his nightmares were the product of a snapped mind, the way his parents wrote them off. He didn't want Felix to be the catalyst of the end. He didn't want the burden of uncovering the helmet's secrets.

Except, he realized with a twist, he'd asked for exactly that. Only hours ago, he had longed for an opportunity to prove himself. This was it, and he wouldn't miss his chance.

"No. I want your word that once you leave Pompeii," Loren said, "you won't ever return."

A long, claustrophobic silence passed before Felix finally spat, "Fine by me."

Four days. Loren only had to survive four terrible days. But when he turned from the trunk to find Felix's back to him, his eyes caught on a stitched arm and bandaged calves, and how slanted afternoon light cast copper hair in red and gold, fire on a hillside, and Loren thought—

Easier said than done.

CHAPTER V

FELIX

Four days. Felix didn't have four days to sit still. Staying still screamed danger. Staying still meant a quick end to an already short life. Whatever protection Loren thought he could offer was nonsense. Felix trusted no one but himself to evade capture and escape Pompeii alive.

Naturally, the first thing he did when Loren left, muttering about returning to the temple to start his search, was break his promise and pick the lock.

The helmet greeted him from the crushing dark of the trunk. Shiny silver gleamed with the possibility of wine, bread, a horse, even, if Felix wanted. Oh, Felix wanted. Recognition tugged anew when he lifted the helmet out, that uncanny magnetic pull. Like the helmet wanted him in kind.

Loren was a fool for believing Felix would stay. Warnings about superstitious Pompeiians and whips aside, he'd only needed Loren to lower his guard long enough to offer an opening. The rest Felix could handle on his own. Helmet tucked in the laundry bag slung over his shoulder, he unpicked the locked door and stepped out.

And nearly tripped over the dark-eyed brothel boy. Elias sat on the tiny landing, blocking the stairs. He gazed up through his lashes, saccharine and venomous.

"Fox was only a nickname," said Elias. "But you're crafty when cornered, aren't you?"

"I bite, too."

"Another word for whore is *lupa*. *Wolf*. Shall we trade teeth?" Elias grinned. "Loren said he's keeping you out of trouble, but I think you *are* the trouble. That's something he can't resist. Usually to the detriment of everyone around him."

"So move. Trust me, I'm not trying to stick around."

Elias rose, if only to use the rest of his body as a barrier. "Tell you what. Come drink with me first. Play a game."

Felix sized him up. Elias was pretty, he'd give him that, but debauched. Short, with a head of loose brown curls, round cheeks, and charcoal-smudged eyes, he resembled a devious cherub. "You don't interest me."

"Wasn't offering, but I bet I can figure out what does interest you. Give me an hour of your time, and after, I won't stop you from leaving." Elias turned to head downstairs, then shot a glance backward. "Leave the helmet. When this explodes in your face, I'd rather not witness it."

"How—"

"I told you, Loren can't resist trouble. The same day the helmet goes missing, he decides to hide a stranger in his room?" Elias arched a brow. "Or we could skip the drink, and I'll fetch the guards now. Gods know I need the reward money. Up to you."

He flounced away, curls bouncing.

Felix knew Elias would do it. Prostitutes loved city guards as much as thieves did, but Elias seemed the sort to compromise his antiauthoritarian principles over a slight.

Felix left the brothel frustrated and empty-handed, tying his headscarf as they walked. Alleys grew grim around them. Every city had a seedy underbelly, and Elias was leading Felix to the pit of Pompeii's. A few more turns, and an unseemly building loomed ahead, stinking

VESUVIUS

of liquor. Disguised as a bar, only an engraving of dice in the door's keystone indicated it offered more than drink. The rattle of tin cups and tossed stones echoed to the street.

Elias beckoned Felix inside.

For such an early hour, the place was packed. The bar advertised wine but doled out beer, the vice of the truly plebeian, and men drank deep from sour jars. Along the wall hung faded theater masks, their exaggerated faces—comedy and sorrow—pulling strange shadows in the half-light. A frazzled barmaid wove between tables, topping off cups. No one gave Felix or his bloodied clothes a second glance.

At the counter, Elias batted his eyes for two beers, then herded Felix to the corner. Felix was no stranger to places like this, but usually in towns where the threat of execution wasn't so heavy. He scooted as far back as the sticky bench allowed, eyeing the crowd. One group caught Felix's attention, men dressed in neat tunics, heads bent in hushed conversation. These men looked too expensive for such a foul place, but rich folks loved pretending to be poor—and intruding where they didn't belong.

They reminded Felix of the statesman. Repressing a shiver, he tried to shut out the memory, but the statesman's breathy murmur brushed through his mind—*Once you remember what was taken from you* . . .

Did everyone in Pompeii know something about Felix that he didn't?

"Do you know the rules?" Elias asked, and at first, Felix wondered if he, too, was prodding around in his head. All Felix ever thought of were his rules—*Don't get attached. Reject belief or pay the price. Stay in the present.* But Elias only gestured to a handful of dice.

"Sure," Felix said. "What's the wager?"

"Let's trade something more fun than coin. Question for question."

"Loren tried a game like that already."

"Who do you think taught him to play?" Elias gave a flat smile. "Roll."

The game began.

For a seasoned player, the rounds moved quick. Dice were matched and swapped in a heady mix of luck and strategy. To Elias's credit, he had a fair dose of both, but when the last round rolled, he couldn't compete with Felix. Few people could.

Face stony, Elias stared at Felix's winning sweep. Clearly, he hadn't anticipated losing.

"I think I won an answer," said Felix.

After a slow drink, Elias reset the game. "I said you could ask. Remind me where I promised a response."

Felix's lips twitched despite himself. Elias was sharp. In other circumstances, they might have got on. Dropping his dice one by one into the cup, Felix's attention drifted back to the rich men in the corner.

"This city. Who runs it?"

"The duoviri, of course."

Heads of the council, Felix's ass. At best, the duoviri ran their mouths. "A *real* answer. I wasn't born yesterday."

"May as well have been. You're, what? Fifteen?"

"Seventeen." Felix bristled. He might be many things, but a baby face he was not. Besides, Elias could hardly be older than him.

"You like your head attached to your neck?"

"Ideally."

"Then reconsider that question. Better off asking, who holds the power?" Elias followed Felix's stare across to the group. "Pompeii caters to a specific bunch. Senators. Ex-senators. Lawyers. Rich bastards who travel here from Rome at summer's end, and the council bends over backward for them. They have no choice. Pompeii is a Roman colony."

"They're tourists?"

"Worse. Tourists with an agenda. I was a child, barely bought and brought here by my first master, when the last big quake wrecked the place. Wiped out most of the town, and we still haven't rebuilt. The council is scrambling to put together the taxes Rome demands, so there's nothing left for local repairs, and the quakes this summer are driving more people out."

"So you have a long line of rich tourists traipsing through a broken city while the capital demands more money, with few actual residents left to tax."

"Smart fox. Rome's envoys keep pressuring the council to levy deeper taxes. A couple strongholds are resisting the proposals, land-owners and merchants, but it's only a matter of time before they give in too. Or are wiped out."

Felix studied him. "How do you know all this?"

"Secrets of the trade, and you're out of questions this round." Elias smirked. "Roll."

The game continued. Matched. Swapped. Matched again. Once Elias adapted to Felix's style, he proved a formidable strategist, skill wasted throwing dice in a tavern. When he won, Felix was only a little sore. He swallowed a mouthful of beer to wash away the taste of losing—and the spike of nerves that came when Elias's gaze turned calculating.

"Don't look so nervous." Elias winked. "I'm saving my question for later."

As if that made Felix feel better, but he didn't intend there to *be* a later. "Take your time."

"I will." Leaning closer, Elias cupped his chin in his palm. "You know, your questions remind me of conversations I've had with Loren. Politics. Local affairs."

The comparison rankled Felix. He and Loren had nothing in common. Felix's interest in politics revolved around knowing who to avoid. Loren wanted to *be* the type of man Felix avoided.

Elias continued, "It's enough to make one wonder about you."

"Keep wondering." Felix pushed Elias's dice at him. "Again."

Sparing the pieces a cursory glance, Elias locked eyes with Felix. His were blisteringly dark. "Just ask what you mean to ask."

"Why did you really bring me here?'

"To stall you until Loren returned. Obviously. Why did you follow?"

"You threatened me," Felix hissed. "Over the . . ."

The crowd was loud enough that he didn't fear being overheard, and both being street scum, he and Elias blended in. Besides, thieves protected their own. But naming his crime would carry finality, regardless of what Elias already knew.

"Please. You followed because you were curious. I know that because I know Loren. He isn't a liar, but he holds a mess of secrets in his head. You can't ask him a question and expect a straight answer. Whatever he told you about the helmet, you couldn't possibly be satisfied." Suddenly suspicion twisted Elias's face. "But you wasted your question asking after tourists. As if, maybe, you've already made up your mind about the helmet. And what use you might make of it."

"A bath," Felix said dryly. "Food. A roof."

"You aren't thinking big enough."

The words, though casual, sent a chill down Felix's spine. He eyed Elias in a new light. Outside, day had turned to dusk. Without stray bars of sunset streaming through slitted windows, shadows fell harsher. They dripped down the planes of Elias's face, aging him before his time.

Loren and the statesman both called the helmet divine. Powerful. Deadly. A tingle raced across Felix's palms, a craving to touch, to hold skin-warmed silver again. To make the helmet his own.

He wet his lips. "Do *you* want it?"

The spell cracked when Elias snorted. "Gods, no. I want you—and it—far from Pompeii when you use it."

As if it wasn't just a glorified piece of metal. Magic was still horseshit. It had to be. Or else—

The air thickened until Felix couldn't breathe. He shoved back, bench legs screeching, and stormed off. Dice weren't the only thing being played that evening. He shouldn't have followed Elias. He shouldn't have been curious.

Curiosity led to caring, and caring never won Felix favor.

The statesman had also said *Your father is dead.*

Even if he brushed the comment off as a lucky guess, Felix couldn't shake how it rattled in the hollows of his mind, where memories should be, but weren't. An emptiness with only a fearful ache to fill it.

Whatever once fit there was no longer his to hold. But that never stopped him wondering.

Maybe Elias had been right: Felix did have an interest in Pompeii's politics beyond self-preservation. That if he asked the right questions, caught a fraying thread about the statesman's identity, Felix might trigger an answer to what he lacked. But his story was nothing special. In the end, all threads snapped. He was one in a long line of fatherless boys, and the statesman was some no-name tourist, and Felix should know better than to dwell.

Out in the muggy evening air, where rain clouds hung heavy, Felix's headache returned in full force. Mind muddled like this, picking out the details that mattered, the lifesaving details, proved impossible. The city sparked with nightlife, sounds stacking on his frustration. Farther down the street, a handful of boys circled in the careless way only close friends could. Something throbbed low in Felix's gut as one boy burst into laughter and slapped his friend's back. An easy gesture, foreign to someone like Felix.

Dangerous for someone like Felix.

Elias's hand landed on his shoulder, not gripping, but not friendly, either. The impact echoed down his vertebrae, like an earthquake.

"You feel like an omen," Elias said. "I can't have you lurking around my city."

"I'll be gone by morning."

"Then here's my question: What do you intend to do with your time left?"

But Felix had no real answer. Intentions never counted for much. Rain began to patter, and he tore his eyes from the laughing boys to face Elias. Before he could formulate an answer—or an excuse—a man twice their age sidled up. No words were exchanged, but Elias's eyes drooped, seductive but threaded with reluctant resignation, and the man pushed him against brick. Felix took that as his cue to leave.

"Hey, Fox?" Elias called. Felix looked back to see the man lick a stripe up Elias's neck. "Loren can be self-righteous, but he's a good person. I don't want to see him hurt."

Envy raked through Felix's gut. Clearly Elias had a tense history with Loren, but he still looked out for him. What must that be like? To count on someone to watch your back? By design, by his rules, Felix would never know.

Elias turned back to his client, and Felix walked alone.

CHAPTER VI
LOREN

If Felix wouldn't offer answers, Loren would find them himself.

He loved the temple best in the after-hours hush, when fading light stretched over the courtyard, and the columns cast shadows spindly and searching as fingers in prayer. When he sat alone with the cats and quiet reverence. When he could untangle thorn-snared thoughts and riddle through how to turn his curse into a gift.

Castor and Pollux greeted Loren at the entrance, winding between his legs as he pulled on his robes. The altar bowl still smoldered with slow-burning incense. Just that morning, he'd smashed this same bowl over Felix's head. Loren winced at the memory as he stamped out ashes. At the supply cabinet, he thumbed the cork of a jug of pricey Lassius wine. More satisfying to take it, certainly, but he was breaking enough rules. Besides, the bottle of Eumachius was already open, leftover from when they bled Felix.

Poor battered Felix. Loren hardly blamed him for wanting to leave. The sooner Loren figured this out—the sooner he stopped whatever disaster loomed—the sooner he could let Felix go. Even if it took all night, Loren would uncover what the helmet could do. Because the longer the helmet stayed within Felix's grasp, the worse the danger grew.

Bowl and wine in hand, Loren unlatched the cella door.

Isis glowed in the ever-lit lamp, marble features soft. Loren was drawn to her the way a night lily tilts to find the moon, and for a moment, his anxiety ebbed. He knelt on the dais and touched the stone-cool hem of her gown, inhaling deeply. He could do this.

Wine pooled into the bowl, swirling, murky as an unrefined ruby. He sat cross-legged, bowl on his lap, and rotated his finger sunwise across the surface of the wine, willing his mind to open. That morning, he'd been so close to scrying something, scenes moving deep in the liquid, but he lost his grip when the quake struck. He needed to reach that point again to ask the wine about the cataclysms. About Felix and the ghost. About how the helmet tied them all together.

Most important, Loren needed to know how he could change the outcome.

In his dreams, Felix always died.

When he first slipped into Loren's dreams years ago, the details were vague, shapeless, a wall of black descending on them both. Felix would cry, or sometimes offered Loren only an empty stare, and the world rolled out to nothing.

Then came Felix's anger. Months of silent tears and dead eyes turned into nights of copper-streaked chaos. He burned in a wave of destruction, turning everyone Loren ever loved to ash. Aurelia and her mother, Livia. Nonna. Elias. His parents. His childhood nurse, his favorite tutor—all made dust. When Felix finished, he'd turn on himself, and Loren watched that, too.

Each dream brought new details, until finally, six months prior, a city materialized around them, a change from the void Loren had come to expect. Red and yellow awnings, pomegranates in the sun, knee-high crossing stones. Nonna's bakery.

That's when Loren knew: Felix intended to bring about all of Pompeii's doom. Not just Loren's.

Felix would look at Loren straight on. Lift a wood-and-iron knife. Slit the seam of the sky. Bury the city alive.

Once—the night before Felix tripped into Loren's life—Felix floated, suspended in the blast of a great force, and Loren crawled to meet him. Stretched his hand. Their fingers brushed. He noted each of Felix's eyelashes, the lay of every curl, tiny details—the finest, clearest yet.

Then Loren drove the knife home.

The memory soured his stomach, and his shaking hands shivered the wine.

"Open," Loren urged. "Show me."

Wings splayed across the wine's surface.

The cella door swung open, and light streamed stark against the dim chamber. Loren startled. Cold wine sloshed over his lap, shattering the image.

"Working late?" asked Camilia.

"What are you doing here?" Loren demanded.

He immediately regretted asking. She was angry. Beyond angry. Fists clenched at her sides, she shot him silent with a gorgon's stare.

"The Priest," she said, "asked me to help him consult the smoke. An emergency reading. Imagine my shock when I arrived to find the altar bowl missing. Again."

Her tone was lethal, but her words made his heart flutter like a bird's last hope. Loren latched on to it. "Let me help with the reading. I saw something just now. Wings, or—"

"Clean up. Bring me the bowl."

Camilia spun and strode out.

Loren nearly knocked the lantern off the dais as he scrambled up. What a sight that would've made, to watch the temple catch fire from one clumsy act. Story of his life. He stabilized the lantern and poured what remained of the wine back into the jug.

At the altar, Camilia crackled like a summer storm. Loren approached her cautiously, bowl held as a peace offering. She snatched it, slammed it down, and busied herself lighting a fire.

"Your hands are trembling," Loren said after her third attempt to strike flint failed. Wrong move. He had never solved a problem by talking more.

She rounded on him, eyes glossy. "Hold your tongue for once. I warned you to mind yourself months ago. I told you not to follow this path. Still, you sneak around and pretend we don't notice. You reek of desperation."

"I'm only trying to help."

"Help yourself, you mean."

Tear pricked the corners of Loren's eyes. Wine dripped a slow beat from his sodden robes. "I am *not* selfish."

Camilia huffed and pressed the flint into his hand. "Light it. Go on."

Loren clutched the sharp stone until it threatened to pierce his skin, add a trickle of blood to his mess. "I don't know how."

"Right. You never had to learn. Someone did it for you."

Loren tugged the cord around his neck, twisting it in his fingers. She didn't know the truth about where he came from. Nobody did. But Camilia was always quick to notice little things, like how Loren couldn't do laundry when he was new to the temple but knew the difference between weaves of fine silk. How he could write in three languages but couldn't mail a letter.

"I see things, Camilia." His throat bobbed. "Horrible things. And I know they're set to happen. I came to Pompeii to learn how to stop them."

"You have bad dreams. Not visions."

"Why don't you believe me?"

"Because you're delusional. Because you think you're an oracle, and you aren't. You can't have a nightmare and decide it's the future. That isn't how it works."

"But just now—"

"Look around you." Camilia jabbed at the altar, the cella, the door that led to the rest of Pompeii. "Look beyond yourself for a moment. Quakes shaking the city, that helmet going missing—the gods are angry, yet you continue to disrespect them. There are tracks to become an augur for a reason. Go beg Umbrius to let you into the Temple of Jupiter if you're that desperate to pursue it. Or if you want to playact so badly, join the theater."

Unsurprising that they were rehashing the same argument from six months ago when Loren first tried confiding in her, after his dreams showed him, concretely, Pompeii's doom. Back then, she'd laughed in his face.

Now she'd sooner slap him.

Loren set the flint on the altar. Wordlessly, Camilia lit the flame with a single stroke, and the crackle-pop of incense filled the silence. He kept his lips pressed in shame. Something soft brushed his ankles. Pollux. Or Castor? Telling them apart was hard enough even when tears didn't blur his vision.

"I wish Celsi hadn't left. I wish you hadn't replaced him." Camilia scrubbed her face and hastened to procure more herbs to burn.

Loren stood rooted at the altar as her blow crept beneath his skin. Her story had never been a secret: A child when her family died, the temple had stepped in to raise her. Celsi became like a younger brother to her, but his father soon struck it rich and moved up in society, taking his son away from the dregs of Isis. For Camilia, the wound of losing Celsi never healed. As much as Loren tried to fill Celsi's absence in the years since, he was cut in a shape that didn't fit.

"Loren," said the Priest of Isis.

Habit drove Loren to turn and dip his head in obeisance, a motion he hardly felt. The Priest leaned heavily on his walking stick, quietly stern. Loren hadn't heard him enter the temple at all. He wondered how long the old man had stood there, how much of their fight he'd heard.

"Good evening, Priest." Loren nodded again for the sake of doing something. "I'll fetch a stool."

A gnarled hand gripped Loren's forearm before he could dash. "Where is the boy you are protecting?"

"I left him in my room. We thought it best he stays out of sight for now."

Which made it sound like a mutual decision, and not Loren keeping Felix in a tight cage while he puzzled through the mystery alone.

"Out of others' sight, or yours?" The Priest frowned. His eyes, normally clouded by haze, shot an arrow straight through Loren. "You should be with him."

"I was hoping I could help you with the reading. I saw—" Loren cut off, thumbing the fabric of his robes he tended to so carefully, blue linen now soaked purple. Here was a chance to confess his dreams to the Priest, his visions, what he was certain would happen. The Priest might listen. Might take Loren under his wing, train him, believe him.

Or write Loren off as mad, the way his parents had.

"I have an interest in divining," he finished, sounding as pathetic as he felt. "In augury."

"Your time would be better spent taking care of your friend. He is as lost as you are right now." The Priest's frown deepened. He pressed a kind, condescending hand to Loren's elbow. "Loren, this was never the place for you. You suspect, same as I, that your path never ran parallel with Isis. Go home."

Loren split down the middle.

He opened his mouth, but no sound came out. He wanted to wail. He wanted to beg. He wanted to drag the Priest into the cella, show him the spilled wine, paint the wings for him. But one of the few things Loren carried with him from home was the ability to take heartbreak with a stiff upper lip. He was intimately acquainted with dismissal.

Humiliation followed him to the closet where he hung his robes for the last time. Camilia's eyes bored into him as he tripped over Castor—or Pollux—keeping watch at the door. He should have spent more time memorizing their differences. Now he'd never trip over them again.

Casting a last look at the altar bowl, the smoke, and the Priest's farewell nod, Loren blinked back tears and left.

Dusk brought a sprinkle, rain rinsing surface grime from the streets, but Loren still felt like gutter sludge. He looped the merchant district, dodging shopkeepers closing stalls for the night. Stopping at Nonna's door didn't make him feel better, even when she passed him a basket of leftover bread, pears, and dates.

"Take the empty basket to Livia. Tell her I need more waxed cloth." Nonna waved Loren off before he could utter hello.

Errand boy.

He took the long way back to the brothel, even as the shower worsened, crossing through the Forum. A dozen or so councilmen had convened before the Temple of Apollo, likely fostering rumors about the helmet thief. A boy stood among them, Celsi, the constant thorn in Loren's side, rubbing sleep from his eyes like he'd rather be anywhere else. Terrorizing the town with Aurelia, likely, or clinging to Camilia.

Still, Celsi had managed to get where Loren could never: in the council's good graces.

Unable to help it, Loren inched nearer. Still too far to discern their conversation, but he could pick out faces. Three scribes etched frantic notes onto wax tablets. One older councilmember dozed while standing. A man in a red tunic leaned lazily against an arch, staring sideways. Priest Umbrius, a short, balding man gowned in purple, led the conversation. Each time he emphasized a point, he brought his hand down on Celsi's shoulder. Celsi wobbled on impact, face pinched.

Loren should be there at Umbrius's elbow. He worked harder than Celsi, cared more than Celsi. He should be hearing their theories about the helmet, what they thought its disappearance meant, what they planned to do next. For Apollo's sake, it was *Loren*, not Celsi, who had the helmet piled under his laundry at that moment.

A dark possibility skittered across his mind, a scenario where he approached Umbrius, revealed the thief's hideout, and catapulted into the public eye as a city hero. He'd be one step closer to cementing himself in Pompeiian society, another barrier to his father dragging him home.

Felix, of course, would be executed.

Quickly as it passed, Loren killed the thought. Maybe if Felix were as cruel as in the nightmares, turning him in would be a given. But Loren had witnessed Felix's death enough times. Couldn't this world—the real world—be the one where Loren saves him?

Frustration, his default feeling lately, simmered anew, and he sidled closer, straining his ears. One of the onlookers spotted him, her head snapping to lock eyes with him through the drizzle. She stood beneath the shelter of a weeping awning, and if not for her pale pink silk dress, Loren would have thought her a ratty eavesdropper, too. She had drawn up her white wool palla to protect her hair, but a long golden curl dangled free.

Her stare pinned him in place. He waited, heart stuttering, for her to nudge a nearby guard, point at Loren, humiliate him for his desperation. She didn't. She merely gazed, curious but oddly knowing, as if—impossibly—she had expected to see him standing pathetic in the rain.

What was she doing there? Married to a councilman, maybe, but wives didn't get involved in council affairs. If Loren had seen her before, it hadn't registered in his memory.

Her lips parted. Foolishly, Loren thought she meant to address him, like they weren't separated by yards of distance. Embarrassment heated his neck.

He'd overstayed a welcome that hadn't been his to begin with. He needed to leave.

Tearing from her stare, he turned to dash—and crashed into a wall of leather armor. The guard caught Loren's arm to steady him. For a terror-soaked second, he panicked that the statesman's soldier had come to demand where the thief hid. But no. That man wore red, and besides, Loren had been veiled. No chance of recognition.

"Watch your step, sweetheart." Rain dripped off the guard's long, thin nose.

Mumbling an apology, Loren slipped free of his grasp and stumbled back, sandals sliding on wet stone. The man tried to say more, but Loren had dealt with enough guards and gatekeepers that day.

He hurried off.

Light greeted him from the brothel's doorway, but Loren lingered in the drizzle, gazing at the closed shutters of his room. If Felix had lit a lantern in Loren's absence, he couldn't tell. He wondered if Felix had eaten, if he'd talked to Elias, if he was still awake at all. Loren hoped not. Cowardly, yes, but after his bold promises to figure Felix out, returning empty-handed and jobless was like choking on a bite bigger than he could chew.

Surely Felix would offer sneering words, too, like Loren didn't carry enough shame already. He didn't want to face that. But, dutifully, and because he had nowhere else to go, he went inside, counted the creaky stairs, paused outside his door. Rolling his shoulders back, he made to unlock it.

The door was already cracked.

When it swung open, Loren's blood iced over at the emptiness that met him. The basket of soggy bread slipped from his numb fingers.

Loren hadn't needed to worry about facing Felix. He ought to have feared the opposite.

Felix was gone.

CHAPTER VII
FELIX

When Felix started up the brothel stairs, he almost wished the underworld were real, if only so he could curse Elias's name to it.

Somehow, Elias had timed Felix's return for the helmet perfectly with the arrival of the last person he wanted to run into. Which meant Elias had outwitted him twice now. Felix couldn't let that stand. But Loren didn't seem interested in any score Felix kept. He glared from the landing, drenched, splotchy, and bursting with self-righteousness.

"For someone whose head is inching toward the block," Loren bit, "one would think you'd be more careful."

Felix cast Loren a cool look, slipping past to pause at the door of his room. "You shouldn't leave this unlocked. Who knows who might invite himself in."

He pushed inside.

"You're a—an—" Loren said in a shaky gust when the door shut behind them.

"Ass?" Felix supplied. "You're allowed to curse."

Loren's face flushed all the way to his freckles. "You were missing. I thought you ran. Or that the council had come while I was away."

"Right, and brand you as my co-conspirator, gods forbid. Sink your political career before it begins." Felix rolled his eyes. "I'm not a fool, and I wasn't escaping. Elias and I went to play dice. Is that so unforgivable?"

"Gambling is illegal."

"I don't bend over the table to get screwed by laws."

Rain dripped from Loren's frazzled braid. "You're vile."

Felix stared. "You live in a brothel. Surely you've heard worse."

Loren's nostrils flared. Felix tensed, waiting for him to swing a fist, but he only crossed to the washbasin and tossed over a rag.

"Wash. Food's in that basket." He made a shapeless gesture. "Fruit, bread. Sleep in the bed if you want, I don't care."

"The floor is fine."

"Fine. And don't . . . don't speak to me." Loren rubbed his eyes, then propped open the shutters. He climbed onto the windowsill, legs dangling, stared at the street, and went silent.

Felix stripped and scrubbed dried blood and grime. He didn't have other clothes to change into, so he donned his filthy tunic again. It'd have to do until he was far enough from Pompeii that he could risk pausing to wash it. Then he scarfed half a loaf of olive-studded bread. Almost had the other half, too, until he remembered Loren likely hadn't eaten.

Felix traced Loren's silhouette at the window. Defeat radiated from his slumped shoulders. Evidently, whatever answer he hoped to glean while prostrating himself at Isis's foot hadn't materialized. This should have heartened Felix. He didn't want Loren poking around in his business. Most days, Felix didn't poke around in his *own* business, since that only led to dead-ends of disappointment. But to his surprise, he liked sullen Loren far less than chatty Loren.

Besides, if Felix was leaving tonight, they might as well part on decent terms.

Awkwardness stretched as Felix settled on the sill backward, feet firmly planted in the room, and held out the bread. Loren furrowed his brow, but slowly accepted the offering.

"Thank you," Loren said, picking at the crust.

"Your food, not mine."

"Still." Rain picked up again, a half-there pitter-patter. "I hate this weather. Either commit to the storm properly or don't bother."

"Are you giving the sky an ultimatum?"

Loren's nose twitched. "Truthfully, I'd prefer the weather clear all the time. Like this, you can't see the stars. You can't see the moon."

Twisting around, Felix squinted. "It was a sliver last night. You'd barely see it anyway."

"I suppose that's why I like it. You always get to watch the moon come back."

Loren lapsed into silence as he finished off the bread. They sat shoulder to shoulder, not quite touching, while the night grew clammy and chill. A sea breeze whistled in from the coast, teasing a change in the weather, a break from the unseasonal autumn heat.

"Felix," Loren broached, brushing crumbs off his lap. "If I ask a question, will you be honest?"

"Depends."

"I should have anticipated that answer." The corner of his mouth pinched. "But I'll ask anyway. You turned down the statesman's offer because you thought he'd kill you once you fulfilled your end of the deal. But you're wrong, I think."

"That isn't a question."

"The helmet hasn't been moved in three hundred years. Until now. What I'm asking," said Loren, "is why would he kill the only person who can handle it?"

He had a point. But the idea of the statesman taking Felix alive made him shiver. He had a sense that whatever the statesman would use him for would cost more than bleeding out in an alley. *Collaborators*, he had said. *Cassius and Brutus of a new age.*

Felix couldn't. He couldn't dwell on the statesman's grip on his face, or he would lose himself completely.

"The kind of power a relic like that holds is . . ." Loren trailed off with a shaky, reverent breath. "That you can touch it must mean something. Have you had divine experiences before? Ritual training? A priest's blessing?"

Felix tensed. "I don't remember."

"Don't you?" Loren urged.

The thing was—it was both true and not. The memories were there, Felix knew because they dogged his footsteps, invisible and unnamed. He knew because he felt the *lack*. But no matter how hard he tried, what questions he asked, they were gated and bricked, his mind refusing to recall. Most days, he didn't know where to direct his grief, or who to channel his anger at, or where that anger stemmed from.

Impressions of a life lived, but not remembering it by half.

Crinkly hazel eyes. A kiss pressed to his forehead. His father's footsteps against pavement, and curly copper hair retreating from sight. Half-light from an open cella door, glinting off a marble face long after nightfall. Sweet wine saturated bitter. Sleepy.

But if he did remember in full, if he found the missing piece— how quickly would the absence become an abscess? How would swapping one wound for another help? Maybe some memories were best forgotten. Maybe Felix was right to be afraid. Maybe he was lucky.

He ran unsettled fingers through his curls, swallowing against his dry throat. In the corner, the trunk with Mercury's helmet stashed inside cast a darker shadow than before. A prickle crept up Felix's spine, phantom fingers pressing in.

A siren's song: *Use me. Use me, and I'll explain everything.*

Horseshit.

"No, I don't," Felix snapped, wrenching back to Loren, pulse racing and lungs tight. The rain was a lukewarm spray against his back. Grounding. "Whatever your fascination is with the helmet, I can't tell you more. Talk about something else."

Loren recoiled. Gently, he said, "Sorry. I won't ask again."

But the one-sided pinch of his mouth suggested otherwise. He plotted, and that plot would spell disaster. But Felix had work to do. Treasures to sell. He couldn't afford to be lured down fruitless memory paths by clueless temple boys or provoked by lucky guesses from some statesman.

"Another question, then?" Loren said, fiddling with the cord he wore. "Not about the helmet, I swear."

"Go on." Gods, Loren talked a lot. Better to listen to his rambling than dwell in memory-land, though. Besides, filling the silence wasn't such a bad change of pace.

"If you were about to do something awful, would you want to be warned? So you could change your path."

"That supposes anyone could predict the future."

"Can't they?"

Felix snorted. "Priests, augurs, oracles, it's made up. They'll say anything to get paid. The only way to change your path—control your path—is to keep running."

"The gods would take exception to that."

"The gods would take exception to most of what I say."

Loren looked at Felix straight on. "You know what I think? You're more truthful than you let on."

"Being blunt and being honest aren't the same," Felix said. "I lie to survive."

Loren had nice eyes. Kind eyes. Warm as cinnamon to match the spray of freckles across his nose. When he stared, he studied, and Felix couldn't shake the feeling that his skin, his muscles, his ribs had gone transparent. That Loren could see right through him, see every twinge and scar of Felix's heart.

No. Silly. Loren knew no part of him. If Felix stuck to his rules, they'd separate as strangers.

Felix shook his head to clear it, the day finally catching up. This time last night, he'd been eyeing the Forum guard in the tavern, wondering how best to pull off his theft. The guard had been the one to pay for it. Guilt swarmed in Felix's chest, but he forced it down. Regret, remorse, recompense—those feelings brought a quick end to any thieving career. Another lesson from his father.

"It's late," Loren said, reading the sweep of Felix's exhaustion. "You should sleep."

Felix stood, arms and legs and skull aching. He made to walk from the window, but he paused. Lingered. "See you tomorrow."

He could survive a few more hours here. He could endure Loren's scrutiny until he drifted off to sleep. He could outsmart the streets and make it to the gate. Then Felix would peel off, run far and free, leave Pompeii and politics in the dust, onward to a future with the helmet as his prize—where no one knew a damn thing about him.

Felix wouldn't look back.

CHAPTER VIII

LOREN

Loren hoped the nightmares would stop, that whatever strand connecting Felix's psyche to his was satisfied now they'd met in the flesh, but that was before he blinked awake—not awake—to a knife running through his chest.

Cold pain punched a hole in his core. Loren gave a rattling gasp, the act ripping him in two, and fought for context. Details didn't immediately solidify. He stood suspended in a void while his pain-lagged brain slowly filled in the rest, staring at the blurry handle protruding from his ribs.

Revenge, Loren thought with sour irony, for stabbing Felix in his dream the night before.

More details trickled in, mist wisping into shape, and the image of Felix stepped from the darkness ahead, lifeless and ragged as ever. Ghostly. Seeing him after meeting real-world Felix gave Loren a startling sense of dissonance.

The ghost said something, but, as usual, Loren heard nothing—frustrating to no end. If he could only hear the ghost, figure out what he needed, maybe Loren could put the specter to rest.

He swayed. Black spots bloomed across his vision. The dream world inched toward clarity, familiar cobblestones forming underfoot, buildings lining the street, colorful awnings sending a throb through his heart that had nothing to do with the knife.

They were about to be destroyed.

"Why?" he demanded in a bloody choke. Every part of him blistered from icy shock. He fought to take a single stumbling step forward, and Ghost-Felix mirrored it backward, stepping onto one of the road's crossing stones.

Loren had hopped across those stones yesterday. Nonna's yellow shop was ahead. The Temple of Isis stood a street over. This was his sharpest dream yet, accurate to the cluster of dandelions growing through the curb.

Of course. Because Felix was in Pompeii now. He'd seen these details himself.

Dark clouds churned. Heavy. Noxious. Smoldering ash drifting down singed Loren's braid.

Vesuvius distilled last, peak visible amidst the storm. Loren looked to it with futile, desperate hope. If only it could stop this. If only it could form a shield against the ghost collapsing the sky.

The ghost's face twisted, mocking. His mouth moved again, and Loren could *almost* hear him, but his voice was muffled and distorted, the way sounds vibrated underwater.

"Why?" Hot tears burned Loren's cheeks, the only warmth in a body cold as stone. "What did I do to you? What do you *want*?"

Another step. Then his legs gave out, so he crawled. He wanted to grab Ghost-Felix's face, close the distance, force him to whisper his demands straight into Loren's ear. Gravel dug into his flesh. He hardly felt it.

Still on the stone, the ghost stooped. His flat gaze held enough edge to be cruel. More words. Loren stared at his lips, reading the shapes. *You.*

"You." Loren coughed. "You do this every night. To me. But I'm close, Felix. I'm so—close to figuring you out. When I do—"

The ghost pointed at Loren's chest. Loren followed the jab of his finger. At first, what he saw didn't register. Rather, it registered as impossible.

His own hand gripped the knife.

Fear, confusion—he wouldn't—Loren jerked up in time to catch the ghost's mouth form one last sentence.

You did this to yourself.

Black caved down. All went still, a crushing, soundless tomb.

When Loren jolted upright, he felt the knife in his ribs. A phantom.

A ghost.

His chest heaved, and he blinked rapidly to dispel the tears he'd carried with him. His ears buzzed. The room was dark. Abruptly, Loren missed the moon with such a raw ache, it reverberated in each of his fingers.

"Loren?"

He nearly jumped out of his skin, but it was only Felix. Real Felix, kneeling beside the bed, hand stretched to shake Loren awake. Felix who, yes, bore a slant to his mouth, but not one of cruelty. One of sardonic self-preservation. The Felix who dropped curses like a first language but had promised to see Loren tomorrow. And here he was. Loren's thudding heart skipped.

At night, Felix's copper curls tangled like a storm-tossed ocean. Loren stared at their waves, letting the soft, sleep-mussed swoop drag him back to shore.

"You were thrashing," Felix said, tight with something that Loren almost placed as worry. "Shouting."

"I don't talk in my sleep," Loren insisted even as the back of his neck heated.

"You said my name," Felix pressed. "You said I do this every night."

Loren dragged his attention from the edge of Felix's cheekbone, illuminated by the faintest sliver of lamplight seeping in from the street. He pressed his palms into his eye sockets, then dropped his hands to twist in his lap. "Forget it. Bad dream."

"Sounded like it. Have you dreamed . . ." Felix frowned, but Loren could infer the rest of the question. *Had Loren dreamed of him before?*

To Felix, the answer would be impossible. They'd known each other less than a day.

"I said forget it." Too snappish. Loren softened. "Sorry I woke you."

Felix shot a glance at the door. "I was up already. Had to piss."

Loren would've bought the lie if the teller had been anyone else. As another grounding exercise, he picked out a handful of clues, like how Felix's sandals were strapped on and the trunk lid was ajar. Felix had meant to leave. He would have, too, if—ironically—his ghost-self hadn't intervened. Hadn't made Loren call out in his sleep. The soft glow that lit when he believed Felix worried for him extinguished.

When Loren looked to Felix, stoniness met him. Felix knew Loren knew, he must, but he also didn't walk his fib back.

Loren swallowed anger. It would do no good to fling accusations of broken promises. He thought—hoped—Felix shared some of his interest in solving the helmet's mystery, whether he admitted so or not. But it was clear now Felix's desire to leave outweighed any bargain. Loren had been a fool for trusting him at all.

Now both had to sit in the discomfort of a plan foiled. Dawn couldn't be far off, and sleep was no longer an option with Felix's intention to flee revealed. Instead, Felix left the bedside to sit against the wall and stare, eyes reflecting in the dark, faintly animal. Loren shuddered, drew his knees to his chest, and pretended none of this was happening.

You did this to yourself. Loren tried to riddle out the implication, that he'd fallen on his own blade. In a way, Ghost-Felix's accusation reminded him of Camilia, blaming Loren for worsening things by meddling. Maybe Loren had finally stuck his nose in one too many places. Maybe Ghost-Felix didn't want Loren figuring him out either. They were far from friends. Whatever he had done to make Felix, or the ghost, rather, hate him so badly, Loren wondered if he would ever know.

Or if he'd be forever doomed to silence.

Sunrise didn't bring answers, but it did bring resolve.

Reality intruded with the stirring of early risers outside, birds and bakers alike. Loren crawled from bed when it was light enough to see without tripping, looked anywhere but at Felix, and fished in his trunk for his only clean tunic. The hair on his arms prickled when he brushed the cloth-covered helmet.

Directing his anger at the helmet helped. He could blame it for worsening an already bad situation. He could blame it for the dreams, the failed scrying, and how now that he needed divine help most, he found only silence and shut temple doors. What a useless ability: to see the future, but never with the time or clarity to change it.

Sighing, he slammed the lid shut.

Shaking wrinkles from his spare tunic, Loren peeled free a scrap of navy silk he'd been gifted by a follower of Isis the other week. He'd meant to bribe Aurelia with it, but the shuffle of days had buried it deep in the clutter. Now it sparked an idea.

If the gods turned away, Loren could shoulder the mystery on his own. And he knew exactly where to start looking.

"I meant to ask last night," Felix started, eyeing Loren as he changed. "Is that wine you were covered in? If all you do is drink, maybe I *should* join your cult."

Loren bit his tongue. He'd managed to last this long without stewing on his dismissal from the temple. No chance would he reveal that defeat to Felix.

"Bad news if you hoped to convert. We aren't going to the temple today," he said as crisply as he could muster. "Besides, you hardly look better, all blood-splattered and filthy."

"If you want me to strip, you could just say so."

"Grab your scarf before I let you rot in those clothes," Loren snapped, cheeks flaming. "If we don't beat the crowds, you'll be seen."

Felix's snicker chased him to the street.

For a mid-autumn morning, the heat settled in unusually early from all sides, cloaking the city in a damp, woolly blanket. Merchants worked in the shade of their awnings, though it wouldn't be long before they pulled their wares to continue business inside. The roads swelled in the slow roast as if, at any moment, they might rupture. Sympathy panged in Loren's chest for Felix, swaddled in his headscarf and bandages, sweat rolling off his brow.

"Hotter than Pluto's ass and smells like it." Felix fanned himself. "How are you not sweating your balls off?"

Sympathy gone. Loren took off at a brisk pace.

Nonna's near-empty basket swung from his elbow as he led Felix to the eastern quarter of the city, past the cheesemonger and cobbler who both waved. By the amphitheater, workers were busy plastering posters to brick.

"What are they advertising?" Felix asked as they neared.

Loren slowed. "We can stop to look."

Felix shifted restlessly. "Just tell me."

"You can't read?"

"You can?"

"Of course, it's—" Loren stopped. In Pompeii, he was a lowly temple attendant. In the minds of most, literacy wasn't a given for him.

He cleared his throat. "It's the festival I told you about, the reason the city is busier than usual, why guards are everywhere. Gladiator games, wine, dancing. Isis has the honor of performing opening rites tomorrow morning."

He said it so instinctively, he forgot he wouldn't be involved until his stomach twisted in reminder.

"Let the Priest know he can't use my other arm as the sacrifice." Felix sniffed. He sounded so indignant, Loren had to laugh. For a moment, the knot eased.

They made it another block, and a rustling was the only warning Loren had before a weight dropped onto his back from a ledge above. Not so surprising. Aurelia's favorite pastime was ambushing him. But it'd been one thing when she was eight and scrawny, and another in the middle of her growth spurt.

"I knew you'd come today," she said, arms locked around his neck. Loren wrestled with her, trying to slip free, and she only relented when he pretended to choke. A satisfied grin split her face. "Mamma said you wouldn't, but I know everything."

"It's been one day. You can't have missed me that badly."

"Miss you? Never." Aurelia hopped up, wiping dusty palms on her dress. She'd tied the long hem for ease of being a nuisance. "I only wanted to show you what I'm working on. Besides, it proves I'm right and Mamma is wrong. Who's this?"

Sometimes she changed directions so fast it gave Loren a headache.

Felix had plastered himself to the wall, watching their exchange with some degree of horror, like he didn't know what to make of children. When Loren introduced them, Aurelia wrinkled her nose at Felix's grubby clothes.

"Does he bathe?"

"Never," Felix said. "Take a whiff."

She faked a gagging fit.

Loren rolled his eyes. "Is your mother home?"

The diversion worked. Aurelia beckoned them to follow and burst into her mother's tailor shop with a victory cry.

Livia poked her head from the side room. "Aurelia, inside voice. Who—oh, Loren!"

In two strides, she crossed the room to pull him into a massive hug. Loren melted into it. Her hair, dark and curly as Aurelia's, smelled of honey and clean water and everything else right in the world.

Which, these days, wasn't much.

When Livia withdrew, she kissed each of his cheeks, but Loren couldn't meet her eyes. "It's been far too long, love. I worried you were avoiding me."

"You scold like Nonna."

"Good. If I can be half as formidable as she is, I'll have lived a good life." She joked, but a sad crinkle formed between her brows. Quieter, just for him, she repeated, "Far too long."

Questions lurked in her tone. Loren didn't know where to begin.

Blessedly, Aurelia saved him. She hopped onto the counter, feet swinging, and pointed. "Loren brought a friend. A smelly friend. He's called Felix."

Livia released Loren when she followed Aurelia's finger to Felix, hovering half out the door.

"Oh dear," she fretted. "Dreadful-looking thing, what happened to you?"

Felix grimaced. "The Priest of Isis."

"Horrible old man." Livia tutted and moved to hug Felix, too, but he shifted back, and she stopped herself. Switching tactics, she clasped her hands and beamed, though Felix didn't relax his defenses. "Well, worry not. We'll clean you up."

"I don't have the savings to cover more than half right now," Loren said. "But I could run errands until—"

"Have I ever asked for pay before?" Livia ushered a stiff-limbed Felix behind the counter, patting Loren's cheek as she passed. "Next time, don't insult me by offering."

They disappeared behind the threadbare curtain blocking off the tailoring room, and Loren rubbed the cord around his neck. Livia was the last person who would keep score, but Loren added this to his tally of wrongs to right.

"You like him," Aurelia said, mouth full of dates scrounged from Loren's basket. "I saw you laughing together."

"Stop spying," he said, "and chew with your mouth shut."

She slipped off the counter. "Come see my project."

Aurelia took him upstairs to the bedroom she shared with Livia. Common for Pompeii's working class, their living space was small, most of the unit belonging to the shop. A single bed, slightly wider than Loren's own, stood neatly made and covered in pillows. Old dolls sat beneath a weaving loom, and above the window hung Aurelia's father's military gladius, sheath carefully dusted.

Livia made any place feel like home. It lay in the little touches, hand-stitched tunics dressing the dolls, embroidered poppies on bed linens. This had been Loren's room once, too, his first year in Pompeii, until he noticed the strain with all three of them packed in. But by then he had his place with Isis, where he made enough to rent the closet at the brothel. He made his excuses to Livia, and he left.

She had never forgiven him for growing up, but Loren likewise couldn't forgive himself for taking advantage of her when she knew nothing about where he came from.

Focus. He shook off the nostalgia.

"I got you something," Loren said, fishing out the silk, and Aurelia's eyes lit. She grabbed, but he held the scrap above her reach. "If you help me first."

She glared. "I hate being bribed."

83

"And yet." He sidestepped her stomping foot. "You spend a lot of time in the Forum. Playing, snooping, whatever you call it. What can you tell me about the stolen helmet?"

"Mercury's helmet?" Aurelia bit the skin around her thumb. "It can't be touched. I dared Celsi to try once—"

"Aurelia."

"—but he told me his pappa would never stop nagging if he came home with burnt hands. Then I said that's only a rumor, and *he* said he knows because he saw someone try once, and now the man has to wear gloves. Sounds awful, hiding your hands all the time. Imagine trying to weave." She scrunched her nose and flounced to undo the covering on her loom.

"Did Celsi say who?" When she only blinked, Loren huffed. "The man with the gloves."

"Oh. Some smuggler who lives in town." Her face twisted impishly. "But if you want the real story, Celsi told me he's a pirate on the run from the emperor."

"Celsi says whatever gets him attention." Loren's mouth pinched. Aurelia's story offered little of substance. A divine helmet was utterly priceless; it would attract anyone with sticky fingers, pirate or not— Felix was proof. But that told Loren nothing about Felix's connection to the helmet. Defeated, he let the silk flutter into her hand, and she grinned.

"Try Nonna next," she suggested. "She must be as old as Mercury himself by now. She might know more. Now, *look*."

Without further ado, she yanked the cover off her loom, and Loren's blood ran cold.

The wooden frame held Aurelia's latest project, yarn interwoven in an abstract tapestry. She pieced her weavings together with threads from Livia's scraps, collecting colors like a crow collected trinkets, but she had a way of making something greater than its parts.

Her tapestries told stories. Told visions.

Now the loom depicted the swallow of a wave, but not of the sea. Black surged in a noxious curl, cut through with red, strands of twisting gray—

"There's an ending hidden here somewhere," Aurelia mused. "But I can't quite find it."

Copper and silver, woven throughout.

Loren's stomach soured. He'd seen plenty of those colors lately. So, it seemed, had Aurelia. This was precisely what he feared, why he never shared specifics about his own dreams with her. A single vision was a single possibility. Two was confirmation.

Copper and silver. A thief and his stolen treasure at the end of the world.

Knees shaking, Loren sank onto the edge of the bed. "It's . . ."

"Missing an element, I know." Aurelia raised the navy silk. "This, maybe? How would you finish it?"

"I'm not a weaver." He fought to keep his voice steady as he tore his gaze from the loom. "Perhaps you should shelve it awhile. Work on something new."

"I'm afraid I won't have time."

"You're young, Aurelia. You have all the time in the world."

"Mamma says I have an old soul." She rolled her eyes. "She says the same about you."

Loren frowned. "You need friends your own age."

"I have Celsi."

"You hate Celsi."

"Not true. It's Celsi who hates everyone. Except me, of course. But especially you." Aurelia plopped at his feet. "Braid my hair."

Her rambling shifted to idle street gossip, critiques about Nonna using too much salt in her flatbread, fights she'd picked with other children lately, but Loren didn't miss the way she left the weaving uncovered, a blight in the room he once called home. Nor could he shake Ghost-Felix's silent words, looping his mind and winding tighter with every pass, a thread tensing to snap—

You did this to yourself.

CHAPTER IX
FELIX

Whatever bond Livia and Loren shared was beyond Felix's understanding.

It wasn't that he didn't miss his mother. More like, he didn't have a mother to miss. She left soon after he was born. End of story. Felix's father never spoke of her, so he didn't know what she looked like or what her favorite flowers were. And if sometimes he pictured the twisting road leading from Rome—the same road he took eleven years later, in the after times—and wondered if she had his same eyes, well. That was his business.

Once Livia herded Felix into the fitting room, she wasted no time ordering him to remove his scarf and strip, leaving him in nothing but shorts. Discomfort lodged in his throat, but when he clutched his old tunic to his chest, a last shield, she pried it gently from his grip.

"You're safe here. I'm a seamstress, I've seen it all." She laid the tunic across a drafting table and studied old stains, mending stitches, blood splattered along the too-short hem. "How long have you had this?"

The tunic had been his father's, still oversized on Felix when he fled. Intervening years wore it ragged as he ran between towns, fabric shrinking against his growing body. Still, he hadn't shed it, even if that broke his rule about attachment.

Tangible items frayed, but they didn't muddle the way of memories.

"A while," Felix admitted.

"You've taken good care of it. Clothes tell a story, love. Yours must be a rough one."

His mouth dried, and he turned his cheek. "It's only fabric."

Livia folded the tunic neatly, then riffled through a closet to find a piece that might fit. A burgundy wool piece drowned him, while an expensive cotton shift crept past his knees and made him itch to pull it down. Finally, she withdrew a navy garment.

"Aurelia wove this fabric herself," Livia murmured, smoothing the hem. "Dyed the fibers and all. I thought I might save it for Loren, but he's so slender in the shoulder . . ."

She draped it over his head, gathering and pinning and securing it around his waist with a leather belt. The linen brushed softer than the others he'd tried, like a cool breeze in the dead of summer.

"Look, it has a pocket." Livia touched the pouch fastened to the belt.

"I can't afford this," Felix said as she made him turn for her, checking the fit.

"Nonsense. You heard my warning to Loren. Besides, it seems you could use a kindness." She smiled, wide and warm, and he thumbed the expensive fabric and couldn't meet her eyes.

Shooed from the fitting room, Felix reentered the shopfront as Loren and Aurelia clomped down the staircase. Aurelia's hair was freshly braided, and her scowl had turned triumphant. Loren, on the other hand, looked ill, mouth pinched and skin pasty. Before Felix could read into it, his expression changed.

"You look," Loren said, swallowing, "nice."

"Navy suits him." Livia fetched a stack of fabric squares and added them to Loren's basket. "Run along. Deliver that fabric to Nonna before she chases me down."

Loren turned to embrace her again. Two hugs in less than an hour—Felix's stomach roiled. Leaving them to it, he mumbled his thanks and made for the door, winding on his scarf. Despite the heavy late-morning heat, he could breathe easier out here. Livia's shop wasn't just cramped, it was *close*. Felix would take sweat over cloying tenderness any day.

The walls of Pompeii threatened to seal him in, keep him as the city's own. He needed to leave. Soon. But before Felix could make a break for it, Loren tripped into the street.

"It's easy for you," Felix blurted.

Loren gave him a funny look. "What is?"

Hugging. Touching. Asking simple favors without fearing the cost. But Felix's stomach churned again, and he said, "Forget it. Where next?"

"Nonna's, to drop this off." Loren held up his basket. "I have questions for her, too. But I'll walk you to the brothel first. I thought you could spend time with Elias until I'm back."

Gods. Felix nearly groaned. What Loren meant was to stick him with Elias like a child who couldn't be trusted—which, in all fairness, Felix couldn't be. Elias's focus was keen as a hawk, and though Felix still hadn't parsed the exact nature of their relationship, Elias would do anything Loren asked. Sneaking off under his watch would prove impossible.

Loren, on the other hand, was more distractible.

"Let me join you," Felix said. When Loren began to argue, he rushed to add, "I'll go mad caged in that place. Or I'll drive Elias mad. On purpose. I'll do it, swear to Jupiter."

Loren bit his bottom lip. "It isn't safe, Felix."

"Safe as life." Felix pushed from the wall. "Show me your city."

Felix knew he'd thrown Loren for a loop by asking for a tour. Tactical advantage. Loren was easier to deal with like this, so consumed by talking about this and that and everything between that he left Felix ample opportunities to escape. A sidestep down an alley while Loren was locked in conversation. Pushing over a cart of cabbages to cause a scene. Vaulting across the street just before a rush of cart traffic hit. All so tempting. Felix's fingers twitched with anticipation.

But whenever he nearly committed, Loren would glance back and catch his eye with a grin. Or ask his opinion on a vase in a potter's stall. Or pass him a sample of fruit. It was maddening how Loren treated Felix as a friend. Then again, he was friends with everyone in Pompeii, and everyone knew him. Worse, they liked him, in that baffled-but-amused way adults indulged chatty children. If Loren wasn't talking taxes with a merchant, he was shouting a greeting or gripping a hand. Knowing people didn't pose a risk to him. He doled out smiles without fear of being recognized as a pickpocket. When city guards patrolled by, Loren didn't cringe.

Felix kept his head down, scarf tight despite the heat. Loren had no idea. No idea how good he had it. Maybe Felix should have taken his chances with Elias.

An ancient woman dozing outside a bakery—Nonna, he guessed—wasn't amused when Loren nudged her awake to deliver Livia's fabric. Felix winced when her pinch left an indent in Loren's cheek.

"Who is this?" Nonna demanded, turning her glare on Felix. "I do not like the look of him. Shifty. Reminds me of my husband, may Charon carry the old bastard's soul swiftly."

"This is Felix," Loren said gently. "He's a ward of Isis. I'm showing him the town."

"Bah! That priest stuck a criminal with you? May Charon carry his soul swiftly too."

"The Priest still lives."

"For now," Nonna said darkly. She heaved upright, bones and chair creaking, and brought a covered dish onto the table. "Come into the shade, sit."

Felix caught a slab of flatbread when she tossed it his way. He blinked at her, then at Loren, who grinned.

"If you hover enough, she feeds you."

The wrinkles around Nonna's mouth deepened, and she beckoned Felix with a crooked finger. "Let me tell you a thing about Loren. This will help you."

Felix scooted his stool close as he could with a table in the way.

"He is a sweet boy. A good boy. But he hasn't a seed's worth of sense. He is like a sparrow. Flits around, head empty, pecking for scraps." She waved her hand, a loose-wristed gesture, as if warding off pests. Still, she threw flatbread to Loren. "We must eat good bread while we can, and I fear that time runs short."

Loren's face twisted in the middle of his bite, like the bread turned to ash in his mouth.

Felix's own hunger vanished. He knew that look—Loren's superstitious, doom-foretelling look, same as he'd met the helmet with, same as he wore before he hit Felix with the bowl. The look that left Felix questioning what Loren knew but wouldn't say.

"Don't—" Felix started.

"You heard about the helmet," Loren said in a rush, leaning forward. "You think it means something."

Nonna scoffed. She worked a lump of dough with deft hands, kneading it into a round. "You do not live as long as me without learning to recognize a divine sign. What have I said for years now? Only a matter of time, but Livia says no, no, surely nothing. Foolish woman."

Loren flicked a glance at Felix. "Do you, ah, that is—who do you think might have taken it? And how? Clearly, the gods didn't want it touched."

"My grandfather's grandfather saw it given to the city, brought to us from bloodshed in Corinth and left to be ogled at here. By Rome. Conquerors stealing *from* the conquered to gift *to* the conquered." She spat over her shoulder. "If Mercury did not want it moved, it would not have been moved."

Mercury. The name flitted through the void of Felix's memory again. Teasing. Mocking. Like peering through the shutters of his own life, unable to open the window, while others faced no barrier. He bit his tongue against the frustration.

Loren's mouth pinched. "Mercury is a trickster. Stirring trouble for trouble's sake?"

"Your mistake is rationalizing the actions of gods with what you as a human would do. They are not like us, and Mercury is different from even his brothers. Remember, he alone can traverse between the living and dead."

"That's right." His frown deepened. "He's a psychopomp. He escorts souls to the Underworld to face judgment. Do you worry that power could be accessed through the helmet?"

"I am less afraid of the helmet than I am of the pawn able to take it. Whether the thief knows it or not, he has more in common with the dead than the living. Two boundaries that should not be blurred." With a knife, Nonna split an X into her dough. "What is a house dog if not a wolf stripped of its wild? Dream-walker. Plane-crosser. Power waiting to be used."

Enough.

Her accusations coated Felix's skin with a sticky veneer. He was none of those things. He was nobody. He was a child of the streets. He had no power, tamed or otherwise, and he wouldn't allow himself to be used by a god he couldn't afford to believe in.

Enough.

Destiny was a crock, but when Nonna rose to transfer the dough to the oven and Loren fumbled the tray in the process, Felix took the ensuing scolding as his own divine sign and made a break for it. Stepping off the high sidewalk, he slipped into the traffic of a city waking from its afternoon nap.

Business as usual. Stalls reopened, goods spread on tables. Carts trundled past, pulled by cranky mules. Felix scooted between crowds, ducked under a litter carried by some rich bastard's servants, pushed through the linked arms of friends. His pulse crested with the same thrill stealing the helmet earned him.

Nonna could keep her superstition about gods and pawns. Felix paved his own path.

He emerged across the street, victory thrumming. Once he reclaimed the helmet, he'd be golden. He only needed—

"Felix, stop!"

His mistake was turning to look.

A flustered Loren, halfway across a set of crossing stones, swayed on his feet.

And collapsed.

Felix froze. This was his chance to leave, to break from Pompeii at last. The precious seconds he'd waste doubling back would be better spent rushing to the brothel to collect his prize. Besides, by the time he could pick his way over, Loren would've recovered, stood, brushed off dirt. Or someone else would stop to help. Felix didn't owe Loren anything.

But he watched, and no one spared Loren a second glance as a cart careened toward the intersection.

Cursing through gritted teeth, Felix flew for the street corner, bursting through onlookers.

A gap in the crowd revealed Loren on his knees, palms pressed against stone, the same fainting spell that had toppled him the day prior, when Felix pantomimed wearing the helmet. Dehydration, exhaustion, or something worse. Something Felix didn't want to consider.

Loren straightened as Felix hopped across the stones. Their eyes locked, Loren's wide and unfocused. Tugging him up by his underarms, Felix hauled them both to safety just before the cart, manned by a distracted driver, rumbled over the crossing.

He had no chance to catch his breath before Loren took the lead in a panic, dragging him into an alcove, crammed nearly chest to chest. The nearness made Felix itch.

"Look," Loren hissed. He gestured to the road opposite the intersection.

Twin swaths of scarlet hung vibrant and vicious half a block away. The capes belonged to a pair of armored men stalking down the street—Darius, the statesman's guard, and a comrade. Neither had noticed the commotion of Loren collapsing.

"Is that"—Loren panted in Felix's ear—"the soldier? Who chased you?"

Felix squinted at the guards, blood turning cold. "I was headed down that street. I would have run right into them."

"Gods," was all Loren managed before he slumped to the ground.

Darius and his partner turned out of sight. Felix looked to Loren. "Are you hurt?"

"No, I . . ." In an instant, he snapped back to himself. His crossed eyes refocused. "Are you?"

"I'm not the one who passed out."

"From the heat."

"I hadn't seen them," Felix said. "But you knew. You warned me. How?"

"I didn't," Loren said weakly. "You were running away. I only meant to—to stop you. Our agreement."

"Loren," Felix insisted, but he had nothing else to say. This mad, impulsive boy had foreseen danger and saved him. No one ever stuck their neck out to help him. "Thank you. For that."

At first, Loren looked confused. Then his eyes widened. "*I* did that. I changed what I . . . *I did that*." He leaped up and stumbled from the alcove, wobbly as a hastily made table. "Come on. We should go—"

"Not back to Nonna." Felix planted his feet. "Anywhere else."

"But—I had more to ask—"

"Then go alone. Leave me here, and ask her whatever you want."

A stalemate. Felix knew Loren wouldn't leave him alone. Too many of his escape attempts lay between them, spoiling any naive trust Loren ever held.

"I . . . suppose we should avoid the market for now, with the guards." Loren's mouth pinched. "But Felix . . . if questions alone make you uncomfortable, how will you react when we find answers?"

Loren staggered away—opposite Nonna's shop and away from the statesman's guards. Felix waited a beat longer, feeling stung. He won this round, but Loren's parting remark landed like a slap.

With a sigh, Felix followed. Tonight. He'd leave tonight.

After he made sure Loren didn't trip into traffic again.

In the Forum, Loren exchanged coins with a stall-keeper for two hunks of honeycomb, dripping with syrup. He presented one to Felix, who let it melt on his tongue and leave his fingers delightfully sticky. Then they hurried to the harbor to watch the last ships of the day sail in, as far from the market and its wandering guards as Pompeii permitted.

A wooden dock stretched over the water. The tide was up, and when Felix sat beside Loren on the boards, his toes skimmed cool water.

"Nonna told me once that the coastline changes," Loren said. "A thousand years ago, where we sit now was deep underwater. Maybe in another thousand, the water won't be here at all." Honey trickled down his wrist, and he chased it with his tongue.

Sucking in a sharp breath, Felix tore his gaze away, "Sounds like horseshit. How would she know?"

"Old people know things." Loren shrugged. "I wonder if we should tell her we have the helmet."

Felix stared. "Did you hit your head when you fell?"

"It's only that I can't stop thinking about what she said, that the thief must be a pawn of Mercury. That Mercury wanted it moved."

"I don't care what Mercury wants. I took it because the payout was worth the risk." *Should be* worth the risk, Felix amended privately, if he could ever sell the thing without meddling statesmen and temple boys interfering. "You keep asking questions, implying wild ideas, but you aren't satisfied with the answers I can give. The helmet was shiny. I'm a thief. I take shiny things. Why can't that be answer enough?"

"Because. Because—" Loren squeezed his eyes shut. Across the harbor, a dockworker shouted something crass at a ship coming in to port. "It simply can't. Look at every myth out there. When humans act on behalf of the gods, it's in ways that bring about their own ruin. If Mercury willed you to take the helmet, we could work with that. We could figure out *why* before the consequences worsen."

"That's another thing. You're convinced there must be consequences. What if there aren't? What if you let me take it and run?"

"There are always consequences when mortals cross paths with gods. Icarus ignored the warnings and flew too close to the sun. Achilles wouldn't fight when ordered, and his pride cost him Patroclus. Hercules—"

"Stop," Felix snapped. "I'm not Hercules. Or Achilles. I'm just Felix."

"If I can't figure out how to stop what's coming," Loren said, voice small but serious, "you'll be Patroclus. Dead while wearing another's helmet."

"Shit choice of a metaphor. I don't know who that is."

"Achilles's lover? Be serious. You haven't read *The Iliad*?" When Felix arched a brow, Loren had the decency to look sheepish. "I could teach you, you know. I've done it before."

Felix only grunted, but his plan had worked. He felt a sting of guilt for derailing the conversation on purpose, anything to steer away from the damn helmet and the damn gods and the doom and gloom Loren seemed adamant was destined, all because Felix had done what thieves do. But Loren was so easily distracted, he would have lost his train of thought soon anyway.

"Might expand your vocabulary at the least." Loren kicked at the water. "I have a scrap of the poem I can show you, though it's in Greek, and my tutor couldn't read a lick of it. I had to teach myself. The piece isn't anything special, but it's the part I liked best. You know Achilles, then?"

"Everyone knows Achilles," said Felix.

"Well, yes—"

"Is it a battle scene?"

"Well, no—"

"A sex scene."

"*No,*" Loren said, and—yes, there. That agitated flush, spreading from his cheeks down his neck. Satisfied, Felix sat back, resting his weight on his palms, face tilted toward the sun. The angle strained his stitches, but the warmth was nice. A gull let out a sharp cry as it soared overhead, shadow distorted on the waves.

"All right," he relented. "Tell me."

Loren huffed. "You're mocking me."

"Swear it, I'm not." Maybe a little. "Go on."

Drawing a knee to his chest, Loren propped his chin. He still scowled, but he started talking, and his brow smoothed again, like their spat over the helmet never happened. Felix wished he could be so forgiving. Or forgetful about anything except what mattered.

"Most wouldn't call it exciting, but to me . . . Did you know Achilles played the lyre? He could hush a room with his talent, but the other men only wanted him for battle. Except Patroclus. In this scene, Patroclus sits and listens, the two alone in their tent. Their own shelter from a storm they only knew the start of."

"That's all? Of the entire story, that's the only scene you kept?"

"You *are* mocking me."

VESUVIUS

Felix straightened too quickly. "No. It's nice, but it is strange. Why that part?"

"I think I'd like that, someday. That intimacy." Loren tucked a loose strand of hair behind his ear. "I know I tend to talk a lot. Too much. For once, I want someone who won't mind listening."

Felix eyed Loren as he gazed at the waves, his straight-nosed, sharp-cheekboned profile that begged to be immortalized in marble. The hem of his gray tunic had hitched up his thigh. Felix refused to notice. A breeze wafted in the sharp tang of brine and ruffled Loren's hair free again. Everything about Loren was free, and none of Felix's feelings made sense.

His fingers twitched. Tucking the strand back would be one of those simple gestures. Easy for anyone. Steeling his nerves, Felix reached. Then froze, mortified, when Loren caught the movement and turned, eyes big.

"What are you—"

Felix's hand dropped back to his lap. "You were staring at the water as if considering jumping in. I don't want to be blamed if you drown yourself."

"Stop exaggerating." Loren let out a breathless laugh and clambered up, tunic draping back down his legs. "Come on, I bet those guards are long gone. Let's get dinner."

Boards creaked as Loren dashed away.

Easy for anyone, except Felix.

He felt again the pressure of Pompeii closing in, the sensation of being cornered by more than just guards. The longer he stayed here, listening to Loren talk about gods and heroes, about consequences and a doomed future, and all the things Felix fought to ignore but Loren implored him to confront, the more Felix wondered—

He stopped his straying thoughts. That path was littered with broken rules.

One last meal, and he'd leave for good, like he should have that afternoon.

Squinting against the red sunset, apprehension spiking for the night ahead, he followed Loren's chatter back into the thick of Pompeii.

CHAPTER X

LOREN

"If you keep shifting," Loren said, dragging bread through his lukewarm bowl of mystery stew, "they'll know you're hiding something."

"I feel eyes on me." Felix's grip on his spoon tightened. "It can't be helped."

Loren sighed through his nose and straightened. They stood at a tall table near the counter, ignoring the suspicious glare cast by Nicias, the bar's owner. Loren should've insisted they take their food to his room, but Nicias, much like Nonna, had read Felix's shifty disposition and declared they'd eat in-house that evening. All to spare the risk of Felix stealing a dish.

Elias had a phrase to describe Nicias, but he used words Loren didn't dare repeat.

The bar teemed with folks catching an early dinner before the night's festivities. Laughter drifted light, tipsy on the way to drunk. Nicias's dog thumped his tail against the counter, hoping for dropped scraps, and pots steamed and simmered. Nothing struck Loren as out of place, but Felix's mood had only worsened since they left the docks. Skittish, tense, quick to snap.

"You had eyes on you all afternoon," Loren pointed out. "And last night you went gambling."

"Around the gambling table, everyone is a criminal. Everyone has something to hide, so we all know better than to look. Here, these are normal people. It's different."

"The world can't be divided into normal people and criminals. That's too simplistic."

"Right, I'm forgetting the wealthy." Felix blinked, unimpressed. "And politicians, who straddle wealthy and criminal."

Loren's stomach clenched, chasing away hunger. Another assumption, which Felix proved awfully good at making. "If it makes you feel better, I'll be the first to admit my political ambitions are frivolous. But I could do without the jabs."

"Frivolous. Like it's a game." Across the table, Felix turned to stone. Gone was the boy who had teased and snickered and listened to Loren blabber, evaporated with the warm mist curling off cobblestones. "At first I didn't understand the angle you play at. You complain about lacking power but didn't hesitate to claim me. You live in a brothel yet talk of tutors. I could take coins from your pocket right now, and you wouldn't notice. Because you don't *have* to notice."

"What are you saying?"

"You belong in a brothel and cheap bars as much as I belong in Pompeii. Which is to say, not at all."

Loren's heart skipped. Someone bumped his back as they squeezed past to the bar. Abruptly aware of curious ears, he ducked low and hissed, "That isn't true."

"You'd make a great councilman. Doling out pity masked as charity. Did your father teach you that, or did he send you here to learn the art of manipulation?"

"My parents have nothing to do with my business here."

"So they still live? Does Livia know that? Nonna? Or did you weave some sad story, make them feel sorry for you—"

"Enough," Loren snapped. "The world isn't half so despicable. I came to Pompeii to make a difference. To make change. I'm sorry *your* father didn't teach you decency."

"My father is dead."

The confession startled him. Felix's walls weren't made of bricks and mortar; they were unscalable as the sheer cliffs on the Amalfi coast where Loren's family used to go on holiday. This was the closest Felix had crept to revealing where he came from, what molded him.

Guilt panged in Loren's chest. "I didn't mean—"

"I'll tell you what he taught me," Felix said. "The only difference between politicians and thieves is who lives and who dies. When his smuggling ring turned on him, I learned from that, too."

"Felix, I'm sorry." Loren reached for the hand curled tight on the table, but Felix wrenched back. His spoon clattered into his bowl, splattering them both. A fleck of gravy landed above Loren's brow, but unlike the swift sting of rejection, it didn't burn.

Voice flat, Felix said, "I have to piss."

He stormed off. Disturbed by the outburst, several patrons watched him go. Nicias's dog growled low, then slunk to lap the dripping stew.

Loren stayed frozen until the temporary hush broke and idle gossip resumed. He wiped his forehead. Bits of meat were caught in his braid. At the counter, Nicias cleared his throat and gestured sharply at the mess.

Loren needed to follow Felix. He knew that.

Humiliation kept him rooted in place.

Whatever others might say, Loren wasn't clueless. That afternoon, he'd had a breakthrough with his visions, he was certain of it. Behind his eyelids, he had seen the guard's sword slash Felix on a crowded street, and for once, Loren reacted in time to change the outcome. He hoped that meant he was falling in tune with Felix, that it implied hints of friendship or at least an end to animosity. Anything that might crack

Felix open and help Loren figure out the mystery of who he was—why he was here. Underneath it all, he even suspected he might like Felix, his kindness concealed within his prickly exterior, if they had time to get to that.

But time was running out. Felix didn't want to be friends. He wanted nothing from Loren.

Forget the mess. Felix might be halfway to the brothel by now. But when Loren stepped around the table to follow, a man in leather armor blocked his path.

"Need this?" He offered a damp rag.

"No thanks." Loren attempted to duck under his arm. Blocked again.

"Too bad," the man went on, leaning closer. "Lovers' spats make for unpleasant nights, if you catch my meaning."

"He wasn't—we aren't—"

"Just friends?"

His tone prodded Loren's defenses. Loren eyed him: taller, spindly, and older by a dozen years, dressed in the armor of some villa owner's private guard. He leered down his thin nose, and Loren's breath caught. He knew this guard. He'd smacked into that chest the night before, in the Forum.

Fear washed over him. Was he being punished for eavesdropping? Had someone recognized him, turned him in? Celsi?

Loren stepped back, crashing into the table. Dishes clattered. He made to dart, but the man's heavy hand locked on his shoulder.

"What's the rush? Name's Ax. Let me buy you a drink. Nic's got the good stuff."

At the counter, Nicias, having heard his name, glanced their way, expression bored. Loren sent a silent plea for an intervention, any intervention, and after an agonizing wait, Nicias rolled his eyes and turned to fill two cups.

VESUVIUS

"Wait here." Ax left to collect.

No time to waste. Loren dashed from the bar's pavilion and didn't dare breathe until he made it to the next street over.

Dark had settled over Pompeii, signaling the close of another wretched day. From a few blocks away came the faint stirrings of the street fair, but Loren was far from a partying mood. Chest heaving, he fought to silence his nerves, force himself to think, but he was never good at that. Felix could be anywhere. Doing anything. Loren guessed he hadn't gone to play dice this time.

No, Felix would be skipping the city gate, helmet in hand, off to cause some cataclysm.

A predatory drawl sounded from behind. "Running? That's no way to be."

Cold shot through Loren's blood. He jerked around. Ax approached from around the corner, hand on the pommel of his sword. A second, broader body lurked behind, face cast in shadow.

"Come with us, sweets," Ax called. "We only want to talk."

Nothing else to do. Loren ran.

Pompeii's layout lived in his heart, her centuries-old layers familiar as childhood stories. Alleyways, alcoves, dead ends, hidden doors. The brothel wasn't far. Only a few blocks west and down. He raced over uneven pavement, bricks over stone, arms flailing to stay steady. He would make it. He'd—

When Loren tripped, he sprawled like a rag doll.

Hot pain exploded from his ankle. He landed hard, hands shooting out to brace the fall, but the impact bent his wrists so far back they nearly snapped. Knees and palms scraped raw, he pushed to a half-sit, stifling a cry.

If Felix had been there, he would've sworn on Loren's behalf. But he wasn't there. It was just Loren on a quiet street, ankle screaming, as languid footsteps neared.

104

"Look at that, Gus," said Ax. "Didn't need to buy him wine after all."

The other man, Gus, snorted.

Shivering, Loren drew his limbs close. "My friend saw you chase me. He went for the guards. They're on their way now."

Ax crouched and tugged Loren's braid. "Your friend who left?"

Loren kneed him where it hurt.

"Jupiter," Ax wheezed, staggering back. "You'll regret that. Gus, lift him."

"Touch him, and I'll run you through," said a girl.

Loren's racing heart stilled. That was the last voice he wanted to hear, but he'd recognize it anywhere. Brave, stupid, brilliant Aurelia.

Somehow, he didn't think chance had led her here this far past her bedtime.

She'd materialized from the night, brandishing her father's old gladius, and approached Gus from behind. Expression fearless, if she knew the real danger Loren was in, the only clue was her shaking fingers.

Ax looked Aurelia up and down with a wolfish smile. "Your grip on that blade is all wrong, little girl. You sure you know how to use it?"

"Aurelia," Loren bit. "Go home."

Aurelia's face tightened. She slashed the blade, technique clumsy, and the sword clattered to the pavement. Gus snorted again—maybe the only sound he knew how to make—and with a swift grab, forced her to her knees.

"Let her go." Loren crawled toward her, useless leg dragging. "She's harmless. A child."

"I'm not—" Aurelia started, but Gus clapped a hand over her mouth.

Ax's eyes flickered between Loren and Aurelia, unamused. Addressing Gus, he said, "We're only meant to deliver the temple boy. But give her a twist, a reminder why little girls have no business in the affairs of adults."

"No!" Loren cried without thinking. Both men turned their attention on him. He wanted to shrink again, but he forced the tremor from his voice. "We don't harm children. It's against city code."

"Against code." Ax's brow arched.

Loren sucked in a deep breath. *Don't show emotion*, the first tactic of politics—and the one tactic he still struggled to master. Never show the enemy what you value. Inevitably, invariably, they'll use it against you. Slowly, he rose, wincing when he put weight on his ankle—sprained, not broken, a small mercy.

"She has no idea what she's doing. In fact," Loren said, holding Aurelia's gaze with a stern glare, "if you let her go, she'll run home, and no one will believe her story. You can take me undisturbed."

"Says the boy who kicked me." Ax glowered. "What do you say, Gus?"

Gus grunted, bringing his vocabulary to an impressive two sounds. He hauled Aurelia up as easily as he would a kitten, then shoved her. She stumbled forward, glancing back with fresh fear.

"*Home*," Loren repeated, praying to Isis and Mercury and Jupiter himself that for once in Aurelia's life, she'd obey.

Her lip trembled. She took off, sandals slapping stone, in the direction of Livia's shop.

Loren deflated. "You're under orders? Take me to who issued them."

If Felix wanted to discuss lessons from fathers, Loren had his fair share, and it started with this: Keep your spine straight, no matter your circumstance. Anything less would degrade the family name.

Loren limped along with the dignity drilled into him from his first steps as a child, gaze trained ahead. Ax led the way through alleys untouched by streetlamps. Gus followed, gripping the sword he'd stolen from Aurelia. These weren't the statesman's guards, Loren was positive, but Ax had called him *temple boy*. If this was connected to the helmet—to Felix—Loren couldn't fathom how. A migraine settled in to match the ache of his ankle.

They headed to the eastern edge of the city, close to the amphitheater, a few streets above Livia's shop. A single estate dominated this block, bordered on all sides by high walls. Silence clung thick, the residents asleep or out at the street fair—but Loren would put money on the former. The owner was said to be a recluse. No one ventured past these walls.

When Ax strode inside the front gate, Loren froze. "You can't be serious."

Gus grunted again, jamming the pommel into Loren's mid-back. Swallowing, he passed under the arch. It opened into a small receiving atrium, lit by a sconce. A still plunging pool waited in the center, and if not for orange light playing on the water's surface, he would've fallen in. Beyond stretched a corridor leading to an interior courtyard.

"This is as far as we'll take you. Our master waits in the garden."

"What does he want?" Loren tried.

But Ax only gestured. Gus moved to guard the exit, shoulders wide, though Loren didn't plan on running—couldn't, because of his ankle, and wouldn't, because he wasn't Felix.

No sense delaying. Loren pushed his shoulders back and entered the courtyard.

Despite his nerves, he couldn't ignore how lush the place was. A portico of slender columns surrounded the rectangular central green, where stone paths wove between flowering bushes. Water cut down the middle, a canal with bridges spanning its width. The sliver of moon overhead barely illuminated the sea of soft grass.

Everything was still.

Loren knelt by the water's edge to splash his flushed face. It didn't help. When he glanced at his blurred reflection, frightened eyes stared back. Felix, wherever he was now, would never know what happened to Loren here. Probably wouldn't care if he did. The thought settled sad on his shoulders.

"There's an old tale," a woman said, and Loren nearly toppled forward. Silhouetted by moonlight, she cast a tall, impossibly elegant figure between two columns. "About a young man called Narcissus who fell in love with his own reflection. Need I be worried about you, little priest?"

Shock rocked through him. It was the woman from the Forum the night before, who had stared at Loren like she found him far more interesting than council chatter about a missing helmet. She offered the same look now, but without the veil of rain, her gaze was infinitely more piercing.

Knees aching, Loren rose. "I'm not a priest, my lady."

"Loren, yes? I've been waiting awhile to talk with you alone."

Talk?

Anger flushed through him in a bright flare. He'd been scared out of his mind for this? For a chat? She'd picked a grand time for it. He should be out searching for Felix. Loren tamped his bubbling fury down. *Don't show emotion.*

"Why did you bring me here? Who are you?"

"My name is Julia Fortunata," she said. "I own this estate. Come."

Julia disappeared into the shade of the portico, skirts trailing at her ankles, a complicated drapery of sheer lavender silk. Loren paused, counted to ten, and limped after her.

Illuminated by lamplight was a summer triclinium, overlooking the garden. An impressive spread of fruit and bread had been arranged on the low center table, and feather pillows cushioned the three surrounding couches. Dressed in his rattiest tunic, braid still sporting bits of stew, this was far too lavish a place for someone like Loren.

The Pompeiian guise of him, anyway.

"Augustus and Axius are given to theatrics," Julia said, sinking onto the left couch. The light cast her features into greater relief—sharp eyes, a classic nose, burnished gold hair pinned in an extravagant updo, graying at her temples. "If they went about their task too enthusiastically, I apologize. I gave them orders to escort you here, not drag you. Will you sit?"

Loren remained standing, even as his ankle throbbed. "They chased me through the streets. I thought. . . It doesn't matter."

Julia had raised a cup of wine to her lips but lowered it untouched. "Tell me."

If she hadn't been the first person to inquire about Loren's well-being in days, maybe he could have resisted the command. But her gaze was steady and curious, and Loren so badly wanted someone who would listen.

He caved.

"I have . . . a friend. He ran into trouble with another patrician in the city. I worried they found us out. Trying to protect him from the executioner's whip is Herculean." Talking felt freeing, but Loren pinched his inner elbow to keep himself in check. He wondered how much Julia already knew about Felix's "trouble." How much the council had already guessed about their thief—and the helmet.

And what Loren might persuade Julia to divulge in turn.

"Do you often befriend troublemakers?" she asked.

"He isn't exactly my friend. I'm afraid I don't have many of those."

Fewer and fewer by the day.

"We have that in common." Eyes sparkling, Julia relaxed into a traditional sprawl, legs tucked to the side. She popped a grape into her mouth, nudging the fruit bowl toward Loren. "Tiresome, isn't it, to offer your best to the world, only to be spit back out. Oh, don't give me that look. I told you, I've had my eye on you for a time."

Releasing a shaky breath, Loren finally sank onto the couch across from her, leg unable to bear weight any longer. "I cannot imagine you're impressed with what you've seen."

"The contrary. My associates tell me you lurk in the back of every public forum meeting. You're the right-hand man of the Priest of Isis, and foreign cult or not, that's no small feat." When she paused to sip, Loren didn't bother correcting her. "Last night, you stood in the rain just to hear Umbrius's plan for catching a thief. You're bright, and you care, and that's more than can be said about half the old councilmen. Tell me what's holding you back from joining the council properly."

This conversation was straying too close to the accusations Felix had flung over dinner.

Frankly, Loren was tired of repeating himself.

"What else besides Pompeii? Its barriers prevent commoners from creating change. Cicero was spineless, but he was right when he said power is under control of the wealthy, not the masses. My family—" Loren huffed. On reflex, he rubbed the cord he wore, his gold ring skin-warm. "I can't prove I come from wealth or authority. I'm not from the city, my lady. Running for office is a fever dream. And even if I earned funds to *buy* a position, I'd be laughed out."

Loren broke off when his eyes stung, years of irony crashing down—irony that the only tool that would help hung heavy around his throat, but in Pompeii, it was the tool he swore he'd never use. He blinked hard and busied himself with the fruit, if only to occupy his trembling fingers. He bit into a pomegranate seed, let the too tart juice ground him. "Sorry, my lady. It's frustrating."

Julia's face stayed blank for a moment, then she barked a laugh. "Listen to you. I knew I picked you for a reason."

"Picked me?"

"Last night, you looked surprised to see me with the council. What business does a woman have listening to the affairs of men?

Even councilmen's wives tend not to get involved. But"—she swirled her wine—"I am no one's wife. What I am is a landowner, and that grants me some sway over decisions affecting the city. Imagine how the council feels listening to a woman's opinions."

"They resent you," Loren guessed.

"My position is tolerated at best. Tenuous at worst. With no male heir to lend me legitimacy, I worry how much longer my influence can last." Her expression turned rueful. "Last week, a proposal was brought forward to challenge the rights of a woman to inherit property."

"That's unfair," said Loren, wary. His patience was wearing thin. Nothing Julia said offered substance about the helmet. If Felix was long gone from Pompeii, Loren had bigger problems to worry about than council meetings and inheritance. "But I don't understand how this involves me."

"You and I have more in common than you realize. I need an heir, someone capable. Educated. Ambitious. You need someone to unlock doors for you. Otherwise, your hope of creating change is fruitless." The reminder stung, but Julia continued, "Loren, you need a family name."

"What are you saying?" Loren asked slowly.

"I think, my doll," Julia said, smile honeyed, "we have much to discuss tonight."

CHAPTER XI

FELIX

When all else failed, at least Felix could run.

He craved the physicality of it, the stretch and pull of his muscles. Running created the illusion of progress. If he only ran far enough and fast enough, he could outpace any problem.

He hurtled from the tavern toward the brothel, willing his feet faster, until the snarling irritation Loren had provoked faded to background noise. Until his rattled nerves stitched back together, and he remembered his purpose: shiny silver wings, proof that one thing—this *one* thing—could be his.

Felix ran until he burst onto the market street and smacked into a street fair.

The cacophony hit him like a wall. Throngs of people occupied the street, laughing and shouting and singing, drunk, spirits high. Stalls sold spiced wine and honeyed nuts and cheese pastries. Guards escorted wealthy attendees around clusters of those less fortunate, because even at a street party—the least prestigious of affairs—class lines held firm.

Heavy coin purses dangled from belts. Felix's fingers twitched with temptation to indulge in his favorite form of stress relief. Screw Loren's moralizing.

He slipped into the party and worked the crowd like clay.

A sleight of hand won him a jeweled hairpin, plucked from the updo of a giggling girl, whose mouth he laughed against before slipping away with a wink. A conveniently timed cup of wine earned him a wooden-handled knife, poached from the pocket of a wobbly-drunk patrician boy who tried to reel Felix closer by his waist. In another town—in another mood—he might have welcomed the distraction. Dealt with the sticky shame later.

A necklace here, a handful of glass beads there—no one noticed, and why should they? Why notice some dirty street kid brushing past, new clothes or not? He was forgotten the moment he strayed out of reach.

Whatever others thought they saw in Felix—that he was built of bad intentions, that he had stolen the helmet at Mercury's bidding, that bad fortune chased him—wasn't true, and this proved it. Felix was nobody. He passed through unseen, a spectator. A specter.

All of it, the running, the pickpocketing, the eyes skipping over him, should have made him feel like himself again. But Felix couldn't melt into it. None of it helped. A whole pocketful of new treasures couldn't dull the echo in his brain. Careless flirting made his skin shrink. His shoulders crept higher, agitation cresting. He wanted . . . he wanted—

He wanted to know why Loren looked at him with recognition when other gazes skated past.

Which was exactly why Felix needed to get out of Pompeii before it stole the last of him for good. Loren had dared tread too close, plucked at too many of the fraying threads of Felix's memory. If Felix pursued the questions lurking in his mind—that Loren knew something about him that Felix didn't know of himself—Loren might unpick a seam that couldn't be mended.

But admitting that would break his most important rule, and Loren wasn't worth the price of belief.

Hemp burned mellow and earthy from nearby sconces, but Felix's head only ached. Snatching a raisin roll, he slipped down a quiet alley, shaking off the press of the crowd. Phantom hands seemed to crawl over his skin, fingers he couldn't bat away.

Blank gray eyes met his when he passed by a door. Felix stilled. A god's carved stone face stared from the keystone of an arch, framed by a winged helm and a staff wound with twin snakes. Nonna's words came back—*If Mercury did not want it moved, it would not have been moved.* Superstitious nonsense. He made to move on.

Deep in the recesses of Felix's mind, a faded memory tugged of too-tight sandals and pockets of coins and bitter, sticky wine. Of that same cold, impassive stare, watching and doing nothing.

Taking a step back, Felix wrenched free from the past, even as wordless chattering picked up, restless voices belonging to no one. The sound was maddening. Relentless. Desperate.

"This is your fault," he found himself saying, though he couldn't put a finger on what compelled the accusation now. Mercury meant nothing to him. *Nothing.* "Everything is."

The murmuring stopped, and the memory flitted away.

Felix cursed, to no one in particular. To Mercury, maybe, if he thought for a moment the gods ever listened. Temple goers could keep their superstition. His devotion belonged to luck, and he created his own.

He'd barely stepped onto an adjacent street when the little girl from Livia's shop barreled into him, slamming him against brick.

"Jupiter, slow down," Felix said, rubbing his reeling skull. "Late for curfew?"

Aurelia glared, eyes puffy and face shiny with snot and tears. "Why weren't you with him? Where have you been?"

"Minding my business. Give it a try sometime."

Snatching his hand, Aurelia tugged. "They took Loren away. Hurry, we have to find him."

Felix dug his heels into cobblestone. "If Loren got himself in a mess, he can work his own way out."

"I thought you were his friend. He said you were his friend."

Friend. Even the word set Felix on edge. "His mistake."

Aurelia stomped her foot like the child she was.

"Listen," Felix said, "and let this be a lesson to you both. Don't pick fights you don't intend to finish. Or learn to run fast. Either way, his problems aren't mine."

He turned to leave, but Aurelia drew in a deep, rattling breath and rasped, *"Dream-walker. Plane-crosser."*

Felix froze. Only hours earlier, Nonna had used those same words to describe the helmet thief—a conversation Aurelia, unless she was even sneakier than Felix, hadn't been privy to. But Aurelia looked beyond herself. A glazed look washed over her, slackening and shifting her features until she seemed both younger and more ancient than she was.

"Where did you hear that?" Felix demanded. Aurelia wobbled, but he caught her shoulders, trying to catch her unfocused gaze.

"Escort of the living," she said, lips pale, *"and the dead."*

She was a thousand miles away, the same way Loren's eyes drifted when he had his episodes. For a moment, Felix worried her limbs would collapse, leave her jerking on the ground in a fit, like he once witnessed a woman do in Rome. Felix was a child at the time, and his father was quick to rush him from the scene, whispering that she must have seen more than she should. That part never made sense to Felix. How could simply seeing something fracture a mind? Years later, he realized his father meant a different type of *seeing*.

The kind Felix never allowed himself to think possible.

"His hand," Aurelia whispered. *"Take his hand. Pull him back."*

Felix's hair stood on end, a chill rolling down his spine. He snapped his fingers beneath her nose. "Aurelia, stop. *Stop*."

She blinked, eyes clearing.

Then she kicked his shin.

Pain replaced the chill. "You're a little terror," Felix hissed. "What did you mean by that? Whose hand?"

But she merely looked confused. It hit Felix that wherever Aurelia had slipped, she hadn't carried back memories when she resurfaced. Interrogating her would do no good. He knew better than anyone that some memories could not be coaxed out.

"He's in danger," she said at her normal bratty pitch. "Because of you. If you won't help because he's your friend, do it for that."

Felix wanted to protest, wanted to shout that he owed Loren nothing, that Loren could shove his questioning up his ass, and that if he wanted to waste money on food out of pity, it didn't mean a thing. Attachment invited vulnerability. Attachment led to a swift end, either of time or freedom, and that mantra had kept Felix alive this far. He wanted to say all that.

But Loren had charged into traffic for him. He'd watched Felix's failed escape attempts but still trusted him enough to confide secret musings about Achilles. And after dinner, despite Felix lashing out, Loren had followed him—and stumbled right into danger.

Guilt crawled through Felix's belly. Maybe he did owe Loren a favor. Maybe this could clear their debt.

"Whatever," he said. "I'll make sure he's safe. But then I *am* leaving. And you won't breathe a word of this to him."

"Coward," said Aurelia. "They took my father's sword. Bring that back too."

They crept through alleys, quiet as cats. For all Aurelia's brashness, at least she was capable of silence when they needed it most. She showed Felix to a walled estate, where they took stock from the shadows. An ox of a man holding a gladius guarded the entrance.

"That's one of the men who took Loren," Aurelia whispered. "I don't see the other."

"What did they want with him?"

"I attacked. I was too preoccupied staying alive to find out."

Felix tried to picture Aurelia wielding a weapon against a grown mercenary, but the image was too ridiculous. "Where did your father's sword end up?"

"Oh," Aurelia said brightly. "He's holding it."

Felix's eye twitched. "Aurelia, look at the size of him. How am I meant to get past?"

"Around the corner"—she pointed—"the garden wall dips. Even someone short as you shouldn't have an issue climbing."

"My height is average." Felix sniffed. "You're shorter than me."

"Yes. But I'm twelve. And still growing."

"I suppose you aren't coming?"

"As you pointed out," Aurelia said, "it's past my curfew."

Felix stepped onto the street. No harm being seen, not yet. Ox Face's eyes tracked him until he turned the corner and scooted down a side alley.

Aurelia was right. Here the imposing barrier was lower. He'd scaled hundreds of walls before. All he needed was a handhold. Scrambling up took no work, even when it strained still-fresh stitches. From the roof, he scouted out the building. Steam curled from a private bath, nearly masking a manicured interior garden.

Careful not to dislodge any tiles, Felix crept until he could drop into the open window of a bedroom, then slipped into a corridor. Empty. A place like this should have servants and slaves and children and guests. Instead, he found only silence but for the buzzing in his skull. Sweat rolled from his hairline. From his pocket, he drew his stolen knife.

Two dark hallways later, he caught the flicker of a sconce. Voices, muffled around a corner. Felix flattened himself against a wall, hardly daring to breathe.

"I was told to cut you off past a jug," said a woman, "and you've had two."

"It's not even the good stuff, Clovia, c'mon," drawled a man. "Mistress'll be tied up with the boy all night. She won't care if I have another."

The boy. Felix's heart skipped.

Clovia said in a low murmur, "She's been so eager to meet him. Talks about little else. I worry about her nerves these days, anxious all the time, checking over her shoulder. I wonder . . . Forget it."

"Go on. I know everything that happens around here."

"Is that so, Ax?" Clovia's voice turned coy.

A polished silver vase in an alcove gave Felix a distorted glimpse of the two, nestled on a bench in a lovers' nook. Clovia wore a servant's garb half pulled from her shoulders, her legs draped over the lap of a thin man in oversized armor.

"Rumor has it the boy isn't who he claims." Ax's hand crept up her thigh. "That he has a secret, and Mistress found out."

Ice dropped into Felix's stomach. Loren was a labyrinth of secrets, made more complicated by how readily he revealed everything else to the world. Felix didn't know what all those secrets entailed, but if any led back to the helmet . . .

Who was their mistress, and what did she know?

Wine-hazy eyes caught his in the vase's reflection.

Jupiter.

Felix fled, Clovia's cry echoed in the hall as Ax gave chase, boots hitting the tile. Felix was faster. He flew through halls, ducking left and right in the maze until the steps faded. His legs burned, wounds searing, and he collapsed against a wall to clutch a stitch in his side. Blood trickled from the reopened gash on his calf.

Mistake. Ax strolled around the corner ahead, adjusting his belt. "Enjoy the show?"

"Seen better," Felix panted.

Ax sneered, nostrils flaring. In a surprisingly swift motion, considering the alcohol curling off his breath, he grabbed Felix's neck and slammed their foreheads together. Felix stumbled, dizzy, head throbbing.

"I should run you through for interrupting." On his chest, Ax straightened a crest etched with laurels and a loopy letter. *F*, Felix recognized, if only because it was part of his own name. "But Mistress is sensitive to killing in the house. Let's ask her permission before I gut you."

For the second time in as many days, Felix found himself at the mercy of an angry guard. Ax kept a blade at the small of his back, hand steady despite the wine, on their trek to the garden. A lovely moonlit stroll, Felix reckoned, except for the knife prodding his midsection.

"Better show her respect," Ax hissed as they crossed the green. "Piss her off, and she might make an exception to the no-killing rule."

A triclinium overlooked the lawn. Warm light washed over a spread of picked-through food. Two figures reclined on the couches. A woman, half-drowned in a purple confection of a dress, laughed at something her companion said and popped a grape into her mouth.

"Mistress," Ax announced. Both occupants turned.

Sitting there, wining and dining and . . . *wooing* this woman was Loren.

Rage sparked. Felix's vision went red. *"Es stercus."*

The last thing Felix saw before Ax forced his face into the dirt were the woman's arched brows shooting up.

Down in the grass, waiting for Ax to make good on his promise, it came as a comfort to be proven right. Right that Loren was some idiot rich boy playacting poverty. Right that Felix was a bizarre charity case, a lesson on interacting with street scum. Every budding politician had to practice manipulating the lower classes at some point, after all.

The blow from Ax's knife never came.

Instead, the pressure on Felix's neck released. Grass fell from his hair as he straightened slowly. Ax had retreated, and now Loren hovered over him, hands fluttering uselessly.

"He's mine," Loren was insisting. "A friend."

"Interesting choice of company," said the woman, tone drier than a Roman summer. She still lay draped across the couch, unbothered, as if strange boys tempted execution in her presence regularly. "Your troublemaking friend, I presume?"

"He's . . . protective."

Am not. But Felix held his tongue.

"Please, Julia," Loren said. "He didn't mean harm. Or offense. He's a ward of Isis. Killing him would displease her."

Julia frowned. She had the dignified, sour face of an empress, and frowning only accentuated the crow's-feet around her eyes. Gods, Felix itched to steal from her.

"He's important to you?" Disdain colored Julia's voice, like she couldn't fathom how Felix could be important to anyone.

"Very, my lady," Loren insisted.

"Like a little pet. Will he be spending the night too?"

"If he may."

Felix tracked the way Julia's eyes devoured Loren as he knelt. An uncomfortable chill rolled across his shoulders, but Loren was moon-eyed and oblivious. Julia could've been a goddess, the way he gazed.

Finally, she nodded. "Very well. You'll both bathe, and tomorrow we'll attend the games."

A servant—Clovia, Felix realized, embarrassed—materialized from a doorway. She gestured for them to follow, and he shook off Loren's offer to help him stand.

Felix felt Julia's piercing, hungry gaze trace them into the shadows.

Bathing would've been awkward if the hot water hadn't felt so good.

Loren didn't say a word as they each washed, didn't so much as glance in Felix's direction. Fine by him. The bath complex was enormous. Easy to pick a corner and stick to it.

But when Clovia returned to show them to their rooms, Felix's hopes fizzled. For one, it was *a* room, singular. Two, the narrow beds stood inches apart. Small mercy Julia hadn't expected them to share. Three, once Loren shut the door behind them, their temporary truce evaporated with the bath steam.

"I know you trip your way into any mess you come across," Felix said, "but why are you here?"

Loren huffed. For the first time that night, he met Felix's gaze, coolly arrogant in a way meant to make anyone lowborn shrink. "Julia has connections. It was worth my time to speak to her—for a number of reasons, not the least being she has access to information about the helmet. The council's theories about it. Their plans. Information to keep you alive."

"I keep myself alive. Forget the helmet. You aren't here for the helmet."

"I said the helmet was one reason. *I'm* trying to fix my city, as it seems no one else cares to, and funny enough, I have a life beyond you."

"Do you? You haven't shown it." Felix eyed him. "She's rich, she lured you here at night, and nothing about that strikes you as odd. So either she offered something you want, or you really are that clueless. I don't know which is worse."

"I can handle myself." Loren's long hair curled, damp from the bath, several shades darker brown. Ridiculous, foolish, arrogant. "I'm not a child."

"I'm not your pet."

"Julia's words."

VESUVIUS

"Screw Julia." Felix's lip curled. "Or was that the plan? She's a little old for you."

Loren's mouth snapped shut, disgust and fury spoiling his features, and Felix's pulse quickened. This was it. He'd pushed Loren too far, and now Felix had to flee the fallout, whether that came from stinging words or swinging fists. Loren didn't seem the type to take a physical approach to anything, but Felix's bones were shaped by history proving the least likely perpetrators caused the worst hurt.

A polite knock interrupted the brewing storm.

Loren's shoulders slumped, tension bleeding from the room, and he cracked open the door. Felix couldn't see their visitor, blocked as they were by Loren's stupid head, but a moment later, he returned clutching linen strips.

"For my ankle," Loren explained flatly before Felix could ask. "Twisted it running. Go to sleep. I don't want to talk."

The dismissal rankled. "I'm not a pet."

No response. Suddenly bone-tired, Felix picked a bed, kicked off his sandals, and curled under the fine wool blanket. Sleeping here was the last thing he wanted to do, but to his surprise, neither did he want to leave. He wanted to figure out the weft and weave of Loren, pick at *him* until he unraveled, the same way Loren wore holes in Felix's nerves. He wanted to unstitch Loren from his life, so when Felix finally fled for good, there would be no loose threads.

Loren sank onto the other bed, drawing up his hurt ankle to wind linen around. His hair fell as a curtain between them.

"What point are you trying to prove," Felix said when he couldn't stand the silence a moment longer, "by keeping your hair so long?"

Loren stilled. "I said I don't want to talk."

"Pity." Felix propped himself on his elbows. "I do."

"Has my hair offended you?"

Felix frowned. "No."

122

"But it bothers you." Another pause. "You wouldn't understand."

"Try me."

Loren considered it for another beat, then resumed wrapping. "My family has—had—expectations of me. One of which was that I must marry, and I must marry well."

When Felix tried connecting the dots, his tired brain came up short. "And?"

"It would seem frivolous to you. Privileged to turn from a comfortable life with a woman as beautiful as she is wealthy. I imagine I'd even grow to love her, in a way." Deep breath. He tucked his hair behind his ear. Water dripped onto tile. "But I'm not . . . for women."

"Not for women. As in . . . ?" A red flush traveled up Loren's neck in the half-light. "Oh."

"Yes." Loren tied off the strip and stared hard at the opposite wall. "But not the way you think. Not an eromenos, a boy-lover. I'd want a companion. Like Achilles and Patroclus—without the tragedy."

"You read too much."

"Can you blame me? Heroes make something of their lives."

Felix picked at his thumbnail. "It isn't unheard of for married men to take a lover."

Loren sniffed. "There's no authenticity in that. I'm tired of living with secrets. I want one thing I don't have to hide."

"You'd sacrifice stability to chase after, what, your principles? That's a fool's dream."

"So call me a fool," said Loren.

For all he didn't care, Felix burst with questions. Surely the prospect of marriage couldn't be that distasteful. Guaranteed companionship, money and land and a solid foundation—a level of ease out of reach for a thief. Something permanent.

And Loren's certainty when he spoke of wanting the company of a man came as a bright shock. Felix himself was indifferent toward gender. When he needed a distraction, anybody would do, but some men only wanted men, and the same with women. Except dalliances were for youths, not adults. When it came time to settle, a man found a woman. Rather, their parents arranged a handsome transaction. Should the man be wealthy, he'd have a boy on the side. An eromenos.

Never someone equal. Always much younger. Lesser. A display of power, not love.

Loren wanted the impossible.

"I still don't see how this relates to your hair," Felix said.

"Cutting it feels like giving in to expectations of what a man should be. I'm stubborn enough to hold out."

Felix watched Loren finish his preparations for bed: tying his bandages, braiding damp hair, checking the locks, snuffing the candle. He crawled into the bed opposite, facing the wall. His tunic dipped, and Felix could count the knobs of his spine.

Quiet, until—

"What Julia and I discussed tonight . . ." Loren hesitated. "She thinks I have potential to be her heir. She offered a contract. Her estate in exchange for legitimizing her political presence."

"Her heir?" Felix sat up, but Loren didn't turn over. "Do you know her?"

"We only met tonight."

"Then why you? Of everyone in Pompeii, why . . ."

"Why some errand boy of a disreputable foreign cult?" Loren's voice took on an edge. "Is it so impossible that someone might take me seriously?"

"That isn't what I meant." Mouth dry, Felix wet his lips. "Did you agree?"

A pause. "No. No. Of course not." The dark all but swallowed Loren's words. "I told you. I'm here for the helmet. The rest is—I'm not *that* distractible, whatever you think. Nothing will shake me from figuring you out, so don't get your hopes up."

Felix huffed. "You keep saying that."

"Because I believe it." Loren flopped onto his back, wrist cradled against his chest, other arm splayed above his head. "Thank you. For coming after me. With how you stormed from the tavern, I thought you'd be long gone by now."

A question lurked in Loren's tone. Felix suspected he knew which. He picked a stray thread on the blanket, thinking back to the street party and the gazes sliding past—and the startling, sudden awareness that Loren looked at Felix and *saw* and didn't look away.

Heat crept up Felix's neck. "We have a deal. Three more days."

"Since when do you do as I say?" When Felix stayed silent, Loren hummed and continued, "Thanks for staying, if nothing else."

"Loren?"

"Yeah?" Loren breathed.

"Go to sleep."

He did face Felix then, offered a sleepy, sweet smile, and shut his eyes. A moment later, the rise of his chest evened beneath blankets.

For all his exhaustion, Felix stayed awake, stomach in knots. What had he told Aurelia, just hours before? Once Loren was safe, he would do whatever it took to ditch the city, clear of the debt between them. But he remembered the starved way Julia watched Loren, sizing him up to swallow whole. And Loren, who had no instinct for deceit, as Felix was coming to realize, hadn't batted an eye. The fact was that neither were safe, not here in this empty, labyrinthine estate.

He'd told Aurelia, *Once Loren was safe.*

He'd promised Loren, *Till week's end.*

Felix stared at the ceiling, confused and conflicted, and didn't sleep.

CHAPTER XII
LOREN

Loren wished he was surprised when he blinked awake—not awake—at the edge of the world, but the novelty of his dreams wore off many years and many horrors ago.

Darkness pooled thick, stars blotted out, moon absent. Hot wind whipped through empty space, cascading off the cliff edge he toed. Jagged white spires rose like teeth from the black yawn below, the open jaw of a beast. A red storm raged over a peak in the distance. This place was barren. Lifeless.

"Why did you bring me here?" Loren asked the hopeless silence.

"You tell me. This is your dream," said a voice from behind.

Loren may as well have been stabbed again, the way his breath punched from his lungs. The last thing he'd expected was for Ghost-Felix to answer. And it *was* Felix's voice, Loren didn't need to turn to see, even if the ghost spoke through flat, hollow vowels, and not in the real Felix's knife-sharp cadence. The dissonance squeezed his heart.

Ghost-Felix edged nearer until he stood beside Loren, a careful distance apart. He stared blankly through unhappy eyes, his body faded like over-laundered linen. Hissing steam pooled around bare, bloody feet.

Loren released a splintered breath, misting despite the swelling heat.

"So you can hear me," the ghost said. "But will you listen?"

"I've listened for years," Loren said. "It's you who wouldn't talk. What have you been trying to tell me? What are you planning? What—"

Ghost-Felix flickered, blinked in and out. "You are close to the answer if that encourages you. You hold the pieces. But you're running out of time."

"What answer? What pieces?"

But understanding washed through Loren in a cold slide. Yesterday, Aurelia showed him her tapestry. Black wave. Copper streak.

For the first time, silver.

"The helmet," Loren said, words a sour spread.

Ghost-Felix's lips parted, hungry, but he said nothing.

"Why? What purpose does Mercury have for Felix?" Except that wasn't the right question. Like Nonna warned, the actions of the gods weren't meant to be understood by humans. Mercury guiding Felix to take the helmet could have an underlying meaning—or equally likely, Felix had simply been in the wrong place at the wrong time, swept by the whims of a fickle trickster god. Loren reordered his thoughts. "What would the helmet tell us? What will it make Felix do?"

"Close to the answer," the ghost repeated. "But you never ask the right questions."

"Tell me."

"Listen," he snarled. From his pocket, he withdrew a knife of wood and iron. Panic rose in Loren's ribs, a twinge where the knife had buried last, but Ghost-Felix continued, "Where will you plant this tonight? Me? Or yourself again?"

He held the hilt out. An olive branch.

When Loren didn't accept, the ghost let it slip from his fingers. Striking the cliff's edge, it bounced, then fell in a deadly spiral down, down. Loren didn't hear it hit the bottom.

"Bring the helmet," Ghost-Felix rasped, "and I'll do more than tell you. I'll show you."

Loren made to protest, tried to cry that the helmet was cursed and dangerous and he'd never put that power in this Felix's hands, but the ghost stepped forward, and words evaporated. The earth trembled. Another step. An arm's length away. Less. Their chests were nearly pressed, noses brushing. Empty heat flooded the gap. Still, Ghost-Felix didn't touch.

For his part, Loren's shivers turned to shakes. He wanted to press his mouth to Felix. He wanted to cast him over the edge. He wanted to follow all the way down.

The ghost breathed, "If you want to stop this, come find me."

The seam of the black sky tore, and ash, again, rolled out.

Loren woke with his lungs burning. He whipped to look across, neck straining, only to find smooth sheets. The bed looked unslept in. Unsurprisingly, Felix was gone.

Or not. Loren's darting eyes landed on ratty sandals. Felix had been so delighted to recover them the other day, his only pair, that Loren couldn't imagine him abandoning them here. Something eased in his chest. He knew he shouldn't, but he took it as a sign Felix planned to return.

Fool. When had Loren started hoping for any future moment together, no matter how brief? Two nights ago—when Loren turned the knife on the ghost—he would have done anything to be rid of Felix. Anything to protect his city.

That was then. Now, Loren had shared bread with Felix. He'd seen Felix's clever mind at work, shown him the places his visions doomed to destruction, confessed secret wants to him. And Felix listened. The prospect of him dying after all that struck Loren in entirely new places.

How could this be the same boy as the ghost haunting Loren all these years?

"Idiot," he said out loud for good measure. He smoothed his braid before ducking from the room. The dream cast one reminder into sharp relief: Time was running out. Two more days until his bargain with Felix expired, and Loren had to let him go. Two days until he lost his chance to prove himself.

Julia expected him for breakfast in the garden, but surely she wouldn't mind if he poked around first. After all, if he agreed to her offer, the place would belong to him soon.

He sidestepped down a different hall in search of her study.

During the day, the house was less desolate, but still so curiously empty. Each room he stuck his head into, servants' quarters and kitchens, storage rooms and lounges, held nothing but dust and cloth-draped furniture. Aside from a snoring Gus stationed outside what must be Julia's wing, not a soul stirred.

The door to the study had been left ajar, and after a furtive glance around, Loren slipped inside. Of all the rooms he'd examined, this struck him as the most lived-in. Shelves held pyramids of papyrus scrolls, and Julia's white palla lay tossed over a chair. A candle burning on the windowsill suggested she had been working recently.

No time to waste. He couldn't be caught. Julia didn't know he was here about the helmet, and asking her directly would set off alarm bells. His investigation required subtlety.

He dove for the desk and began digging.

Letters and scrolls and neat stacks of parchment—but no luck. No convenient dispatches from the council, no notes detailing Umbrius's plan. Not even a journal entry with her agenda. That would be too easy. His gaze slid to the work she'd been doing: a wax tablet, etched with legalese, next to flattened parchment. Loren's father used to do this too, spend hours shut in his study, copying over language to construct watertight contracts not even the wriggliest of creatures could slip through. The comparison tasted of oversweet wine.

But that was the core of a life in trade or politics. Here or back in his family villa, it didn't matter; Loren's future would always lie in an office. At least with Julia—*if* he agreed—it'd be an office of his choice, where people would listen. Not only about politics, but his visions. Maybe they'd even believe him.

No. Loren shook off the selfish fantasy and tugged the cord around his neck. He was here for the helmet. He hadn't lied to Felix about that. If Pompeii survived the next two days, maybe he could entertain the rest of Julia's offer.

"I would have shown you if you asked," said Julia. Loren startled upright. She smirked from the doorway, bearing a wine cup. "Oh, relax. I'm not angry. It's your contract after all."

Her tone was teasing, but the rest of her sighed exhaustion. Her same lavender gown from the night prior sagged on her frame. Golden hair tumbled free from pins, circles heavy below her eyes. If she'd slept, she didn't show it. The servants of Julia's estate should have attended to her by now. Loren's mother would never be caught so disheveled.

"I was looking for you," Loren said carefully, inching back. "You weren't in the garden."

Julia arched a brow and swept over to blot ink off a drying stylus. "I'd respect your answer more if you admitted to nosing around. Tell me honestly, Loren. A stranger whisks you away in the dark, promises to make your ambitions a reality—it's what I would do in your position."

"I haven't agreed." Still, something eased in his chest.

"Not yet." Her eyes gleamed, and she fetched a wrapped package tucked under her palla. "I took the liberty of having clothing delivered for you. Expensive on such short notice, believe me, but I won't have you dressed so common, not today."

Loren accepted the bundle and undid the hemp string. Inside the packaging lay a butter-yellow tunic. Intricate embroidered flowers of red and blue decorated the neck and sleeves. He flipped the hem to find an unfamiliar stitch pattern. Not one of Livia's creations.

"It's beautiful." Loren bit back a curl of guilt. "But—"

"If you plan to protest every gift, I fear you'll run out of breath. Go on, there's more."

Taking care not to crease the linen, Loren set aside the tunic. Next, he unfolded a crisp white sheet. His eyes widened. "A toga?"

She'd busied herself uncorking a jug, but he caught a hint of a proud smile. "Your first, I assume."

Instead of answering, Loren smoothed his hand down the wool. Togas were reserved for full Roman men, and in Pompeii, he straddled that uncomfortable line between citizen and not. That was the thing about leaving your identity behind: You lost all it came with, too.

By gifting him this toga, Julia proclaimed, unspeaking, that she took Loren seriously on his own merit—the first person to since he arrived in Pompeii. Perhaps even the first in his whole life. The Temple of Isis hadn't. His parents certainly hadn't.

He didn't realize his grip had tightened, crumpling fistfuls of white, until Julia uncurled his hands from the fabric.

"As my heir," she said, neatly swapping the toga for a cup of wine, "and thus my representative, I would prefer if you didn't wrinkle your toga hours before our appearance at the games. You'll forge connections today. No better place to discuss politics. We'll sit in the box and eat expensive meats. And Jupiter knows Pompeii needs some fun before half her citizens abandon her, gods help this corrupt town. I'd be lying if I said I wasn't tempted to leave myself."

Loren frowned at the drink Julia handed him, the knot in his stomach twisting afresh. He hated when people spoke of the city this way, as if Pompeii were in her death throes. It felt like a joke everyone was in on but him, while he frantically tried to stop the punch line from landing.

"Pompeii presses on," he said tightly. He couldn't help the defense from slipping out, but regret followed swift when her mouth slackened. "Sorry, my lady. That was out of turn."

131

"Don't apologize," she said. "I value your counsel. And call me Julia. Goodness, even my servants aren't this deferential. Just the other day, Clovia had the nerve to suggest I need a good . . . Ah. Inappropriate anecdote. She thinks I ought to seek a suitor. Marry." Her nose wrinkled, and she paced to the other side of the desk.

Loren gaped.

Absently correcting a mark on her tablet, Julia continued, "Not that I haven't had offers. When my father was alive, he rejected them all. They want the estate. The name. Never me. You understand now why I prefer our alternative means of securing an heir. I despise the entire institution of marriage."

"I'd drink to that," Loren said weakly.

"Shall we?" Julia tipped her cup in his direction, and Loren met it with his own. Metal clinked. "A toast to forging our own paths."

"To partnership," he added, "that means something."

"To families built, not born."

Fragile hope dared take root in Loren's chest as they each took a sip, emboldened when familiar sticky sweetness washed across his tongue. Lassius wine. For once, the taste didn't drag him down.

Heavy footsteps interrupted from the hall, and a gasping Ax stumbled into the study.

"Axius, what's this?" Julia said, affronted.

"It's the boy," Ax wheezed. Julia's eyes darted to Loren, but Ax grunted, "The other one. And Clovia. You better come quick."

Sprawled like a discarded doll, Clovia lay in the atrium, face submerged in the plunging pool. Her head bobbed in the water, loose hair writhing in ropy strands.

Felix was kneeling beside her.

Loren's throat seized.

Julia inhaled sharply, and Felix's head jerked up. Loren took stock of his face, searching for a clue to prove he couldn't have done this, but his expression gave away nothing. Only the tight line of Felix's mouth exposed him affected at all.

The dreams of a Felix let loose on the city. Was this how the end began?

"Augustus!" Julia shouted as Ax crumpled.

Gus lumbered in, blinking away sleep. When his slow brain caught up to the scene, he grunted, reaching for a weapon. Aurelia's father's sword had hung from his belt last night. Not anymore. Undeterred, he lunged for Felix and wrestled him from Clovia's body.

Felix didn't struggle. Just stared at Julia with hard eyes.

"I thought it strange," she said, meeting Felix's gaze, "when she didn't arrive to dress me this morning. I dismissed it. Perhaps she was tired."

"We were drinking," murmured Ax. "Last night."

"Tripped, did she? Interesting she landed face down in the pool with no one to help her. I believe, Axius, I instructed you to stay off the wine."

Ax scrubbed a palm across his forehead, smearing nervous sweat.

"Interesting," Julia continued, nostrils flaring, "that she seemed sober enough when she brought me parchment before bed. Are my guards so lax that not even my staff is safe in my own house? She's lain here for hours, and the street boy found her first. Disturbing."

Ax swallowed.

"It hasn't been hours," Felix corrected. "And she didn't drink herself to death. Or drown."

Julia's expression didn't stray from cold impasse. "You know this how?"

"She wasn't here when I left earlier. Feel her. Her blood is warm. This happened moments ago."

When nobody moved to prove him wrong, Felix squirmed free to pull Clovia from the water. Rivulets streamed down her pale face. "Poppy sap. Can't you smell it?"

"I can't smell a thing."

"Nose-dim, all of you. Then look. Bruises."

Fighting nerves, Loren inched closer until he, too, knelt by the woman. Felix wore a guarded expression, protective almost, for the corpse under his hands. His wariness gave Loren pause, an attitude for this dead stranger he simply couldn't place, but when he reached to pull aside Clovia's hair, Felix made no move to stop him. Deep welts of purple and red mottled her throat, a violent necklace. Gingerly, Loren brushed her cheek, wincing at the chill.

"She was strangled," he confirmed.

"Poisoned and strangled." Julia's lips pressed tighter, and she gestured to the guards. "Clear her from the room."

Ax and Gus trudged forward to gather poor Clovia and shuffle her somewhere private. Sickness filled Loren's chest. He wondered what would become of her body, if she had family outside Julia's estate, where along the road from Pompeii she might be buried. If anyone would care how a serving-woman met this gruesome end.

"Wait." Loren fished in his pocket and pulled out a coin. He slipped it into Clovia's slack mouth. It paled in comparison to rituals he'd seen at lavish funerals he'd attended as a child, but it would at least pay her passage with a psychopomp, Charon or Mercury, to the underworld. When he dragged his eyes from hers, fixed in death, it was to find another pair studying him.

Again, that wariness. Felix carried a somberness at odds with his flippant nature. Reverence from the least reverent in the room. Suddenly Loren was struck with the impression, unfounded as it was, that Felix felt Clovia's death most keenly of any of them.

At last, Gus and Ax carried Clovia from the atrium, and silence settled.

Felix broke it first.

"Before you ask," he said, "I didn't kill her."

Julia held up a hand and ducked her head. "I know."

It was the last thing Loren expected her to say. But her certainty didn't waver, even as the frozen set of her mouth thawed into a politely cool smile.

"Are you accompanying us today, Felix?" she asked.

"The games aren't my style."

Her lips quirked. "Too bloody?"

"Something like that," said Felix.

Loren's mouth opened, but no sound came out. There'd been a *murder*. Yet they spoke of gladiator games casually as the weather.

"Shame." Julia turned. "They ought to be entertaining. Loren, get dressed. We leave within the hour."

Sharp footsteps receded from the atrium. The instant they faded, Loren scooted from Felix's side. "Where were you when I woke?"

"I had business in the city. Does it matter?"

"Does it—" Loren's chest heaved. He braced a hand against his heart. "Yes. Because."

Because murder. Because Julia hadn't made a lick of sense. And because Felix's new tunic dripped with corpse-water, and he was barefoot like the ghost in Loren's dream.

"I didn't do it," Felix repeated. "You know I didn't."

That was the trouble. Loren wanted to believe he wouldn't, but since the moment they met, Felix had done his best to keep Loren from knowing any part of him. Irony rang hollow in Loren's ears that, if it came down to it, he knew more of the ghost's truths than he did the real Felix's. At least the ghost made his intentions clear.

"Felix," Loren said, half a plea, "I don't know a thing about you."

"Then you haven't paid attention," Felix said, cold as marble. "I watched my own father's murder. Do you honestly think I could have done this?"

Like shushing a candle, Loren's anger fizzled. Again with the Felix-induced guilt. Any time Loren gained ground chipping through those walls, it came at the expense of hurting Felix. Now he felt like Pompeii's biggest *culus*.

"I didn't know," Loren tried.

Felix cast him a scathing look. "Spare me the pity and go dress. If Julia wants to parade you around, you better look presentable."

Loren thumbed a streak of mud on the tile. "You should come with us."

"So you can keep an eye on me. So you can ask questions when I've told you to stop." Felix's fists curled. "Because you don't trust me."

You haven't given me a reason to, Loren nearly said.

Except that wasn't true. He flashed back to last night: Felix breaking into the estate, if only to ensure Loren's safety. Felix listening to him ramble in the dark. How, despite the many holes Loren left for him to slip through and end their agreement, Felix kept coming back.

His bed was empty that morning. But he was here now.

"Trust my experience if you trust nothing else from me. It's never a good sign when a rich person takes an interest in you," Felix said. "I know what it's like to be used."

He stormed from the atrium before Loren could work past the conflict in his chest.

CHAPTER XIII
FELIX

Ditching sandals to silence an approach only worked if the target wasn't waiting in anticipation.

Dawn streamed thin over Pompeii, and no sooner had Felix turned onto the street of the seamstress's shop than a flash of curls disappeared from the upstairs window. He carried the sword of Aurelia's father, having reclaimed it from the belt of Julia's snoring guard. Unsheathed, it glinted flat and gray in the morning light. Too old to fetch much coin—so what if Felix considered pawning it rather than returning it?—but the fantasy died when Aurelia barreled out the door.

Only his growing familiarity with how she never acted by half reminded him to stand back.

"Where is he?" Aurelia demanded.

"Morning to you, too," he said, dodging a shin kick.

"Don't joke." Hair a thundercloud, frizzy and falling from its braid, she looked a puffy-eyed mess. Felix wondered if she slept at all, or if nightmares had her tossing all night. He remembered her episode in the alley, her glazed expression and grave pronouncements, forgotten the moment she said them, but Felix didn't know where to begin questioning her.

She was strange. Strange as Loren. No wonder the two got along.

Sighing, Felix relented. "He's fine. Didn't need me. Didn't need either of us."

"Not true. Mamma says we all need each other."

"For some, that's hard to admit."

Aurelia stared dead-on. "Some like you?"

Felix felt again that odd effect, the same one Loren had on him, that his skin had turned invisible, and his vitals were exposed. He itched to cover up despite being dressed. Slowly, he said, "Part of my trade is working alone. I'm a thief, not a smuggler."

"That's not it. I think thieves are the loneliest of us all." Aurelia sniffed, then snatched the sword and slammed the door in his face.

For a long moment, Felix stood in the street, trying not to feel the press of her words. *The loneliest of us all.* Aurelia didn't know the first thing about what loneliness meant.

Or what the alternative could cost him.

He took the long way back to Julia's, hoping Loren was still asleep so Felix could creep back into bed like he'd never left. A first for him. Anything to avoid a confrontation.

But as he came around the corner, a swath of scarlet motion at the far end of the alley stopped him in his tracks. Apprehension flooded his veins. He had seen that color before in Pompeii. Red dye, especially a shade so vibrant, cost a pretty penny.

Felix knew one man who could afford it.

Footsteps light, he clung to the shade as he approached the main road. He leaned out past the bricks, only enough to see the same scarlet cape turn a corner. *Gods.* Last time Felix saw that profile, he'd been at the other end of an arcing blade. Darius, the statesman's guard—the man rapidly becoming Felix's least favorite Pompeiian—was lurking in the early daylight in a part of the city he didn't belong to.

Something was off.

His nerves prickled. Did the statesman know Felix had stayed at Julia's? Had he dispatched Darius to break into the estate? Part of Felix itched to follow him. Itched for another glance at the statesman, to try—futilely—to place him in his blank memory. He gripped the wall, chewed his tongue, teetered.

But something dark twisted in his gut, a sense of disquiet, scratching his brain and calling him to Julia's house. Felix needed to check. To see. He hadn't survived these terrible days in this terrible city for Loren to die by some guard's hands.

He headed for the estate.

Where he found Clovia, bobbing in the water, purple welts around her neck.

Later, Felix watched from the shadows as Loren left for the amphitheater, escorted by Julia and her guards. Conflict clashed in Felix's chest, the urge to keep watch on Loren warring with the need to gather proof. Felix was in no position to accuse Darius of murder, not to Julia. Pointing fingers never worked in a thief's favor. Usually, it got them cut off.

His initial assumption, that Darius targeted the estate because the statesman knew Felix was there, no longer struck him as right. Not after witnessing Julia's reaction, her knowing gaze and cool confidence that Felix hadn't killed Clovia. Like she'd expected it. Like it had happened before. Darius had wanted to be caught, wanted the murder to be recognized. Felix recalled the press of Darius's fingers around his neck and the bitter stink of poppy sap the statesman poured. Those marks on Clovia's body screamed of a signature style. A message.

There was a connection between the statesman and Julia, and Loren had tripped into a worse mess than Felix thought. *That's* why

Felix needed proof. To convince Loren that Julia's danger wasn't worth any information she could offer about the helmet, and unless he cut ties with her, it'd be Loren's body, drenched in bruised poppy, that Felix found next.

Not that Felix cared. He only wanted to get back on track, so when he left the city he could make a clean break. No lingering regrets. No ghosts.

Then Loren looked over his shoulder one last time, familiar mouth pinched, before the crowd swallowed them, and Felix's stomach fluttered. Worry, or something like it, reordered his priorities.

He didn't care for the sensation at all.

Felix left the estate too, in the opposite direction.

The streets brimmed with folks ambling toward the festivities. Spirits ran high, voices jubilant. Everyone would be there, craving a break from Pompeii's recent sour luck. Felix banked on it—though for once, he wasn't escaping. Not when he had a point to prove.

No one noticed him moving against the flow. Again, he ditched his sandals to grab later, then followed changing bricks onto a too-familiar street. Ignoring the front gate, he made for the side door he'd entered before. He twisted the hairpin he'd pinched from last night's party in the lock until it clicked and the door swung free.

The fresco of Vesuvius, in all her grape-crowned, writhing-snake glory, welcomed Felix into the statesman's lararium. The lares posed in their alcove, begging for gifts and gold. Spilled wine had dried into a sticky purple smear across the floor. Even days later, Felix still felt cold tile bruising his knees, the cradle of his jaw in the statesman's hands.

But that was the past. He shouldn't think about the past. Swallowing, he moved away.

Silence reigned. A pin would echo from across the house if there'd been another soul to drop one. Secrets thrived here, Felix could taste them. Dangerous secrets. He wished he had the knife he'd stolen, a meager defense, but when he checked his pocket, it had vanished. Lost. Damn.

Picking a corridor at random, he began his search.

The next door he tried was locked, too, but not for long. With a smirk, he slipped the hairpin away and pushed forward.

His grin died quickly.

Jupiter and Juno, the room held a lot of shit. The statesman called himself a collector. *Hoarder* was a better word. Felix's fingers flexed. It would be a thief's perfect cache, a smuggler's wet dream, if it didn't ring so . . . *wrong*.

Gingerly, Felix stepped over the threshold. Tables against the wall groaned under tons of bronze and silver trinkets, and mounds of discarded treasure dominated the floor. Stacked towers of dull cups, clusters of leering statues. Shields, crowns, a scythe. He picked up a sword coated in rust or blood, stomach lurching. The room buzzed with a frenetic energy he couldn't source, and it vibrated to his fingertips, a building static charge.

One wrong touch, and he'd light the place up.

Worst were the helmets. Empty eyed, they glared from every angle. Shiny helmets, crushed helmets, gore-spattered helmets. All these, and the statesman still wanted the helmet Felix had stolen. The one stashed in Loren's laundry bag. The one the statesman was willing to pay for. Kill for.

Whispering tickled Felix's ears, more wordless chatter. The sensation of being watched, eyes dragging down his body, set off gooseflesh on his arms. Delicately, he replaced the sword and backed away, nerves strung. Whatever the statesman's entanglement with Julia, surely a room of relics didn't factor in.

The next room wasn't better. These were the statesman's private quarters, Felix could tell from . . . well, he could tell. He stood dumbstruck in the statesman's study, surrounded by mountains of scrolls and papyrus sheets. Stacks on stacks of paperwork. A half-finished document waited on the desk, inkpot left uncapped to dry. All that predatory self-control the statesman had shown, but he chose to live in chaotic mess.

Felix closed the door behind him. Unsure what to search for, he riffled through the nearest pile. A hint, a sign, a word he recognized. Anything. Loren could've translated if he weren't busy playing politician. Huffing, Felix slumped at the desk and pushed curls off his forehead. A room dedicated to random old objects, a guard with a grim message, poppy sap and paperwork. So much paperwork. How did it all tie together?

A heavy bronze box, more like a coffer, occupied one corner of the desk. When Felix dragged it closer to inspect the lock, something shuffled inside. He tinkered with his hairpin again, and the latch popped.

Inside was more damned paper.

The top sheet was folded in thirds and a different texture from the paper scattered across the desk, expensive parchment instead of reedy papyrus, ink black as the day it was laid down. It must've been written to impress the reader. Or written by someone with money to waste. Felix scrutinized the text, but comprehension didn't dawn until he reached the seal at the end.

F, looped in laurels.

He'd seen that crest before, emblazoned on Ax's house pin. This letter had been penned by Julia. His mind whirred with possibilities, heart leaping that he had been *right*.

His shock nearly caused him to miss the voices.

"Utter waste of time," a man said from outside, and Felix thanked the gods he'd shut the door. He stuffed the letter down his tunic, shoved the box in place, and dove for the closest hiding spot, an adjoining bedroom. No sooner had he ducked below an unmade bed than the study's door slammed open and in strode the statesman.

From this angle, chest against the floor, Felix could see only the states-man's leather boots as he paced the study in sharp strides. Something had him agitated. A second pair of legs joined, red hem just visible. Darius. He stood at attention near the door, an obedient watchdog.

"Leaving early, won't that strike the others as odd?" Darius asked.

"You saw Umbrius's condition. I'd wager half my worth he didn't notice."

Dust swirled under the bed. Felix's nose tickled, and he bit his tongue to tamp a sneeze down. Light fell in slats across the floor to his right, filtered through shutters. Slowly, so slowly, he inched toward it.

"I didn't mean Umbrius, sir."

The statesman's pacing paused. Paper rustled. "Ah. If our dear lady believes her new boy makes a fraction of difference, she's more addled than I thought. Or more desperate."

Felix stilled.

The morning Felix fled to the Temple of Isis, Loren wore temple robes and a veil. Unrecognizable from the boy in fancy clothes Julia swaddled him in today. But Felix spent that encounter unconscious. He didn't know what Darius walked in on, how much of Loren's face he'd seen. If Darius put the pieces together, realized Loren, draped on Julia's arm, bore a connection to Felix . . .

"Seen him before," Darius grunted. "In the Forum. A whore, I think, from the lupanar."

"Spend much time there?"

Wisely, Darius held his tongue.

The statesman continued, "Easy to pick off, in any case, no one weeps for whores. It's unsurprising Julia would stoop so low. Her mistakes grow sloppier by the day. I imagine we'll finish her soon. Of course," he said, tone shifting from idle amusement to one far more pointed, "if I had the damned helmet, none of this would be necessary."

"The guards at the gate have no news," said Darius.

"He must be biding his time in town," the statesman murmured. "I dealt with boys like him in Rome, I know the lines these thieves think along. Their uncanny good fortune, their ability to blend in. Almost magical, isn't it?"

Felix tensed. Always that. Always magic. And the statesman had accused Pompeiians of being superstitious.

He slunk toward the window, emerging from the bed and crouching low as he edged for the shutters. He didn't dare breathe.

"Darius," the statesman said, "did you unlock my letterbox?"

Heavy footsteps clomped toward the desk.

Felix flung himself over the window ledge into the alley. He didn't stick around to learn if Darius caught sight of him. He booked it to the street, swift as a cat, and never glanced back.

Felix found Aurelia in an alley near the Forum. She knelt by a chalk circle, head bent with another child. But where Aurelia's clothes were plain and lived-in, the boy's were formal—a crisp white toga over an orange tunic, a Roman senator in miniature, wholly out of place crouching on dirty cobblestones. The two were conspiring about something, overthrowing the empire or taxes or whatever else devious children colluded over.

"I need your help," Felix announced, tugging on his sandals as he neared.

The two separated abruptly.

Aurelia glared. "I'm busy."

"Seems like it." Felix surveyed the ground. A handful of marbles adorned the circle. Aurelia's friend used his thumb to launch a glass shooter into the ring. It crashed and scattered a cluster of smaller marbles. Two rolled out of bounds, and the boy cheered.

Aurelia slapped the ground and groaned. "See what you did? Distracted me. Now I'll lose."

"You won't." Felix did a quick count, then squatted next to her. "Aim this way"—he mimed shooting—"and you'll knock out all three."

Skepticism twisted her mouth, but she snatched her shooter. "Like this?"

"Angle it more."

She let it fly. It hurtled through the ring, striking the other orbs. As Felix predicted, the final marbles rolled free, securing the game. "Yes! Where did you learn that?"

Felix shrugged with sudden discomfort. It shouldn't bother him that he couldn't remember where he'd learned a game, but it was another piece stolen of his childhood. Trapped behind the gate in his mind he couldn't pick the lock of. It seemed everything in Pompeii wanted to taunt him with what he couldn't recall. He pushed the frustration aside for later.

"Cheater," the little boy huffed, face turned in a pout.

"Mamma says those in glass houses shouldn't throw stones, Celsi," Aurelia said.

His scowl deepened. "What?"

"It means you can't call me a cheater when your whole family comes from cheaters."

"We're *not*—"

Felix didn't have time for this. "Aurelia, game's over. Help me with something."

She dropped her marbles one by one into a leather pouch with a satisfying *click-clack*. "Why should I?"

"Because I helped you win. And I risked life and limb bringing back your sword."

"Hardly."

"And if you help," Felix said, digging in his pocket, "I'll give you this."

He presented the treasure, a yellow blown-glass bead he'd siphoned from a stall last night. He'd figured he'd pawn it for a coin or two later,

145

but Aurelia's game struck inspiration. Her eyes glinted, and she snatched it with greedy fingers.

"I want to see," Celsi whined. Aurelia relented, holding it out, but he grabbed, and she yanked it back. "Hey!"

"It's mine. Besides, your pappa doesn't allow toys."

Chin lifted at a haughty angle, Celsi stood and smoothed his toga. "Whatever. I have more important things to do, anyway. The procession is due to start any minute."

"Then shoo," Aurelia said.

With a final envious glare at the bead, Celsi spun and marched stiffly to the Forum.

"Procession?" Felix asked.

Aurelia's mouth soured. "That was *Councilman* Numerius Popidius Celsinus."

"He's a child."

"He's nearly my age."

"So, a child," Felix said. "What do you mean by 'councilman'?"

She rolled her eyes. "Not a real one. Not a proper ordo. Celsi's father can't hold office himself since he's a former slave, so he bought his freeborn son's way onto the council. You know the earthquake? The big one, not these little ones we keep having."

Elias had mentioned it when they played dice, Felix remembered. "Fifteen years ago?"

"Seventeen. It destroyed the Temple of Isis, and no one had money to fix it for a decade. Celsi's entire family was devoted to Isis, and his pappa raised money to fund the repairs—in Celsi's name. So the city rewarded him with a council position and moved him to Jupiter's temple. He was six at the time. Now he's ten. He was more fun back then. Lately he's just . . ."

Instead of finishing, Aurelia grabbed a lump of chalk and began doodling on the pavement. The outline of a face appeared, a sharp jaw, frowning mouth. When it was clear she'd say no more, Felix sighed and withdrew the folded parchment.

"Can you read?" When she shrugged, Felix continued, "I need you to tell me what this says. It's important."

"About Loren?" She drew loops of hair, an ear.

"Not exactly. Well, he's involved."

"Show me." For the first time in a while, she looked up, dark brown eyes startlingly sharp. Felix passed the sheet over. Chalk powder puffed as she took it.

"A letter, maybe," he said. "I recognize the form, if nothing else."

Silence fell as Aurelia scanned the writing. "I know that signature. It's—"

"Julia," Felix said. Aurelia stared over the parchment edge, puzzled.

"*Julius*. Julia Fortunata's father. He owned an estate in town, dunno which. But I suppose now that he's passed, Lady Julia would've inherited." Her eyes flicked down. "This doesn't make much sense. A business deal, or a favor, but it fell through."

Felix sighed. "Read it out loud."

Aurelia pursed her lips and began, voice unsteady:

> "*My dear friend Sen. M. Servius R.,*
>
> *It grieves me to hear of your dismay at the termination of our trade negotiations. I imagine such transactions are handled differently in Rome. As expressed in my last letter, I am both unfit and unwilling to conduct exports of this nature. Regardless of promised earnings, I'm simply past the age where reward outweighs risk. I expect to live out the remainder of my days in Pompeii, alongside my daughter and household. As for the future of my estate—and my dear man, I am old but still sharp—I would see it kept within my family.*
>
> *Do pass my regards to the emperor.*

"Sincerely," Aurelia concluded, *"Spurius Julius Fortunatus.* He was a wine merchant, I know that much. That must be what *exports* means."

"No," Felix said, realization hitting with a sick lurch. "It's a mask-term smugglers use. I heard it too often growing up not to recognize it now."

It made sense. The room of relics, his so-called specialized interest—if the statesman had a history of *exporting*, no wonder a divine helmet had caught his eye. Felix's mouth dried. Rome was full of smugglers. But he rather hoped he'd left that lifestyle behind.

"How did you find this letter again?"

"Stole it, how else? What do you know about Julia?"

She passed back the letter and resumed her sketch, detailing an eye, shading the nose. "Mamma says she's a recluse. After her father died, nearly five years ago, Lady Julia stopped going around, shut herself in the house. Comes out for festivals mainly. Voting and council meetings, sometimes."

"But she's a woman."

Aurelia shot him a withering look. "And? Oh, don't explain yourself. I'm too young to be so exhausted by boys. As long as Julia owns the house, she has a say in how Pompeii is run."

Felix examined the letter again, hoping another look might reveal more answers. What mess had Loren tangled himself in? Worse, how much messier would it become before Felix could *untangle* it? Smugglers, politics—when he promised four days to Loren, Felix hadn't agreed to this.

Neither had Aurelia. How she stomached living among Pompeii's snakes and wolves was beyond him.

"You know a lot about this city," he said, "don't you?"

Again an eye roll. "I live here."

"There's more to it than that. You collect details like they'll save your life someday."

"Not only mine," Aurelia said grimly. "I'm smart. I can piece things together. Things I see and hear. You know how it is to live by your wits."

Felix studied her, the way she oscillated between childlike and piercingly keen. The way she tied her skirt to the side so she could run faster, climb higher. Her messy braid and scratched knees. How she gathered stories, and worried, and never slowed.

That's what Felix didn't understand. She lived comfortably, didn't she? With a mother, a home? Loren treated her as his sister, if not by blood. She had friends, too.

What was Aurelia so desperate to run from?

Somewhere both distant and too near for comfort, bells began to clang. Under the sound hummed a low current of footsteps, chanting. The procession must be approaching.

"You know, this is all wrong," Aurelia muttered, her voice nearly drowned by the growing cacophony. She scratched another chalk line. Felix peered down, startled to see his own face, rendered in white streaks with surprising depth, staring back. But it wasn't like seeing his reflection in a mirror or pool. Here, his face was distorted, carved and hollowed by something he couldn't name. Twin protrusions, like wings of a dove, splayed from his curls.

As though he wore Mercury's winged helmet. As though he had become the helmet.

With a snarl and a swift movement, Aurelia scraped the broad side of her chalk across Felix's face, sweeping it away entirely. She hurled the chalk against the wall opposite, and it shattered into a thousand fragments.

"Hey!" Felix cried. "What was that for?"

But Aurelia spoke as if she hadn't heard. "One day I think this will all go away. Disappear. Where will we be when the tide comes?"

CHAPTER XIV

LOREN

Gladiators battled it out in the arena below, but Loren quickly realized the real maneuvering was relegated to the stands, where the most vicious battles fought were bloodless.

"Stay at my side," Julia muttered, smile plastered tight. They paused outside the private row, reserved for the upper class. "Some in this audience will be interested in you. Too interested."

As if that weren't ominous. Nerves swirled in Loren's stomach.

"You'll be stunning, dear. No need to worry." Julia patted his cheek and linked her arm through his. Together they pushed through a heavy curtain.

Pompeii's amphitheater adhered to strict class lines. The lower in society you were, the higher you sat. Loren had never been so close to the action. The roar hit him first, concentrated in the belly of the bowl-shaped stands. Above the elite bench, men and boys had their pick of the plebeian seats, while women and slaves were on the uppermost outskirts.

Women, with one exception. Not a soul blinked at Julia as she drew Loren along.

Unlike the crammed public stands, the private row had room to spare, with wide aisles and cushioned benches. Even giant Gus could comfortably walk, silently bringing up the rear of their party as Ax had lurked off to lick his wounds. Loren tried not to gawk at the faces they passed. Politicians, patricians, rich Romans here on holiday—men he recognized from the Forum meetings he'd crashed. His nerves amplified.

Julia led Loren to the center front, above where the champion fighters emerged, and dismissed Gus, who retreated to stand with the other private guards. A handful of men, all robed in togas, glanced up.

"Lady Julia!" A portly man stumbled up from his sprawl, gold circlet askew. He clutched a half-empty goblet and threw out his other arm in welcome.

Loren took a swift breath. Here was his chance.

"Umbrius," Julia said, cool as ever. "Pleasure. Might I introduce you to—"

"Come, come. Sit." Umbrius, Priest of Jupiter and head of the council, flopped down, wine sloshing. He patted the cushion beside him with excess enthusiasm. "The drink is truly excellent, our sponsor outdid himself. Have your servant bring a glass."

Julia tucked her skirts neatly as she sat. "Loren isn't a servant."

"I was about to say, he does look different. Where's your regular? The woman?"

"Incapacitated, unfortunately."

"Shame." Umbrius beckoned to nobody, and a cupbearer appeared to refill. "Who did you say this boy is?"

"He's my—"

"It's Loren, sir," he blurted. If he thought his nerves agitated before, now they boiled over. "I don't know if you remember, but we met, not quite a month ago."

Umbrius frowned, unspeaking. Sweat prickled Loren's palms. He wiped them on his toga.

"In the Forum," he continued. "After a meeting."

"Part of the council, are you? I don't recall seeing you before."

"Ah. Well." He sucked in a deep breath. "No, sir. But I follow the council's votes avidly. It was after you gave that speech on cutting education funding—"

"Oh dear," Umbrius said.

"—and I know you said not to approach you again, but I must urge you to reconsider—"

"Now that you mention it, I *do* remember you." Umbrius clutched his wine tight to his chest, a wrinkle between his brows.

"Do you?" A spark shot through Loren. He nearly floated.

"Of course, of course. Let's, ah, talk after the games. Have a seat, won't you?"

Loren sat, breathless, simmering. Last night, he promised Felix he wasn't distractible, but here he'd wasted his chance to ask the questions bursting on his tongue—things like what Umbrius made of the helmet's disappearance, whether he took it as an omen or message, what his worries were. What his plans were. But he could ask none. Not with others so near, who might cast a suspicious eye for curiosity above his station and not trusting the plan of the gods. He fought to play cool, to not let his impulses snare him in deeper trouble.

"Well," said Julia, lips quirked. "Lovely that we're all acquainted."

"Refreshing to see a young man take such an intimate interest in local politics," a voice drawled from the other side of Umbrius. "What did you say your family name was, boy?"

Julia stiffened, whole body turning to stone. "Servius. I hadn't noticed you."

Servius smiled, a slow, relaxed thing, and leaned forward. For a hot autumn day, he wore odd clothes, all tall boots and tight gloves. His toga was crisp as they came, draped over a deep red tunic and pinned with a hawk crest. Something about him tickled Loren's memory, as though he'd seen Servius in passing.

Umbrius latched on to the topic change. "Julia, did you know our dear senator is sponsoring today's games? From his own pocket, mind you."

"Is he." Julia's smile didn't waver. "How generous."

Servius waved dismissively. "Umbrius exaggerates. It was nothing. Between the quakes and theft, the city needs its spirits lifted."

"Spared no expense." Wine splattered from Umbrius's goblet, narrowly missing Julia's dress. "Now, Julia, about that donation we discussed. One must wonder if the Forum had been in better shape, the guards might be more incentivized to, ah, guard."

"Discussing temple repairs on a festival day? Leave the woman alone. The games are about to start." Servius gestured for more drink, and the cupbearer acquiesced, which proved an adequate distraction. "Alcohol, always the great mediator. Advice for your new ward." His eyes gleamed as he tipped his cup to Loren.

"Loren is a clever boy, Senator." Nails dug into the meat of Loren's arm, half-moon pinches of pain, and he barely suppressed a wince. "He hardly needs to dole out wine to get what he wants."

Servius's jaw clenched, a tiny motion. "The games are about to start."

Julia faced the arena. "Indeed they are."

Loren wondered what, exactly, he had missed.

"Weak stomach?" Julia asked after the last match. They were taking a turn around the garden outside the amphitheater, waiting for Priest Umbrius to sober up.

Camilia used to drag Loren here on festival days, once they were released from temple duties. By the time they'd arrive, even the worst seats would be picked over, leaving them to sit on the highest wall, feet dangling. The distance made it harder to see the gore.

"Perhaps gladiator events aren't to my taste," Loren admitted in a small voice.

"You've turned green."

"He licked blood off his sword."

Laughing, Julia clutched his elbow. "Games are among the most crucial aspects of your political career. How do you win over the masses? Pay for entertainment."

"Like Senator Servius did." When Julia didn't respond, Loren rushed to add, "I've seen him before, I think, with the council. I didn't realize he was part of it."

"He isn't," Julia said carefully. "Servius advises the council. Influences policies. But he belongs—belonged—to Rome."

"You don't like him much."

"Was I that obvious? Servius and I go back." She sighed. Under a sprawling fig tree, a bench offered privacy from other early leavers, and she beckoned Loren to sit. "Do you know how I can tell you're a clever boy, Loren?"

He blinked, his ears heating. "I'm not, really. My father thought me dim."

Julia snorted, an inelegant sound. "Lend yourself more credit. You notice feelings. You perceive what others pass over."

"There are terms for that. Oversensitive. Thin-skinned."

"Don't discount the power of reading others' emotions. But you must be wary, doll. Politics is a game where your opponent will do anything to gain the upper hand. Exploit any weakness. You mustn't let this be one of yours."

Loren frowned and shifted on the bench. "How does this relate to Servius?"

"By virtue of being an unwed woman with the nerve to own property, I have enemies. And as I said, our visiting senator and I go back a long way." Julia's smiling mask faltered, mouth pressing a touch too tight. "Servius is nearly impossible to shake off. It's enough to drive anyone to the brink. Make them do anything to win."

"My lady?" A shadow passed over the garden, sun dipping behind a bank of clouds.

"It's a festival day, Loren. Put Servius from your mind."

"Telling me not to worry only makes my worry grow."

She barked a laugh. "Funny how that works, isn't it? The arrangement you and I now share eases my own burden, at least."

Right, their arrangement. Loren should tell her. About his parents, his visions, the responsibilities waiting back home. The truth of where he came from. The helmet. Gods, his secrets strangled him. Fiddling with the ring around his neck, he opened his mouth—

A trumpet blare cut him off. All around the garden, people hushed.

"The procession begins," Julia said dryly.

Bloodlust satiated, the real celebration could start.

Sweet smoke from burning beacons filtered over the heads of those walking. Drums beat a steady rhythm, bells chiming along. Priest Umbrius summoned Julia from the throng of spectators as easy as pulling in a fishing net. Julia indulged him, and with Loren on her arm, they marched down the Via dell'Abbondanza near the head of the parade.

"When we get to the temple," Julia muttered, again with her unmoving smile, "position yourself next to Umbrius. Offer to help."

Loren stared. "Why?"

"He's performing the afternoon augury. If you want to be noticed by anyone, it would be him."

"Surely I'm not qualified for that."

"You're sweet when you're nervous. If I consider you qualified, you are."

Loren's mouth pinched.

With clanging and chanting, the crowd shoved into the Forum, where those who hadn't attended the games had staked an early claim to the festival space. Umbrius tottered up the cracked marble steps of the Temple of Jupiter. Under his breath, he grumbled about bloody renovations and damned earthquakes and spoiled little boys named Numerius Popidius Celsinus, whose father picked the wrong temple to sponsor.

Julia nudged Loren, and with a nervous backward glance, he left her side to join the elite men on Umbrius's tail.

"I can see Camilia," came a child's voice from Loren's side, "and she looks like she wants to cut your balls off."

Loren jumped. Celsi himself had appeared from nowhere, his short legs working hard to keep stride. Chalk powdered his black curls, and dirt smeared his toga. Celsi met Loren's surprised stare with a haughty lift of his chin, then nodded to a shaded space beneath the portico.

Camilia's familiar cropped bangs nearly masked her angry brows, but she wasn't the only one glaring. The Priest of Isis leaned heavily on his walking stick, a deep frown underscoring the grooves in his face. Sera and Shani, at least, were too preoccupied bickering with each other to direct their ire elsewhere.

Loren's insides turned to lead. He raised his hand halfway, a meager apology, but the Priest only shook his head. Camilia sneered. She spun on her heel and disappeared, and Loren's heart dipped.

But against the shame came an indignant spark. The gap the Isis temple workers expected him to fill had never been Loren-shaped. It'd been cut for someone else, long before he came to Pompeii. And when the Priest turned him away, Julia opened her arms.

Everything was poised to fall into place, so long as Loren played the game right, solved the ghost's riddles, saved the city. He would prove what his visions were worth, and once Felix left, Loren would sign Julia's contract.

When his father tried to drag him home, Loren would be untouchable.

"Look, you've made them angry," Celsi chirped. "How does it feel to be an utter disappointment?"

"Charmed to see you, too, Celsi."

He grabbed Loren's hand. To anyone else, it might've looked sweet, like a pair of brothers. The sharp dig of his nails told the truth.

"I don't know why you're here," Celsi said, "but you aren't good enough to be."

"Aurelia is right about you. You're a little beast."

"Careful." Celsi pinched deeper. "You won't take my place on the council if that's your plan. My father paid for my chair. Sitting pretty with Spinster Julia won't get you anywhere."

Loren sighed, despite it all. "I'm not trying to take your place."

"Really?" Big eyes swam through Celsi's lashes. Then he stomped on Loren's toes. "Because you've done it before. I could have had both, you know. Isis and Jupiter. Until you came along."

Pain radiated from Loren's trampled foot, and he gritted his teeth. "That wasn't my fault."

"Camilia always liked me better. Even now, you're nothing but my replacement." Celsi squeezed Loren's hand one last time and pulled away, ducking to the other side of the procession line as they reached the wide-flung temple doors. Loren itched to chase after him, but the weight of Julia's expectations held him back.

The Temple of Jupiter was grand and regal, and Pompeii's most important worshipped here. Loren only visited at his most desperate, when he playacted having status, but under the stern eyes of Jupiter's statue, he always felt like nobody. Even now, bundled in his expensive toga, Loren couldn't shake the heavy shadow the king of the gods, flanked by Minerva and Juno, cast.

Swallowing his discomfort, he trailed after Umbrius to the altar and tapped his shoulder.

Umbrius did a double take. "You again. What is it? No more talk of funding now."

"N-no, Julia told me to help you, if permissible."

Umbrius grunted. "About time she took an interest in the temple. Very well. You may hold the cage. Celsinus, pass it over."

Celsi had materialized from nowhere, clutching a wicker trap holding a deeply unhappy raven. At Umbrius's command, Celsi's face screwed up. Loren could tell he wanted to argue. Or cry. Or strangle the bird.

"That isn't necessary," Loren protested, but Umbrius gestured again, and Celsi shoved the cage into Loren's arms. He stomped off, little sandals slapping against stone.

The raven cawed, beady eyes glittering, and Loren fought back an uneasy twist.

"Father Jupiter," Umbrius rumbled. His words blanketed the assembly with a hush. "As we offered food, wine, and bloodshed, let us now reveal your gracious will."

He carried on, rattling demands: prosperity for the city, a respite from the heat, the earth to cease its quivering, the helmet to reappear, its thief to meet swift justice. On and on through Pompeii's many problems. At its end, Umbrius issued a cue, and Loren fiddled the cage's latch.

When the ground lurched, it was almost unsurprising.

Almost. Startled, Loren dropped the cage, and its door sprung free. The spooked raven soared for the ceiling. Umbrius stared, stunned. Then the earth rolled again, and any scolding he intended to lay upon Loren for his fumble lost its urgency.

Nervous chatter erupted as men abandoned their piety, stumbling for shelter or gripping another's arms for stability. Stone rumbled, tiles splintering. A crack cleaved marble in two. Torches flickered with the threat of falling. The statue of Minerva lost her grip on her spear, and it tilted at a precarious angle. Loren stood rooted in place, heart kicking, even as Umbrius fled the altar.

This was normal. This was no different from the quake two days ago. Two weeks ago. Two months.

Across the panicked room, Loren locked eyes with Felix.

Even disguised in a bulky palla and scarf, there was no mistaking Felix's storm-cloud stare. He leaned against the back wall of the temple, partially hidden by a column. The lines of his face were rigid. Hollow. In the half shadow, juxtaposed with white marble, nearly ghostly.

What had Nonna said about the helmet thief? *Dream-walker. Plane-crosser.*

Closer to the dead than the living.

Loren's stomach hit the floor.

Nearly smacking into Celsi, who'd picked that moment to dart across the room, Loren beelined over unstable ground, trepidation spiking. If something had happened—

He herded Felix around the far side of the column.

"Where is it?" Loren hissed, searching Felix up and down, as though the helmet might be hidden beneath the drape of his shawl. "What did you do?"

"What?" Felix spluttered. "Nothing—I didn't—"

Rationality snapped back into place, quickly as the earth settled underfoot. Of course Felix wouldn't have the helmet. He valued his skin too much to parade around with it, he'd said as much. Loren simmered down, though his insides still quivered like an aftershock. Amidst it all, relief spread. Relief that Felix was here. Was still *Felix*. Loren's hungry eyes devoured him in the fresh light, cheeks a human pallor, mouth softly skeptical. No ghosts here.

They stood awfully close. Heat rolled off Felix. With a flush, Loren recalled the near-press from his dream last night, the space between their bodies a mere fraction. How badly he'd wanted to bridge that gap. How he still did, even awake.

"Coincidence," Loren admitted, hoping torchlight concealed his fluster.

"Thought you didn't believe in those." Felix hitched his shawl higher on his shoulder.

A man's loud laugh echoed through the temple, Pompeii pressing on, as always. But this time, the energy had shifted in a way Loren couldn't pinpoint. Even though Umbrius had ended the ceremony, high-ranking men lingered all over, murmuring in clusters. Agitation colored their voices like Loren had never heard.

Partially hidden by the column wasn't good enough. Eyes and ears were everywhere.

"You shouldn't be here," Loren whispered. "Someone could see."

"Embarrassed to be spotted with me? Worried I might damage your reputation?"

"I'm worried about *you*. You're meant to be lying low. Surely this can wait."

Across the courtyard, Umbrius cracked open a barrel of wine. Now was Loren's opportunity to talk to him about the helmet. About his visions.

"Not this." Felix's stare pierced Loren to his core. "I wouldn't be here if it weren't important. I found something that will change whatever you're planning. About Julia. And—*it*."

Wine cascaded from the barrel, pooling ruby on tile, and nervous mutters turned to cheers. Umbrius toasted the sky and threw back a swallow. Loren was torn. Julia had done exactly as she promised: granted him the opportunity he desperately craved. He'd be a fool not to take it. But Felix had come here, despite the risks, despite his distrust of temples. He'd sought Loren out. For once, Felix wanted to help Loren's search for answers rather than hinder it. It startled Loren how frightened that made him, but his choice, when it came down to it, was no choice at all.

Tomorrow. Loren would find a way to speak with Umbrius tomorrow, away from shaking ground and watchful eyes. Felix needed Loren now. The rest could wait.

As he beckoned Felix to follow, a flash of movement caught Loren's attention. From the next column over, Celsi was dashing for the exit, but skidded to a stop. Suspicious eyes landed on Loren, then snapped to Felix.

"Celsi—" Loren started, but it was too late. Celsi fled.

"That's the little boy Aurelia is friends with," Felix said. "I ruined their game of marbles. Do you think he heard much?"

Loren shook his head, even as his tongue dried. "Come on. Tell me outside."

Surely they hadn't said anything implicative. He didn't know about any marbles game, but something in the way Celsi had stared at Felix made Loren's hair stand on end.

It was the type of look that said *I know a secret you don't.*

CHAPTER XV

FELIX

Outside the cramped temple, the festival was in full swing despite its shaky beginning, again proving Felix's theory that madness plagued every Pompeiian.

He followed Loren along the edges of the Forum, weaving between stragglers. He kept his head low, pulling his stifling palla tighter. A last-minute addition to his disguise, he'd swiped it after distracting its owner with a kindly offer to carry her laundry basket—before promptly dumping it to tail Loren into the temple.

They ducked down the same alley where Aurelia and Celsi had played marbles. Felix repressed a shudder when he stepped over the scraped chalk remnants of his own face. It touched a nerve he couldn't explain. He lived. He breathed. The drawing, haunted and inhuman and crested with wings, was no more than dust.

"Felix?"

Fingers brushed his wrist, a question, and he jerked like Loren had pinched him. Maybe it was how for once, he wished the touch went deeper. Down to his bone. Anything to prove he wasn't transparent.

"Sorry." Loren pulled back. "You were drifting. What did you need to tell me?"

Felix's breath gusted out. *Focus.* "Clovia's murder wasn't random. It was a message."

Loren's mouth opened in a perfect circle.

Felix regurgitated how he'd spent the afternoon. For the first time since they'd met, Loren kept silent, eyes round as coins. "I didn't tell you before because I didn't have proof," Felix said at last. He withdrew the letter, dog-eared from rough handling, and slapped it against Loren's chest. "But I do now. I took this from the statesman—the one who wants the helmet."

Loren caught the parchment before it slid. "You said you'd lie low. Not trespass into the house of the man hunting you down."

"Just read it."

"I'm surprised you know what it says."

"Aurelia helped." A muscle tightened in Felix's jaw. "Read it."

Painfully slowly, Loren unfolded the letter and scanned the writing once. Twice.

"But the names—" His mouth tugged down.

"Julia's father, I know."

Braid flopping, Loren shook his head. "Not who it's from, who it's for. You have no idea who you took this from, do you?"

"I thought we were past the trespassing."

"Felix, you aren't listening." Loren tapped the header. "*Sen. M. Servius R.* He's your statesman? The guard you recognized at the estate, are you certain he's the same?"

"He cut me with a sword. My memory is shit, but that's not something you forget."

Loren huffed and tucked loose hair behind his ear. "Senator Servius is powerful. You don't understand. I met him today. He and Julia . . . she said they have history. I didn't realize how much. Or how deep their feud goes."

"Murder-deep, apparently."

"Isis, this is bad." Slumping against the bricks, Loren pressed his palms into his eyes, weary as the world. "When you said a rich man was after you, I thought a merchant. A lower ordo at most. But a senator of Rome?"

"Worse," said Felix. "He's a smuggler. I recognize the phrasing. My guess is he failed to rope Julia's father into his ring, and now Servius holds a grudge."

"Aurelia told me a story of an exiled smuggler, a man who wears gloves perpetually, who tried to move the helmet and was burned. I should've listened. Servius wore gloves at the games."

"No wonder he wants the helmet. Imagine what that would fetch on the market."

"If Servius had a true divine relic, I doubt he'd sell it off so easily."

"You think he'd use it." Felix kicked a crack in the wall. "Right. Who wouldn't want more power?"

"You wouldn't." Loren dropped his hands and stared at Felix hard.

"You would." Felix leveled his gaze. "Power abuses. You can't trust anyone who has more than you."

An agitated flush spread over Loren's cheeks. "That isn't true. A good politician should be someone you trust more than anything. Someone who acts for you. If they fail, you vote them out."

"Because it's so easy to get rid of a bad politician."

"It isn't a perfect system. But with the right intentions—"

"Intentions? Loren, politicians don't act for me. They act for whoever has the deepest pockets. And I'm worth nothing to either, not the council, not the rich folks funding them. What am I worth to—oh, forget it." Felix couldn't stomach listening to Loren defend a system that'd never once given a damn about him. Not again. Instead, he flicked the letter, still in Loren's tight fist. "What will you do about that?"

The diversion worked. Deflating, Loren tried in vain to smooth the rumpled parchment. He read it again and sighed. "What choice do I have? I should warn Julia he's after her."

"You saw her face when she found Clovia. She already knows. I brought you this as proof dealing with her is dangerous. Anything you think she might know about the helmet isn't worth it. Find another way to figure it out or drop the matter. Whatever you have with Julia, end it now."

"She's in danger, Felix. As her heir, it affects me, too."

Loren might have continued speaking. He probably did. But Felix's scope narrowed to a pinprick. Three words: *as her heir.*

"Her heir?" Felix breathed, cutting Loren off mid-sentence. "You signed?"

Loren shifted. An odd look came over him, glowing and proud and blushing for all the wrong reasons. "Not officially. Yet. You don't have to care for politics, but what she offers—"

"You said you wouldn't. That you were only there for the helmet." Felix swallowed. "Gods, Loren. I thought you didn't want to be controlled."

"Julia isn't trying to control me. She's—she's like me."

"What, a liar? She snared you in her political mess. Sorry, is *use* a better word?"

"Since when do you care?" Loren snapped, eyes bright and damp.

It caught Felix off guard, yanked the cobblestones from under his feet. He'd made Loren cry. He shouldn't have lashed out. He should apologize. It'd be simple. One of those easy gestures, the kind friends shared.

"Damn if I know," Felix said instead.

Loren's lips parted in fleeting surprise, but his face turned to stone. With crisp, even motions, he folded the letter and tucked it into his toga. Shoving off from the wall, he headed for the alley's exit.

"Loren, I didn't mean that," Felix tried. "No, I did. But I shouldn't have said it."

"Whenever I start to think you're halfway decent, you ruin it." Loren's mouth tightened at the corner: his signature expression. Felix hated that he recognized it. "I'm going to find Julia. Take the coward's way out if you want, but I don't cut ties when a situation stops serving me."

Gods. Felix watched helplessly as Loren was swallowed by the swarm of the Forum.

Lurking in the shade of the alley was far more comfortable than confronting . . . that. After all, Felix wasn't supposed to care. But Loren had slotted into all his rules, easy as reaching back for a friend's hand in a crowd so as not to be parted. No one had ever reached for him before. Felix wasn't ready to lose grip, even as he felt the fingers slipping away.

He thought back to the statesman—Senator Servius, rather. Darius sneaking from Julia's estate. Clovia's head bobbing in the atrium pool. And he thought of everything they could do to Loren now that he'd tangled with Julia.

Smugglers were bloody. And they never hesitated.

Gods. Felix steeled himself, then dove after Loren.

For a thief, a festival crowd was less a party and more an opportunity.

Felix's father would take him to the Circus Maximus on festival days. Not to celebrate. To pickpocket. They had a routine: Little Felix, all curls and dimples, would scream that he'd lost his da', and kind strangers would swamp him. He'd be scooped up, cradled and comforted. Then, tucked against their chest, he'd sneak his fingers into their pockets and rob them empty. One of his few remaining memories of childhood.

Now that he was older, sharper, less dewy-cheeked, Felix adjusted his strategy. Preying on the generosity of middle-aged strangers didn't work the same at seventeen. These days he looked for drunks with wide pockets.

Pity Felix didn't have time for petty theft. Today in Pompeii, alcohol flowed free.

He scanned the crowd, shouldering through pressed bodies, all somewhere between sufficiently tipsy and absolutely blitzed. Cups passed between hands and steady music thrummed beneath a current of excited babble. Felix's fingers ached to grab something. Anything. Deep in his pocket, he found another marble, but a body jostled him, and he seized at the contact. The marble slipped and bounced away between sandaled feet.

No more bribes for Aurelia.

Across the Forum, Felix caught a familiar shade of blue, the robes the attendants of Isis wore. Camilia, short-haired and short-tempered, slumped on a set of crooked steps. Felix hadn't seen her since the Priest of Isis sliced his arm, but she and Loren were friends, right? If anyone might talk sense into him, maybe she could. He shifted directions, skirting a cluster of girls.

When he straightened, Camilia was no longer alone.

Curly hair and a tiny toga. Celsi again, the fussy boy, and his hand was cupped around Camilia's ear in the way children believed inconspicuous. Her brow scrunched.

Felix stilled. Not wise in the crowded Forum. More bodies bumped him, and a gaggle of children half Aurelia's age did their best to bowl him over. He stumbled, skin itching. Camilia and Celsi's duo turned into a trio. A middle-aged man, skin the same olive as Celsi's, stormed over. He grabbed Celsi by the arm and jerked him away.

The phantom sensation of a hand curled around Felix's own wrist. He blinked. Blinked again. His lungs tightened. The sway of bodies, the echoing pulse of a drum—*his own father dragging him down temple stairs, feet tacky with blood on white marble, a cooling body robed in sacred purple splayed behind—*

VESUVIUS

The memory thread snapped, and with the next drumbeat, disintegrated. Felix yanked himself present, shivering with anger at his mind for pulling him through time like that. He rubbed his wrist, the ghost of long-faded bruises. His father hadn't meant to hurt him. He'd pulled Felix away from the hurt, he was sure of it.

Not what Celsi's father had done. Dragged him—Felix's stomach soured—toward worse.

Camilia rubbed her eyes. A second later, she fled in the opposite direction, walking faster than Felix could hope to catch up to. He couldn't shake the feeling he'd intruded on a scene he shouldn't have witnessed. If he were braver—if he were Loren—he might have intervened, if only to wrench that man's hand off Celsi's little wrist.

The ebb and flow of the crowd dragged him back in, though he felt more on the outside than ever. He couldn't relate to these strangers. He wasn't like them. A mystery cup of liquid appeared in his hand from an equally mysterious source. Alcohol would only dampen the senses Felix needed sharp, but between the press of the crowd and the lingering pinch in his chest, a sip couldn't hurt. He brought the cup to his nose. Nothing unusual. Good.

He threw it back. All of it.

Bitter hops burst across Felix's tongue, searing his throat. Within seconds, a fresh cup was exchanged for the old. This was a mistake. He swallowed another mouthful and turned. And promptly spit it back out.

He had found Loren.

Beer dribbled down Felix's chin. With a grimace, he scrubbed his sleeve across his mouth. In the quarter hour after storming off, Loren had melted into a group of townspeople letting loose, spinning and laughing and clapping in rhythm. Some type of folk dance, the type everyone was somehow born knowing.

Everyone except Felix, anyway. Because while other children got to practice dancing, he was cutting his teeth as a prodigy pickpocket.

The leather band holding Loren's braid had fallen out, long hair tumbling down his back and catching the light when he spun. A stranger's arm linked through his and danced him away.

Dumbstruck, Felix passed his cup elsewhere.

All his life, Felix had kept a tight grip on his feelings, determined to keep them in line. If he was angry, he stayed angry until he ran or drank it from his system. But Loren wasn't like that. Felix pictured it with perfect clarity: Loren, angry and shiny-eyed and bursting with self-righteousness, storming through the Forum, not realizing he'd cut through the middle of a dance until he was pulled in. Getting swept away. Switching his feelings on impulse. Determined to get the most out of every beat of his heart, even when it didn't make sense.

Gods, Felix yearned to live that way, where he could put his heart's desires over the demands of his head. Where he ran into the moment, instead of from it.

Across the space, their eyes met. Loren's face lit up, their earlier spat forgotten, and he skipped close to extend a hand. As if to pull Felix in. To dance with him. Felix only managed a blank stare. Another stranger, a boy with pretty eyelashes, materialized from nowhere to whisk Loren off. Sharp heat curled in Felix's rib cage. A moment passed before he placed the feeling.

Jealousy.

"Gods," Felix said, teeth gritted.

When an opening appeared, a girl's timid smile, Felix let himself be tugged in. She mumbled her name, and he tried to remember, but the buzz of alcohol hit his system at last, a soft filter between him and the crowd and her hand on his.

Her hair was all wrong. All pinned and complicated. Not free to cast his fingers through. Still, she showed him how to move his feet, and she didn't mock him when he stepped on her toes. They whirled to the drum. If he were anyone else, he might've held on to her.

Partners switched. Felix reached, but the boy Loren danced with swept in, twining their fingers and grinning against his neck. Partners switched. Now Felix swung an old woman, near Nonna's age, and she laughed a creaky thing when he dipped her low. Somewhere in the mix, Felix's palla pulled free, scarf unwinding, exposure coming as a luscious, nervous thrill. Partners switched. And switched. The music picked up tempo, spiraling and lilting and clapping to—

At last, Loren's hand landed in his, and Felix reeled him close, gripping him tight at the waist. The touch burned him to cinders. Cinnamon eyes. A dusting of freckles. Sunshine.

—the end.

"Felix," Loren said, and he didn't move away.

"Do you want," Felix started. Stopped. His mouth went bone dry. "I mean. Can I."

A sudden, breath-stealing urge to linger in the moment for the rest of his life, frozen in this spot as a pair of statues, cascaded through his system. Loren's lips formed the most perfect bow, parted in confusion or surprise.

Felix found himself tilting forward.

A shriek split the din. Chatter died. Felix jolted back as a streak of long curly hair burst from the crowd, barreling toward them. He missed the heat of Loren's palm the second it slipped from his grasp.

"Aurelia?" Loren said, frazzled, his eyes unfocused.

She said nothing as she collided into him at full force. Loren tipped back, and on instinct, Felix moved to catch his arm. Too late.

Aurelia pulled Loren's hand to meet her cheek.

His legs gave out. He folded. His eyes rolled back into his head, and Loren was gone.

CHAPTER XVI

LOREN

Loren was split between two realities, this world and—

Cobblestones digging into his knees. Heat blazing on his back. Acrid air searing his lungs.

A swallow of black.

Copper ducking into silver. Slipping the helmet on.

White.

This world, and the one where he died. Images flickered in and out, switching between Aurelia's vision and the festival crowd. Loren couldn't tether himself to either. He felt—

"Take his hand," Aurelia rasped, glassy eyes a thousand miles away. "Take it."

Fingers gripped his wrist.

Pulled.

Felix's ghostly face shattered.

Loren tore his palm from Aurelia's cheek with a cutting gasp, fingers blistering. She wavered where she knelt, as if she might tip sideways. He'd never seen her do this before. Not once.

Hysteria choked him. "What does that mean? What are you trying to show me?"

He didn't know who he asked. Aurelia, the gods, did it matter?

"Loren," she whispered. "He was there. I see you, too."

"What"—his voice broke—"am I doing?"

But Aurelia only shook her head. "Loren, I think . . ."

"Aurelia."

She looked at him with a sadness far beyond her years. "You can't stop the fire."

"No." Loren recoiled. "No."

Of all things Aurelia could have said, that burned the worst. All his years spent toiling in Pompeii, facing dead ends and mockery by day and murder and catastrophe in his dreams, but Loren was doomed to fail anyway. He couldn't. He wouldn't.

Felix said something. Something urgent. Worried. But it was like Loren was submerged in a bath, head underwater, all sounds muffled except for Aurelia's somber tone, alone in a bubble all their own.

"Loren!"

His ears popped. Music, laughter, talking. It came back in a sudden rush: where they were, who they were, the fact that Felix was gripping Loren's shoulders tightly, stopping him from slumping. Felix's hands seared imprints into Loren's skin, through the layers of fabric. He wanted to lean into it, let Felix hold him here, grounded, forever.

They didn't have forever, and Felix wasn't his to keep.

Loren lurched up, knees shaking, dimly aware he pushed Felix off him, and his dizzy mind mourned for the lost contact. People gawked. Of course they did, he'd had a fit in the middle of a festival. When he glanced down, Aurelia had slipped from his side like she'd never been there to begin with.

"What happened? What did you see?" Felix asked. For the first time since Loren jolted back to reality, he looked at Felix properly. Felix's skin had drained of color, gray eyes urgent. He was scared. It looked all wrong on his face.

They'd been dancing, Felix's hand on Loren's waist.

Loren swallowed, throat parched. Too late, he realized he was staring. Face burning, he dropped his gaze to the pavement. Thoughts raced, tripping over each other. He needed something to do. Something to center the energy boiling inside him before he burst.

"I need to find Julia," he blurted, then dove into the crowd, desperate for distance. To keep his fingers from shaking, he braided his hair. Picked it apart. Started over. Voices raged in his mind, all demanding attention. Aurelia. Julia. The letter. A city on fire. Felix's hand *on his waist.*

The memory replayed over and over, a tune Loren couldn't put from his head. What had he been thinking, getting distracted by a dance like that? Distracted by Felix, the boy Loren used to fear? Maybe Loren's father was right. His brain was addled beyond hope.

In Loren's dreams, Felix always died. He started the fire.

Now Loren knew how: by wearing the helmet.

He wasn't working fast enough to solve Felix's mystery. He needed something he could fix right *now.* Something straightforward, to get Servius off Felix's back for just a moment. Something like the letter.

Julia stood outside Apollo's temple, speaking with one of the councilmen. Rather, the councilman spoke. For her part, Julia merely watched, bored. When she caught Loren's approach, she brushed the councilman aside and slipped away.

"My brain nearly oozed from my ears listening to him," Julia said. "Gossip about that helmet, as if that helps the situation any." She squinted. "Are you ill?"

"I need to speak with you," Loren said. "It's urgent."

"Urgent?" Glancing over Loren's shoulder, her smile soured. "Ah. Your pet is here too."

Loren couldn't bear to look back at Felix for fear he'd vanish, Eurydice in the Orpheus story. If he never looked, never wanted, Felix couldn't be taken from him.

"Felix found something," Loren said. "It concerns your father."

Her posture changed, hand dropping from Loren's elbow, spine straightening. Warm Julia disappeared. Statue Julia took her place.

"I see," she said, chilly as a winter sea storm. "Come with me."

"Mention this to nobody," Umbrius warned as he handed Julia the key to his study, eyeing Loren and Felix hovering behind her. "A woman in the office. Unspeakable."

She offered a tight smile and led the way inside. The small study was too cramped to be called cozy, but private enough. A desk and pair of chairs crowded the space. Along the back wall, a shelf held a pitcher and goblets, perfect for men settling in to play a long game of politics.

Julia sank into Umbrius's spot. Loren chose the seat across. Felix, after a lengthy pause, perched on the arm of Loren's chair, and Loren did his best to ignore his fluttering insides. He had to play it cool. More skittish cat than boy, Felix was warming to him. One wrong move, and Felix would bolt.

"We won't have much time," said Julia. "Show me what you found."

Loren passed the letter over. She skimmed it, stony face not shifting. When she reached the end, she tossed it on the desk with a dismissive wrist flick.

"Is this all?"

"No," said Loren. "Felix saw Servius's guard moments before he—"

"Found Clovia," Julia finished. "I'm aware of Servius's techniques, believe me."

"But at the games—"

"Yes, I knew then, too. Hold your protest, Loren." She busied herself decanting wine. "There's more to this story than you can possibly predict."

Julia plucked a scroll from a basket under the desk and unfurled it, a portion of a map. She weighed three corners with her filled goblet and two apples, leaving the fourth to curl back over the sea. Finally, she withdrew a pouch, concealed by the drape of her dress, and emptied out a scatter of coins.

"Our friend has hands in more places than you realize." She set to work arranging the coins, placing them one by one over points on the map.

Loren recognized some of the cities. Rome, their capital. Surrentum. Stabiae. Even Salernum. Then Julia began filling in the gaps, setting coins over places even Loren, with his education in trade, hadn't heard of. Two dozen markers soon cluttered the map.

"A pattern," Felix said, flushing when both Loren and Julia looked up in surprise. "Look. Rome in the center. The coins surrounding it."

"Keen observation," Julia said, not quite begrudgingly. Her eyes slid to Loren. "Perhaps your dog does have a brain."

Felix's lip curled. Loren shot a warning glare, and Felix slouched back against the chair.

"Anything Servius wants, he will stop at nothing to get." Julia placed a final pair of coins over Pompeii and Herculaneum, side by side, like covering a corpse's eyes for passage to the underworld. "What he wants is this city in his pocket."

"I don't understand," Loren said. "His end goal is, what? To be elected here? You said he's from Rome."

Julia snorted. "Pompeii could crumble into the sea tomorrow and Servius wouldn't flinch. No use drizzling trash with honey. He hates this city. Hates it for holding him hostage here. He crept onto the councils of these other towns, swayed the vote, and turned them obedient to the capital within months. Pompeii has held out for four years. Do you think that endears us to him?"

"He should leave," Loren said hotly. "If he thinks so poorly of us."

"He has nowhere to go. The emperor won't allow him to return to Rome until he fulfills the conditions of his sentence. Servius has been in exile for six years."

Felix scoffed. "Most smugglers aren't let off so easy."

"You know about his hobby? You keep surprising me. But yes, why is anyone ever exiled? You fall from good grace but are too important to assassinate. A useful strategy to keep yourself alive, I'll allow him that. Servius entangled himself with a smuggling guild and got caught with his hand in the honeypot. Former Emperor Vespasian offered a deal—bring the colonized towns in line, and Servius would see his station restored."

"Raising taxes," Felix said. "He's one of Rome's envoys."

"I track the council's votes," Loren said. "Session after session, the answer hasn't changed."

"Hasn't changed yet," Julia corrected, "because I have stood in the way every time."

"You—of course." Loren sat back and studied the map. "Your estate gives you sway with Umbrius and the council. And if you continue pressuring against a vote to raise taxes, Servius can't leave. It's an impasse."

"When Servius faces an impasse, does he strike you as the type to relent? To bargain?" Julia grabbed her goblet, relieving its duty as a map weight, and swallowed a mouthful of wine. The freed parchment corner curled. "I'm afraid it's more complicated."

"Then what is it?" Felix snapped. "I hate politics. Life ought to be yes or no, none of this complicated shit."

Julia arched a brow, unamused. "You wouldn't survive a day in Rome."

"I survived eleven years in Rome."

"Yet you're here, meddling in the politics you despise."

Felix muttered a series of barely audible curses. The hem of his tunic brushed Loren's elbow.

Julia turned back to Loren. "Before my father retired to his estate here, he was a traveling merchant. His contracts took him throughout the empire and landed him the favor of Vespasian. This was how he met Servius, who, if you recall from the letter, tried to strike a deal with my father. Rope him into his ring. My father wasn't pious by any means, but the objects Servius sought . . ."

Loren's stomach sunk with the suspicion he already knew. Still, he said, "Valuable. Priceless."

"Divine," she corrected. "Have you noticed his gloves? They cover scarred palms, burned from handling relics beyond what humans can stand. Even so, he persists. Servius has a lust for it, the idea that mortals can touch hands with gods. He went so far as to operate his dealings out of a temple in Rome. And *that* was too scandalous for my father. He tipped Vespasian off, and within weeks, the smuggling ring was scoured."

On his perch, Felix stiffened, rigid and lifeless as an amateur painting. A question formed on Loren's tongue—a shapeless interrogation that somehow would draw a link between Servius, smuggling, and Felix—but Julia spoke first, and the thought faltered.

"Servius's ire with me is as personal as it is political. You read the letter. Once Vespasian declared his punishment, Servius saw the opportunity to sink Pompeii and thus sink my father, if only he got his hands on the estate. My father was elderly. Servius decided to bide his time."

"But you inherited the estate when your father died," Loren said.

"An untraditional arrangement. Servius didn't expect it, certainly. I imagine he didn't see me as a threat, but I'm everything he hates in a person. A woman, educated, and clever enough to stay two paces ahead."

"So he should kill you. What's stopping him?" Felix said, voice flat. Loren winced, but Julia only smiled, cold as ever.

"If Servius has ever erred," she said, "it's by underestimating me."

Loren fiddled with a coin, spinning it on its side. "How many times did you reject him for marriage?"

"More times than appropriate. He thought I'd relent eventually. But now he's grown impatient. Clovia was an unfortunate casualty."

"Julia, if Clovia was only a message, surely he'll do worse to you." Loren cast an eye to Felix. Unless justice was delivered and Servius stopped, he had the sinking feeling Servius would keep hunting Felix. Even after he put the helmet back. Even after he left town. Felix's ability to handle such a relic would be too valuable to let slip away. "And I have reason to suspect he still smuggles, despite his exile. We have evidence. Go to the council. Go to Umbrius."

At last, Julia's mask crumbled. Eyes lit, she straightened and gave a shrill laugh. "My power is tenuous. I'm a woman who owns property by the skin of her teeth. Were I to accuse a senator from Rome, of all places, of wrongdoing, we would test how thin that skin is. Do you think for one moment they would believe my word over his? Damn the evidence!"

"But it isn't right. What does the council stand for if not the people? How can we fix injustice if we choose to do nothing?"

"We can't." Julia slammed her goblet down. Wine sloshed over the rim and onto the map, spreading across Pompeii in a bloody streak. "You are no hero, Loren, and your political ambition is at odds with your ideals. You must lose one."

"If I don't?"

"The alternative is obscurity. Or death if you're lucky."

"Go to the council. They'll listen, we can show them."

"Lorenus, *enough*."

Loren's world halted. In an instant, it pared to a singular moment: Julia's face, purple and furious, shoulders trembling with barely restrained rage. Felix's body tensed to flee. Wine saturating cities. His full name on Julia's lips.

The name Loren hadn't heard in four years. Not since his father last drawled it.

"You knew," Loren said. "This entire time."

"Of course I knew," Julia hissed, pinching the bridge of her nose. "I grew up in trade. You thought I wouldn't have met your father? I wouldn't recognize your mother in you? That I'd pluck any random temple boy off the street? I want to solidify my family line, not destroy it."

If Loren's carefully constructed false identity hadn't just been wrenched apart at the seams, he might have laughed. How could he have missed it? The wine jug in her study, how she hadn't questioned his lacking backstory—of course she knew.

She had never wanted him. Just his name.

Loren stood, nearly overturning his chair. The cord around his neck hung heavy.

"I'm not your doll," he bit through clenched teeth, "to manipulate. Find someone else, Julia."

He stormed out. Behind, Felix's footsteps were close on his heels, but whatever he had to say, Loren couldn't stomach it. He burst into the Forum, where the party still thrived, infectious, careless joy. A jolt shot through his veins. Sitting in the study, surrounded by maps and money, it'd been so easy to forget that this was Pompeii's beating heart.

This was his home. He'd struggled here, cried here, true, but Pompeii had been the first to offer him any chance at existing on his own terms, outside his father's villa. Pompeii gave him hope.

Ghost-Felix's words rang back: *You did this to yourself.*

Aurelia's next: *You can't stop the fire.*

His uselessness tore him apart.

Loren loved this city the way Icarus loved the sun. Bold. Bright. Willing to burn for it.

"You're all in danger," he breathed.

Felix crept up quietly. Gentle fingers curled around Loren's wrist, a rare touch that emboldened him to act.

"Damn it all." Loren pulled away and strode forward.

Government buildings and temples surrounded the Forum on all sides, stuffy halls of law and order, but the point of the place was to open the floor to the common man. Any free citizen could speak, and even if Loren had objections to who that list excluded, by the gods, he'd use this platform for all it was worth.

Because Julia wouldn't do anything about Servius.

Because Loren could do something.

He hitched the hem of his toga and clambered onto the nearest stone block.

"Stop, everyone, stop!" he shouted. "You must listen!"

A group nearby shot Loren dirty looks, but the crowd danced on. It was too loud. Thinking fast, he pulled off one sandal. *Apollo help him.* He threw it.

He'd aimed between the flutist and the drummer, only to get their attention, but his shot was off, and the shoe smacked the kitharist square in the face. The boy stumbled back, music grinding to a halt. The dancing slowed. Heads turned. Sudden, stunned silence.

Loren stared, hand over his mouth. But he got what he wanted. He pulled his palm away, and said, loud and shaky, "You'll all die if you don't leave the city. Now."

A thousand pairs of eyes fell on him. Well, if his political career hadn't already withered, it had surely crumpled now. He pressed on.

"It sounds absurd." A few people in the crowd shifted, shot each other apprehensive glances. Encouraged by the possible stirring of belief, Loren raised his voice to carry across the square, despite his panic. "But a horrible catastrophe is about to fall upon the city. The quakes are no coincidence. They're a warning. Days, weeks, I don't know when. You must leave. Immediately."

"What evidence?" a man shouted back.

Loren paled. What evidence indeed. His parents had urged him from childhood, ever since he first dreamed of a woman from town drowning, only for her bloated body to wash up days later, to keep his visions secret. They were an embarrassment, a defect, a sure sign he was mad or cursed or both. His father once said, *There is no tolerance for madness, boy. Not here, not out there.*

Across the Forum, Loren locked eyes with Julia, haloed against the open door of the lantern-lit study. She was all marble and glowing gold, cold and furious as a distant star. Strange, friendless Julia. In the end, he supposed they weren't so different.

Two people dripping with privilege, but neither had power when it mattered.

And Felix, who had nothing at all.

It slapped Loren with brutal irony that Felix, a flighty thief, had become the true constant in his life. Not just in the past days, but years now, ever since the angry ghost first stepped into his nightmares. Because if no one else believed his visions, Ghost-Felix did. Loren searched for Felix now with a desperate ache, for any sign he wasn't some fool alone in the world, but his thief was long gone.

Felix had no reason to stay. He wasn't Loren's friend. He'd made that clear.

Finally, Loren turned back to the gathering. These were people he saw daily in the market and tavern, exchanged smiles and handshakes with, but they glared now with anger and distrust. The cheesemonger he waved to only yesterday flashed a crude finger-sign.

"I don't have any," Loren admitted. The crowd tittered. Any rapport he had garnered quickly faded. "No, but you must listen—"

"Start the music!"

The kitharist, having recovered from the sandal assault, shot him a horrible glare, made uglier by his freshly bloodied nose. He strummed his kithara defiantly. After a beat, the flutist and drummer joined in.

"No," Loren whispered. Then, louder, "Please, trust me."

"Get out of here!" A cold, wet splat hit Loren's shoulder, fruit that dripped and stained his toga. Snickers erupted.

Loren fled.

He hopped from the speaking stone and ran. The crowd didn't part for him, forcing him to weave and stumble as people jostled and shoved and laughed. Loren kept his face down, fighting back the humiliating sting of inevitable tears. One foot was still bare. Somehow, that made everything worse.

Finally, he crashed outside Isis's temple, the only place he could think to run to. With Julia's manipulations revealed—that she only meant to use him for his family name—returning to her estate was unthinkable. Facing Elias at the brothel would be worse. Here, Loren could at least be quiet for a while.

He shut the door behind him and leaned against it.

"Tell me," said a gratingly familiar voice, "are you finished humiliating us yet?"

"Don't, Camilia." Loren opened his eyes to find her braced over the altar. She wouldn't look at him, just stared at embers in the bowl. "Please. I can't bear it."

"*You* can't bear it? You overstepped your role, so the Priest dismissed you. Now you gallivant around with people far above your station." Camilia shook her head, lips pursed. "You mock us, but still you come for sanctuary. You used us as a steppingstone into the council and the Temple of Jupiter, like Celsi did. Worse, because he had the excuse of being a child with no choice."

Loren crossed the courtyard. Smoke filtered the air with gray haze. "You know I'm loyal to Isis. You know me."

"Do I?" She looked up at last, eyes ringed with smudged black liner. "I thought I did. We were friends once. Now I'm not convinced."

"I've never lied to you. Not when it mattered."

"Everything about you is a lie, Loren. When was the last time you were honest? Not with me. With yourself. And don't say a damned thing about your visions." Herbs snapped and sizzled. Shapes seemed to twist in the smoke, but Loren's eyes were too tear-blurred to make any out. "Everyone knows you in this city because you can't keep your nose out of things. Everyone knows you as Isis's temple boy, and everything you do reflects on us."

"You didn't want me here in the first place," Loren said, flushing hot all over again. "None of you did."

"We tried to include you for years. But from your first day, you looked beyond us." Camilia shoved off the altar and stripped her temple robes. "Our reputation has suffered enough. You should go."

"I still follow Isis. I have the right to be here."

"I don't mean back to the brothel, or wherever you sleep now." She paused hanging her garments. "I meant go home. Back where you came from. Don't bother us here anymore."

His gut clenched. "Why are you saying this?"

The cabinet door shut with a resolute snap. "Because I'm not the only one tired of indulging your savior complex."

Camilia left without looking back. Loren waited until the door slammed and her footsteps faded before he let the last of his walls crumble. Eyes burning, he stumbled for the cabinet and what he knew was stashed inside.

A clay jug of wine, stamped with that familiar emblem: a stern *L*, looped in vines.

"Cheers, old man," Loren said. He popped the top and drank.

CHAPTER XVII
FELIX

Felix's plan revolved around a missing shoe. That should've been his first indicator he was destined to fail. The second came from the knowing look Livia delivered him when he showed up at her door just after sundown.

She was sweeping the walk, still dressed in day clothes. Aurelia crouched on the stoop, rolling marbles between cobblestones, but the moment she saw Felix, she blanched like she'd seen a ghost and scampered inside. Livia glanced up at the slam of the door.

"Oh, hello." Her face lit up, as if seeing Felix was the best thing that had happened all day. "Have you eaten?"

"I—"

"Of course not, you boys don't look after yourselves." From her apron, she withdrew a half slab of flatbread. "Have this. Why are you holding a shoe?"

Surely Felix still had time to flee. "It's why I'm here. Have you seen, uh . . ."

There. That look that said Livia knew exactly who Felix was and what he wanted.

Her smile turned sad. "No, love, but Aurelia told me what happened. I imagine he's feeling quite low right now."

Felix shifted his weight, palms sweaty where he gripped the sandal and the bread. It was fresh, baked by Nonna. How he'd become so acquainted with these people in only a few days, he couldn't say. Maybe when he left, his piss-poor memory would work in his favor for once. Maybe soon he'd forget them all.

"You know," Livia said, "it's a good thing Loren has you."

Oh, this was bad.

In truth, tonight was Felix's worst escape attempt yet. After Loren stepped on the block to speak, Felix fled, not able to stand the brewing fallout he sensed, the shift in the air pressing on his nerves. Attention, conflict—too risky to stick around for.

He hadn't made it three paces from the Forum before he turned back. Each step from Loren's side felt like wading too far from shore. He couldn't leave, and this time it wasn't the fault of city guards or Darius or the helmet. Felix *wanted* to stay. He wanted Loren safe, not torn apart by a pack of political dogs. Wanted Loren with both his shoes on.

That scared him worse than magic or memory ever could.

Felix took a steadying breath. "I'm only returning his sandal."

Livia still gave him *the look*. "It isn't about the shoe."

"Isn't it?"

"You should find him."

"I'm trying.

"He could use a friend."

"Right," said Felix.

She hummed. "I was only a girl when my parents kicked me out," Livia said, the change in topic so abrupt, Felix felt dizzy. "I thought to myself, that was it for me. No more trusting. Care is hard to accept when all you've known is hurt. Until I moved here, and Nonna took me under her wing. She helped me open my shop. And I met someone else who proved me wrong. He's gone, but you know what I learned?"

"I don't think I want to," Felix said, defenses creeping higher.

He must look like a proper fool, standing on her step like this. Livia set her broom aside and pulled him into a crushing hug, squashing the bread. This type of touch set off alarm bells, but for once, he forced them silent.

"I learned," said Livia, rubbing Felix's back, "that love doesn't mean losing yourself. You don't have to sacrifice anything by letting someone in."

"It isn't that easy." The admission burned. "Not for me."

"Your walls exist for a reason, I imagine. Start by finding someone willing to make the climb." Livia released him, but kept a hand at his flaming cheek. "I meant what I said. I'm glad Loren found you. He's a good boy, but he needs a tether."

Only a mother could get away with saying these words. A little thrill shot through Felix that Livia had murmured them to him, as if he and Loren were more than two boys thrown together by bad luck.

"Run along, love. You'll find him." Livia ruffled his hair and swatted him away. She returned to her sweeping, and Felix returned to his search, and that was that.

Felix ate the bread as he walked. Drunk and cheery folks lingered on every corner, dancing, sharing wine, kissing. A buzz spread through Pompeii, twilight air punctuated with chatter. They were happy, and their obliviousness disturbed him. Change hung heavy in the atmosphere, bubbled in the city's core, a grim haze hovering low, and Felix might not believe in omens, but he trusted his gut.

All his instincts screamed *run*. While he still could.

The brothel loomed ahead, orange lights beckoning. Felix's skin tingled as he stepped through the door. Musky air greeted him, cut through with the sharp scent of—

"Fox!" Elias perked up from where he reclined on the stairs, a fat blunt of herbs pinched between two fingers. "Interesting, I was wondering when you'd return to our humble home."

"That smells horrible," Felix said. "What is it, roadside dandelions?"

Elias tilted back and laughed, eyes rimmed red. "A new strain of hemp, sweet thing, for refined tastes. Breathe it in for a moment, and tell me it isn't intoxicating."

Felix crinkled his nose but stepped closer, despite his better judgment. "Where's everyone else?"

"The women? Out with the others. Celebrating. Like any good Roman." He squinted at Felix through the low-lit smoky filter. "Y'know, I'm surprised to see you here alone. Festival not enticing enough?"

"I was hoping"—Felix winced—"that you'd seen Loren."

"Who? You'll have to describe him, Fox. You see, I've passed the point of remembering, well, anything."

He was taking the piss. "I'll check myself."

Elias sprawled on the stairs, blocking Felix's path. "He isn't there. I would've seen him come home."

"How long have you been sitting here?"

"Hours and hours. Sit with me, why don't you? Maybe we can solve this puzzle together, work through all the places he might be. Promise I'll make it worth your while."

Felix hesitated, but Elias shot him a wild little grin and scooted over. Gingerly, he sat, but kept his feet planted on the ground, ready to flee at a moment's notice. Elias offered the blunt, shrugging when Felix shook his head.

"Tell me where you've looked already."

"Well." He picked at the worn leather edge of Loren's sandal. "The docks. The tavern. The weaver's shop. Here."

"If your method is to search all the places Loren wouldn't be first, you have an awfully long night ahead of you. Can I pose something?"

"No."

"Part of you is afraid to find him," Elias said anyway. When Felix bit his tongue, Elias barked a laugh. "I'm right, aren't I?"

The tops of Felix's ears burned. He hoped against hope Elias was too blissed to notice. "Shouldn't you be out pulling someone?"

"It's my night off. Well, from that part of my job. Now you've stumbled onto the other half of my profession: doling out relationship advice and soothing broken hearts."

Groaning, Felix dropped the sandal to bury his face in his hands. "I'm trying to return his shoe. That's it. After, I'm leaving. For good."

Elias blinked, thoroughly unimpressed. "You're pathetic. And oblivious."

"Piss off."

"You want my advice," he drawled, and Felix was certain he didn't, but he continued, "stop looking where you know he isn't, and go where you know he is."

"If I knew that, I wouldn't be here," Felix said.

Elias smirked and leaned heavily against the step. In the flickering sconce light, he was smudgy and lean, like a hastily drawn figure study, ink bleeding around the edges. Imperfectly crafted in a careful way. Lazily beautiful. In another town—and pliant with enough drink to dull the discomfort of touch—Felix would have pulled him into a dark corner by now. Impermanent intimacy, a distraction.

A hand on Felix's shoulder pushed him back from where he'd been leaning forward.

"It would be a yes to you," Elias said, "if I thought I was what you wanted."

"Why wouldn't you be?"

"Because I'm easy, and you aren't meant for that. Because soon, I'll pay my way out of here, and I won't leave anything behind when I do." Smile widening, Elias took a long drag from his blunt. Smoke cascaded between their faces. Maybe he was right. The herb was a slow burn, hard to stomach at first, but it grew on the senses, given time. "Perhaps in another life. Go find your boy."

Felix took Loren's sandal and left.

The brothel wasn't far from the Temple of Isis, and it came as both a relief and a disappointment to find the temple door unlocked. But it was always unlocked. That was the way of Isis: She welcomed the downtrodden, the miserable, the dispossessed. Felix fit all three categories.

Orange streaked past his feet. He froze, but it was only one of the cats, Pollux, the most useless sentry. At the altar, incense crackled, but unlike Elias's smoke, these fumes were sweet and mellow and didn't blur Felix's mind. Otherwise, the courtyard didn't stir. For a moment, he thought he had it wrong again. Then he caught a sliver of light spilling from the cella door. He followed it up the short stairs and paused.

This place made Felix shrink so very small, a boy who'd never outgrown the feeling of not belonging. The cella was sacred, reserved for the devout. Nothing about it should feel familiar, except . . . flashes. A memory tugged again. Another temple, another cella, another time.

There was a temple—the Aventine Hill—

Lantern light. Solitude.

Wine laced bittersweet.

Felix rubbed the prickle from his arms. He didn't have time to chase stray thoughts. He braced himself and pushed inside. Isis's dark eyes tracked him, but she didn't seem angry. A gilded sunray fanned from her hair. The cult performed their mysteries in this chamber, the secret rites of Isis's followers who swore their lives in return for nothing, at worst. Comfort, at best.

Temples had only ever left Felix hollow.

A too-familiar figure slumped at the statue's feet.

"Move," Felix said to Castor, nestled on Loren's rib cage. Castor's large yellow eyes blinked once, and Felix feared he'd have to fight the animal off, but he stretched, yawned, and padded to curl on the goddess's sandals. Cat-free Loren somehow looked more pathetic. Felix pursed his lips and knelt, shaking Loren's shoulder until he stirred.

"You're drunk," Felix asked, "aren't you?"

With all the grace of a newborn fawn, Loren hauled upright. His eyes drooped, cheeks tearstained. Strands fell from his mussed braid, framing his face. "If you came to tell me off, don't bother. Can't take being called a fool by you tonight."

"I'm not here for that." Felix held out the shoe.

For a long moment, Loren only stared.

"It's yours," Felix said.

"I know," Loren said, still struggling. "Why d'you have it?"

"Because you threw it. At the kitharist. A good hit, though perhaps not for him."

"I *know*. But why do *you* have it?"

Of course this couldn't be easy. Felix dropped the shoe and sat beside Loren on the dais. "I looked for you after your speech."

Loren snorted. It sounded all wrong. "Generous to call it that."

"Your only pair of sandals, right? I'd want it back if I'd been up there." Which wasn't precisely true, given that Felix nearly ditched his own sandals days ago, but it seemed a reasonable excuse.

"Wouldn't have been you." Loren screwed his eyes tight. "You understand, don't you? Only I'd lose control like that. In front of everyone. I'm ruined."

Felix couldn't help it. He rolled his eyes. "You think Patroco—"

"Patroclus."

"—never embarrassed himself? You aren't the only fool in history."

"I'll never *he* in history," Loren insisted. "I threw all my ambitions in the gutter tonight. And Patroclus died when he made a fool of himself."

"Should I use Achilles as an example?"

"Also a fool. Also died."

"I can leave, if you'd rather." Felix shifted to stand, but Loren flailed in protest.

"Don't. I would rather listen to you talk poetry than be awake with my thoughts." Fumbling with an amphora, Loren squinted at the maker's stamp, then passed it to Felix. "I was under the impression wine was meant to help."

"How much did you drink?" Felix said, sloshing it around. Nearly dry from the sound.

"Opened it new."

"Jupiter, Loren, what were you thinking? You're supposed to water this anyway, not drink it straight."

"I was thinking I didn't want to think. But it only made everything louder."

Felix took a draw from the jug. Sickly-sweetness washed over his tongue. "Horrible. Who made this? Lassius?"

That startled a pained laugh from Loren. "You have no idea, do you?"

"I don't care what you rich folk say. Lassius wine is swill." A smirk curled Felix's face. "I stole from his villa once."

"No." Loren still giggled, a drunken babble. His whole body shook with it as he pressed his forehead to Felix's shoulder, and Felix felt the burst of each laugh echo warm and sharp down to his fingertips. "Tell me that's a joke."

Strangely proud, Felix nodded. "He owns the big vineyard south of here, a day's ride by the main road. Has more property than he knows what to do with, so I took as many bottles as I could. Doubt he noticed them missing."

"Felix." As abruptly as it started, Loren's laughter died. "You can't tell me these things."

"Why not?"

Weight retreated from Felix's shoulder. Not that he cared.

"Because Lassius is my father."

Felix waited for the joke to drop. And waited. But Loren fished under the neckline of his toga-tunic-abomination and withdrew a gold ring fastened to a cord. With a sharp tug, he snapped the leather.

He dropped the ring into Felix's palm.

"I didn't want to tell you," Loren said, which Felix took to mean *I'm only telling you because I'm drunk out of my skull.* "But Julia knows, so. Fuck it."

Felix's mind melted. "Julia knows?"

"You didn't hear her?" Loren's pretty mouth twisted into a grimace. "Not a soul in Pompeii should know my real name."

"Your real name." Not melted. Disintegrated.

"Lucius Lassius Lorenus. Ridiculous, isn't it?"

Neither laughed. Felix stared at the signet ring, emblazoned so clearly with the Lassius family crest. Reversed, so when pressed to damp clay or puddled wax, it would face correctly. For a long moment, Felix found he couldn't make any sound at all.

"Say something, Felix. Say you were right all along, that I'm some rich boy choking on privilege. I know you think it already. May as well air it. Or tell me—"

Felix slipped the ring on. Loren cut off with a strangled cough.

"Keep it," Loren choked out. "I don't need it. Don't know why I kept it this long. Figured I'd flash it someday to get myself out of trouble, or into trouble, but obviously this was a mistake. I'll crawl back to them. I'll leave tonight."

The thought came over Felix, in a slow spread, that for all he thought he and Loren were different, perhaps those differences linked them. After all, weren't they both searching for a place to belong? Where rules didn't matter?

"No," Felix said. "You aren't going back there. Pompeii is your home."

The chamber fell eerily silent. Felix dragged his eyes from the ring, turned to look, and—

Loren kissed him.

And, oh. *Oh*. Dry at first, then soft. Soft and clumsy and unco-ordinated. Loren tasted of sweet and sticky wine, but the sugar was tempered, somehow, honey left to caramelize in a simmering pot. Felix cupped Loren's jaw in his palm, guided him to a better angle, and pushed his fingers back into braided hair. He ached to unpick the twists, let dark strands fall free, so he could comb through it, all the way down.

He wanted to kiss Loren until he went cross-eyed.

He wanted to slip into this boy and not resurface.

He wanted to unwrite all his rules.

Loren's hand settled somewhere on Felix's chest, his touch a thousand tiny sparks. Felix's whole body lit, and he trembled with overwhelm, and their mouths slid together. Sugar-wine faded, and all he could taste was *Loren, Loren, Loren.*

When Loren sighed hot against his lips, Felix jerked back. "We can't."

A crease appeared between Loren's brows. He still leaned in, even as Felix pulled away. Blown pupils swallowed his cinnamon eyes. "But . . ."

"We can't." Felix's heart pounded against the fingertips grazing his collarbone. Suddenly the pressure suffocated him.

"But." Loren blinked. He straightened, noticing Felix's discomfort, and dropped his hand to scoot away. Even in the low light, Felix caught his face flush deep. "Oh. You don't like me that way. I assumed. Read you wrong. Or is it . . . you prefer women. I'm so sorry, Felix, I—"

This boy needed to stop talking. Felix searched for a place to touch him that wouldn't imply something improper, but his shoulder felt patronizing, and his waist was more intimate than he could stand. He settled for Loren's knee.

It worked. Loren, indeed, stopped. Not just stopped talking. Stopped everything. He stared at Felix's hand, mouth parted. The signet ring winked beneath the lantern, heavy on his finger.

"You're very, very drunk," Felix said.

Nor was Felix drunk enough, but he didn't dare reduce Loren to a distraction.

"I'd kiss you sober," Loren breathed, and gods if that didn't send a bolt of lightning down Felix's spine. "It isn't the wine."

"But you're drunk now. I won't take advantage of you when your mind isn't clear."

Loren's fingers hovered, feeling out their welcome, then tangled with Felix's own. Touch was a careful, convoluted conversation that Felix wished he didn't need to constantly negotiate.

"I trust you," Loren said. "I'd let you do anything you wanted to me."

"That's why I'm concerned." Felix frowned and stood. "Come on, I'll walk you home."

With uncoordinated fingers, Loren strapped on his recovered sandal. Felix pulled him up, catching him when he promptly tipped back over. Cat eyes glimmered from the shadows, Castor and Pollux scrutinizing, almost like they didn't trust Felix half as much as Loren did.

Maybe the Egyptians had that right: Cats could see what humans couldn't.

Silent streets accompanied their walk to the brothel. The city had tired of its festival at last, or at least moved it indoors. Loren leaned heavily against Felix, but the weight wasn't such a bother.

Some god in charge of small mercies had sent Elias away, off to kiss some stranger or procure more hemp. Felix shoved Loren upstairs in a mess of limbs. Finally, after an awkward pocket search while Loren teetered and gazed at his hair, Felix unlocked the door of their room. Loren's room. Whatever.

Loren wasted no time flopping into bed, fully clothed.

"You're a wreck," Felix muttered. He reached to remove Loren's sandals, but Loren's hand shot out. Grabbed his fingers again. Felix froze.

"You aren't who I thought you were," Loren confessed.

It could seem casual, a reference to strangers and first impressions, but Felix remembered the look of recognition haunting Loren's eyes moments before the bowl crashed down. The mutterings of his name in sleep. Felix had known Loren for two days.

But he wondered how long Loren had known him.

"I want to understand," Loren said, brow furrowed over shut eyes. "You. Want to help."

"There's nothing to help," said Felix.

"What Julia said," Loren started as though he'd only just remembered, here on the brink of wine-sleep. "'Bout. Smuggling ring. Temple. Servius. D'you think . . .".

Felix gently broke the hold as Loren mumbled into unconsciousness.

Do you think. No, thinking was one activity Felix strove to do as little of as possible. Thinking only complicated his life. Especially when it came to temples and smuggling and memory. Besides, he suspected what Loren meant to ask. His mind had gone there, too. Of course it had.

But this Felix knew with certainty: No matter how shrouded his other memories were, Servius was a man he wouldn't have forgotten. Chasing coincidence was a waste of time. Felix discarded the thought. Forced it down, even as it threatened to bubble back up. Now he only hoped Loren's impending hangover would erase it from his mind too.

Felix jiggled the latch of Loren's trunk until it popped to dig for the spare blanket tucked at the bottom. But when he pushed back the lid, he stilled. The laundry bag had drooped open. Silver glinted in the dark of the room, reflecting nothing. Delicately, Felix scooped up the helmet, cradling it in his palms.

Such a strange thing for Pompeii to prize and fear in equal measure—and such a strange thing to have pinned Felix in one city for the longest stretch of time since fleeing Rome. Yet there was something familiar about the helmet, a beckoning he couldn't name. Wasn't sure he wanted to name. Loren called it Mercury's helmet. The shape, the weight, the style . . . but the harder Felix considered it, the farther the answer seemed, flitting away on swift, winged feet.

And now he itched to follow.

His thoughts returned to the questions he'd considered on the docks, all those impossibilities he hadn't allowed himself to wonder about before. That he had been drawn to Pompeii for a reason. That he was meant to pursue an answer here—one he had been too afraid to face.

Felix had no family name. He had no vineyard to return to, no heir-ship waiting. But he had the helmet. Something all his own. Something that understood what it meant to be untouchable.

Something to run to, instead of from.

Under the press of his fingers, Felix could have sworn the metal hummed.

CHAPTER XVIII
LOREN

Morning brought Loren two things: a hangover and the sick realization that the world moved on. How could it, when Loren knew how Felix's mouth tasted, had felt the planes of his chest under his palm? It should've been impossible. Everything had changed.

But when Loren woke, sunlight blaring through the shutters, to find Felix standing at the door, a third realization hit: Loren had messed up spectacularly.

Their four days ended tomorrow. Tomorrow, Felix would leave.

Loren stood on unsteady legs, forcing back nausea, head throbbing dully. Julia's toga still swaddled him, a suffocating mass of crinkled, wine-stained wool, and he fumbled for the pin. Distant-but-still-too-close memories teased him of Felix hauling him up the stairs, putting him to bed, unstrapping his shoes. Of Loren drowning in Felix's curls.

If these were the memories Loren still held, what didn't he remember?

He groaned and clutched his abdomen.

"If you plan on vomiting," Felix said, offering out Mercury's helmet, upside down, "aim for this."

Loren glared.

Felix pulled it back. "It was a joke."

VESUVIUS

There was no saving the moment once it passed. Loren stumbled to the washbasin, expecting to see days-old water with a veneer of soap scum, but found a fresh bowl instead. "Did you—"

"Wash up," Felix snapped, ears burning red. "You slept half the morning away. I want to leave before night comes around again."

Comprehension dawned as Loren reached for a washcloth. *Felix held the helmet.*

Panic seized him. "But it's too early. You promised four days."

"Not *leave*. I want—I hoped you and I could—" Felix ran a frustrated hand through his hair. "I'm tired of hidden truths. Of others knowing more about me than I do. You said I'm the only person who can touch the helmet. I'll hold to my promise to return it tomorrow, I swear. But first I want to know why I was able to take it at all."

"You want to help." Loren blinked.

Wasn't this what he wanted? He should be excited Felix might stop dodging questions.

But Loren's stomach churned all over again at the way Felix clutched the helmet to his chest. He wanted to figure Felix out, but he'd been terrified of Felix figuring out himself. Flashing visions lurked behind his eyelids. *Black wave. Copper streak. Ghost-Felix at the crux.* The helmet was there at the end of the world, connected to Felix. Learning more would come with a cost.

Except Loren was already doomed, though not by any silver helmet. By a smart mouth and stormy eyes and his ring still on Felix's finger.

"I don't know how much I believe," Felix admitted. "About what you say the helmet can do. But if I'm not allowed to understand anything else about my life, I'm willing to try to believe. I need you to show me how."

Loren had been selfish. He couldn't deny Felix this. All Loren's work figuring out what the helmet foretold so far had been done alone—all amounting to nothing. Maybe a different approach was needed.

198

One that required Felix's cooperation.

Downstairs, Elias was awake and stretching in the corridor between cubicles, back a perfect arch. When he spotted them, he dropped with a wicked smile.

"Sleep late? It's near noon," he said. "Glad you made it home, Loren. You had Felix all out of sorts."

It shouldn't have stung, but it did, the idea that Felix had confessed anything to Elias.

"Yes, and now we're leaving," Loren replied, clipped. He ushered Felix hastily toward the exit, Felix seeming all too happy to comply, tying on a scarf and escaping to the street.

"Wait," Elias called before Loren could follow. "Stay a moment. These days, it seems like you're always leaving. We never talk anymore."

Loren closed his eyes. Turned, smile tight. "I see you daily."

Elias didn't return the smile.

"Three years. That's how long I've known you." Elias rose slowly. At his full height, he barely met Loren's chin. He scrutinized Loren, stepping right into his space. Such proximity used to swoop Loren's stomach, but now he only felt tired. "So why is it that I understand Felix better in three days?"

Loren could think of a lot of reasons, like how Elias and Felix had more in common with each other than with a rich winemaker's son, or that Loren had tried to get closer to him and was swiftly shut down, but he had the sense neither would prove sufficient.

He sighed. "What do you want?"

"I thought he was the one I should worry about," Elias continued, "but I wonder if I should reconsider. Between the two of you, you're the one with ambition. You're the one I can picture wearing wings."

The accusation cracked like a hit to the jaw, and Loren would've preferred a physical blow. Any surprise he should have felt that Elias knew about the helmet was an afterthought. Dropping his voice, he hissed, "You think I'd use it? For myself?"

"Use it? Or use him?"

"I'm *trying* to help the city."

"And I'm trying to warn you," Elias said. He caught Loren's wrist and jerked him in. For a deluded second, Loren thought Elias was going for a kiss, they were that close. "I'm telling you to be careful. For his sake too."

"What do you want?" Loren repeated, except it spilled out as a plea.

Abruptly, he missed Elias with a scorching ache. They stood sharing breath, but Loren had never felt the distance so keenly—though it had been him who drove the wedge home. After admitting his feelings and facing rejection, Loren thought creating space was a favor, a sacrifice on his part, but he never thought to ask Elias what *he* wanted. Loren couldn't shake the feeling time was running out to make amends.

When this was all over, he would fix what was broken.

"I told you a long time ago," Elias said at last. He let go and took a measured step back. "I want nothing from you."

If Felix overheard anything, he had the tact not to mention it when Loren stumbled outside. Neither spoke as they set off. The laundry bag swung from Felix's shoulder, helmet nestled inside. They almost passed as normal friends doing normal chores on a normal day, except Felix was drawn tight as a lyre string, and Loren had never felt so messy in his life. Discomfort swelled between them, worse than the intense morning heat.

"We should start with Nonna," Loren managed to say. "Pompeii has no library, but she's Etruscan to her core, the first settlers of the city from before Rome's sack on Corinth. If anyone knows the helmet's history, she will."

"I believe you that she won't turn us in. That doesn't mean I trust her."

"Trust me, then." Loren sidestepped to let a basket-bearing man squeeze past, and Felix tensed when it brought them too near. "Last time you didn't like what she had to say, and I kept pushing the issue. I won't do that again. If you say stop, we leave."

"I am not fragile," Felix insisted, then averted his gaze farther, a feat Loren hadn't thought possible.

There he went, putting his foot in his mouth again.

Half the city was still sleeping off its hangover, but Nonna sat outside the bakery, molding dough into rounds. When she saw them, her eyes lit up.

"Loren, sweet sparrow." Nonna let Loren kiss her smiling cheeks, her face soft and creased as fresh dough. "Sit, sit. You and the shifty one. Help me knead."

She moved a basket off a second stool, and Loren procured a third from the shop. Felix looked like he would rather stay standing, ready to flee at the slightest whiff of burnt bread, but Nonna shot him a stern glare and he acquiesced, arms tight around his middle.

Nonna put Loren to work stretching a lump of dough, repetitive, mindless work that numbed his lingering headache. Flour coated his hands and dusted his face. In another life, he could be a baker. Forget politics and priesthood, vineyards and visions, and become Nonna's apprentice. He'd live out of her storage closet, and she'd teach him to bake, and he wouldn't have to cut his hair or move home or marry.

"Don't lie to Nonna, now," she started after a measure of comfortable quiet where her eyes didn't leave Felix once, "because I see it in both your faces. You got yourselves in trouble."

Loren watched her wrinkled hands expertly fold her loaf. He bit his lip and copied her tucks, but his came out lumpy. "We may have caused the trouble. I need you to help us out of it."

"Use your wrists more. Like that. Good." Nonna hummed. "I suspected so, the moment I first saw you two together. You attract trouble like flies to honey, sparrow."

Puffing his cheeks, Loren chanced a glance at Felix, who still sat coiled tight. *Now or never.* Before he could change his mind, he plunged. "Nonna, what would it take to steal Mercury's helmet? And what might one use it for, once they had it?"

A beat of silence. Then a flour-powdered pinch bit his cheek. Dropping the dough, Loren clapped his hand to his stinging face.

"Tell me you didn't, boy. Tell me you had nothing to do with it." Nonna dove for a second pinch, and in his haste to scoot away, Loren toppled off his stool. Cobblestones rushed to meet him.

Arms caught under his. Loren stared, dumbstruck. He hadn't seen Felix move, but he'd flown to stop the fall faster than the beat of a hummingbird's wings. A slow blush crept down Loren's chest.

"It wasn't Loren," Felix said, voice carved cold.

"Yet the company he keeps reflects on him. Humans are not meant to fiddle with divine power." Nonna sat back, seething. "Unless . . ."

Felix's jaw clenched.

Loren carefully extracted himself from Felix's grasp before he did something foolish, like melt into it forever, and fumbled to right his stool. This was the breaking point. Nonna's trailed-off accusation had, once again, pushed Felix too far, and now the conversation must end, still no answers given. Still no nearer their aim.

Then Felix surprised him. With his foot, he dragged the other stool closer to Loren's and sat. Sat so their arms brushed, tiny, temporary contact. Loren's breath caught, pulse tapping fast.

Permission.

Loren turned to Nonna, swallowing thickly. "*Unless* he had already been touched by the divine. A priest's blessing, maybe."

"Or a curse. The life of a mortal who has caught the eye of a god is no easy path. They cease to be human and turn into a tool. An object to be manipulated."

"Strangely enough," Felix said, "I still feel plenty human."

"Then Mercury is not through with you yet," Nonna warned. "The helmet is called dangerous for a reason. For three hundred years, it has not moved, not since Rome thought it a fair exchange for stamping out my Etruscan ancestors in their own city. What energy do you think that bears? How many souls of the restless dead it holds? I have no answer for why you could take it, but gods, I fear the fallout."

"Unless," Loren repeated, "I could find the answer. What if I stopped the consequences before they started? Where would I look?"

"Your brand of curiosity could spark a war. I pray you have thought this through. I pray he is worth the risk." She lowered her hand, but Loren knew better than to trust. Old Etruscan grandmothers struck faster than a snake. "What do you want to know?"

"Everything," Loren said breathlessly. "Tell me—us—everything."

"Even I do not know all ends," Nonna said. "But I will tell you where to search."

Getting through the gate proved the easiest feat of the day. The two flustered, baby-faced guards were already overwhelmed by a merchant disgruntled over their search through his cabbage cart. All Loren had to do was explain he and Felix were disciples of Isis on the way to burn the linens of a plague victim before the guards exchanged fearful glances and ushered them through. A dirty trick to be sure, but an effective one.

Leaving Pompeii always felt like kissing it goodbye. Like once Loren strayed too far from its gates, they would never open for him again. Being on the road meant he had no walls to hide behind. Still, he pushed on, with a wanted thief at his heels, an obscenely powerful artifact tucked in a laundry bag, and desperation clawing his spine with every step.

He hoped there would still be a Pompeii to return to come morning.

"How much farther?" Felix asked. He lagged several paces behind, kicking small stones at Loren's calves.

Another pebble struck. Loren rolled his eyes but didn't rise to the bait. "Nonna said it's perhaps a half-hour walk from the gate. Have we walked a half hour?"

Felix's sulk was audible. "No."

"Then you have your answer." Loren made the mistake of glancing back. "Do you—"

He hated the way his words faltered.

Out here, Felix wore no headscarf, and daylight transformed his copper curls into flaming laurels and lit his skin gold. He looked like a young Apollo in the prime of his life, fast and clever and fierce. Loren ached to bask in his sun, soak it up before it dipped behind cloud once more.

He only tore away when he stumbled over a rock. His arms flailed to reclaim balance, barely catching himself before he fell. These damned weak ankles would be the death of him.

"Careful," Felix said with a snort. "If you twist an ankle, I'm not carrying you back."

A flicked stone smacked Loren's heel to drive the point home.

Loren sighed and stared at Vesuvius ahead, crisp against the pale sky, clouds ringing the peak. The day really was beautiful, despite the heat, the bare hint of a breeze rustling fields of wilting poppies and tall grass.

Shame they were due to spend the afternoon underground.

Ahead, a pair of crooked standing stones peeked through a cluster of pines, exactly as Nonna said to look out for. Loren veered off-road. Weeds crunched underfoot.

"The Etruscans raised stones like these near important places," he said. "Places charged with energy. I bet we're close. Is the helmet . . ."

"Reacting?" Felix arched a skeptical brow. "No."

Loren fought for a smile. "Then we aren't close enough."

Beyond the stones, the underbrush opened into a bowl-shaped grove, hewn from the hillside and concealed by overgrown trees. Mist clung stagnant to the branches, the grass. A stillness lingered here, one Loren wasn't keen to disturb.

"Through there?" Felix nodded to the back of the grove, where a jagged gash in the hill begged exploration. "Give me the torch."

Before they left, Nonna had pressed a leather satchel of essentials into Loren's hands. Now he passed the tools to Felix, and a moment of fussing fingers later, the torch flared to life. Loren said a silent goodbye to the breeze.

Together, they ducked into darkness.

The tunnel stretched forever. Loren held the torch aloft, illuminating a scant few feet in front and back, but otherwise they might as well be walking into Tartarus itself. His anxiety spiked with every pop of the flame. People weren't made for this, lurking in suffocating tunnels. Foul things made their homes underground, monsters and beasts. A place to hide wrongdoings from the watchful gods.

Fitting, maybe. Loren had been doing a lot of wrong lately.

"The air's clammy," Felix said, cracking the quiet. Loren startled, nearly dropping the torch. "Can you smell that?"

Loren inhaled, in part to settle his racing heart. "Doesn't smell unusual to me. Musty, perhaps."

"Well, you'd be used to it. Pompeii stinks, like eggs left to rot. Not so bad in town, but on the road, it got worse. Down here it's intolerable. And the walls hum, can't you hear?"

Loren frowned. "Just how sensitive are you?"

"Too. Hard to filter out the chatter." Felix sighed and briefly squeezed his eyes shut. "Whatever the cause is, let's hope we don't find it."

Again with the uncomfortable silence.

These were the final hours before Felix would skip town. Loren knew he should savor them, but a mental wall had gone up between rational thought and acting normal, *gods, Loren, can't you act normal?* The disconnect panged. He'd kissed Felix. Kissed him. And despite the distortion of the wine, Loren was certain—

Felix had kissed him back. But Loren didn't have a great record for kissing boys and keeping them. Tomorrow, Felix would leave. Would he look back once he cleared the gate?

The torchlight cast shifting shadows on the rough rock ceiling to match the stir of his stomach. Loren released a shaky breath in the dark.

Unfortunately, Felix took it as an invitation to talk.

"So," he started, a valiant attempt at sounding casual. "Lucius Lassius Lorenus. Interesting name."

Loren dropped his gaze forward, glaring at the smothering dark. "It's mine. What of it?"

"I know better than to stick my nose where it doesn't belong—"

"Could fool me."

"—but that's quite the secret. You weren't going to tell me, were you?"

Sweat dampened Loren's braid. He turned sideways to shimmy between the tunnel wall and an outcropping. "You saw through me from the start. Rich boy playing at being poor. Why hand you another arrow for your quiver?"

Felix hummed. "Strange to give that up in exchange for scraps."

"You wouldn't understand."

"Help me to."

Loren chanced a glance back. Felix's face wasn't mocking, but he almost wished it was. Anything would be easier than this. "I told you that night at Julia's, there are expectations of me. My parents have a framework for how the world ought to work. They don't tolerate much beyond it. When you're Lucius Lassius's son, there's no room for being different."

He wet his lips, then added, "Four years with the Temple of Isis got me nowhere. Umbrius and the council wanted nothing to do with me until I caught Julia's eye, and you saw how that ended. I ran from home when I was twelve. Now on the edge of seventeen, I've done nothing to cement myself in Pompeii to stop my father dragging me back."

"Your father knows you came here?"

"You don't become one of the wealthiest men in the empire without connections. He has eyes everywhere. He's indulged me, letting me stay this long." Loren's thoughts were scrambled. He tried to sort through them, order them in a way Felix might understand. "My father has no other heir. Unlike Julia, he'd rather be run over by the Roman cavalry than have the Lassius name passed to someone not of his blood. He needs me trapped."

"Would that be so terrible?"

"To have no say in your life? To have everything about you dictated, from the way you wear your hair to who you sleep with? To restrict your world to a few acres of land when you know you could do more, if only they'd listen? Yes, Felix. It would."

Silence. The torch flared.

"See," said Felix, "that's where we differ. I'd give anything to have what you gave up. Stability. Something certain. A home."

"It was never a home to me."

"Easy to say when you chose to walk away."

Loren swallowed, eyes stinging. He blinked rapidly, but his vision blurred.

"But I meant it," Felix said. "You aren't going back there."

He had no idea how dangerous it was to say things like that. Had Loren not been on the verge of tears or holding a flaming stick in a dark, smelly tunnel, he might have confessed how afraid he was to add Felix to his list of burned bridges.

Gods, Loren was sick of losing.

Another beat of silence.

Felix asked, "Is it me, or did it get lighter?"

Lowering the torch and squinting only worsened Loren's headache. "How could you possibly tell?"

"Maybe your eyesight is shit."

"Maybe you're full of—" Loren bit his tongue and wheeled around, scowling. "I don't curse. Stop trying to make me."

"You said 'fuck' last night."

That smirk was insufferable. Loren wanted to shove Felix against the wall. Better yet, have Felix crowd Loren in, press their chests together and—

He kept walking.

But maddeningly, Felix was right. Not a full minute later, Loren realized he could make out the texture of the wall beyond the torch's reach. What started as a handful of degrees became a shock of brightness as they emerged from the dark into an open-air pit. Stone spires jutted from the ground, crooked as broken fingers and riddled with minuscule, blistered pockmarks.

"Oh." Loren's hand shot to his mouth, and the torch dropped, sputtering and rolling. Vertigo rushed over him, like the wooze he felt before slipping into a vision, but he remained fixed in the present. He grasped for the wall. "This place is horrible. I feel—"

"I've never seen anything like it," Felix murmured, stepping past and entering the chamber proper.

"I have," Loren realized with a jolt. "I dreamed it the other night. You were there, too, but we stood up top. I thought we were at the edge of the world, and when I looked down, I saw only . . . teeth."

How mad he must sound. Verbalizing his dreams was an exercise in explaining things he barely understood himself. Usually best if he said nothing at all. But here he was, spilling his guts to Felix, who already must think him deranged.

Felix ran a hand up pockmarked stone. "They weren't teeth. What else did you see?"

Something in his tone rattled Loren too close to honesty. He blurted, "Nothing. This is last night's wine talking."

"Loren. What did you see?"

"You said I was close to the answer," Loren said in a rush. "That I held the pieces." *And asked who I'd run through with a blade. Me or you.* He swallowed.

"Do you dream about me a lot?"

It should've been an innuendo. Any other time, it would have been. But for all Felix's lewd comments, his question didn't ridicule. It said, *I believe you.* And, *I trust you to tell me the truth.* A spark ran the length of Loren's limbs, heat blooming in his belly despite the chill of the pit.

"Yes," he breathed.

Felix's clever eyes met his. "Before you met me."

"How did you know?"

"When you saw me in the temple, that first morning." Felix stepped closer, sandals crunching silt. "You weren't surprised I was there, but that I was there at that moment."

"For the record, I'm sorry for hitting you with the bowl."

Felix was near enough to touch. In the dreams, he'd stepped in until their noses nearly brushed. Loren remembered how breathless he'd felt and found—desperately—he wanted to gasp for it again.

"In your dreams," Felix said, "what do I do?"

The moment, like so many fragile things, shattered. Loren bit his tongue and tripped away, needing the distance. Felix's gaze tracked Loren as he edged around the chamber, still waiting for answers. *Tell him,* whispered the ghost lurking in Loren's shadow, but he forced him back into the dark.

Then he did what he did best: He started talking and simply didn't stop.

"This is like a place from a myth, where a great fire or flood swept through and carved these tunnels out." Loren traced tiny stone divots.

"It makes sense why Nonna told us to take the helmet here. The old settlers of the land worshipped Mercury in strange places like this. Places where the veil between the living and the dead thins, where it's easy to believe he could flit among humans. Bring us messages in ways other gods cannot."

Messages from ghosts, though the thought stirred sour. He had meant "Ghost-Felix" as a nickname, a way to differentiate between real and unreal, but now . . .

His heart stuck in his throat, a pained lump.

No. Felix was alive. One only needed look at his glow as proof.

"How does the helmet feel now?" Loren asked, half dreading the answer. "Is it telling you anything?"

The question felt foolish the moment he asked, but Felix obediently unslung the laundry bag and pressed his palm against silver. He closed his eyes, listening, sensing. Loren held his breath.

But Felix shook his head. "I still think Nonna is full of it."

Loren's laugh bounced empty around the spires. "I thought you said you wanted to give believing a try."

"Loren, I—" Felix's mouth flattened. "Forget it."

"No, tell me."

His thumb worried the bag strap. When he spoke, it was carefully even. Forced control, swallowed emotion. "Your belief is so easy. Your feelings are so easy. I don't understand it."

"Why wouldn't they be? Trust is easy." Loren frowned. "What made you lose yours?"

For a moment, Felix bore the expression of someone who badly wanted to confess. As if the words hovered on his tongue, dying to plunge. Loren waited, ready to dive with him.

"Forget it." Felix looked away. Then he paused. The bag hit the ground with a soft thud, and he strode for the center of the pit. "Did you drop this?"

When he straightened, he held a knife. Wood. Iron.

Loren felt the blood drain from his face.

"Funny," Felix said. "I took a knife like this off someone days ago, but I lost it."

"Common enough design. Coincidence."

"You say that an awful lot for someone who doesn't believe in those," Felix teased, then his lips twitched down. He held the blade to the light, tilting it this way and that. "I swear the etching was the same. Almost looks like the mountain."

Daring to inch nearer, Loren squinted at the afternoon sun reflecting off the blade, catching on an engraved squiggle: an inverted V with a cratered top.

You are close to the answer, Ghost-Felix had said in the dream.

Loren's eyes drifted up. From the bottom of the chamber, he could only see only its crown, a silhouette ringed with clouds. The mark could be any mountain, really.

Except Ghost-Felix had dropped this knife here for a reason. Had said, *If you want to stop this, come find me.* The realization struck in a sting of lightning, a blast of steam, quicksilver eyes locking on a target—a target that had been there all along. The mountain, at the edges of Loren's dreams. The mountain under a red storm. Always the one constant. Frustration mounted in his chest, swirled with the flush of an answer at hand.

Years of taunting visions were about to end.

"Remember when you said you don't believe in fate?" Loren murmured.

"Fate can screw itself."

"In my dreams, I see a mountain."

Felix stepped closer, following Loren's stare. "Don't say what I feel you're about to say."

"I think," Loren said regardless, "I know where to go next."

CHAPTER XIX
FELIX

When Felix asked for help with the helmet, he didn't think it would involve batting off clouds of gnats and dodging stinging nettle as he chased Loren through fields of grass.

Loren always wore his heart outside his skin, but this took chasing his impulses to a new extreme. Knuckles bloody from climbing from the spire pit, he'd sprinted through thickets and brush, gaze locked on Vesuvius, a boy possessed. Felix was naturally speedy, but even he struggled keeping pace with Loren's long legs. Ridiculous. Reckless. If Felix weren't so annoyed, he might find it attractive.

By the time they stumbled back onto the road leading to the mountain's base, the scorching heat had peaked. It'd be a hell of a climb armed only with sandals, a fact Loren seemed oblivious to. The last dregs of Felix's draining self-preservation roiled.

"Changed my mind," he called. "I don't care about the helmet after all."

"Pity." Loren was six strides ahead. "My mind is set."

"We can't scale a mountain like this. Remember when you hit me with a bowl? And sliced my arm open? I'm in no condition—"

"It's calling me, Felix." Loren's heels dug into dirt, and he spun to glare. His cheeks were flushed, eyes bright with discovery. "We were

led to the spire pit. We were meant to find that knife. The answer I'm—
we're—looking for is on the mountain. Go back to Pompeii if you want.
I never said you had to follow."

"Well. I am." Felix shifted the laundry bag to his other shoulder.
"Following."

"Oh." Loren blinked. "Good."

"But it's a bad idea."

"You've said." Loren made to keep walking, but as he turned, he
wavered. Swayed. His knees buckled, and only barely did Felix slow his
fall. Slowed it, but didn't prevent it. Loren's palms braced flat against
the warm earth.

Felix swore and gritted his teeth. "Not again."

Loren had done this too many times for it to be explained away
as caused by exhaustion or heat. Until now, Felix had always thought
prophecy was horseshit, but he was starting to wonder if Loren defied
those rules, too. Gripping his shoulders, Felix heaved Loren upright.
His eyes were glassy, focus a hundred leagues away, like Aurelia's had
been in the alley two nights ago.

"Snap out of it." Felix pressed his hand to Loren's burning forehead. "Come back."

With a choked gasp, Loren shuddered and flailed, shoving until
Felix sprawled on his ass.

He spat out, "Riders."

All at once, Felix understood. His hearing sharpened, picking up the
steady rhythm of hooves against packed dirt, a mile or less away. Distant,
but nearing quick. His nerves spiked. Could be innocent passersby.

Could be worse.

"They're close." He dragged Loren up and jumped for the shoulder
of the road, where they landed in a cluster of bushes. For a moment,
rustling branches and thorns consumed Felix's senses, limbs so tangled

VESUVIUS

he wasn't sure where his ended and Loren's began. The proximity of skin and sound saturated him, too much at once.

"Felix, how did you hear—"

"One horse. Maybe two. Half a minute at most."

"But how?"

"Shut up. Don't move."

Loren stilled. The rustling silenced seconds before the horsemen rounded the corner. Felix held his breath. In the close, dappled shadow of the bush, he made out a trickle of blood running down Loren's chin where a thorn had pricked his lip.

Move on. Keep riding.

"Look! Prints," a man exclaimed.

Felix mouthed a curse.

A horse whinnied. Two sets of feet dropped to the ground to investigate. Twisting his neck past the point of comfort, Felix watched filthy sandal-strapped calves tromp around where he and Loren had argued on the road moments earlier.

Warm fingers intertwined with his. Felix nearly shot out of his skin, but Loren only squeezed his hand. Another easy gesture. Something Felix would never have thought to do himself.

"Keep looking," a different speaker grunted. His voice rang familiar. Felix riffled through his memory but came up blank when Loren's thumb brushed his. Felix's brain may as well have grown legs, sprinted off.

"They end here."

"No." The soft *schnick* of a blade drawn. "There."

Many things happened in the space of a heartbeat.

A sword hacked through the bush. Felix's head should've rolled, but he wasn't in the underbrush anymore. He was on his feet, being dragged into the trees bordering the road. An angry shout echoed, and the firm *plunk* of an arrow hitting its mark followed. Felix looked up, expecting to see a shaft protruding from Loren's back, but no, he was still running, and Felix ran, too, and ahead, an arrow shivered in a tree trunk.

Crashing feet thundered behind. Then Felix's thief instincts kicked in. He took the lead. He pulled Loren, hands clasped, and they hurtled through the forest as if hellhounds were snapping at their heels. Mercury's helmet, swaddled in its bag, knocked against Felix's back, rhythm like a heartbeat.

Trees thinned. The landscape changed from forest to a field of plants in uniform rows. They burst into a vineyard, one of several in the countryside around Vesuvius, where black soil let grapes grow heavy. Felix had sampled some the other week, until a worker chased him off. It felt nice to reminisce about old times, when he was chased for nothing more than petty theft, and his chaser wasn't armed with lethal weapons.

Banners embroidered with a familiar vine-cinched *L* hung listless in the dead air. Felix moved his thumb, tucked inside his fist, to rub the ring he still wore. A plan teased his mind.

Tactically speaking, a vineyard was a poor place to flee through. With straight rows, another arrow fired would find a clean shot. If their pursuers wanted the bag, Loren, empty-handed, was collateral damage. A victim of circumstance. Only one logical thing to do.

"We need to separate," Felix panted.

Loren turned on him, eyes horrified. "Are you mad? I'm not leaving you."

"It's our best chance. Cut diagonally across the field. You're less bulky than they are, you'll have an easier time at it. But with any luck they'll follow me."

"With any luck?" Loren's breathless screech shot in pitch. "Felix, no!"

"I have a plan," he said, then shoved Loren sideways through an opening in the trellis. Loren fell with an indignant cry, tripping over his feet, but Felix clenched his teeth and kept moving.

He had years of practice at that. *Keep moving,* his father used to say, *and sooner or later they'll tire of chasing you.* Keep moving and survive another night.

Felix hoped that would hold true.

Not daring to look back, he plunged deeper into the field, sandals striking season-hardened soil. Veering sharp, he took his chances with a promising gap. From there, it was a matter of keeping a row or two of space between him and the guards, zigzagging across the empty vineyard. In the hottest part of the day, the fieldworkers had abandoned half-full baskets of grapes, seeking shade.

Eyeing these, another plan struck. He emptied a basket into the laundry bag. If this failed, at least he'd have a snack on the way to his execution.

Felix had barely slipped through the next gap when a reedy cry stopped him.

"You there, stop!"

Two men stood down the row, one trim and proper, the other hunched over a basket. Baring his teeth in what he hoped resembled a smile, Felix raised a hand in peace, then jogged to meet them.

"Greetings! Are you the grape-keeper?" A bullshit term. But he had long since learned that if you bullshitted confidently enough, anything sounded authentic.

"Aye," the upright one said. He wore the fine linens of an esteemed director, someone good at ordering work without lifting a finger. He clasped his hands, heels together at a sharp angle. A badge glinted on his shoulder. "I am Master Adolphus, caretaker of these lands. I assume you are a thief?"

"Depends on your definition," Felix said.

The hunched man paused harvesting fruit long enough to snort. He wore the wide-brimmed hat of a field slave, the skin of his arms seared bright red. Adolphus kicked his leg.

"Silence, Stravo. This is no time for laughter." He turned to Felix. "You realize trespassing is a crime?"

Felix shot him his most disarming grin. Three more beats. That's all he needed.

Adolphus didn't waver. "And that such a crime is punishable by—"

Tragically, Felix never received his sentence. Behind him, a trellis crashed to the ground, and a man in leather armor wielding a sword burst onto the scene.

"Why, sir, I never," Adolphus squawked, stepping back into the chest of the second guard, emerging on the other side. "No weapons in the vineyard!"

"Apologies, Master," the swordsman said. For once, he wore no identifying colors, and his signature hawk crest was absent, but beneath the iron helmet, Felix would recognize him anywhere: his old friend Darius. "We're pursuing this thief. He's wanted in the city."

Poor flustered Adolphus fought to regain his composure, while at his feet, Stravo snickered. Smoothing his tunic, Adolphus said, "Very good. It seems you came just in time. He is here to steal our prized assets."

The second guard, the one with the bow, frowned. "Grapes? I'm afraid this is a bit—"

"Do you think," Felix interjected, adopting a mask of cool indifference at odds with his racing heart, "my father will be pleased with the way I've been treated, Master Adolphus?"

He held out his hand. In the high afternoon sun, Loren's signet ring winked.

The effect was immediate and fully consuming. Adolphus's flushed face transformed from red hot to pasty pale. Stravo muttered a curse. Darius and his comrade stared, confused.

"My father owns this vineyard." Felix dropped his hand before the ring could be inspected. Authentic as it might have been, it was crafted for Loren's slender fingers. Anyone with half a brain would notice how tightly it fit Felix. "He sent me here for samples. A quality inspection. Anonymous," he added for Adolphus's benefit.

Word didn't need to make it back to Lucius Lassius. If Loren had kept his head down this long, no sense alerting his father he was now conducting spontaneous inspections on their outlying properties.

"Samples my ass," Darius said. "Lying bastard."

Adolphus bristled. "You dare insult my employer's son?"

Felix shot him a fond look. Adolphus might be an idiot, but he was a loyal one. Or a bootlicking one. In the moment, Felix would accept either.

"This boy is no one's son. He's a criminal." Darius gestured with the point of his sword. "Open the bag."

"And spoil the samples?" said Felix.

"And spoil the *samples*?" spluttered Adolphus.

The other guard grabbed, but Felix danced away. "Fine. Have it your way, but if wine stops flowing in Pompeii, on your head be it."

The bag thumped to the ground, and Felix untied the strings. Lifting the flap, he allowed Adolphus and the guards and the gods themselves to peer inside.

Grapes spilled out. Hundreds of them.

Adolphus gasped. "Oh, wonderful samples. You have an eye for detail, like your father, young master."

Felix filtered him out, holding Darius's piercing gaze. Darius's eye twitched. A bead of sweat dripped off his nose and splattered in the dirt.

Adolphus was fooled, but Darius knew too much. Felix unmistakably wasn't the son of Lucius Lassius, and if Darius pressed the issue, the deception would unravel. Felix would face worse than Servius; he'd be turned over to Lassius himself for fraud once Servius had the helmet. Not exactly how Felix imagined meeting the parents of the boy he'd kissed would go.

Fumbling and stomping broke their glaring contest. Loren stumbled through the gap.

"Wait!" He staggered between Felix and Darius. "You cannot harm him on these lands. I order you—"

The sweet, clumsy fool was about to ruin it all.

Felix snarled, "Silence, Felix!"

"What," said Loren, and it wasn't a question. Silently pleading he would catch on, Felix twisted his hand until the signet ring flashed.

"Who is this?" Adolphus puffed his chest. "Who is this, issuing orders?"

"I," Loren said, hesitation scraping. He swallowed. "Am Felix. His assistant."

"He's Greek," Felix offered. "Speaks little Latin."

Loren looked like he'd swallowed a wasp. "Yes, I—"

"In fact, he hardly speaks at all."

His mouth shut with an audible click.

"Interesting," Darius said, "that you two match the descriptions of the thieves we're chasing. You should know guards talk to each other. Perhaps it wasn't wise to throw around your affiliation with Isis at the city gate."

"On whose authority?" Adolphus snapped. "You trespass onto the land I tend, accuse my master's heir of theft, demand access to time-sensitive samples. I would like to know, who do you serve?"

Darius's thick fingers tightened around the grip of his sword. Felix held perfectly still. One well-aimed swing, and his head would roll with the grapes. But anyone with even a passing knowledge of trade knew the power Lassius commanded. Even when Felix's identity was revealed, the scandal of killing the vineyard's heir unarmed on his own property would sink Darius's reputation. And by extension, Servius's. The line Darius toed was thinner than papyrus.

Slow, so slow, Darius inclined his head. Bowing to Felix must rank among the most painful tasks ever asked of him. "I meant no offense, wine-master. We'll leave you to your business. Come, Maxim."

Tilting his chin to his companion, Darius strode down the long row of trellises. Maxim shouldered past Adolphus, nearly knocking him over. Loren steadied him.

"Horrible man," Adolphus said with a sniff, shaking off Loren and snapping his heels together to preserve his dwindling dignity. "Are you all right, sir?"

It took Felix a moment to realize the question was for him. He nodded and released the breath he'd been holding as Darius finally disappeared.

"It is a sad day when a boy cannot fetch grapes off his own land without being harassed," Adolphus continued. "Why, when your father finds out—"

"No," Felix said. "Don't breathe a word to him."

Adolphus frowned. "But—"

"Do you think my father is a patient man? Or a forgiving one?" Felix squished a grape between finger and thumb. Juice and pulp splattered. "If he found out you allowed his son to be chased by armed men, he may question what else you let happen. Lax on patrol, lax on quality."

"Sir." Adolphus's receding hairline trembled. "My work is my life. Allow me to set this right."

Felix stood, hoisting the bag over his shoulder. "You've done enough."

"There must be something more."

"My assistant and I were on our way to inspect the upper pastures."

Behind Adolphus, Loren's nose crinkled. *Pastures?* he mouthed, but Felix shot him a warning glare.

If Adolphus thought the phrasing strange, he didn't dare mention it. Instead, he brightened. "We shall go together. Stravo has a cart."

Beneath the brim of his hat, Stravo grimaced.

"No, no," Felix said. "It's delicate work, these inspections."

Loren pulled another face. It didn't help Felix stay in character.

"Besides, my father did want this done anonymously," he continued. "Though . . ."

"Anything. Anything at all." Adolphus adjusted his badge, a reminder of his station.

Resisting the urge to raise an unimpressed brow, Felix looked toward the sun's position. The ambush had cost precious time. Making it up the mountain before sunset had been a stretch already, but now it'd be impossible on foot. Scaling Vesuvius in the dark would surely prove deadly.

If only there was a faster way.

Stravo seemed to draw the same conclusion the moment it clicked for Felix, but he didn't look happy about it. "Shall I hitch the mules?"

"Oh," Adolphus said to Felix, "what a brilliant idea, Master Lassius. Full of them, you are. Just like your father."

Full of shit, more like.

Adolphus fretted and fussed, a last-ditch effort to impress, until they left him at the edge of the vineyard. He waved a linen handkerchief as he faded from sight.

"We aren't sailing to Troy," Loren muttered. "The theatrics are unnecessary."

Felix pretended he understood that reference.

Stravo's rickety cart was little more than planks tacked together and set on four wheels. Felix didn't trust the contraption not to fall apart, considering he was much heavier than its usual grape-y occupants. Despite the ominous creaking, it held firm, even when the road turned from packed dirt to lumpy rock farther out.

He and Loren dangled their legs in tandem off the open back, the laundry bag separating them. Damn laundry bag. Felix couldn't believe the deceit had worked. The risk he'd taken was calculated, and for someone who never learned mathematics, extraordinarily foolish. Had Darius kicked the bag, looked beyond the surface layer of grapes, everything would've ended then and there.

Would Darius have let Loren go? Or would his blood have spilled, too?

A whistled tune from the driver's bench shook Felix from his mental spiral. They were on the mountain proper, halfway up one of the trails only grape farmers used.

Loren cleared his throat and spoke for the first time in a long, silent while. "It was clever, what you did back there with the ring. Brave, too."

"Brave? It's your ring. I stole your identity. You should be angry."

"If you want to be Lucius Lassius Lorenus, be my guest." Loren pulled his knee under his chin, like he had the day at the harbor, when he spoke about Achilles and Patroclus, and Felix lacked the nerve to tuck his hair. Even now, eyeing the strands mussed by their sprint through the vineyard, he clenched his fists to stop from reaching.

Instead, he picked his thumbnail and watched the ground disappear below. "I ruined it for you. Darius saw the signet ring. He'll tell Servius, who will tell your father. It's over."

Loren's brow furrowed. "You're a thief, Felix. For all Darius knows, you murdered Lassius's real heir and stole the ring for this purpose. In fact, I hope a rumor of my brutal slaying does make it back to my father. Delay the inevitable, at least."

"Or hasten it, if he came to see for himself." Felix studied Loren's profile, the sharpness and softness of his lines, the translucent glow of peach-fine hair on his cheek. "Darius saw you at the games. Now Servius will know you both as Julia's heir and my accomplice. Two axes against your neck."

"Just one, I think." Loren sighed. "I spoiled any chance I had with Julia when I made fools of us both in the Forum. No one takes a mad boy as an heir."

Felix sniffed. "Never liked her anyway. You can do better."

"I hope so." Loren shot a sideways glance, and Felix's heart skipped.

He busied his hands by popping grapes in his mouth. When he held out a handful, a peace offering, the corner of Loren's mouth tilted. Together they ate until they'd emptied the bag and only Mercury's helmet remained.

With careful fingers, Felix drew it out. It seemed safe as anything out here on the side of a mountain. Stravo wouldn't know a thing about it, wouldn't care even if he did. The lower class didn't get involved in the affairs of the rich. Too messy. Too much to lose.

Case in point: Felix, with this headache of a helmet.

"They were after this," he said. "You called me clever, but I'm not. I'm lucky. Lucky Adolphus was there to stop them. Though, if what you said the other night is true, I suppose Servius wants me alive anyway."

Loren hovered his hand a scant inch above the metal. "The one element I keep returning to is—why you? I know I asked before, and I know you don't want to discuss it, but . . . what makes you special, Felix?"

"You also said you wouldn't ask again."

"Let me help you," Loren said. "Let me in. What does the helmet mean to you?"

When Felix looked, Loren's whole body was turned to him. The scrutiny shook the foundations of his walls, made him itch to build higher, reinforce his weaknesses. But Loren was the type to come back with rope for climbing. He saw Felix when other eyes skated past.

A spark of a memory flared to life, deep in the recesses of Felix's mind. He followed it down. "There's a temple to Mercury in Roma, on the Aventine Hill. Mercury has a soft spot for thieves. My da' and I spent a lot of time there."

"You're a ward of Mercury? And you never thought to mention this before? *Felix.*"

"I didn't remember until now, all right?" Only a partial lie. Of course Felix remembered, now that he thought about it. The connection lurked, fizzling out of sight, but obscured. Veiled, like most of his memories. "My memories . . . they come and go."

Loren pinched the bridge of his nose. "I wondered. It was my first theory, actually, that perhaps you're able to handle the helmet because you have a divine association to Mercury. A priest's blessing."

Priest. Nausea swelled. Felix turned the helmet to inspect the interior. Another memory thread tugged, this time of curled fists and booming voices. Bitter poppy sap on his tongue. He could unravel this one. Pull the string, see how it loosened. See where it sprang from.

"That can't be it." Felix swallowed back rising bile. "My da' killed the priest."

"Oh."

"My da' wasn't bad." Suddenly, it felt of utmost importance that Loren understood. "He did it for a reason. He wasn't bad."

"I believe you."

"I—just . . ." Felix kicked the empty air. "I don't recall the reason. But sometimes I remember being at the temple without him. He left me with the priest while he worked. Stole. Whatever."

The memory snapped, refusing to unspool into clarity.

"And?"

Felix shook his head. He had reached that gate in his mind, beyond which was only a poppy-sap-muffled blur. This time, no prodding thumbs materialized to coax more out.

"That's all there is. So you see, that's why I don't know how to believe. Memories of any faith I had are no longer mine, and what I do have . . ." Felix's throat tightened, the corners of his eyes itching. "I'm afraid of what I'm missing."

"So you choose not to think of it," Loren finished.

"Easier not to dwell, not to look too far ahead, but faith demands both. How do you give yourself to devotion, and trust you won't be used?" Humiliated, Felix scrubbed his face.

"It's a comfort, I suppose," Loren mused. "Believing there's intention behind what happens. Trusting that hurt isn't random."

A humorless laugh tore from Felix's chest. "That pain is supposed to mean something isn't a comfort. I never asked to be part of that story."

"Oh, that's not what I meant at all. It's less that I think there is a reason for hurt, and more that faith gives us grace to heal. To come out the other side to try again," Loren said. "I follow Isis for a reason, you know. Livia used her connections to get me into the temple, but I chose devotion on my own."

"Why's that?"

Loren smiled. "Remember why I like the moon? It comes back. Isis symbolizes that, to me. No rebirth without death. The sky will be dark tonight, but give it time."

Felix wondered what that would look like. *Try again*. Except when Loren said it, it sounded more like *trust again*. That, despite the hurts he had known, there were other things worth believing in. Other people, even.

Warm fingers brushed his knuckles, featherlight. Touch often settled sticky over his flesh, and even gentle hands triggered his instinct to flee. But there was something different about Loren. He didn't touch in order to take. Felix wanted to flip his hand over, press their palms together, languish in the simple sureness of a gesture like that. Wanting carried a price he couldn't afford.

It felt greedy, but he let Loren's touch linger. This, and no more.

"You said you recall some," Loren broached, delicate as vellum. "You told me your father died. Do you remember that?"

"Yes." Closing his eyes against the sun, Felix's vision washed red. "I remember that."

Because for all he fought to live in the moment, that was the memory he couldn't escape. His mind blocked out other pain from his past but kept this within reach. It left too much room to wonder. Speculate. For a little clawing voice to scratch the back of his mind, to burrow in, mutter.

To suggest Felix hadn't decided to forget. Someone else made that choice for him.

Felix hadn't realized how tightly he was clutching the helmet's edges until Loren pried his curled fingers loose. Red welts carved canyons across Felix's palms.

"Thank you," Loren said. "For telling me."

Another shrug. "You told me your secret. Figured I owed you one back."

The wheels of the cart creaked and groaned. One of the mules brayed. Down the slope, Pompeii shone like a beacon. From here, Felix could see out to where sky met sun-brushed sea. He thought the conversation dead, but then—

"Sorry again for kissing you," Loren blurted, all in a rush. When Felix only blinked, he hurried on, "I should have asked first. And I'm not very good, am I?"

"Maybe," Felix said, drawing out the word, "you need more practice."

"Practice. Yes." Loren's face flushed scarlet. "Now?"

Felix fought back a little grin. "Survive the mountain first. Then we'll talk."

CHAPTER XX

LOREN

Just when Loren's thighs went numb from the rumble of the rough wood, splinters pinching, brain rattling in his skull, Stravo pulled the reins.

"This is as far as I can take you," he announced. "Beyond here, the trail is impassable by cart."

They'd stopped at a fork in the trail, where one branch narrowed as it wound up Vesuvius's flank, past where trees withered and only sparse grass grew. The other path dipped to a mountainside terrace hosting a special selection of grapes. Loren knew all about them, an experiment with higher-altitude wines, still in its infancy when he'd left home. He hadn't realized how far north his father had expanded in the years since.

It made sense, in the twisted way Lucius Lassius's logic tended to work. He wouldn't drag his son home yet, but he'd hover a hand over Pompeii to ensure Loren stayed within reach.

Felix stumbled a little when he slid from the cart, Mercury's helmet tucked beneath his arm. It was almost a relief to have that freedom up here. On Vesuvius, they didn't have to hide or sneak.

If Stravo thought anything suspicious about the helmet, he didn't mention it. Instead, he gave Felix a cautious once-over. "Don't return to the vineyard."

Felix asked, carefully neutral, "Why is that?"

"You may think you fooled Adolphus, but he's shrewder than he appears."

"There isn't anything to suspect." Felix flashed the ring again.

To Loren's surprise, Stravo didn't quell under the show of authority. Instead, he raised a brow, half-hidden by his hat. "You're a talented actor, I'll give you that. But you're not our master's heir."

Wind rustled the grass. "How do you figure?"

"The real son of Lassius doesn't want to be found. Wouldn't stroll onto his father's field midday and announce himself, would he?" With a snap of the reins, the cart creaked back down the mountain. Over his shoulder, Stravo called, "Rest easy. I won't tell Adolphus more than he knows."

Loren gave him a moment's head start before he tripped along the path after him. "Wait!"

Stravo shot him a bemused look when he drew even. "So the assistant can speak."

"How many of you are there? Workers, I mean."

"Slaves," Stravo corrected.

Discomfort clenched Loren's belly. "Slaves."

"Twenty or thirty, counting the women in the house." Stravo shifted his shoulders. He was broad and strong from years in the field, skin toasted red by the sun. He might be from one of Rome's upper provinces, Gaul, perhaps, or farther north to Londinium. Either way, he didn't belong here. None of them did.

Loren had little power when it came to his father. But this he could do. "Gather them As many as will go. Leave tonight."

"Orders from an assistant?"

"Tell Adolphus you were released on good authority." Loren leveled Stravo's skepticism. "By order of Lassius's son. And if Adolphus resists, remember he is only one man."

Stravo hesitated. For a moment, Loren feared he would laugh him off. But he nodded, a single motion. Reins cracked. The cart rumbled on.

Loren was left in the dust, hoping he hadn't done more harm than good.

Slowly, he trudged back to Felix, whose expression was unreadable.

"Until you started speaking," Felix said, "I thought you were begging a ride back. You're a bit unpredictable."

"Me?"

"Yes." Felix tilted his head. "Though I think I've figured you out. If someone set a fire, I would run away. But you live by your heart. You would run toward it."

"Yet you followed me here."

Felix's mouth twitched. "Someone has to make sure you don't get burned."

Warmth spilled across Loren's face, but he forced his mind back on track.

Even if Stravo hadn't taken them all the way, he'd easily cut their journey by half. The air was thinner, and when Loren breathed in deep, his lungs came up short. He was made for the balmy coastal breeze, not sheer mountain wind. And the heat. Stravo may have spared them a long walk under the sun, but the mountainside boiled, assailing from all directions. Steam curled from the ground. Thick silence settled, not a birdcall to break it.

"The stink is worse," Felix said, reading Loren's wrinkled nose.

"It's no perfume."

"We could turn around. Go back. I don't know what you expected to find, but there's nothing here."

The suggestion shouldn't have been so tempting. But Loren rejected it. He had what he wanted, the peak of Vesuvius in his grasp, where his dreams had led him all along. Answers lived there, and Felix confiding his fears only made Loren more determined to demand them. He would solve the mystery of the helmet for the city.

And for Felix.

"No." Loren pursed his lips. "But we haven't reached the top."

In truth, Loren had no idea what he thought to find on the crest of Vesuvius. He was certain it would reveal itself once he arrived. All the pieces would click into place, turning the right key in a lock. The answer would present itself.

Until he stared into the depressed crater of the mountain—a desolate valley of hissing steam and gravel, bulging in the middle, like something was trapped inside and trying to break free—and he realized he had no clue what he was doing.

"My feet are on fire," Felix grumbled. Sweat trickled from his hairline into reddened eyes. Loren could empathize. He, too, felt like bones set to boil. "So, we're here. Now what?"

Loren opened his mouth to say something, anything, but bit his lip instead. Noxious fumes clouded his mind. His ankles ached, and dirt clung like a second skin. What he wouldn't give for a bath. A cool bath with orange slices and mint leaves floating.

Vesuvius had no baths. Only an empty crater and unnatural heat and two boys who shouldn't be there.

"Don't tell me you don't have a plan," Felix snapped. "Don't say you dragged me here for nothing."

"Not for nothing."

"Gods. I can't think past the ground's hum. Like voices I can't parse. Driving me mad." Felix flopped onto a boulder at the crater's edge, planting the helmet firmly into the loose gravel beside him. It glared at Loren. "Pass the water."

"You drank it all."

"Gods. I'm leaving." He stayed sitting.

What had Loren expected? A vision? Clarity, truth, a grain of salt in a mound of sand? What an ugly place to look for it. Vesuvius was beautiful from a distance, but up close, it writhed like an angry, sick beast.

Maybe he wasn't close enough.

"I wonder," Loren said.

Hands shielding his eyes, Felix replied, "What?"

If Loren didn't stop biting his lip, he'd gnaw it off.

Felix waited. When Loren offered nothing more, he dropped his palms from his face. "The one time I ask you to talk, and you won't."

"I think," Loren said, "I should go down there."

"Go—" Felix jerked around. "There? No."

Too late. Loren swung over the edge of the crater, fixed on the peak of the bowl's center, where the land swelled. Carefully, he began picking his way down the slope.

"Stop!"

Stone scattered, and a hand yanked Loren's elbow. He jerked free, but it threw his balance. Arms whirling, he teetered. He nearly steadied himself, but Felix made another grab. Loren dodged and hit the ground hard. Momentum carried him forward.

He slid.

Hot gravel snagged his tunic and bit his palms. Silver flashed in his peripheral, a round object knocked free and sent tumbling down. By reflex, he reached.

Fingertips brushed cold, stinging metal.

Loren gasped, and in an instant, everything changed.

Loren's dreams weren't dreams.

He had come to terms with that as a child, when he'd wake from a nightmare with paint-covered hands smearing his bedroom walls. Red dripped down his wrists and puddled on the tile. Then he'd scream until his lungs burst and a servant came running. His mother fancied him an artist, indulging him with colors and brushes, instructing him to paint all sorts of lovely things. Fruits in baskets. Flowers. Things to cover the horrors he splattered in his sleep. Nothing helped.

Loren wasn't mad. He wasn't.

But against the pounding heart of Vesuvius, hand still brushing metal so cold it burned, he began to second-guess himself.

Time stopped. The helmet, tumbling free, halted its trajectory. Felix, who seconds earlier had been grappling with Loren, disappeared. As though he'd never been there at all.

A shiver racked Loren's spine. All his hair stood on end. In the stillness of this sweltering world, the breath he released was loud enough to shatter stone.

Movement. White mist wisped into a figure, legs and arms and hair flying loose. A phantom child, running carefree. Loren grasped at the boy's ankle as he passed, but his hand slipped through.

A ghost. Not real.

Head swimming, he watched the boy launch into the arms of a second figure, face murky but with the same head of curls. A parent, maybe. The two spun, then dissolved.

Another spirit formed, one Loren recognized, gangly limbs and skinny knees: himself, sitting cross-legged, eyes closed. Smiling. From the mist emerged a disconnected hand, and Loren's ghost-self allowed himself to be pulled up with a silent laugh. And vanished.

His heart skipped, and the crater filled. Pompeii's Forum on its busiest occasion might've been transferred to the peak of Vesuvius, except those figures were as real as his ghost-self. Gods, they looked happy.

And—oh, there he was again. Ghost-Loren. Older now, shoulders a bit broader, but his hair still hung long, cascading unbraided down his back. He wore the toga of a lawyer or senator. He was happy, too, face split in a wild grin, arm looped through that of a faceless figure. A man's figure. Loren drank himself in, a Loren in a future with no vineyards, no marriage, just him and his lover in a crowded city. He tracked their path as they moved between playing children and stray dogs until they were lost. But he hadn't seen his fill.

His sandals slipped on loose gravel as he skidded down. His pulse quickened. A bit closer. He passed through other ghosts, invisible. His ghost-self's hair swung with his stride, beckoning him forward. A burning trail. A promise.

He stumbled to the top of the mound of the crater's center and stopped short. On the other side sprawled a dense field of poppies, sheer white but for their bright red caps waving him on. The people had vanished, except—there. At the far end of the field. Loren squinted. A boy, curls tousled, stood with his back facing Loren, but he'd recognize his form even here, at the edge of the earth.

"Felix," Loren breathed, then broke into a sprint. Sharp grass stung his legs, and his lungs burned with sour vapor. Poppies erupted into bloody showers of petals when he batted them aside. Felix took a step forward, away. Loren panted. "No!"

The word shattered the spell. He blinked, and the visions vanished. Gasping, Loren slowed, whole body shivering. An illusion, but his stomach ached for—

Felix spoke from behind. "Stronger men than you have lost their minds chasing ghosts."

Loren spun, daring to hope.

His hopes were dashed. The boy staring from the mound, translucent and frayed, face twisted bitter, wasn't his Felix at all. This was a phantom. Something cruel and haphazard, pulled apart and stitched together wrong. Fumes flooded the space between them, shifting and blurring the ghost into a haze.

"Bring him back. I want to see—" Loren stopped in a ragged choke. The Felix at the far end of the field. He wanted—needed—to see if . . .

"If it was me," Ghost-Felix finished.

Loren's fists clenched. "Not you. Him. Mine."

"Yours?"

"You're a murderer. I've seen you. Dreamt you."

"You think your Felix wouldn't do the same?" Ghost-Felix's lip curled. "Sweet. Loyal. You've known us for, what, three days? We must have won you over somehow."

"Stop." Steam seared his face.

But the ghost only began a slow descent of the slope, carving a path to where Loren stood frozen, then paced an unhurried circle. The lazy spiral of a hawk before it dove. "Tell me what we did. How we listened. Said what you wanted to hear. Pretty words in the dark. Did we make you feel like we could be your home?"

He paused behind Loren's shoulder. Loren didn't dare glance back. The ghost said, "Tell me how we kissed you. Touched you. Made you beg for more, always more—"

"*Stop.*"

"—always hands on our skin, never clean. Years and years of it." His voice slipped into an earworm of a mutter, creeping into the gaps in Loren's body to wriggle him apart. "How desperate were you for a friend?"

The words were to him, but the inflection had turned inward, leaving Loren wondering who, exactly, was being accused. Slowly, Loren turned to find Ghost-Felix cradling the abandoned helmet, tender despite the acid dripping from his mouth.

"It always comes down to this," the ghost said to empty sockets. "Us. My helmet. The mountain. She understands me. She knows how it feels to hold something in."

"What are you?" Loren whispered, skin crawling.

"I am the Felix who didn't forget."

The image rang too familiar: Felix gazing at the helmet like it held answers he couldn't grasp alone. Felix, vulnerable but guarded. Aching

234

to be known but fearing anyone who dared tread too close. An impossible puzzle. *My helmet.*

The mountain, the one constant.

"He said he had trouble remembering," Loren said cautiously. "That his memories come and go."

Only that made it sound like the casual ebb of the tide, not most of a life lost to time.

"Not lost," said Ghost-Felix.

"Stay out of my thoughts."

"But they're such a nice respite. So little going on in your mind, it's almost peaceful."

"Good one. Yes, Loren is dim. Very original." Loren breathed to cool his temper. Rancid air left a tang on his tongue. "If his memories aren't lost, why can't he take them back?"

"Exactly like you to assume he had a choice. That either of us did. They meddled with our mind. Took it away. Told us it was for our own good." Ghost-Felix stepped closer, voice hissing sharp as the steam shooting between jagged black rocks. He flickered in and out, as if tethered by an unsteady connection. "They—he—stripped it from him, not realizing doing so created me to hold it. All the memories, and all the anger they contain. Wasn't that monstrous?"

"Who? Who did it?"

"Keep up," he snarled. "Our—*my* father, he's mine, only I remember him. I'm who suffered when we were wrenched apart. To protect us, Da' said."

None of this made sense. The ghost spoke in riddles. Protect Felix from what? What good would tearing memories from him do? Suspicion thickened in Loren's mind, fear that his brutal, bloody visions weren't warnings. They were threats. Somewhere, dormant deep inside Felix, was a power or plague, raw as the paint Loren smeared on the walls as a child. Something others felt best locked away.

Loren stared at the ghost with fresh horror. Despite the slow roasting of his skin, the realization cast cold water through his blood. "If he remembers, he'll become you."

"I am not what his memories make him," Ghost-Felix said. "But I'm angry at being trapped alone with no way to reach him. I've held this on my own since we were eleven. When he learns, it will be his turn to hold the anger. It would remake him."

Or unravel him. Bile rose up Loren's throat. "I want to help him. Tell me how."

"You won't. You're afraid." Sneering, he turned his cheek, hugging the helmet. "By now you've realized there are pieces he won't recall, and there are pieces he cannot, and his line between them blurs. But wouldn't you want to remember? To have that choice?"

"I want to help him," Loren repeated, weaker than before.

"Then you understand what I ask."

Loren wanted to scream that he didn't, that the ghost hadn't said a single helpful thing, that he'd been trying to help Felix all along, but the ghost stood in his way. But his eyes dropped to the helmet, held by pale, familiar hands. *My helmet,* the ghost had said. And Loren understood. Whatever memories Felix couldn't access, the helmet must be strong enough to destroy what stood in the way.

"He thinks coincidence drew him to Pompeii," said Ghost-Felix, "but a far greater power called him here. I cannot say the role he's to play. It's not my grief to share. But I can tell you yours. Days ago, you told him never to put the helmet on, and he won't, unless you say otherwise. You are as much a part of this as he is."

The role he's to play. Nonna's warning crashed through Loren's mind, that the wielder of the helmet was doomed to be a pawn.

Fear burned away until Loren had nothing left but fury.

"Felix resists control at every turn," Loren snapped, impatience bursting. "He won't play a role he doesn't want to play. I've spent my life having my words dismissed. They have no power. That he hasn't put it on has nothing to do with me."

"Then you're more oblivious than I thought. Everything has to do with you. Destiny demands you be together when he comes into his power. Our fates have always been tied."

"I am not part of the destruction. I won't let you twist me into a villain. Let me go if I worsen your situation. For years you've haunted me, not the other way around."

"You think I wanted this? You are the only one whose mind is open enough—or empty enough—to receive me. You say you're cursed, but I'm cursed to be stuck with you to hear. Hear, but never listen."

"Then let *Felix* go."

"I don't want him either," Ghost-Felix seethed. The ground jolted, shuddered, and Loren fought for balance against the sudden quake. "I hate him. I am him."

"You are not"—Loren panted—"him."

Ghost-Felix coiled tighter, and Loren glared him down, anger shooting sparks to his fingertips. If he wanted a fight, Loren could give him one. Stones rocked, a cacophonous groaning in the mountain's belly. Scalding jets of air bit and scratched.

No lunge came, no lash fell. Loren stood his ground.

Instead, the ghost crumpled the way all unloved things did.

He folded his body in, made himself small, bracing for a blow that, though dreaded, would not be unexpected—as if the ghost feared Loren's swing. Sizzling gravel crunched when Ghost-Felix dropped to sit, knees pulled close. The helmet rolled away, freed from loose arms that came to cover his face. The ground stilled.

Loren's ribs ached. He hated that he felt even scraps of pity for this phantom after so many years of torment. But as he stared down his nose at the boy on the ground, chest heaving, for the first time he struggled to separate this Felix from his. His eyes stung. He couldn't stand to see any version of Felix so shattered.

His brain screamed to run. To claw his way from the crater and leave the ghost huddling alone. But Loren wasn't in the business of listening to his head over his heart. He stepped forward, sandals sliding. Sweat rolled down his neck into his already-drenched tunic. Stepped again. Knelt. Tiny rocks nipped his skin.

Waited.

Ghost-Felix froze at the nearness, and moments dragged by, but slowly he peeled his face from where he hid. His eyes, barely visible over his forearms, shone quicksilver. Distrustful mercury. Mist coalesced on either side of his head, fanning in the splay of bird wings. White as doves.

Gingerly, unsure of even his own intention, Loren stretched a hand, then paused until Ghost-Felix relaxed his arms farther. Lifted his gaze higher.

Permission.

He cupped the ghost's cheek.

The ghost's lips parted in a soft, surprised choke, and the misty wings fluttered and flexed. For all the cold marble he projected, his skin was soft. Flushed. Blood roared in Loren's ears, pulse thrumming unsteady. Pressure against his palm increased, the ghost leaning in. Shivering, asking for more.

A twinge in Loren's heart sent an aching reminder that Ghost-Felix had been alone all these years. *Since we were eleven,* he'd said. No one had touched him in as long.

"What happened to you!" Loren whispered, so low his voice cracked. "What will Felix remember if he puts the helmet on?"

Silver slipped from the corner of Ghost-Felix's eye, a damp trail.

"I will not speak of it. Not on my own."

"Tell me how to help. Tell me what to do."

"Give me back to him," he begged. His warm breath fanned the inside of Loren's wrist. "Give me back."

Icy dread replaced the flutter in Loren's stomach. He chanced a glance at where the helmet had landed on its side, an arm's length away. The pull of its power hummed magnetic, a lodestone drawn to iron. A knife demanding to break skin. Its silver wings mirrored those framing the ghost's face, symbols of Mercury and all he represented, the carrying of souls down, down, where light couldn't touch. The helmet wanted to belong to Felix, Loren sensed it. It wanted to make Felix its own, release his memories, let them burst like a busted dam or split artery, and unleash a power he had long been divorced from.

Felix had confessed, not an hour before, that what lay behind his memory block terrified him.

Part of Loren wanted to do anything, give anything, to piece these halves back together, if only to mend the fractures marring the boy whose face he cradled, whose pulse tapped weak against his fingers. But doing so would wreck Felix—the Felix whose realness Loren never needed question.

He couldn't take that risk.

Loren swallowed sharp, hot gravel wedged in his lungs. "I can't do that to him. I can't watch him break."

Against his palm, Ghost-Felix stiffened. Hope drained from his eyes, the last dregs of it.

Searing steam blasted Loren back. He landed hard, pain ricocheting up his spine, arms flying to shield his face from the burning spray. Stones singed and tore his flesh. The ground trembled again. Holding back a sob, he squinted through the hazy uproar.

The ghost had risen, hovering a foot off the ground. Another pair of wings flurried at his ankles. Mist convulsed and took the form of many disembodied hands, grasping at his legs, his flesh, the hem of his tunic. His lips drew back in a snarl, the rawest he'd been, the least human. If the ghost's skin split now, Loren wondered dizzily which would flow, blood or ichor.

Dream-walker. Plane-crosser. Power waiting to be used, and Loren finally grasped what that entailed. A drumbeat pulsed deep in the earth. Dire. Steady. He scrambled to stand, but a gust knocked him down. Misty hands crawled toward him, searching, reaching, and Loren kicked at them to no avail.

"You never heard my voice," Ghost-Felix hissed, sound whirling around the crater in a shivering death rattle, "until I showed you turning the knife on yourself. That is what it took to make you listen. Do not pretend this has ever been about Felix."

Stinging overtook Loren's vision, tears spilling free, eclipsing all else in a hot sweep. "As if you're better. You lured me here to taunt me, not to help him. Say something useful or vanish."

"Always an ultimatum. This or that. But this is far bigger than just you. A haze of death hovers low over the city, and only he can shoulder it. When it breaks and no one can bear the fallout, the guilt will be yours." Spectral feet backed away, light as the padding of a fox over empty air. The helmet hummed, chattering against rubble, then shot into his grip. "You stand at a crossroads. Everything you do from here on out is a choice. Learn to live with the consequences."

Understanding hit a beat too late. "Wait—"

The ghost ducked into the helmet, polished silver against swirling mercury. The instant it settled on his brow, he vanished.

With a hollow clang, the helmet fell to earth.

When Loren came to, he was back where he'd started. Sliding into the pit. Reaching for the helmet. Recoiling his stinging hand. Then he was caught beneath his arms, momentum halting.

"Loren? Are you with me?" Panic. Worry, muttered in his ear.

Felix had stopped Loren's slide, held him, was still holding him.

"Oh," Loren gasped. He twisted to touch Felix's cheek, skin so much hotter than the ghost's that it stung the pads of his fingers. "You're still here."

Felix shot him a funny look. Annoyed, yes, but fond, maybe, too. He brushed sweat-damp copper curls off his forehead, and when his hand lowered, it paused against Loren's. "Where else would I be?"

"Felix," Loren breathed, canting forward until their foreheads pressed together. Heady heat rolled through his body, a sweet bloom of warmth that said *here* and *yes* and *stay*. Forget the sticky mountain and the ghost who stared with such fervent hate. This was Loren's Felix. Felix who'd followed him up here. Felix who'd kissed him back in the quiet temple.

"We need to go," Felix said. "These fumes make me sick."

"I'm having an epiphany."

"Now? Can't it wait?"

Loren shut his eyes, lingering in the moment. *A crossroads*, Ghost-Felix had hissed. Maybe he was beginning to understand. Either he told Felix to put the helmet on, learn his memories at the risk of him turning cruel as his murdering, phantom counterpart and using the helmet's power to destroy the city, or Loren lied to protect Pompeii—and lost Felix anyway when he left the helmet behind tomorrow. The choice dangled, but neither option tempted.

Night after night, his visions had dictated his actions. Here was his turn to reclaim control.

The helmet, cast against black rocks, struck a more sinister figure than ever. Ghost-Felix *wanted* Felix to put it on. Wanted to merge. But Felix was holding Loren as if he alone mattered. Perhaps there was a different end to this story, after all. A kinder end. One where Felix picked Loren over any shiny helmet. One that kept them together. One that protected Felix from the truth.

This was Loren's crossroads. Whatever set him on this path had meant for it to end here, with him turning to find that someone had chosen him, too.

Relief sank slowly into his bones. Ghost-Felix had made one thing clear: Loren *could* change the outcome of his visions. He had a choice. So long as he chose not to tell Felix about the helmet, its power would stay dormant, and they—and the city—would be safe.

"If I said I could see the future," Loren said, words a shaky gust against Felix's mouth, "how would you respond? Would you call me mad?"

"I'd say you dragged me up here to tell me what I already knew." Their noses brushed. "You aren't mad, Loren. Strange. Brilliant. But not mad."

"I thought you didn't believe in magic."

"I don't," said Felix. "But I believe you."

He withdrew and stood. Gravel tumbled loose as he picked his way to collect the helmet. On the return trip, he paused, offering his hand. Loren blinked, brain turned to mush.

"Let's go home," Felix said.

It sounded like a promise.

CHAPTER XXI

FELIX

Descending the mountain proved far easier than the journey up, and the sun hung low when Felix and Loren joined a stream at its base. Every inch of Felix's skin itched, sweat and dust and dirt caked thick. A quick plunge would do wonders. He made to kick his sandals off and jump in, tunic and all, but Loren pulled him back.

"Not here," Loren said. "These streams have been sour for months."

"I'm already sour." Felix tugged his neckline, and dust puffed. "I smell like an egg gone off."

"A little road dust won't break you. Come on, I know a place."

He led Felix farther downstream, through a rich grove of olive trees, limbs bursting with fruit begging for harvest. Shade shielded them from the relentless evening heat. At a point, Loren stretched back a hand. A mindless gesture on Loren's part, but one Felix hadn't dared consider. When he accepted it, their fingers tangling, warmth that had nothing to do with the weather settled deep in his belly.

The grove opened, and the sea spread before them.

Beneath the setting sun, the water glistened yellow and orange, fire licking the surface. Felix sucked in a breath. Brine filled his lungs, driving out Vesuvius's stench. Low waves foamed and sloshed. There was no beach, just a field to the edge of the land, where the bank dropped into waist-deep water. Thick grass thronged the coast, tall and green and lush. In the distance, to the south of this quiet nook, Pompeii glimmered.

"This is . . . ," Felix said, swallowing. "Nice."

Loren smiled, and Felix had to look away.

He wasted no time disrobing, shucking his tunic with a grimace. Tossing the helmet to the side, he dove in. After the scorching afternoon, the seawater came as a cool relief. With handfuls of sand, he scrubbed his skin until it tingled. Then he let his hair writhe in the current before surfacing for air.

Loren had perched on a tree stump, legs crossed. Dappled light filtering through leaves cast freckled shadows across his shoulders.

"You stink, too," Felix said when he kicked back to shore to drag his tunic in the water. He scrubbed a mystery stain with his fingernail.

"Thanks," Loren said dryly.

"Are you shy?"

Delicious red washed across his face, wine overturned on table linen. *"No."*

"Then swim with me. I don't want to smell you all night." Cackling, Felix ducked to avoid the pebble Loren threw. If he was offended, Felix wasn't sure, but he watched from the corner of his eye as Loren stood and—fingers fumbling—pulled off his own garments.

Felix forced his gaze to drift, counting the handful of clouds in the pink sky.

Another body joined his with a splash.

"I won't look," Felix said. "Swear it on my mother's life."

"Your dead mother?" Loren asked. Then, "I didn't mean—"

"She isn't dead. She's a nymph, I bet."

Felix fell back until he was floating, vulnerable in the current. Weightless. This felt safe, somehow, water muffling the earth's hum and offering respite to think. So much had happened on the mountain, and he couldn't tell if he understood more or less than before. Could both be true at once?

For a long while, no words were exchanged, only the sounds of Loren's ablutions and the sea's quiet lapping.

Until Loren said, "I dreamed this."

Frowning, Felix righted himself. He'd been so lost in the trance of floating, he hadn't realized he'd drifted so near Loren. Loren, who studied his face like trying to read a particularly impossible text. Or any text, if you were Felix.

"What do you mean?" he asked.

"You were floating to me."

"Another vision."

"Maybe." Loren's mouth pinched. "But my visions aren't normally so peaceful."

"Maybe I'd drowned, and you hadn't realized yet," Felix said.

Loren shivered. "Don't speak like that."

"Worried I'll will it into reality?"

No response. Instead, Loren began undoing his tangled braid, slender fingers working.

Abruptly, Felix's mouth dried. Fishing his tunic from the water, he hurried to land, wearing nothing but damp shorts, and sprawled in the grass.

"I could stay here for ages," Felix mused. "The sea, the breeze, damn, it's nice."

"Your mouth is a sewage pit," came Loren's response, closer than Felix expected. He cracked open one eye to watch a figure climb from the sea, a silhouette against the slow burn of sunset. "And you have no shame."

Unbidden, Felix grinned, a little wild. "Can't afford shame."

"You could try for modesty."

"Thievery is the humblest profession."

A weight settled beside him. Loren had dressed again, donning the embroidered yellow tunic Julia gifted the day prior, now stained and unpolished. Felix liked it better that way.

Pushing to his elbows, he said, "Your hair is a rat's nest."

"You always know what to say." Loren dug in Nonna's satchel until he withdrew a comb with a victory cry and set to work detangling.

Felix studied the narrow slope of his shoulders. He could drink his fill of this, watch Loren the way a thirsty man begged for water, toe the surface of his depths, so long as Felix didn't let himself drown.

"You seem happier," he said after a time, "since the mountain."

The comb slowed. "Do I?"

"*Happier* isn't the right word. *Lighter,* maybe. Like a burden was lifted."

"I wasn't honest before when I told you nothing happened in my dreams. In truth, they're nightmares. Horrible visions. Things I can't repeat, but—you heard me in the Forum yesterday."

"Pompeii. You worried—saw—something happening to it," Felix guessed. "Something involving the helmet?"

Loren picked at the tines. "Even I underestimated what its power could do."

It sounded like another half-truth. "And now?"

"Now I have an answer. Everyone will be safe once you put it back come morning." He hit Felix with his burning smile, sunshine made tangible in the sweet upturn of his lips. "I think everything will turn out all right."

He resumed the steady drag of his comb.

Felix's nerves, meanwhile, felt flayed.

He had done all Loren asked, hadn't he? Felix had talked to Nonna, trekked up and down a mountain, confessed fears he had never divulged to anyone else. Yet Loren kept the truth obscured. Whatever answer he found on Vesuvius about the helmet, he wasn't telling Felix in full.

Felix had a sick sense those answers would come out the hard way before this ended.

Rules clashed in his head. *Avoid attachment. Stay in the present. Belief is never worth it.* Felix lived by his mantras to keep from dying if he went against them, but in the span of three days, Loren had systematically sorted through each one, pondered it, then flipped it on its head. Still, even through the jumble, Felix kept hold of the one he'd learned first: *Trust your gut.*

Others could keep religion and magic, augurs and oracles. None had ever served Felix the way his instincts did. What started that night with Servius, when he first felt the ground shake under his knees, had spiked to a maddening buzz he couldn't put from his head. A constant chatter of wordless talking, disembodied hands grabbing his ankles, tripping him. Like a skittish animal, he wanted to lay his ears flat against his skull, turn tail, and duck away until the storm passed. Everything about Pompeii was wrong, wrong, wrong.

Tossed in the tall grass, Mercury's helmet gleamed red. That siren's song still, beckoning Felix closer. A thread of a memory, demanding its knots be unpicked.

An inhuman whisper, muttering the worst was still to come.

He knew he should be angry that Loren posed yet another barricade in Felix's quest to understand himself. He *was* angry. But he didn't want to waste their last night, and if nothing else, Felix had mastered compartmentalizing his feelings. Separating his emotions from the task at hand.

Loren pulled his hair over his shoulder, dividing the strands into three.

"No." In a surge of boldness, Felix touched the back of Loren's hand, fingers prickling. "Leave it loose."

Loren's lips parted. He blushed. "You didn't let me finish telling you before."

"About your floating dream?"

A nod.

"I think," Felix said, "I can guess."

This time he kissed Loren, and they were both completely sober.

Still, Felix thought as his mouth moved against Loren's, a jug of wine may well have been decanted directly into his gut. His veins burned. Loren's movements were still sweetly clumsy, but he caught on quick, lips soft but sincere. Want scorched through Felix, thrill and terror coupled in equal doses. This, now, was all too much. Not enough. Too much. He didn't permit touch like this. He didn't allow it. Another rule Loren upended, simply by noticing—without being told—that Felix had such a rule at all.

When he reached to draw Loren closer, his hands shook.

"Damn," Felix panted, breaking free. He moved, chasing a bead of salt water rolling down Loren's neck.

Loren's breath hitched. "Sewage pit."

"You like it."

"Your—depravity?"

Felix responded with a nip to the tender skin behind Loren's ear, coaxed his mouth open again. Conversation dissolved.

Loren's olive skin glowed in the fading sun, lit from within, and Felix could live off this ichor. He'd make himself the god of easy gestures and spend his immortal hours cataloging every dip and knob of Loren's spine, the curve of his throat, and the way his tunic bunched up his thighs. The mole below his jaw. The arch of his back. He'd map the press of Loren's body against his, where he was soft and where he wasn't. Discover constellations in his freckles, chart the stars anew. How he breathed. How he trembled, and met Felix kiss for kiss, and tangled with him in the field, and nothing else mattered. Tomorrow didn't matter. History didn't matter.

This was a boy worth remembering. Felix wouldn't let this memory disappear.

"You are," he said, forehead against Loren's shoulder, chest heaving, "unreal."

"That wasn't a curse word." A fine-boned finger tilted Felix's chin up.

For once, Felix didn't feel like amending himself. Instead, he smoothed Loren's hair, still damp, away from his face, then ran his thumb over his cheekbone.

"You kiss like a virgin," Felix said.

This time, Loren didn't blush. "You like it."

He grinned, soft and open, and Felix's heart cracked.

"When will I lose you?" Loren asked sometime later. They sat in the tall grass now, and he'd shifted to straddle Felix's lap. In the starlight, his cinnamon eyes were fathomless.

Holding his gaze ached too much to bear. Felix broke it, hiding in Loren's collarbone. "That's an odd question."

"A valid one, all the same."

Coaxing a shiver from Loren was too simple. Felix did it again, skating his fingers across ribs, just because he could. "Why are you so sure I'll leave?"

"That isn't what I asked."

"Another vision?"

"Not quite." Loren ducked when Felix leaned up for a kiss. "You're trying to distract me."

Felix grunted. "It isn't working."

"It's working." Loren pulled back, disentangling their limbs to sit apart. The vacancy hit Felix immediately, the loss of warmth, weight. "I want to believe you speak the truth. That you wouldn't lie. Not you."

"I lie to everyone. It's—"

"How you survive. So you've said." Loren tore a handful of grass, braided the strands with nimble fingers. His hair fell over his shoulder, creating a curtain that blocked Felix from reading his face. "What if there's more to this than survival? We could run away together. Find a new town."

Furious, frantic weaving, but his hands shook so badly that the grass snapped. Felix stilled him with a palm. "You? Leave Pompeii? The place means too much to you."

"I find meaning in anything. I'm sentimental that way."

"Enough, Loren," Felix whispered. "You hardly know me."

Wide eyes met his. "But I know enough to see you want it too."

"I want you." Simple, honest, no promises. A gods-damned easy gesture. Fitting that Felix only caught on to those at the end.

"You have me. My worry is I don't have you in return."

"Come here."

Loren did, crawled closer, and Felix tipped him back into the grass and kissed his neck and shoulders and chest, and stars wheeled overhead in silent cacophony, and insects buzzed and hummed nearby. And the leaves of the olive trees were still. And the world was still.

And Felix could pretend he had it all, for one moonless night.

Dawn broke too soon, lighting the sky in gray and purple, sun hovering below the horizon behind Vesuvius to the east. Felix woke, sticky and sore, and knew Loren would be more so. But he still slept, face softened by the early-morning gloom. Felix dared to kiss his temple.

Their last.

Standing, careful not to jostle Loren, Felix dressed, tunic stiff with salt. Water from the lapping sea cleared his senses when he splashed his face. He ate a heel of bread from Loren's satchel, slowly, crust first and then the middle, as if drawing out this moment would somehow preserve it.

He tugged on his sandals, gathered the helmet, and disappeared into the mist.

A spell of silence cast a net over the road to Pompeii, as if all that once lived had fled. No birds gathered in the trees. No lizards crossed his path. No idle chatter from a friend to fill the spaces. Only his shadow kept him company, a phantom at his side. Tighter and tighter wound that relentless hum of pressure building, waiting for an excuse to burst.

The quiet offered too much time to plan. To consider the terms of the deal he meant to strike.

Fog crept among the tombs outside the city gate. The guards from yesterday were absent, a sure sign the city had lost faith in catching the helmet thief. Ironic, considering what Felix carried slung over his shoulder.

Alone amidst the mausoleums and markers, Aurelia drifted like a ghost, hem of her white nightdress catching on aloe spines and dragging over dead grass. When she spotted Felix's approach, her pensive frown didn't shift. Almost like she knew to expect him out here.

"Can't sleep?" Felix said.

Her face was too empty for a girl her age. "You spoiled everything by coming here, do you know that?"

"So I've gathered."

Felix considered Aurelia, compiling his evidence collected over the past days: her episode in the alley. *Take his hand.* That scraped chalk drawing of Felix's face, framed by the same wings on the helmet he held. The collapse she shared with Loren at the festival, and his frenzied warning in the forum after. Pieces were falling into place, tiles in a misfit mosaic.

Conclusion drawn, he said, "His visions. You have them, too. You knew I would meet you here. What else do you know?"

Aurelia glared and kicked listlessly at a grave marker. When she spoke, it wasn't to Felix at all. "Pappa thought I'd gone mad when I begged him not to leave. He and Mamma wrote it off as fussing from a worried little girl. Until the other soldiers brought back his belongings. His blanket. His sword. If he'd listened, he wouldn't have gone. He promised he'd return, but I knew—I *knew.* Now it's happening all over again."

"With Loren." When her face only pinched, sour spread across Felix's tongue, threatening to bring up the scrap of bread. Confirmation. "Aurelia, he thinks he's stopped it, whatever is about to happen. The destruction. The end."

"He's wrong," she whispered.

"I believe you," Felix said.

"Of course you do." Aurelia cast him a scathing look. Then she snarled, yanking her hair. "It isn't *fair*. I never asked to see these things, I never asked to know. Why can't—why can't I be normal? Like Celsi, or the others. I don't want to live like this anymore."

Stuffing her fist in her mouth, she muffled a furious sob. Her chest heaved. Her outburst, as most things did, died quietly. She screwed her eyes tight and slumped against a tomb, burying her face in her knees.

Awkwardness settled, thick as the surrounding mist. Felix was no good at this comforting business. He didn't have the experience, and opportunities to practice were hard to come by when he avoided attachment for exactly this reason. So he did all he could think to do. He sat beside her. She seized when their shoulders bumped, but she didn't flee. A small victory.

"Most days, I feel closer to the dead than the living," Felix said. Confessing this to her felt both strange and appropriate, like Aurelia alone in the world would understand him. "In every town I pass through, no one sees me, but I see everyone. The shops they run, the friends they share meals with, parents and children and families. I can't fathom how they manage it. How it comes so naturally when it never has for me. That maybe I forgot how to be a person, or maybe I never learned at all. All I know is how to run. Restless."

She sniffled. After a time, she lifted her head to pick at a hole in her dress. "Like you're missing something, but you can't find the piece you lack. No matter how hard you look, finding is beyond your control."

"It's shit, isn't it?" Felix snorted. "If all that separates people from objects, or the dead from those alive, is that we can control ourselves, what does it mean if you can't? What does that make you?"

"I don't want to find out," Aurelia admitted.

"That might not be up to us." Felix knocked his knee against hers, then rose, shouldering the laundry bag. "I have an errand. If you come with, I'll give you a ride."

That was the thing of it. For all that Aurelia existed beyond her time, aged prematurely by visions of futures not yet lived, she was still a child. And although she hesitated when Felix leaned down, she scrambled onto his back, clinging tight around his neck. In an odd way, it wasn't so bad, having someone holding on to him. Trusting him not to let her fall.

Together, he and Aurelia entered the tomb-still city.

Aurelia rested her chin on his shoulder and slipped into a quiet ramble, filling him in on all he'd missed in the city since yesterday. Much, from the sound of it: a fight breaking out in a council meeting, Nonna tripping over a loose brick and hurting her hip, another well gone dry. Seemed Aurelia had eyes and ears all over Pompeii.

"I haven't seen Celsi since our marble game," she said as they turned onto a street of houses. "Do you think he's upset with me?"

Felix hadn't thought about him since the festival, but Aurelia's concern stirred a memory of Celsi being dragged by a man who looked to be his father. No one had intervened, not Camilia, not Felix. He'd watched and done nothing, and that still sat out of place in his gut.

"I bet he's busy." Felix kept his tone light, forcing back a surge of shame.

"I suppose," Aurelia replied, but she didn't sound convinced.

At an intersection not far from his destination, Felix elbowed Aurelia until she slid from his back. She glanced around, eyes narrowed, at the new bricks, the even cobblestones, the freshly painted exteriors.

"This is where the rich tourists stay," she said. "What's your business here?"

"I told you. I have an errand."

"I'm coming with you."

"You can't," Felix said. Aurelia hit him with a scowl. He understood the frustration of being told no without an adequate explanation, but his task was for him alone. "Aurelia, I'm going to fix this. You, Loren, your mother. I'll get you out of the city, but you must promise to do exactly as I say, and neither can find out what I'm about to do. Understand?"

She wavered, softening a fraction. "For Loren?"

"For you, too." He pushed at her. "Go home. I'll find you later."

With one last calculating look, Aurelia took off. Felix watched until she rounded the corner and her curls disappeared. Some new brand of resolve settled on his shoulders in her place.

For the third time, though he doubted that number would bring him luck any more than his name had lately, Felix entered the house of Senator Servius.

The building was as void of life as Julia's estate, but the telltale sound of a stylus scratching drew Felix to the study. The door stood ajar. Servius hunched over his writing table, dressed immaculately as ever, gloves tight and hawk crest fixed, despite the early hour. Even at the sound of Felix's footsteps nearing the desk, Servius didn't budge from his work.

"Awfully quick," Servius said. "Umbrius must have made it easy."

Felix waited. He pinpointed the precise moment Servius realized it wasn't Darius standing before him. His hand stilled. Bland eyes flicked up. Amusement tugged his mouth.

Servius propped his stylus in its holder, still dripping ink. "You thieves keep me on my toes, don't you? Forgive my mention of Umbrius."

"Don't care," Felix said. "I don't get involved in politics."

"And yet."

Gods, Servius and Julia were cut from the same cloth. It rankled Felix to no end, these petty disputes of the rich. The issues patricians and politicians fought over never mattered. Ultimately, they were each on their own self-serving side, with far more in common than either would admit. What a waste of breath. To Loren's credit, he at least attempted to argue issues that regular folks cared about. Things that made a difference, however slight.

This was all distraction. He willed his focus back to the details that mattered, shut out what didn't. Now or never. He didn't want to give it up, this one thing that proved he was worth more than the flesh on his back, the only power he'd ever held. But he remembered starry kisses. A pinch at the corner of a familiar mouth. Those details mattered.

From the laundry bag, he withdrew Mercury's helmet and slammed it on Servius's desk.

Servius's gloved hands rose, and he scooted back a fraction. But his surprise quickly smoothed over, like he'd suspected this might happen all along. Bastard. He relaxed in his seat, a satisfied sprawl. "You decided you want the horse after all."

"No," corrected Felix. "I want two."

A smile spread. "An expensive demand for a helmet I can't touch. Surely we can find more favorable terms."

Familiar tightness in Felix's ribs screamed at him to flee. Staying would carry the heaviest consequences he had ever faced. He knew what came next, and it boiled down to an impossible choice—one he shouldn't hesitate to make. Flee, or lose. Flee, or be used. The last thing his father said to him was *run*. Felix hadn't looked back since.

But his rules stopped mattering days ago, the same instant a bowl crashed over his head.

Gods, if only his da' could see him now.

Felix inhaled a final breath on his own terms, then dragged a chair to the bargaining table.

CHAPTER XXII

LOREN

"Our wayward son returns," said Ax, straightening from his slouch against the arch that opened into the Forum. He stepped neatly into Loren's path. "About time. Lady Julia's had me searching all over. My instructions are to deliver you posthaste, with no sidetracking, stalling, or... or..."

They could be here all day while Ax struggled to name another *s* verb.

Loren deflated. His morning had been bad enough, and he'd only barely finished the long, sweaty trek back. All he wanted was to complete one last task before crawling into bed and suffocating himself with a blanket. Julia Fortunata didn't factor into that agenda.

He peered past Ax's shoulder into the Forum, more crowded than usual. People jostled and shoved, wrestling to get nearer to a scene or else listen to some proclamation, but Loren couldn't see what. He had hopes. But he didn't dare speak them.

He had learned the hard way lately how voicing hopes ruined them.

"I'm not interested in a scolding." He took a steadying breath. "Tell Julia I apologize for how things ended, but—"

"The way I see it," Ax said, "you don't have much of a choice here."

Loren's blood ran cold. "How do you figure?"

Ax flicked out a knife to clean under his nails. Casual enough. "Word spreads fast in Pompeii. With how you've acted lately—throwing public fits, stirring trouble—I wonder how the Lassius reputation will fare once the council finds out who you are."

"Are you threatening me?" Loren hissed, eyes darting to see who might have overheard.

"Then where will you hide? You've tricked everyone you know, took advantage of their kindness while all along you were a wine-nursed brat." He shrugged. "Up to you. My lady only wants to talk."

Ax wasn't smart enough to piece this threat together. Loren recognized Julia lurking behind his words, and he had no qualms she would act on it. If she revealed his truth, there would be nothing left for him in Pompeii, and he had already lost so much. Elias would hate him. Livia would never look at him the same.

He scanned the crowd in the Forum again, searching for a clue that at least one promise had been made good on. But it was cruel of him to doubt. Felix had sworn he'd return the helmet before he left Pompeii. If he was no longer in the city, regardless of the sour state of Loren's heart, Loren had to trust Felix had seen it through.

He steeled himself. "Fine. Make it quick."

Ax gestured, and Loren turned back into the thick of town.

Let it be said there was no worse feeling than waking alone.

If he shut his eyes, Felix lingered behind them. A phantom sensation, a ghost of a touch. It haunted Loren from the moment he woke and rolled over, smiling, only to see a faded imprint in the grass. Still, he waited. Surely Felix was coming back. Surely.

But Loren's signet ring was back on his own finger. If that wasn't confirmation of Felix's intentions, nothing could be clearer.

When they passed the brothel, Loren considered shouting for Elias to save him, but raised voices inside announced Elias was already having it out with the landlord. Probably over money, how the price of freedom kept inflating. Maybe Loren should be the one to intervene, though last time he'd tried, Elias had been equally furious at him. Something about fighting his own battles. Interrupting now would break what remained of their strained friendship.

Arriving at Julia's estate brought a fresh wave of dread. Ax waved Loren into the atrium and directed him to the study, but the sight of the plunging pool gave him pause.

"Wait, Ax. Clovia, what became of her? Her burial."

Ax's eyes dulled, face hardening. "Lady Julia paid an undertaker to handle the body, but there will be no ceremony. No time."

Loren frowned. "Time could be made. Without a funeral, her spirit can't rest."

"And? Julia's word is final. Don't pretend to care, sweetheart. It doesn't suit you."

Ax slunk off, leaving Loren to wonder how many ghosts this estate held.

He found Julia perched on the sill of a shuttered window in the study, gazing at nothing. She wore a simple gray tunic, hair in a disheveled knot, so far removed from the portrait-perfect statue she'd been at the festival. Her face drooped with exhaustion, creased with worry. But once Loren crossed the threshold, her armor slid back.

"Hello, doll." She rose with a smile that didn't reach her eyes. "Your hair is different. I've never seen you without your braid."

It was so beyond what Loren expected her to say that he tugged a lock by reflex. Silly, really, a child clinging to a toy. But as he'd waited in the grove for a boy who wasn't coming back, his fingers worked by memory to separate into three and weave. Then he pulled the band off his wrist to tie the braid, and—

Felix had said *"Leave it loose."*

So Loren left it loose, like that would coax Felix to his side again.

He shook it off. This was a distraction attempt. Loren wouldn't let her win this round. He drifted past her to survey their battleground.

With the window closed, Julia's study was stifling, dusty and dimly lit by a half-burned candle. Parchment lay strewn across the floor, a series of drafts discarded for whatever disappointments they contained. A platter of untouched cheese sweated in the heat. This wasn't the right setup for a scolding. Loren should know. He'd faced plenty in his father's office.

"Julia," he said slowly, "why am I here?"

He peeked at the parchment centered on the desk, the sole draft to have passed her scrutiny. Even from a distance, Loren hazarded a guess at what it said. After all, he'd seen a version before.

Julia clasped her hands. "I'm prepared to forgive you."

Incredulity hooked in Loren's gut. "For what, precisely? For having the nerve to speak the truth? For not wanting some washed-up senator to get away with smuggling and murder?"

"Settle, Loren."

"Don't tell me to settle. Not when you lied. Not after threatening me."

"You take liberties," she said. "Remember, in Pompeii we're not equals. Here, you are nobody. Do me the courtesy of hearing my case first. You wear the clothes I gifted. You owe me this, at least."

"Speak quickly, then, or I'll leave and not come back."

Always an ultimatum, the ghost murmured. *This or that.*

Loren shook him off his shoulder with a huff he hoped Julia assumed directed at her. She didn't acknowledge it. Instead, she began to pace, slow, even strides.

"Most think me a recluse. Unsociable. If you thought the same, you were too polite to voice it." She shot him a wry smile he didn't return. "But my estate wasn't always so empty. For a time after my father's death, I rented out rooms. I employed more widely. Built new baths. Expanded."

"Was it unsuccessful?"

"The contrary. I was booked throughout the year." Julia paused, jiggling the window latch, but didn't push the shutters open. "Until I pieced together the truth about how he died. I'd been forbidden to visit his deathbed, robbed of my right as his only daughter to anoint him, to arrange his funeral. And the undertaker refused to tell me, believing my constitution fragile. I stole the records months later."

"Julia—"

"Poisoned. Strangled. Clovia's death wasn't my first brush with Servius's methods. I learned quickly there are few people I can trust."

"Yet you deny her a funeral." Loren's lip curled despite his effort to keep accusation from his tone. "You trusted her enough to make her your sole attendant, and now you condemn her to the same fate as your father."

"Disgust spoils your pretty face," Julia said coldly. "So does contempt. If you knew half of what I know, you would not regard me with either."

Loren swallowed hard. "I wish I could help you. But my answer stays the same."

"You still don't see it." When she spun to face him, her eyes brimmed. "You don't understand the opportunity I offer. A route into politics, a stable life in Pompeii, a new family. I could give you everything."

"You want a puppet. You want my father's name attached to yours." Loren stepped back, striding for the exit. "But you are no better than he is. I can't put myself through that again."

"I want you, Loren."

He froze.

Julia smelled victory. "When was the last time someone asked what you desired from your life? And didn't force you into a mold? When someone wanted you, exactly as you are?"

Last night. Loren grimaced. What he and Felix had was different. And the knife it twisted hurt far more than Julia ever could. Not that it counted for much. Felix still picked flight in the end, and Loren was reduced to an afterthought.

His mistake for believing he was worth choosing.

"Not your parents," Julia continued. "Or you wouldn't have run. Not Isis, or the Priest would have valued you as more than an errand boy. And the seamstress-woman and her daughter have their own lives to worry about, you cannot keep clinging to them. Where does that leave you?"

A lump lodged in Loren's throat. With one neat move, Julia had reached into his chest and torn out all the insecurities he harbored. Had drawn the same conclusion he long feared. He was a burden. His visions, his hopes, his love were all too big for anyone else to hold, and he was selfish for asking it.

She crossed the room in three ruthless strides. They were the same height, but she still managed to look down her nose at him, make him shrink. "Fools. All of them. You're remarkable on your own merit, Loren. There's no one more suited to be my heir, no one in the world who can secure my line and protect Pompeii from Servius's influence. This is mutual insurance on both our parts. I need you as much as you need me."

"You can't mean that," Loren whispered.

"I'm offering you a life on your own terms. I'm offering an ear that will listen," Julia pressed. "When your father comes to Pompeii, he'll face the entire council before he can get to you. That I can promise."

Loren thought about what waited for him outside this room. Elias's cajoling, Livia's pity, a position with the Temple of Isis stripped from him. No tie to the city to stop his father dragging him home. An empty bedroom. More visions he couldn't make sense of. No friends.

No Felix.

He turned from the door.

The parchment waited on the table, outlining their agreement. Loren skimmed the language transferring estate ownership, stretching from the home in Pompeii to holiday villas in Rome and Stabiae, into his name. These contracts weren't uncommon. His father protested them, believed blood a stronger bond than ink, but the rest of the Roman world had no grounds to question their validity. Every estate needed an heir. If you couldn't make one, you found one.

Julia passed him a stylus and ink.

Stop, said a scratching little voice. Loren wanted to believe he knew the source, but he wasn't convinced Ghost-Felix was capable of caring. *Don't make this decision with your heart so raw.*

She wants me, Loren thought louder. *She, if no one else.*

The ghost flitted away.

A scrawl of the stylus. He dipped his signet ring into puddled wax and pressed his seal beside his signature. When he finished, he slid the sheet aside so Julia could copy him. Scribble. Dip. Press. All too easy, too quick. Wax cooled, and neither spoke for a long moment.

"Do you think your father will be angry?" Julia said.

"Anger requires feeling beyond indifference. I'm not convinced he's capable."

The ink tipped over. Julia scrambled to rescue the contract from the rapidly expanding black spill, clutching it to her chest as though a newborn. Loren grabbed for a cloth tucked under the tray of old food.

He froze. The plate was rattling of its own volition.

Across the room, a shelf collapsed and crashed against tile. Wood splintered. A jug on the windowsill toppled with a clatter, spraying deep red wine. Outside, something heavy, bricks or tile, broke loose and shattered.

This wasn't supposed to happen. By Felix replacing the helmet, this was meant to stop.

Wasn't it?

"No," Loren whispered. "No, no." He reached for Julia, to hold her forearm as proof he wasn't alone, but she dodged and ducked below the desk.

"Under here!"

The roar of the shaking earth nearly drowned her voice. Loren stumbled over rocking ground to huddle beside her. He gripped the table leg tight as he could, knuckles white. A crack in the wall split a fresco of a politician buying votes with bread. Paint chipped from the plaster in a puff of dust. Loren blocked it from his lungs with his sleeve and screwed his eyes tight.

The quake lasted an eternity.

Until eternity ended. A final lurch sent his stomach rolling.

Julia panted in his ear. "Are you hurt?"

Loren shook his head.

He crawled through the wine puddle and vomited into the empty jug, throat burning. Julia spoke again through a dim filter, maybe expressing disgust, maybe scolding him. Loren couldn't process. Numb, he rose on unsteady legs.

This broken place belonged to him now, per the contract Julia still cradled.

Loren swayed once. Then he bolted for the door.

Pompeii was no stranger to the earth's angry fits, but as Loren staggered outside, today's energy struck him as wrong as the stench of sour eggs flooding the streets—the smell Felix noted in the tunnels. Now it had intensified in the city. That couldn't mean anything good.

Rubble from crumbling buildings littered the roads. Smoke and dust swirled in the air, and Loren drew his sleeve across his face to shield his lungs. People scrambled with urgency, all stomping feet and panicked voices. Some were already at work on repairs, plastering cracks, sweeping debris, hauling aside bricks—Pompeii pressing on— but Loren noticed a few families frantically filling bags and loading carts. They were leaving. Quitting the city before it quit them. He should be glad they were finally heeding his warning from the Forum, but he was supposed to have *stopped* this.

Loren didn't slow until he spotted the familiar paintwork of Livia's shop. Only when he saw Aurelia upright and unharmed did he breathe. He swooped her in a frantic embrace.

"Get off, get off," she chanted, wriggling free, but Loren kept a tight grip on her wrists. "You lunatic, let go."

If Aurelia had the head to act like a menace, the shop must've fared well. "Where's—"

His words fell away like roof tiles when he glanced up and found a horse staring back. Two horses, each with bulging saddlebags and still skittish from the quake. Dazed, Loren straightened, and Aurelia took advantage of his shock, twisting free. "Aurelia, how—"

"Celsi owed me," she said in a rush. "I beat him at marbles, but his pappa doesn't give him pocket money. He paid with these instead."

"Celsi has horses?"

She flashed a dark look. "Not anymore."

One of the horses, a dappled mare, snorted. Stroking her muzzle did little to ease the knot in his gut. "You're leaving."

Aurelia twisted the toe of her sandal. "Mamma wants us on the road by noon. There's nothing good left here. No future worth staying for. Only fire."

Yesterday, giddy and lovesick on hope, Loren might have argued with her. He'd thought he'd found proof that the future could be changed—that he could be the one who changed it. Maybe he'd managed to stop the city's destruction by Felix's hand. But the other

VESUVIUS

future he wanted to build, the one where he and Felix walked together, was out of reach. If Loren chose to stay in Pompeii with Julia, it wasn't because of hope.

Rather, it was because he had to be right that Pompeii was safe, if nothing else.

"Aurelia," Loren said, bile souring his tongue, "there is no fire. I solved it. The stolen helmet—"

The shop's door opened.

"Don't call me a fool, Nonna," Livia said, exiting with Nonna hobbling at her heels. She clutched a fabric bundle. "This place is due to sink into the sea any day now. So many quakes in a week isn't right, on top of all this chatter about thieves and omens, and now Umbrius—Loren! Where have you been?"

Her cloth hit the cobblestones, and she wrapped Loren in an embrace.

As much as he ached to sink into it, a shade slipped over him, distance no hold could cross. The sensation startled him. For the first time since he was twelve and new to the city, he felt like a stranger in Livia's arms. Over her shoulder, Loren caught Nonna's suspicious glare. She leaned heavier on her cane than usual. He had so much to tell her, but he didn't know where to start.

Time for that later, Loren supposed. He wriggled free to collect the fabric Livia had dropped, taking his time straightening the folds before handing it over. She took it but didn't bustle off as he hoped.

"You're terribly quiet," Livia said. She made to touch his face, but he turned his cheek.

"I'm giving silence a try. For once."

She didn't laugh. Her gaze roved over him, all of him, then softened. "Felix left?"

Loren's lungs seized. He tripped in his haste to back away, ducking around the mare. "You know how men are. Fickle. Never settle."

266

Nonna scoffed. "Too true."

"Loren, love—"

"Where are you headed?" Loren asked.

Pity still twisted her mouth, but she resumed stuffing the saddlebag of the other horse. "South. I have an uncle in Alexandria if we can catch a ferry across to Egypt. It will be an adjustment, but I'll find work, and Isis has a temple there. They'll take you on as an attendant. Nothing much will change. New scenery, same life."

"I'm not going."

Aurelia let out a sharp cry. "But—"

"This is not up for debate." Livia clapped Loren with a look that pinned him in place. "I will not raise my children in a city of shaking earth and assassinating snakes."

Loren blinked. "Assassins?"

"Assassins?" Aurelia asked with too much grim curiosity.

"Go pack," Livia ordered her. "This isn't for your ears."

"Mamma!"

Livia cast an imploring look at Nonna, who acquiesced with a threat to pinch, and only then did Aurelia scamper inside.

Dropping to a whisper, Livia leaned close. "Didn't you hear? Nonna brought the news before the quake. Priest Umbrius was murdered in his bed. Bruises all around his throat."

"May Charon carry his soul swiftly," Nonna said with no shortage of glee.

Loren went numb. He must have misheard. No wonder the city was on tenterhooks. Divine signs came in threes, and people could tolerate only so many crises. Thieves, quakes, now murder.

But another source of anxiety pulsed through Loren. With Umbrius dead, Julia's sway over the council was weakened. Servius had moved in for the kill. Did Julia know? Was that why she was so desperate to finalize the contract? *Why hadn't she told him?*

"Livia, I can't leave. I have—"

"You have what?" Livia snapped the saddlebag shut. "You have a little girl inside that shop who will be wrecked if she loses you. So will I. Family doesn't abandon family."

He stared at his feet, blistered from his hike up Vesuvius. Livia said family, but Loren heard only Julia's gnawing term: clinging. Burdens clung. Burdens lied about their true weight, and he couldn't ask Livia and Aurelia to carry him any longer.

Julia was his new family. That decision now dried in dark ink.

"I'll walk you as far as the gate," he said firmly.

He expected Livia to protest, but her lips only pursed, like she didn't believe him. She likely wouldn't relent until Loren was a speck in the distance.

"Besides," he said, forcing a smile, "someone needs to stay with Nonna."

"Bah!" Nonna sunk into a chair by the door. "I have taken care of myself all these years. I look forward to a break from the pestering."

Livia grimaced. "Stubborn, both of you. But if anyone could survive this damned city, it would be her."

Leaving Livia's shop for the last time was a bittersweet goodbye, heavy on the bitter. This was Loren's first home in Pompeii. Now it stood stripped of all things familiar. Old dolls, quilts and weavings, the gladius above the window, all packed away on the horses that would carry Livia and Aurelia far from the city.

He wouldn't weep for it. Not if he wanted to keep firm his resolve not to follow. He swallowed the burning in his throat and turned his back on the shop.

At last, after a long goodbye from Nonna, where she squeezed Loren's hand too tight and he wouldn't meet her eyes, they departed.

Loren guided Livia, Aurelia, and the horses through the chaotic streets, a mix of those few wise enough to leave and the stubborn majority. At a point, not far from the shop, he caught a glimpse of Celsi in the swarming crowd, but when he tried to wave him down, he failed to catch the boy's eye. Celsi's attention was fixed, weaving through the flock toward the wealthy side of town, clutching tight to a bundle of paperwork. Some errand for the council, perhaps. Forms related to Umbrius's death.

Better he didn't see Loren, anyway. When the news broke that he'd signed as Julia's heir officially, Celsi wouldn't be pleased. That pout of his might become permanent.

Aurelia chattered away about everything and nothing, not realizing that these were their final moments together. Loren lacked the spine to tell her the truth. She'd piece it together at the gate, where her tears would be Livia's problem. He hated to end things this way, but throwing another deceit on his already teetering stack was old hat. Besides, he had vowed to figure out his visions to make things safe for her. Whether or not the ground kept shaking in Pompeii, at least she'd be far away when he learned if he'd succeeded. Her visions might ease beyond the city. She could know peace.

At the city gate, Livia left them waiting in the shade while she haggled for last-minute road rations, a poor excuse for giving Loren space to break the news to Aurelia. She'd started a game of balancing on cobblestones knocked askew by the quake. Watching her wobble made guilt swell afresh. He had to tell her. Inhaling deep, he opened his mouth.

Across the street, a flash of copper ducked into shadow behind a fallen awning.

"Be right back," he muttered.

Ignoring Aurelia's shocked shout, Loren dove into traffic, dodged an oncoming cart, and plunged after Felix. He had one chance, and he refused to lose it. Skirting a corner, darting in a zigzag, he chased Felix through narrow side streets and alleys populated only by storage crates and stray cats. Felix might be faster, but Loren knew the city by heart. And even if his heart had misled him at every turn lately, at least he still had Pompeii.

By the time Loren caught up behind a residential block, his lungs burned. He snagged Felix's wrist before he could round another corner.

An empty victory.

Felix's back faced him, but Loren traced the line of his profile. His familiar shape stirred all sorts of tangled feelings—the way his muscles had flexed and softened under Loren's touch, that smooth, strong heat. The cool grass when Loren woke alone.

"I waited for you." Loren slid his grip down Felix's arm until their fingers curled together. His nerves fluttered, dangerous hope taking flight. "You left. But you're here now. Aren't you?"

For a long, honey-drip second, Loren thought he had him.

But the moment dragged, and Felix was a bowstring when angry. He pulled tighter, shoulders seizing, tensing to snap. To let the volley of arrows loose, send the spear hurtling, Achilles bringing down Troy.

Felix twisted free with a jerk. "Don't. Don't touch me. I hate when you touch me."

The sting cracked whip-sharp, stealing Loren's breath. "I don't understand."

"Of course you don't." Lithe even in blistering fury, Felix danced away.

Slanted light cut him in two. With the fresh distance, Loren took a moment to look him over, in all his messy-curled, stormy-eyed, agonized beauty. To watch Felix was to witness a tragedy unfold, and Loren tried to wrap his mind around him, fit him into a mold he understood. Myths he understood. Stories he made sense of. He cycled through the possibilities.

If not Achilles, raw from battle, Felix was the sun itself. The same sun Icarus flung himself at over and over. The same sun Patroclus died under, wearing the clothes of another man. Both sacrifices for nothing. Perhaps Loren was the gap in Achilles's armor, trying—failing—to protect Felix from himself, waiting for the arrow to strike home.

Perhaps his mistake had been attempting to mythologize Felix at all.

"That isn't what you said last night," Loren said, training his voice steady.

Felix let out a cruel snort. "Were you that lonely? That desperate?"

Loren had heard that before, from a mouth both similar and not. *Curls disappearing into a silver helm. Memories, seductive and deadly.* Marble splintered through his stomach. For a moment, a twist of the light, he saw the splay of mist-drawn wings.

"The helmet," Loren breathed. "Where is it?"

"Sold it."

"*Where is it?* Did you—did you put it on?"

Felix's face hardened. He took another step back, crossing fully into shadow. "You told me not to. I put it back. Like you wanted."

"This isn't what I wanted." Telltale stinging warned him: *Compose yourself before you embarrass us further.* But not from Ghost-Felix's scratching voice. It was an old scolding from Loren's father, still hounding him for being *too much*. "You were what—"

"Saying that will only make it hurt worse."

"You could stay. In Pompeii." Pleading now. Loren couldn't help it. "I can't—I can't lose you."

But Felix only shook his head. "You never had me. You saw what you wanted to see."

The accusation stung worse than any words before it. Loren swallowed it in a slow, choking slide, the fears he'd held all along deepening their roots in his gut. Who was Felix? Loren thought he knew a version of him, one removed from his nightmares. One who shared his bread, and listened, and chose Loren back.

Here in the alley, that Felix no longer existed. Maybe he never had. Maybe he'd been a ghost all along.

"Is this why you run from town to town?" Loren snapped before he could stop himself. "You trick, lie, steal, then leave before the fallout. Before you risk caring. Who are you, under all that? You accused me of being a liar. Maybe I am one, but at least I'm honest about what I want."

Felix's lip curled, and Loren hoped, however naively—however cruelly—that the words had hurt him. Hurt Felix the way Loren's heart had been breaking all morning.

Then Felix said, "How much longer will you chase what will never want you back? You never should have left your father's vineyard."

"What are you saying?" Loren said slowly, roots twisting fresh.

"I'm *saying* stop living in your dreams," said Felix, face hard. "I'm saying goodbye."

Desperation mounted, filling Loren's chest with wasps. He tried, "Come with—"

"Telling me what to do again?" Felix stepped once more, another foot of uncrossable distance, saying without speaking, *Here, and no farther.* "Go home, Loren."

Loren fled.

His feet worked mindlessly, carrying him swiftly through the maze of alleys and alcoves, streets and sidewalks. It was a primitive need, to put distance between you and that which hurts you.

Go home.

Pompeii was Loren's home. But as he moved, lungs tight, awareness dawned that Felix was right. Pompeii didn't want Loren either. He had spent so many years clinging to the city that all he'd done was bruise it. Everything he had ever loved bore the indents of his nails.

With that realization came another: He couldn't stay. It blazed through him in a grand sweep that no distance was vast enough to ease the wound Felix tore. The last rational part of his brain, long neglected, begged him to realize his senses were addled, he was acting on impulse, he was breaking a contract, he was throwing away a future.

He would deal with the consequences later. Right now, he needed to leave the city. He needed to let Pompeii breathe, away from the crush of his hand.

When Loren reached the gate again, he said nothing to Aurelia, who gave him a knowing look far beyond her years. At least she held her tongue. He hoisted himself onto a horse just as Livia concluded her business with the merchant and returned. She stopped short at his change of heart.

"Nice weather for a ride," Loren said, even as his ribs threatened to crack from the pressure of holding himself together.

Warm fingers squeezed his numb hand. "Egypt is even nicer. A fresh start."

He stared ahead at the road winding out, unable to meet her eyes. What a truly miserable oracle Loren had turned out to be. Waste of a gift. For the first time in his life, he had no idea what the future held. Nor did he want to know.

Time to take notes from Felix's strategy. Live in the moment, and that's it.

Loren pulled his hair forward and began to braid.

CHAPTER XXIII

FELIX

The finality of what Felix had done didn't crash down on him in the alley. Nor when he watched from the shadows as the horses rode out. Not even when he stepped into the street and stared at the road until his eyes burned from the sun.

It sank in when he turned, nerves raw, to find Darius leaning against a column, arms folded, sword still sheathed because there would be no fight. He wore the smug expression of an eavesdropper who just learned he won.

"If your intention was to leave an impression," Darius said, "I figure he won't forget you anytime soon."

"Good," said Felix evenly. "Means he won't return."

"Our agreement was that you could see your friends off. Make sure my master upheld his end of the bargain. If you're satisfied, he'll want you back now." Darius's hand came to rest on the pommel of his gladius.

No, there wouldn't be a fight. Felix had made himself valuable. Too much hinged on his life now. Darius couldn't kill him so long as Servius intended to make use of the helmet. But that didn't mean Felix had to stop ruining Darius's day.

He sneered, slipped past Darius, and sprinted into the thick of traffic, dragging out his final moments of freedom before he became Servius's tool for good.

Running felt good. Felt normal in a week of anything but. Felix wove between carts and stalls, slid between conversations, let himself melt into the buzz of a restless city. He dodged rubble, leaped over piles of bricks, ignored the shout of a shopkeeper when Felix disrupted his pile of swept plaster. He ran until his senses cleared, until he hopped onto the curb and looked back and no longer saw Darius's flushed purple fury chasing behind.

Any normalcy running brought was tainted with one simple fact: He had nowhere to go.

More than once he caught himself slipping into history, triggered by passing something he recognized, but these weren't frayed threads from boyhood. These memories were ropes, binding him to the city in knots he'd never unpick. Nonna's bakery, closed for repairs. The street leading to Livia's shop. The crossing stones where Felix had dragged—

He bit his tongue, tasted the salty wash of blood. *Don't dwell.* That was another of his rules. But he found it increasingly impossible to stay in the moment when the only future he'd ever wanted rode far from Pompeii.

Halfway up the Via Stabiana, he halted his trajectory toward the Vesuvius gate at the far end. Running to it would prove a waste of energy, and attempting escape would break his deal with Servius—the consequences of which would harm more than just Felix.

Static amplified, shaking the inside of his skull—the city's hum intensifying. He changed course, veering left, and followed the alleys to the only place he had left.

Elias was lounging like a cat on the brothel stoop. When Felix slowed his jog, Elias stretched languidly. Lazy eyes half-lidded, he acted impervious to the commotion gripping the rest of the city, though his shoulders carried an uncharacteristic slump.

"Welcome home, Fox," Elias said. "In all honesty, I didn't expect to see you again. Thought you and Loren skipped town yesterday."

The name prodded a bruise. "We did. Now I'm back."

"Clearly." Elias looked him over. "And he is . . ."

Impressive how only a few words into the conversation, Felix already regretted his choice to come here. Fatigue weighed on him. Spending the hours between dawn and the quake negotiating with Servius for scraps had worn him ragged. Sparring verbal rounds with tricky-talking Elias would shred what was left.

But he needed somewhere to collect himself. Darius would find him here soon enough, but first, Felix wanted proof that any of this had happened at all.

When he made to skirt past Elias, fingers gripped his ankle tight. "Where is he?"

Felix kicked free. "Why should I know?"

"Because," Elias said, rising until their faces were a fraction apart, and Felix smelled wine on his breath. "You took off with him yesterday. Now you return alone."

"He's weepy. I grew tired of listening."

"Liar."

"And he's easy. I got what I wanted."

"Liar." A hand landed on Felix's shoulder, nails digging into flesh. "If you wanted easy, you'd have come to me."

"You're expensive."

Elias snorted. "My rates are reasonable. Practically charity."

"I ditched him," Felix said. "Returned the helmet. It's better this way. For me, at least."

"I believe that." Elias scrutinized him, but not the way Loren tried to read Felix, as a text worthy of careful study. Elias read him like a piece of vulgar graffiti, looking for confirmation of what he already knew. After a moment, he relaxed his grip, and Felix beelined for the stairs. "Where are you going now?"

"Somewhere far from this miserable town," Felix called over his shoulder. "If you were smart, you would leave too."

On the second-floor landing, Loren's door stood slightly ajar. Felix hesitated before pushing it farther.

It swung to reveal chaos, like a storm had coursed through the newly broken shutters and turned everything over. Linens were stripped from the narrow bed, mattress slashed, straw scattered in tufts. The trunk of personal items had been broken into, contents strewn. Clothes torn, winter boots missing their soles. Shreds of papyrus, the scrap of *The Iliad*, stirred in the draft.

This hadn't been a search. This was a threat. This said *You cannot hide from us.*

Felix took a cautious step in, and something crunched under his sandal. Fragments of a jar. He picked up a shard stamped with a familiar emblem, the Lassius crest. Same as the signet ring he'd wrested off his finger and returned to—

Clay clattered back to the floor. Why had Felix come here? *Sentiment?* Had he thought he'd find something to cling to wherever Servius dragged him next?

Screw that. Felix kicked a pile of straw and it burst into a cloud. It didn't make him feel better. Emotion swelled in his chest, bitter, bleak grief. Standing in the room made his skin crawl. When he left, he slammed the crooked door.

Elias glowered from the bottom of the stairs. For a moment, Felix considered turning back, testing his luck with the drop from the window. It wasn't too far. He would survive. Probably.

"I forgot to mention," Elias started before Felix could escape, "some intimidating men dropped by yesterday. Wanted to speak to him."

"So I noticed. What did you tell them?"

Elias's lip curled. "That a private room costs extra."

"I imagine they didn't like that."

"Neither did the landlord when he shouted at me for spoiling potential business." He pulled the armhole of his baggy tunic to the side to show off an impressive purple splotch along his ribs. "Worth the bruise."

So this was what Darius had done after losing the chase in the vineyard. He stalked Loren's trail around town, bullied his friends, and destroyed everything he treasured.

"Before, when I said—" Felix swallowed hard. The hum pierced now, a spike through his skull. "I meant it when I told you to leave."

"And go where?"

"Anywhere."

"With you?"

Felix took his time descending the stairs. "You wouldn't like where I'm headed."

"If it's all the same then, I'll stay. Some of us have jobs. Another month, and I'll have saved enough to leave on my terms."

"Suit yourself." He tried not to shoulder-check Elias on his way to the door.

"It isn't too late, you know." Something in his tone made Felix hesitate. Glance back. Elias wasn't facing him, was still staring at the landing. He said nothing for so long that Felix wondered if he intended to speak at all. Then, "He taught me to read. And the little girl who follows him, what's her name?"

"Aurelia." It came out raspy.

"What I'm trying to say is, if you let him go, you'll never find another like him. So think about that, before you leave. It isn't too late."

It is too late, Felix didn't say, thinking of Loren's splintered expression in the alley, when Felix weaponized his own words at him. He thought of all he'd traded away in the hours before, agreeing to Servius's calculated terms. He thought of the helmet, and the cataclysmic visions, and the churning in his gut that confirmed—*It was far, far too late.*

Felix said nothing. Instead, he ran away, like he always did.

Once he left the brothel, he didn't bother keeping an eye out for Darius. He would catch Felix eventually. Still, Felix ran fruitlessly, dragging out the chase as long as possible. He almost pretended he was exploring a new city. Getting to know it from the inside out. Taking it in for the first and last time.

Especially so, in the case of Pompeii.

The Forum bustled with its late-morning crowd, those too stubborn—or oblivious—to have fled after the latest quake. Felix crossed to the center and stood still. Townsfolk parted around him, all with their lives and businesses and priorities. Repairs were already in progress, workers toiling in the high heat. Across the way, a shingle, shaken loose, separated from the roof of Apollo's temple and smashed on cobblestone. Commotion buried the sound of its shatter.

No one stopped to notice the ragged street boy watching. No one saw Felix at all.

A fight broke out at a shoemaker's stall, voices shouting and fists flying. Somewhere, a child cried. Another shingle broke free. The noises compounded, pushing each nerve in Felix's body. From the offices exited a gaggle of councilmen, bickering in their bright white togas. Taxes, games. One man insulted another, but these were proper gentlemen, and only the lower classes fought. The men laughed it off, then went their separate ways.

All these people had one thing in common. One thing Felix could never have—had never allowed himself to have. He swallowed thick.

A lifetime spent avoiding glances, and now, at the close of his path, he ached to be known. Just once. Felix kept himself alive by running, sure. But what was a life if no one would remember him when he'd gone?

The living, the dead, and Felix somewhere between.

The Temple of Apollo stood like an accusation. Felix never should have touched the helmet. If he'd taken his coins and cherries and run, he'd be far from here by now. If he hadn't crashed into Loren, uprooting his life, Felix wouldn't be frozen in the Forum while the world went on, while the earth below his feet continued to boil, with the blistering knowledge that nothing he did would ever—could ever—make a difference.

His senses crashed, suddenly too much to handle. Breathing felt like swallowing sand. Felix left, nearly bowling over Darius, who had finally caught up, panting. He lunged, but Felix dodged neatly.

Down the street. Across a block. Up crooked steps.

He paused, hand against the sun-warmed door of the Temple of Isis.

"This again?" Darius snapped, palms braced on his knees. "A priest's threats won't shield you now. Stop running, or I'll drag your boy back myself."

Fear gripped Felix, but he composed his face hard as bronze, adopted a tone of pure affront. "You would deny me a final visit to my temple?"

"My master knows what temple you belong to, and it isn't Isis."

"I'm not escaping."

"Forgive me for not trusting your word. You're a snake."

"I'm not half so scaly as your *master*," Felix sneered. "What are you, a dog heeling to its owner? He must have something good on you to keep you so loyal."

"Bait me with words all you want. You aren't half as clever as you think."

"I don't think I'm clever at all," Felix said. "What's half of nothing?"

Darius spat. "Go on. Pray. See which god helps."

Felix clenched his jaw and entered.

The courtyard was silent. But not the silence he and Loren shared two nights before, the comfortable quiet of sitting together. When Loren's hand curled in his. When he first kissed Felix, sloppy drunk and teeth-achingly sweet.

No. This was the quiet before the storm.

Felix took a deep breath and stepped from the portico. Blue smoke curled from the altar into open sky, where it diffused and vanished. Behind the stone block hunched a figure, his gnarled fingers gripping a smoldering bronze bowl. The rest of the courtyard was empty.

"I wondered when I might see you again," said the Priest of Isis at Felix's approach. His eyes, unlike last time, were clear and keen. "Though I am surprised you came willingly. I was under the impression you dislike temples."

"Not temples. But I have a history of bad experiences with priests." When the old man said nothing in his own defense, Felix continued, "Loren left the city."

The Priest passed a hand through the smoke, and it twisted into peculiar shapes: the soft outline of a galloping horse, the spread of a bird's wings, a fox disappearing in the underbrush. A week ago, Felix would have blamed the shapes on whatever alcohol he last drank. Now all his beliefs—the rules that kept him alive—lay dashed in the gutter.

"Left? Or was sent away?"

The Priest didn't say it as an accusation, but it hit as one all the same. It threw Felix back to the alley, the fear that spiked through him when he saw Loren bidding Aurelia and Livia goodbye. Felix had counted on Aurelia to convince Loren to leave with them. His plan hinged on it. But Felix was nothing if not adaptable. He switched tactics. He baited Loren to follow, then used everything he'd learned about him, admired in him: That Loren acted with his heart.

To get Loren to leave, Felix had to break that heart.

The Priest offered a smile kinder than Felix deserved. "Sit with me."

Reluctantly, Felix perched on a second stool. The still-healing gash on his arm twinged. "I hope you aren't about to take a knife to me again."

"The time for appeasing the gods is long past. The course is set, the dice have been thrown, if you will."

"Comforting to hear the gods gamble, too." Felix sniffed.

The Priest laughed. "They have vices, same as humans."

"Then why worship them?" Felix blurted, face flushing hot when the Priest raised a brow. "I only mean, it seems unfair to devote so much to them when . . ."

"When they give little in return? Ah, you've stumbled upon the crux of religion," he mused. "Tell me, how old were you when you lost your mother?"

"An infant. I never knew her."

"And your father?"

Felix tensed. "How did you know? That he's dead?"

"I can read it in the lines of your shoulders, son, that you have been alone a long time."

The familiar urge to bolt surged, spreading thin through his blood. Felix made to slip off the stool and—do what, he hadn't figured out—but the Priest held up a hand.

"I meant no offense. It can be a terribly good thing to share a burden, you know."

Felix's heart pounded, the need to flee driving his bones to move at any cost, but he remembered again—

He had nowhere left to run.

Instead, he hugged his midsection tight. "I was eleven. My father was a smuggler. A thief, a good one. But that time he wasn't quick enough. They sliced him to ribbons, right there in the alley. I watched.

Everyone watched. Nobody did a damn thing, not the people, not the gods. Not me."

"That's enough to make anyone lose their faith."

"I have had only myself since, and even that's—fragmented. Until I met Loren, and believed in him, and lost him. I wasted the morning running around the city, trying to be on my own again. Now I'm here, but no closer to understanding."

"Then perhaps what you need most *is* faith," the Priest said. "Not in the gods, but in your ability to let others see you. You might figure yourself out along the way."

Felix wanted that. He wanted like an ache, a muscle atrophied after years of disuse. Boys like him were not allowed to want. Wanting led him to take the helmet. Led him to Loren. Picked at memories long stripped away. Wanting begged for power. Demanded choice.

Felix wanted to want *more*.

Hot tears blurred his vision. He scrubbed a hand across his damp face with a laugh. "You're a terrible priest. Empathizing with a non-believer. Is that allowed?"

"It is not my job to judge you," said the Priest quietly. "Nor convert you. I only seek to help others find their path, wherever that might lead them. I wouldn't be so certain your path ends here." He waved through the blue smoke, and the hazy bird returned. "Where did you say Loren went?"

Felix drew in a ragged breath. "I sent him away. I said—horrible things—"

"You aren't the first to hurt someone to protect them."

The Priest met Felix's stunned stare evenly. The words sank in slowly, stirring the dregs of memories run dry. Felix learned that lesson long ago. Perhaps the final rule his father taught him, that wine-soaked day he killed Mercury's priest.

To protect Felix, before the rest of their lives fell apart.

"With any luck," Felix said, throat raw, "he'll reach Surrentum before midafternoon. He must never return to Pompeii."

"Good. Now, where do you go from here?"

"I have unfinished business. A debt to settle."

The Priest's brow crept higher. "We have an exit in the back if you want to try your luck."

That should have been tempting. But as Felix sat there, the inevitability of his circumstances hardening his stomach, he said, "This is where I need to be. I'm tired of running."

Before the Priest could speak, a low rumble rolled across the sky, thunder with no end. On the altar, the bowl chattered against stone.

"What—" Felix started.

Another great tremor rocked the ground. With a strangled cry, the Priest lurched, stool knocked unbalanced. Felix dove to catch him, slinging the old man's frail arm across his shoulders.

The maddening hum spiked in pitch.

Pain shot through Felix's skull, an arrow fired clean.

Pressure snapped.

A catastrophic boom ripped the air in two. Some great, ungodly beast had wriggled into the heart of the earth and torn it asunder. Felix's ears rang empty.

"The mountain," the Priest wheezed. "Look to the mountain."

Felix let the Priest go, then whipped around, darting to the door. Screams and shrieks echoed from beyond, muted by a dull, endless roar. He had no time to brace himself before he stumbled from the temple.

Hot air blasted him, a shock wave of scorching wind. On reflex, he shielded his face, then lowered his arm to squint through the sudden storm. Dust and detritus stirred by the gust scratched his eyes, but when he saw the source of the blast, the sting faded to the background.

The ground still trembled, but the world—its people—had stilled. All staring. All stunned.

Collective, silent horror.

Black tendrils like spilled ink twisted through the sky, curling and climbing up, up. The churning, deadly cloud roared and rose. The once-clear sky dimmed. The beast expanded. Ravenous. Hunting, like only the sun itself could satiate its hunger.

When the first flecks of ash began to fall, Felix almost thought it snow. October snow. He held out a palm, numb, truth not yet sinking in.

Then, all at once, it did.

Vesuvius had burst, and it was swallowing the world.

Felix had thoughts only for Loren, riding away from the city.

He tripped back inside, brain lagging. "Tell me he makes it. Don't— it can't—*please*."

Wordlessly, the Priest steadied himself on the altar, then twisted one hand into the fumes. Nothing at first.

Then it shifted. The bird, and a second shape closing in: a hawk, talons outstretched.

Felix had seen that hawk before, pinned to Servius's chest. Hot betrayal replaced cold fear, and he forgot all about the mountain. Clearly it was the lesser of the dangers facing Loren.

"I fear his fate is not so certain," the Priest said. "But from a source I can't parse."

Chest tight, Felix gasped. One breath. Another. His knees shook, even as the trembling earth faded to the background. He couldn't process. He couldn't understand the feelings rattling his bones.

"Go," the Priest ordered. "Do not worry about me."

Their eyes met, Felix searching for approval. Leaving felt wrong, but the Priest's watery eyes hardened with resolve. Felix backed away.

"This does not have to be your end." The Priest settled back on his stool. "Go."

Felix did. He ran for the exit as the sky darkened.

When the shock ebbed, chaos set in.

Felix wove through panicked, clutching crowds. People tripped over each other, stumbling for shelter or escape or for the sake of action at all. The ground still shivered, but Felix had grown used to running over unstable cobblestones.

Darius jolted from his stupor when Felix sprinted past him for the third time that afternoon, but it didn't matter. Not when he was running back into the snake's coil. Anger tinted Felix's vision red, blocking out sure signs that this, of all things, was the wrong course of action.

Servius didn't look up from his papers when Felix slammed into the study. Mercury's helmet glared from its spot on the desk.

"You lied." Felix jabbed a shaking finger. "You promised—*swore*—he had your protection. What did you do?"

Servius's eyes focused first on the finger, then briefly on Felix before casting back to his work, disinterested. With a lazy wave, he signaled Darius, panting at the doorway, to grab, but Felix slipped out of reach, fury making him light on his feet. He danced to the other side of the desk, fists clenched.

"I made no offer to protect them. I said your friends could pass to the nearest town with my blessing and my horses." Sighing, Servius leaned back, arms folded over his chest. "But you broke our deal first, so it was only fair to annul our bargain. I sent a rider after them."

Felix stared at the back of the senator's balding head. "Broke our deal?"

"Our deal," said Servius, "was agreed upon without the knowledge that your friend is the absent son of Lucius Lassius. Lying by omission, however convenient, is still a lie."

Shock stunned Felix to silence. Servius waved a bundle of parchment, and Felix snatched it. His eyes roved over the fresh ink, some contract he couldn't comprehend, until he reached the bottom.

Two signatures. Two wax seals: a loopy *F*, and a vine-cinched *L*.

"Julia Fortunata's estate was abandoned this morning after the quake. She left everything behind, including this transfer of property to one Lucius Lassius Lorenus. Stamped and sealed and in plain sight, she undeniably intended for me to find this. I'll admit to my confusion. News along the grapevine, pardon my wordplay, said Lassius's heir hasn't been seen in years." Servius paused to scrawl in his notes. "Of course, that's where Celsinus comes in."

Felix's focus wrenched from the contract. Surely he had misheard. Then his gaze settled on a small figure perched across the room, sitting so quietly that, lost in desperate rage, Felix hadn't spared the boy a glance.

Celsi met his shock with a pouty frown. "Don't look so surprised, thief."

"Celsinus has been useful," said Servius. "Not only did he fetch the contract, he confirmed Julia's new heir is indeed who he signed as."

"Everyone underestimates me." Celsi's pout became a defensive sneer. "But I'm cleverer than all of you. That ring he wore around his neck has the same mark as the bottles my father drinks. I'm the only one in the whole damn city who knew."

"Language," chastised Servius. "What would your father say?"

Celsi shifted, folding his skinny arms and settling into a deep sulk. A purple bruise bloomed across his forehead, half hidden beneath his mop of curls. "I saw Loren talking to you in the temple at the festival, and I know he's been poking around about the helmet for days. Not hard to piece together. So I thought Senator Servius should know the full truth."

Celsi was lucky Felix had enough dignity not to curse out a boy whose voice hadn't yet broken. Turning back to the contract, his mouth flattened. "Julia set Loren up. She knew you were after her, so she moved your target onto him. Once you killed Loren, Julia would reveal his real identity."

"That I'd eliminated the Lassius heir, thus sinking my political career—and sparing herself the work of taking me down." Servius scooted back his chair and stood, facing Felix with placating palms. "Yes. Clever woman. Oh, don't crumple that. I still need it."

He pried the parchment from Felix's curled fists. As he smoothed it out on the desk, Servius's mouth twitched in a bland smirk.

"Lorenus is now the heir to both the Lassius and Fortunatus estates, establishing him as the wealthiest man in the Campanian province, but I have the contract under his name. With this in hand, I could make him convince the council to pass the vote to increase Rome's share of taxes. Neat how this worked out."

"So you sent a rider to drag him back. Loren won't work with you. He—"

Servius tossed the contract to the side. Sheets burst in a scattered flurry. Felix jerked, stunned, as they fluttered to the ground. Celsi, instincts shaped by years of being around unstable councilmen, dropped to his knees, scrambling to shuffle the pages together.

"Frivolous," Servius said. "Julia's flaw has always been her capacity to overthink. I don't need an estate, nor do I need Pompeii's vote. Not now. I have the helmet. I have you."

Felix's hollow stomach flipped. He cast back to Servius's words the night they first met. *Collaborators. Cassius and Brutus of a new age.* All at once, he understood what Servius meant to use the helmet for—use the power he believed it granted Felix for. Revenge on Rome for exiling Servius. Revenge on the empire. The warnings Felix had spent days denying came back in a cold slide.

Dream-walker. Plane-crosser. Holder of restless souls.

Traverser between the living and the dead.

And what a power like that could do in Servius's hands.

Fighting back swelling panic, Felix forced his mind on what mattered. Not magic. Not memory.

"Then why bring Loren back at all?" he bit out. "If you don't need him, let him go."

Servius's smile widened. "You misunderstand. This isn't about Lorenus. This is a lesson for *you*. My instructions to Maxim are to dispose of them all. No loose ends."

"No loose ends," Felix repeated, numb.

"You said Loren wouldn't be hurt," Celsi piped up, shot with a trill of fear. "You promised."

Promises, promises. Felix snarled, vaulting to fling open the window shutters and reveal the darkening day, the black cloud chewing on the sun. "The world is *ending*."

"I have the helmet," Servius repeated. "I have you."

As if Felix had the ability to make this stop. Mouth dry, head spinning, he lurched forward, bracing on the desk chair. Teeth gritted, he choked out, "When did your rider leave?"

"Not long ago, so rest assured your boy has a healthy head start. Burdened by the shopgirl and her mother, though, it won't be long before he catches up. In fact"—Servius peered out the window—"if my timing is right, it should happen any moment now."

Felix made a break for it, a mad dash to grab the helmet and race for the door, but Servius issued another bored gesture. In a whirl of limbs and a blow to Felix's face, Darius put him on his knees, arms yanked back. The helmet rolled away. Gods, Felix was sick of this. Panting, he bared his teeth at Servius, who observed him like one might indulge an amusing pet.

"You lost," Servius said. "After all these years playing, the game ends here. Can I give you a bit of advice? Not that you need it, your life is very much mine."

"Piss off."

"Next time, don't tell the man holding the chips what you care about. That's where your father failed too." Servius squatted to twist his hand sharp in Felix's curls. "Here's another piece of wisdom I must teach you, same as I did your father—I am not one to fool."

"You know nothing about my father."

"Don't I, Felix? You're the spitting image of him, and I never forget a face." Uncurling his fingers from Felix's hair, Servius brushed a thumb over his cheekbone. "Did Julia neglect to mention why I was exiled from Rome? Your father and I ran in the same smuggling circle. He killed our priest, then double-crossed me. I handed down the orders to kill him. Only by my mercy were the guards called off before they caught you, too."

"Stop," Felix begged, because it was all he had. *"Stop."*

Servius straightened, brushing invisible dust from his tunic, as if Felix's mere proximity had soiled him. To Darius, he said, "He's useless struggling like this. Make him pliant so I can test my theory."

Darius obliged with far too much enthusiasm. He pried Felix's jaw open, and the bittersweet tang of poppy sap exploded across his tongue. It hit his system as a trickle, then all at once. Fingers wrapped around his throat, closing his airway. Felix scrabbled for purchase, fighting to stay awake, but the hands of sleep dragged him down, covering his skin and touching all over.

"That's enough." Servius's frown came as a blur. "I said pliant, Darius, not—"

Black swept Felix's senses, and the last thing he saw was Mercury's helmet, cast in the corner, a silver trophy for losing again.

CHAPTER XXIV
LOREN

"Do you hear that?" asked Aurelia, and only the abrupt silence that followed made Loren snap from his daze.

All the way out from Pompeii, she'd kept up a running chatter. First an analysis of the weather, which morphed into some fantastical romance of nymphs and wine and demigods, clearly invented as she told it, and—well, Loren filtered her out. Nothing personal. But he recognized his own strategy: talking to mask an uncomfortable silence.

Sometimes he saw too much of himself in her.

Now Aurelia stopped, head cocked, and Loren perked up, too.

"Hard to hear anything over your stories," Livia said, not unkindly.

"No, listen." Aurelia tugged the reins in Livia's hands. Their horses slowed to a halt on top of a hill, edged on one side by a steep ravine. The afternoon fell into a deep hush. Wind rustled leaves. Somewhere far off, a dove cooed.

"I don't hear anything," Loren said with a twinge of annoyance.

"Quiet!"

The pounding beat of racing hooves, quiet but growing. Loren turned in his saddle to squint down the road. A dark blur against the pale horizon, an indistinct figure approached.

Livia whistled. "They're in a hurry. What do we think it is? Urgent news?"

"Oh! A war declaration. A flood. A coup in the city." Aurelia nearly bounced.

Loren winced, thinking of Julia and Servius and poor Umbrius. *Anything but a coup.* "Perhaps we should get off the road."

Once their horses were situated in a pine's shade, he dismounted for a better look. That, and to escape Livia's suffocating concern. She hadn't said a word, but between the tender half glances and tilted mouth, her overwhelming motherly energy gave Loren a rash.

He wasn't being avoidant. He was safeguarding his gnawed heart.

The rider disappeared behind a rocky outcropping. Behind Loren came the sound of Aurelia riffling through supplies. She'd returned to blabbering about her nymph story.

Parting from them come morning would kill Loren all over again, though he hadn't yet determined where he'd go. Returning to Pompeii was the sensible choice, but he couldn't force the city to want him back. Fleeing across the sea would offer a fresh start, but one he didn't deserve. If he hadn't shirked his familial duties, tried to pave a path perpendicular to his father's plan, he wouldn't be nursing a hole in his stomach, raw from acid.

He ought to go home, where he belonged. Where his visions couldn't hurt anyone else. Loren deserved this. He'd flown too high, and now he suffered the burns.

Wooziness washed over him, an aftereffect of riding too long under the hot sun. He turned to ask Aurelia to toss a waterskin, but his vision blurred, slipped, and he saw—*a sword slinging through empty space.*

Hooves of a rearing horse overhead.

A determined brow beneath a helmet, and a familiar crest glinting.

Loren gasped awake, palms against the dirt. How long had he drifted?

"Aurelia, go!" he shouted.

The rider burst over the hill, sword glinting cold in the afternoon heat. Loren had no time to think, to scurry from the stampeding horse, before the blade swung. He rolled aside, gravel shredding his tunic.

Livia screamed. Feet crashed through the underbrush.

Let them get away. Please, gods, let them escape.

Ahead, the mercenary wheeled for another swing. Loren lay frozen in the road, terror clawing through his chest. The sword came down.

Something red and round hurtled through the air, striking the mercenary's helmet in a clean shot. Knocked askew, the sword's arc fell short. The horse panicked at the abrupt jerk. It reared back with an angry whinny, and the mercenary lost his grip on the saddle, hitting the ground hard. The thrown object tumbled to a stop by Loren's foot: an apple missing a solitary bite.

Foolish, brave, brilliant Aurelia.

Loren's senses kicked in. He rose, scrambling from the hooves of the riderless horse as it took off down the road. The mercenary pushed to his feet, flinging his helmet aside.

Maxim, Darius's companion from the vineyard.

Terror gripped Loren. He never expected to be followed this far from Pompeii, but in hindsight, the countryside had no witnesses. Only the quiet road, where bloodstained dirt would soon wash clean. Servius must have found out about the contract already. Guilt coursed through Loren. What had he done to Julia, left alone in their empty estate?

Maxim stalked nearer, wicked sword glinting. For every clumsy step Loren stumbled back, Maxim took two strides forward.

"I won't return to Pompeii," Loren tried. "You have my word. The contract—"

The blade slashed, curving where a heartbeat ago, Loren's stomach had been.

"Let my friends walk free, and I'll do any—"

Metal sung through air.

A blade appeared at Maxim's neck. "Don't you touch him."

Livia stepped around as Maxim stilled. Her approach had been so silent, Loren hadn't registered it until she stood right there, shoulders tense in wrath. She gripped her husband's gladius, hand lethally steady.

"You plan to stop me, woman?" Maxim said with a thread of mirth.

Wrong choice of words.

Livia sliced Maxim's forearm, and he hissed. His sword thudded to the ground. Deep purple blood sprayed from the cut. She edged the hilt of his fallen weapon with her foot, then kicked it in Loren's direction. It took a moment to recognize her command. Trembling, Loren picked it up.

Another moment, and he realized the ground was shaking, too.

The horses, tied under the pine tree, stirred. Aurelia, somewhere in the underbrush, shouted a warning. Beneath Loren's feet, the earth rattled, violent.

An aftershock, stemming from this morning.

Ghost-Felix's ragged voice: *This is far bigger than just you.*

Loren turned to face the direction they had come.

Vesuvius, proud and distant as an old stone sentry, shattered.

"Jupiter," Maxim muttered.

Every piece of the world apart from the mountain froze as a plume of debris rocketed skyward, a curled fist punching heaven. Tongues of red lightning forked through the cloud, muffled crackling like faraway thunder.

Watching the storm unfold from Vesuvius's maw, Loren felt both removed and excruciatingly near. He couldn't break away. A tear streaked down his cheek. He'd been there, barely a day prior. He'd stood on those same rocks, walked in the same crater, felt the sting of steam and burning gravel. Had knelt there, touched Ghost-Felix's face, and failed to make the right choice once again.

His first thought: the helmet. Without Loren to stop him, had Felix put it on? But as soon as it crossed his mind, he knew in his heart that was wrong. Felix had said he wouldn't. And despite his claims otherwise, Loren was far more a liar than Felix had ever been.

His second thought: He should have listened to the ghost.

Black wave. Copper streak. His mind raced to sift through what he thought, what he knew, and where those diverged. He filtered his catalogue of visions through this new lens, the death and ash and the ghost's tears. Vesuvius, present in all his dreams, the ghost's wordless warning. Had Ghost-Felix ever been as cruel as Loren accused? Or had he been another victim of Loren clinging to control, desperate to prove himself a hero?

In doing so, he'd doomed them all.

A force barreled into Loren from behind. Though disarmed and bloody and facing the world's end, Maxim wasn't out of the game yet. He tackled Loren, and together they tumbled off the steep hill.

Loren dropped the sword, arms flying to protect his face. Shards of rock sliced his flesh. Momentum propelled him in a tangle of grabbing hands and kicking feet, landscape and sky swirling sick, but Maxim refused to let go. They slammed to a stop at the bottom of a harsh ravine. A dull echo thudded in Loren's ears.

Maxim rolled Loren on his back, pinning him to the ground, knee digging into his stomach. He thrashed against the weight, but Maxim was built like a bull.

Hands closed around Loren's throat.

Panic swallowed his senses. In the back of his air-starved brain, Loren wondered if Clovia and Umbrius and Julia's father felt this same fear, an invisible strand connecting the four of them in death, if nothing in life did. Loren's vision bled black.

He couldn't breathe.

He did all he knew to do. He fell, and let impulse catch him.

VESUVIUS

With the last of his conscious strength, Loren curled limp fingers around a stone and dashed it across Maxim's temple. Pressure on his neck lifted. Air rushed into his starved body. Every inch of him hurt. Loren threw his weight into a roll, so Maxim, face oozing red, now lay below him. Maxim grunted and struggled, big hands grabbing, but Loren brought the stone down again.

And again.

Time blurred.

Maxim stilled.

Loren's throat closed off.

"Loren, love, that's enough." Gentle hands pulled him back, pried the stone from his numb grip. Livia had picked her way into the ravine.

"I killed him," Loren gasped. His cheeks were hot. Wet. A moment passed before he registered he was crying, chest heaving in painful sobs. Nothing felt real. Nothing felt like him.

"Let's get you cleaned up," Livia said, terribly soft.

Cleaned up? Loren looked down and fought back vomit at his own hands coated in bright blood. Impossible to tell how much was his and how much was Maxim's. He gagged, shivering, and emptied his stomach into the gravel.

When it was over, Livia coaxed him away, and they climbed to the road. Neither mentioned the body cooling below.

Up top, a streak of dark curls assailed Loren, arms wrapping tight around his middle. For a horrible moment, Loren flashed back to Maxim's lunge, but it was only Aurelia, seeking comfort. He had none to offer.

Livia drew her off. "Give him space."

Aurelia looked a wreck, but she seemed unhurt, and that eased something in Loren's chest. Maxim couldn't harm her, couldn't harm Livia. Still, Loren couldn't meet either of their eyes. He staggered to the horses, legs quaking. Shame slid sticky over his skin. When he'd driven

296

the stone home over and over, he hadn't spared a thought for Aurelia or Livia. He'd thought only of his own animal desire to breathe again. Whatever had overcome him had sprung from a source truly foul, and Loren feared he knew exactly which one.

When Felix told Loren he lived by his heart, he couldn't have known Loren's heart was spoiled. Poisoned. He was every inch a selfish creature, inside to out.

Loren's mare was still trembling, spooked from the attack and the quake, but he ran a soothing palm down her flank, and she settled. A fat waterskin hung from her saddlebag. Unstopping it, he poured it over his arms, scrubbing with his nails until the trickling water tinted pink, then, finally, clear. When he restrung the pouch, his eye caught on embossed leather tooled into the saddle, a seal he'd neglected to examine before.

Loren could return to Maxim's body, pluck the crest of Servius from the man's still chest, hold it to the saddle side by side, but he didn't need to. The swooping hawk was pressed into his memory, deeper than any embossing.

Soft footsteps crept behind him. Loren knew their owner without looking.

He trained his voice calm. "Who secured us these horses, Aurelia? Because they never belonged to Celsi."

No reply.

"What did Felix tell you?" Loren wiped a palm across his face, flinching when it came back smeared with more gore. Sudden desperation burst, and he rounded on her. "What did he trade away?"

Aurelia's stunned silence melted. "He found me at Pappa's grave this morning, said he had an errand to run, and he'd bring the horses after. H-he knew about your visions. Mine, too."

"He suspected something would happen." Even after Loren, brimming with arrogance, assured Felix in the grove that all would turn out all right. "His senses are that sharp. He offered you an escape. So long as—"

"You came with us." Her face crumpled.

Loren's mind reeled. Felix's cruelty in the alley struck less abrupt now, more calculated. *Go home* hadn't been one final nasty blow to Loren's ribs. It had been a lifesaving plea.

"Jupiter, Aurelia, why did you lie to me? To us?" Livia shook her daughter's shoulders, but Aurelia tore away.

"Because," she said, hiccupping through a choked sob, "if Loren goes, we'll never see him again. And I can't lose my brother."

Her words slid home, and Loren understood her in a way he hadn't before. These weren't the wailing cries of a little girl fixated on the worst-case scenario. They were the wailing cries of a girl who'd seen the outcome.

Loren braced against a tree, staring hard at the horizon. Underfoot, the ground shivered again. Far off, Vesuvius raged, a blight against the clear sky, Pompeii doomed in its shadow, with everyone still stuck there.

Felix, still stuck there.

Slowly, Loren turned back.

"I think you're right," he said quietly. "Our paths diverge here. This is the last time I'll see you. I won't make a promise I cannot keep."

"Don't go," Aurelia rasped. "I'm sorry for lying."

"Aurelia, I'm not angry. But if I can't save the city, I must go back for Felix."

That would have to be enough.

She dropped to the ground and hid her face.

Which left Livia. Livia, who had pulled a terrified Loren to her chest when he was fresh to the city. Livia, who treated him like her son by blood, kept him dressed, and never asked for payment. Who loved him, simply because she felt he was worthy of her love. Now she clutched the reins of his mare.

"I had a vision," Loren lied, "where I get him out. I'll get both of us to safety. Are you going to stop me?"

Livia's eyes watered, lips pursed tight, and Loren readied for a fight. But she shook her head. Taking a deep breath, she placed a hand over his pounding chest. "The Egyptians believed thoughts sprang from here. Now we know better; they come from the mind. But I think, sometimes, it's all right to follow what your heart tells you."

"Mamma." Loren's voice cracked.

She tugged him forward in an embrace that could've lasted forever. He sank into it.

"There are few things worth running to," she murmured. "Love is one."

When Livia pulled back, she curled Loren's fingers around the reins, then unhooked the saddlebags. He swung his leg over his mare's back and guided her to face the mess he'd left behind.

"Wait!" Aurelia shrieked. In a flurry of limbs, she scrambled from her huddle to dash to the second horse.

Alarm surged through him. "You can't come with me."

But Aurelia wasn't mounting. Instead, she fumbled with the saddle until a familiar sheath slid free. Then she fetched her father's gladius from where Livia dropped it after the attack. Aurelia shoved both into his stunned hands.

"Take this." When Loren shook his head, she bared her teeth. "Take it."

Loren looked to Livia. The sword was her last relic of her husband. Surely . . . but she only nodded. He fastened the sheath to his belt and slid the gladius home. It hung heavy, a weight he'd never carried.

Aurelia gripped his knee. With all the wisdom her twelve years afforded her, she said, "Fuck destiny."

Loren spurred his horse without waiting to hear Livia scold Aurelia for cursing. He trained his attention on the black cloud swelling from Vesuvius. He didn't look back.

As Loren urged his horse faster, hooves kicking swirls of dust, he wondered if Livia had read his latest lie on his face. *I had a vision.* What—no offense to his mare—horseshit. His dreams weren't so concrete, nor did his visions project so far out. Livia knew all that, and still she'd let him go.

Despite what Aurelia predicted, Loren swore if he survived today, he'd find them again, and he'd tell them the truth.

Suffocating black devoured the sky beyond, punctuated with orange flares. Ash fell thick as searing snow. Inhaling set Loren's lungs ablaze. Outside Pompeii's walls, refugees, faces terrorized and streaked with grime, huddled in the meager shelter of the tombs. Loren drove past the stragglers and burst into the burning city, dismounting at the gate. His mare was skittish and drained, and tying her beneath a roof was unfair, but Loren couldn't afford for her to bolt. Once he had Felix, they'd need a quick escape.

"I'll be back for you," he promised.

She didn't look convinced.

The Via Stabiana lay deserted. Hours had passed since the mountain exploded. By now, those who hadn't fled had retreated to the safety of their homes and shops to avoid debris and wait out the storm. Smoke billowed from buildings, fires catching from burning pebbles falling. Loren's sandals echoed as he dashed up the road, dodging abandoned carts and ducking below awnings sagging from accumulating ash. His gladius knocked against his hip.

If Felix was with Servius, Loren had no idea where to start looking. He should've demanded to know which house belonged to Servius days ago. Everything was clearer in retrospect. Loren skidded to a stop at the corner near the theater, next to the Temple of Isis, and paused, panting, to collect his thoughts.

"Loren?"

His heart skipped. A figure slumped on the temple's steps. Even with her short hair matted by sweat and ash, Camilia's scowl was recognizable anywhere.

Relief soared in Loren's chest, proof another soul was still alive within Pompeii's walls. He jogged down the walk to kneel before her. They reached out at the same time, and Camilia clutched his hands to her chest. Up close, she looked even more haggard, the kohl around her eyes smeared.

"Are you hurt?" Loren peered through the door. Only the altar bowl inhabited the courtyard now, sending smoke signals never to be received. "Where are the others?"

"Nobody has seen the Priest since this morning," Camilia said, fatigued. "Sera and Shani . . . I looked. I found—they're gone, Loren. Everyone is gone. Even the cats fled last night, like they knew what would happen. I've worked my ass off alone, pulling people from collapsed buildings and putting out fires. Where have you been?"

Off playing victim. That's what Loren would have said, if he were honest. A pebble struck his shoulder. He flinched.

"You can't stay here. You need to leave the city, go as far south as you can."

"There are dozens, hundreds more lives in the city, and you suggest I leave?" Beneath the grime, her cheeks flared angry red. "Gods, you never change."

"You've done all you can. Something worse is coming."

Camilia sneered. "Enough about your visions."

"I was right about this," Loren snapped.

They were locked in a fierce glaring match, Camilia steady but for the trembling of her mouth and the way she still clung to his hands. Loren allowed it. Slow understanding wriggled under his skin.

"You can't find Celsi," he guessed gently.

Instantly, she collapsed, hunching into grief. "I went by their house soon as I could. His father was dead, Loren, crushed by a wall while clutching a bottle. Celsi wasn't there. I don't know where he is. He tried to tell me something, you know, the afternoon of the festival. Something about you, always about you, and his father dragged him away. To punish him. Just for speaking to me." She wiped under her eyes. "He's the closest I have to a brother."

Loren had spent years in silent competition with a child for Camilia's regard, and only here at the end of the world did he realize how silly their rivalry had been. Sulfur filled Loren's lungs. "Camilia, there's nothing more you can do for Celsi. Please. You have to go."

Her nostrils flared. For a long moment, Loren braced for a strike.

Then she dissolved into silent sobs.

Slowly, he coaxed her up and guided her from the temple steps. Back at the street corner, he gave her wrist a careful squeeze, then detached fully. Words formed on his tongue.

But Camilia didn't need a goodbye. She looked incredulous. "You lecture me, but it's fine if you stay?"

"There's something I need to do."

"For who? Julia Fortunata? Priest Umbrius? Haven't you heard? He's dead. Or . . ." She sneered. "Don't tell me you're here for that ratty thief. I saw you two, you—"

"His name is Felix," Loren snapped, then shook his head when she only stared, dumbstruck. He stepped back. "Goodbye, Camilia."

"Stop," she said before he could dash. The word sounded like it cost her. "You should know something. The soldier who chased your thief came back last night. Wanted to know where you lived, what you did."

"What did you tell him?"

Her lip curled. "Piss off."

A laugh bubbled in Loren's throat. "Tell me you saw the direction he went."

"Better. I followed. If some bastard's sticking his nose in my friend's business, I have the right to know who he is." White-hot rock hit her bare arm, and she winced before rattling directions.

For the first time in hours, hope sparked. "If you were a man, I'd kiss you."

"If you were a woman, I might kiss you back." Camilia stepped from the sidewalk, giving him one last squint. "See you around."

They split, headed in opposite directions.

Loren's pulse raced faster than his feet could. He had failed the city. Failed the temple. Fell on his own blade trying to stop the disaster by drawing all the wrong conclusions. But he would find Felix or die trying, that much he knew. Until Loren could finally right his wrongs.

Felix's ruin wouldn't come from Loren's choices.

That was the gods-honest truth.

CHAPTER XXV
FELIX

Felix's dreams took him home.

In Rome, on the Aventine Hill, stood a temple. This was not unique. Rome had many temples, some small, some grand, and Mercury's temple was fashioned somewhere between. Grand, but not overt. A good place to raise a motherless boy, whose father was driven by a compulsive, ancient need to stay in motion.

Felix dreamed of his first taste of wine, the proper stuff, not the weak and watery swill the other children got. This was the wine grown-ups sipped after a good heist. Felix didn't know what they celebrated, and the wine tasted icky besides. Too bitter. Made him sleepy.

He dreamed, and his dreams were pressed by milky poppy sap.

Felix reasoned, beyond all doubt, that if Loren's face swam before him, surely he must have made it to Elysium. Odd. He couldn't remember being particularly heroic in life.

"Thank Isis," Loren said. His cheeks were ruddy, cinnamon eyes swollen. Had something made him cry? Felix would fight whatever had. Felix would... "Sit for me."

Everything hurt. Nothing hurt. "Is my da' here?"

"Your father?" Loren's brow scrunched. "Felix, where are you?"

But of course his da' wouldn't be in the blessed realm. Too much priest blood on his hands.

Where *was* Felix? Half in this world, half the other. Ghosts tugged the hem of Felix's tunic, dragging him, asking, begging—

He should lead them to their rest. He had a job to do.

If only he weren't so tired himself.

Felix's eyes drifted shut.

"No, no, stay with me, Felix, please—"

He ran barefoot through fields of blooming poppies, carnal and red, while the world bled out behind him.

Hands were on Felix's skin, and he was going to vomit.

"Get off," he slur-snarled. *"Get off."*

The touch retreated, leaving him cold in the dark.

"Felix," Loren said. "Please. I know you're tired, but you must wake."

Felix's stomach rolled. Spit and bile dribbled from the corner of his mouth, pooling on the tile. He gagged and shook and choked and shivered. If poppy sap tasted bitter going down, it was worse coming up.

"You'll suffocate on your own spit lying like that. I'm going to touch you, but only to move you upright." Hands returned, and Felix flinched, but they did as promised, navigating him to sit against a wall before pulling away. Scratchy rope bound his wrists.

Loren knelt before him, the worst thing Felix had seen.

"You can't be here," he croaked.

"Nice to see you, too," Loren said with a sniff, but his words lacked heat. "Tell me I smell or that my hair is ugly again, and I'll know you're awake for good."

Beneath bone-deep weariness came a selfish thrill of relief. Loren had defied impossible odds, survived, all to claim Felix from a room of relics as the city caved around them. He blinked rapidly. His fever left him sticky, coated in thin sweat with stomach acid dripping down his chin.

He wrinkled his nose. "Can't smell anything past my own vomit."

"No, keep your eyes open. I'm going to cut you free, all right?"

Loren drew a sword from his belt. Felix recoiled, drawing his elbows back far as he could with his bindings. "And take my hands off? Tools of the trade. I need them. Check my pocket for a knife."

"I wouldn't—" Loren sighed, but patted Felix's side. "Empty."

"Damn." Felix's breath came in shallow, slow pants. If he dipped into sleep, for only a moment . . . He dug his nails into his palms, the bite keeping him conscious. "I liked that one. Wood and iron. The little etching. Valuable. Could resell it."

"Keep talking." Loren stood and disappeared. "I'll find something. Gods, this room is creepy. So many strange items."

"He's a collector," Felix murmured. "This is where he keeps his collection. His things."

"About that." A clatter rose as Loren sorted through a box. "You did a bastard thing. I don't know what deal you made, but—"

"Two horses for the helmet."

"There's more to it than that."

"In exchange for me, then." Felix's eyes had shut again, a detail he wasn't aware of until rope snagged against his wrists. Loren had returned, clutching a rusty dagger.

"You thought you could spoil the place for me. Hurt me so I wouldn't come back."

"Seems I went to too much effort. Look around, the place spoiled itself."

"Don't joke." His pretty lips flattened. Felix had kissed that mouth, licked away the pinch that appeared when Loren was frustrated or overthinking. "You have all these defenses to keep yourself from being hurt or used, but once you dare let someone inside, you'd give anything to keep them safe. That isn't fair. Don't you see? To get inside your walls, I came to know you, too. Am I meant to be flattered you gave yourself up for me? How little you value your life?"

"Nothing to value." Felix's head lolled. "I'm no one's prize."

Fibers snapped as Loren sawed. "Sounds like you were plenty prizeworthy to Servius. Did your clever brain even attempt to escape?"

"No point."

"No—are you listening to yourself? Felix, the point is that I've never known you not to have a plan, and another plan on top of that. The point is that you gave up. Why?"

The floor rumbled, tiles chattering, jostling Felix's thoughts. He squeezed his eyes shut, trying to recall his reasoning for staying. Hours ago, he'd struggled to understand it himself, but here, lost in a haze of poppy sap and stirring memories, it felt the most obvious answer in the world.

"I'm done running," he said. "I have—something still to do. A task."

The dagger froze. "A task?"

"You told me we were meant to meet. I was meant to come here." Felix swallowed another bout of nausea. "Don't you still believe that?"

"You aren't making sense," Loren said, though his face paled like he'd seen a ghost.

"I always make sense. You're the one who—" Felix broke off in a cough as rope fell free. He felt delirious. Beyond himself. "You signed with Julia. *That* doesn't make sense."

"Don't change the subject. I can handle myself."

Felix stared at him as though for the first time. "How did you find me?"

"Now you ask." Loren threw his hands, exasperated. "It's a long story, but we don't have much time. Can you stand?"

A grin twitched. "You're just like those Greek tragedies you love."

"What, dashingly heroic?"

"Melodramatic."

"You've lost it." Loren hauled Felix to his feet, slinging his arm across his shoulder.

The world lurched as they stumbled to the door. In the dark hallway, away from the suffocating hum of Servius's charged and cursed collection, Felix picked up the sound of stones pattering the roof. The air reeked of all things burning, a rankling, sickly-sweet stench. Loren limped Felix along, searching for a way out.

"Wait," Felix gasped, lungs scorched. "The helmet. Not leaving without it."

"Forget the helmet. Do you think I care if you put it back now? Mercury won't mind."

"Mercury will mind." Felix dug in his heels. "I can't lose it. I—I need it. My task. It's mine."

A candle flickered to life against the dark.

"Did you ever stop," said a voice, "to consider why that is?"

Felix nearly vomited again.

Orange flame carved shadows on the planes of Servius's face, reflecting in his colorless eyes. He stood centered beneath an arch, hands gloved and boots laced.

This was the man who killed Felix's father, who made Felix watch, and who hadn't felt a scrap of remorse for either life he ended that day.

"The hunt around town, the stunt you pulled at the vineyard, none of that was necessary," said Servius. "Had you brought me the helmet on day one, I could have told you the truth. Why you alone can handle it. I tried to show you, remember?"

"Move." Loren drew his gladius. "You won't be warned again."

Servius smiled. "Commendable for you to come for him, Master Lassius. Or is it Master Fortunatus? You managed to join two wealthy houses without the complication of marriage. Congratulations."

Loren detached from Felix's side and lunged. His sword flashed in the meager light, aimed true at Servius's chest. A clang echoed down the hallway as a second blade emerged and intercepted Loren's. Time slowed to a trickle, a bead of sap oozing. Darius swapped spots with Servius in a blink, met Loren's next swing easily, kept meeting them as Loren hacked over and over.

"Stop," Felix mumbled. He slumped against the wall, knees threatening to give.

When Loren's fire was lit, by the gods, he was unstoppable. But he was equally an impulsive fool who thought nothing through. One mistimed thrust, and Darius had him pinned, sword to his neck. Loren's gladius hit the tile, and Servius stooped to collect it.

"That was amusing." Servius slid the blade into his belt. "I've been waiting ages for you to wake, Felix, after Darius overestimated the dose. Come, let's discuss this in the courtyard."

"I can't hold them both," Darius said, annoyed.

"You won't need to. Keep a hand on Master Lassius, and Felix won't risk a thing." Servius studied Felix, still half collapsed. "Why don't you fetch the helmet from the study? Nothing funny now, or your boy will bleed out before he hits the floor."

Moving outside, the lighting didn't change. Flashes of glowing amber and red burst in the pitch-dark sky, crackling with thunder. Falling rock pinched and sizzled against flesh. Fetid air scorched Felix's lungs. The courtyard was smaller than Julia's garden, but no less lavish, with lush grass and a long reflecting pool. If not for the dusting of ash and the fact that the world had reached its end, it wouldn't be a bad place for a picnic.

Maybe Loren's diagnosis was right: Felix was losing it.

Servius had erected a makeshift altar near the pool, topped with a burning bowl. Overkill, in Felix's estimation; enough was on fire without Servius's help.

"Untraditional not to do this in a temple, but it appears the Priest of Jupiter is indisposed," Servius said. "No matter. By virtue of my political position, I'm qualified to act in Umbrius's place."

Priests, politicians, poppy sap. The same story cropping up throughout Felix's life.

Darius gripped Loren's neck, sword trained at his throat. He wriggled, face screwed, but Darius forced Loren to his knees. A pained hiss. The noise shot to Felix's fingertips with how badly he ached to reach.

A child darted from the surrounding portico, dropping by Loren's side.

"You're alive," Celsi said breathlessly, relieved in a way he had no right to be.

Loren's pain shifted to puzzlement. "What are you doing here?"

"Betraying you," Felix said. "Choose better friends."

Loren recoiled. Felix half expected him to lash out, curse or plead or question, but all Loren said to Celsi was, "Camilia is looking for you."

Celsi scrunched himself up and crawled to crouch beside Servius, who petted the top of the boy's curls the way one comforts a dog. Felix's skin crawled. The ridges of Mercury's helmet dug into his flesh, he clutched it so tight. The pain grounded him. Kept him from drifting.

Servius beckoned Felix to the altar. When he didn't budge, Darius flexed his hand. Almost imperceptibly, Loren winced.

Felix stumbled forward. "Stop hurting him."

"Control your reactions," Servius said. "You allow yourself to be taken advantage of."

"Maybe others should learn not to take advantage."

Sizzling rock landed inches from Felix's foot. It fumed in the dirt before spluttering out. Another followed, and this one caught, snaring the grass in growing flame.

"Is that what your father taught you?" Servius smiled. "He was terribly young when you were born. An accident, too much to drink at a festival. He almost quit our guild to raise you, but he was our best sneak, so light on his feet. Magical, how he moved. I convinced him to leave you at the temple with the priest while he worked. A solution that favored everyone."

Felix spat. His strength still bogged down by the drug, it didn't fly far, landing in the altar bowl to crackle in the ashes.

"I can't imagine the gods will appreciate that," said Servius.

"If the gods gave a damn, none of this would be happening," Felix said, needing it to be true.

Seconds of silence passed. An act. An effect. "You truly don't remember who he was. Who your father's own father was. The reason you carry no family name."

"He was human." The word fell from Felix's lips without a thought to how strange a defense it sounded. Of course his father was human.

In his grip, the helmet hummed.

"He was the last of a dying breed. The blood that flowed from his veins—the same that fills yours—was priceless. I'd spent years tracking rumors, hoping to find something like him, and he was in my lap in Rome all along. Of course, had I known then, I would've kept him. Kept you."

"Shut up." Felix bared his teeth against another roll of the earth.

"That first night, you didn't recognize me," Servius continued. "But I understand what happened. Your father didn't want you to remember, so he locked the memories away. Heroes' minds were made to be manipulated. How else would the gods ensure their children did their bidding? Wouldn't grow too powerful to be controlled? Think of Hercules. Achilles. What they did when left to their own will."

"Felix," said Loren, "what's he saying?"

Darius kicked Loren in the ribs, and he stifled a gasp. Flames spread through the grass, a hungry, licking animal. If this didn't end soon, they would all be made ash.

Servius's hypnotic gaze locked Felix in place, and he only stared, breathless, waiting.

"Your father," said Servius, "was the son of Mercury. What does that make you?"

Numb.

Felix was numb and cold and silent. The impossible revelation floated on the surface of his understanding, refusing to sink in, his mind's final attempt at keeping him safe.

"Imagine the possibilities, Felix. Who you could be if you were made whole again, with your power intact. Put the helmet on. Find out."

"No, Felix, you can't—" Another kick, and Loren doubled over.

Felix's vision tinted red, but he was shutting down. Words refused to come. Memories tugged at his ankles, his hands, demanding he follow. He couldn't. *He couldn't.* He hated the way Servius said it, like his identity hinged on the past he lacked instead of who he'd grown to be. That what lay behind the gate in his mind defined him, and nothing else.

"You wield power I've searched for my entire life," Servius urged. "We could sweep the empire in days, reclaim what was stolen from us. You would make us legendary. Put it on."

He was Felix. Just Felix. Why couldn't that be enough?

Felix stared at Mercury's helmet, its silver wings and empty eyes, the promises and threats stored in its hollow crown, *Plane-crosser. Dream-walker. Traverser between the living and the dead.* Power waiting to be used.

Abruptly, his question shifted, transformed, glass catching colors under new light, and the helmet echoed with a sharp jolt. He was nobody. He was a pickpocket.

He was just Felix.

But what if that meant something more?

Servius waited, then sighed. He looked to Darius. "Start with his hair."

Loren thrashed as Darius wrenched him forward by the braid. Horror flooded Felix, rooting his bones in stasis. At Servius's feet, Celsi made an aborted attempt to intervene, but a hand on his shoulder stilled him. Darius forced Loren's head into the flames. His hair caught. A wrecked cry tore from his throat, a sound that would ricochet in Felix's mind until the day he died.

Adrenaline surged, and Felix hurled the helmet into a sea of white-dusted grass. Servius's brows shot up, the most emotion he'd ever displayed. Then Felix upended the smoldering altar bowl in Servius's face. A coward's trick, but cowards outlived heroes for a reason. Engulfed by the close cloud of stinging embers, Servius coughed and lashed out. Felix dove for Loren, but a hand dragged him backward across the altar by the neck of his tunic. Stone scraped his skin.

Felix grappled and twisted. He would've liked to think he was the craftier of the two, but the drug still clung like sap to his senses. He gripped Servius's clothes, seeking leverage. Weight jostled in his pocket, his favorite knife reclaimed on the same trip to the study to fetch the helmet. If he could only work his hand down—

"I'll show you if I must." One hand clutching Felix's throat, Servius peeled the glove off his other with his teeth. "I didn't think you would need this much convincing."

Shock rocked through Felix at the sight of Servius's hand, bare at last, bleached white and covered in thick scar tissue. Utterly ruined, damaged past hope of healing. The helmet had done that to Servius. The same silver that welcomed Felix's touch. If the helmet's power did that, what else could it do? What else—

"Impolite to stare," Servius snarled. He cupped Felix's jaw.

—could *Felix* do?

Skin met skin, and Felix fell backward through time.

CHAPTER XXVI
LOREN

When Felix had said Loren ran toward fire, surely he hadn't meant a funeral pyre.

Darius's grip was unrelenting, even as fire licked his hands. Loren twisted, a final effort to protect his face. Not that it mattered. Flames crept up his tunic, his neck, snared his braid. Soon his whole body would burn.

His eyes stung, the only sensation he could parse. The fire's roar swallowed the rest. He thrashed, clawing Darius. Blistering heat ate and ate. Smoke choked him. Tears dried as fast as they formed. Loren had fled all the way to Pompeii, and he still couldn't breathe. He may as well have died beneath Maxim's fist.

The memory inspired fresh conviction, and Loren kicked. His sandal slapped leather. With a quiet grunt, Darius's hold loosened.

Freedom. Loren squirmed free and rolled away from the blaze, patting his braid, his tunic, his flesh. Fiber came away in ashen clumps. The hair on his arms had singed to cinders. Every inch of him smarted. Gasping, he rose to his knees and squinted at the scene.

Something had shifted while Loren was in the fire, a change in energy, but he couldn't put a finger on what, only that a low hum now eclipsed the distant thundering of the mountain. Celsi had vanished, hopefully fled somewhere far away. Ash and embers obscured Felix and Servius at the altar, and bronze glinted in the grass—it seemed Loren wasn't the only one capable of weaponizing a bowl. The two were locked in a grapple across the podium, Servius clutching the sides of Felix's face.

Felix, it appeared, was losing.

Pushing to his feet, Loren took a single wobbly step. His respite didn't last. Darius, recovered from the blow, reengaged. His sword had vanished in the dark sea of rubble, but he had his body. He lunged. Loren sidestepped the grab and used the momentum to swing himself onto Darius's back, winding his arms around Darius's thick neck and tightening. Brutal, but efficient. And Loren learned it from Darius himself.

For a moment, Darius scrabbled. Then his whole body went lax. Loren slipped free. No sooner had he let go than a big hand gripped his ankle and tugged. He fell. Hard.

A feint, Ghost-Felix muttered in the back of Loren's head. *So easily tricked.*

"Shut up," Loren growled.

Darius pinned Loren, forearm to chest. "Didn't say anything."

"Wasn't talking to you." He wriggled. "But if you want a conversation, should we discuss the state of your balls?"

"My—" Darius cut off with a groan as Loren's knee jabbed up. Another thrust, and he backed off.

Loren tumbled free, panting, and scrambled for the flash of iron he'd seen while prone. Not his sword, but it would do. He trained the blade at Darius's chest. "I don't want to kill you the way I did Maxim. So don't move."

Darius stilled. "Maxim is dead?"

"Don't. Move."

Then Loren sprinted for Felix, his only pillar standing in a world turned to rubble.

Or not standing. Felix sagged in the grass, eyes shut, face cradled in Servius's bare palms. Blood trickled from Felix's nose, down his chin, dark droplets on his tunic front. Ice-cold fury washed through Loren's veins. He raised his sword for the final slash.

"Put that down," Servius said, never breaking from Felix. "Don't come closer."

"He doesn't like to be touched." Loren panted.

"No, I imagine he doesn't." The words were a low hiss, ruthless as snake venom and twice as deadly. "For all his razor-sharp posturing, he's a soft thing when helpless."

A thumb brushed the crest of Felix's cheekbone. Nausea curled in Loren's stomach. He had cupped the ghost's face like that, only yesterday. "I'll give you one second to release him."

"He told me he didn't believe in magic. Funny, when I can feel the threads in his mind, the way he slips about unseen. Sharp senses. Uncommon luck. Light on his feet, swift as an arrow. And so easy for others to weave those threads anew. It's how his father made him forget." Servius met Loren's eyes. "Forget his pain, at the expense of also forgetting his power. How cruel to deny him the truth."

Sweat made Loren's grip on his sword slip. Servius's words dripped with accusation—like he somehow knew the ghost had already told Loren all this on the peak of Vesuvius, and Loren had failed to listen. In doing so, he'd denied Felix the truth, too.

"That's the give and take of magic. The more you have, the more others want to wield it to their advantage." Servius's stroking thumb stilled. "Ah. Here are the memories, muted for so long. Should I release them? See what he does once he remembers who he is?"

Don't let him, Ghost-Felix begged, deep in Loren's mind. *He will twist what he releases. Only the helmet holds no agenda.*

Loren swallowed bile. "One."

He swung. Marred by trembling hands, the blow merely grazed Servius's shoulder, but he let go with a hiss. Felix's lashes fluttered as he came back.

"I see Julia turned you arrogant as she is." Servius hauled himself up with a sneer. Blood oozed from his wound. "Not a shock, the way you sniveled for her at the games."

"What did you do to her?"

Surprise flickered before a smirk twisted Servius's mouth. "We didn't touch her. She left you as carrion for the vultures."

That must be a lie. Surely Julia wouldn't—she'd said—

Loren slashed again, snarling when Servius dodged neatly, taking another step back.

"All for nothing. Because with Felix in my power, I won't need her damned estate to pass legislation. The helmet is but a conduit. *He's* the untapped vessel. Power over the space between life and death, can't you imagine? He will make the emperor's *ghost* beg before we're through with Rome."

Life and death and the space in between. Loren stilled. Revelations crashed through his mind of all the clues he'd missed. Felix's sensitivity to Clovia's murder. The ghost's warning that a haze of death hovered over Pompeii, a burden only Felix could shoulder. Felix's incoherent mumbling about his *task*.

Mercury had called Felix—his blood—to the city not to destroy it.

To tend to its dead. Take them to their rest.

Loren shivered against a sudden chill. "Felix isn't cruel. He wouldn't use his power for that."

Servius barked a laugh. "Wouldn't he? After all he's endured?"

A flash of copper hair disappearing into swirling silver.

Years of stagnant anger pouring free.

"You don't care about him," Loren said. "You would use him as a weapon."

"I'm a person," Felix said from behind, wounded voice a quiet punch. When Loren turned, Felix was hunched over the helmet, hugging it tight. He seemed so small in the dark. "Not a vessel. Not a weapon."

317

VESUVIUS

Loren's heart skipped. "I didn't mean—"

"Put the helmet on," said Servius. "Prove us wrong. Finish this now."

For a moment, a shattering, pulsing flash, Loren saw the end.

Not the end of the world, though that was imminent, but the end of Felix. *His* Felix, the one Loren had grown to know and treasure and need in only a handful of days. The Felix who listened and laughed, sharp as a blade, and spoke with cutting precision, wounding with words as often as he spun sweet sentences. Who followed Loren up a mountain.

Unravel. Remake. Hollow boy.

But Felix only snarled. "Make me."

"Darius," Servius said politely. "Help him reconsider."

Darius, pride aching as much as his balls must, glowered from where he lurked. "He's the only one who can touch that helmet."

"That isn't what I asked."

Servius and Darius locked eyes. Something passed between them, and Darius drew to his full height. Loren adjusted his grip on the sword and prepared to throw himself in front of Felix.

Darius said, "No."

Servius wet his lips. Venom dripped. "No?"

"I've done your bidding for years. Anything you asked." Darius fiddled with his badge, same as the one decaying on Maxim in the ravine. "But this is too much. That *thing*—look at what it did to your hands."

"I stalled your legion from executing you. That's a blood debt."

"One I've paid many times over. Same as Maxim."

Servius sneered again. "Once a defector, always a defector."

"He was my friend." Darius winced. "I won't go the same way he did. You'll tear down the world to get what you what. Then what will you have left?"

With a final shake of his head, he dropped his badge in the grass and strode for the exit.

318

"I suppose," Servius said, "I'll do it myself."

He struck like a viper, Loren's stolen gladius in hand. Loren hadn't seen Servius draw it from his belt. Pain erupted down his thigh, a clean slash for a heartbeat, but as he watched, two paces removed from his body, the gash darkened, and out poured a river of sticky wine.

Loren swayed. Crumpled.

The sword he'd taken from Darius was pried from his grip.

A mutter in his ear. "Staunch that."

And Felix charged Servius.

Loren's head spun. Felix wanted him to stop the bleeding, put pressure on the bleeding, *stop the bleeding*. One problem—Loren was locked. Disconnected. There was so much blood. So much, fresh and smelling tangy as iron. He touched the wound, shuddering when his fingers came back stained purple as crushed grapes.

"Would this help?"

Celsi had crouched at Loren's side. He offered a torn piece of scarlet cloth, a shade Aurelia always begged to weave with but was too expensive for Livia to afford. Loren could gift the cloth to her at the shop—later—

There was no later. There was now, and that was all. He snatched the cloth, and Celsi flinched. Loren twisted the fabric tight as he could around the gash.

"There's this, too." Shakily, Celsi presented a folded document and shoved it into Loren's bloody hand. "Senator Servius threw it out, but you should have it."

There wasn't time for this. Loren nearly tossed the papers away—nothing mattered with the world raining hellfire—but Celsi's eyes were intense enough that Loren stuffed them into his pocket.

"Father caught me talking to Camilia," Celsi confessed in a rush, gripping Loren's elbow. His lower lip trembled. "He's had me locked away since. This morning, I escaped, and I know Servius despises Julia, and I was angry. At you. So I told Servius anything he wanted to know about your family."

Metal clanged deeper in the courtyard. *There wasn't time.*

"Celsi, you've done enough damage," Loren said. "I don't care why you told my secret, or how you found out. I want you to get as far from me as possible, and I don't want to see you again."

"But—"

"Go." Loren grimaced as he shook free. "Run. Take the market road. Be fast, and you might catch Camilia."

Be fast, and you might survive.

The air had thickened the way it did before a thunderstorm broke. A heaviness. Tension in the atmosphere, pressing against leaves and bones and all other living things—the hum Felix had complained about for days.

Whatever Vesuvius had left was about to be unleashed.

Loren didn't stick around to see if Celsi followed orders. He took an aching step forward, foot sliding in blood pooled in his sandal. Another. He nearly tripped over the altar bowl, hidden in the grass.

Felix and Servius danced along the lip of the reflecting pool, coated in a dangerous layer of floating ash. The subtle slosh of jostling debris gave it away, but Felix, despite his keener senses, might not realize where he stepped until he fell. Mercury's helmet, abandoned near the altar, watched the scene through empty eyes.

In the heat of a fight, Felix glowed. This wasn't his style of survival, Loren knew that, knew he preferred to flee before the storm hit, hide like a fox in its den. But now, pushed to the brink, Felix fell into a natural rhythm, a lyre plucked by deft fingers, a field-fire leaving nothing but charred land.

He was incredible.

Servius was better.

Most politicians got their start with illustrious military careers, and he was no exception. While Felix's hold on his gladius was confident, it was fundamentally awkward, and Servius had been honed beyond hope of mistake. He never faltered.

"I know how to inspire reaction," Servius spat, blades striking in a burst of white sparks. "Another lesson, since you clearly don't learn."

"You aren't my damned teacher." Felix swept for Servius's neck. Blocked.

Loren caught the mistake first.

Felix shifted back, adjusting his footing, too close to the water's edge. Not a fall, but the time it took to correct cost him the fight. Fear seared across Felix's face.

He stumbled.

Servius saw his opening.

Loren clutched the altar bowl.

Both swung in the same moment.

Bronze crashed against the side of Servius's face, an echo of the blow Loren had dealt Maxim—dealt Felix, even, that first morning in the temple. The gladius faltered from Servius's grasp on its downward arc. Felix darted back, but not before the blade nicked his cheek. The sword fell into rubble.

Servius tottered. Loren's aim landed true, but weakened by blood loss and reeling with panic, the blow hadn't been strong enough to catapult Servius into unconsciousness. Servius's lips pulled back like an animal's, but enough was enough.

Loren brought the bowl down again. For good measure, he threw his weight into a shove. Overbalanced, Servius toppled back, landing in the water with an ash-muffled splash, and sank out of sight.

He did not resurface.

"Is he . . . ?" Loren croaked, throat raw.

"Yes," breathed Felix.

"But—"

"He's dead." Felix swallowed. "I—I sense it."

Loren had killed another man. This time, he was too empty to cry.

Felix stared like he'd never stared before. Red smeared his cheek, copper curls sticking to his forehead. But his gaze was focused, poppy sap finally drained from his system. Even bloodied and wrecked, Loren had never set his eyes on a better sight.

He wanted to reach, to hold and be held, but the words from the alley still played on a loop. *I hate when you touch me I hate when you touch me I hate—*

"We have to leave." Sour grit coated his teeth. "We don't have much time."

"Loren," said Felix, "you killed him."

"I'd do it again."

"I never—I never wanted you to kill anyone. Not for me."

That sensitivity toward death again. Loren's scattered thoughts rearranged at a breakneck pace. Dozens of questions grew and died on his tongue.

"Well, good news. I'm selfish." Loren picked his way over to sheathe Livia's gladius. Adrenaline made him sound braver than he was. "Pretend I did it for myself if it eases your conscience."

Above, the sky churned, noxious grays blending in a heavy swirl. Ready to collapse. Soon. *Black wave. Copper streak.*

Dust coated the helmet, and Felix rubbed it clean. What once gleamed silver was now tarnished. Decayed, if metal could rot.

Loren shuddered at the change. "You should leave it here."

Silently, Felix shook his head, but he offered his empty hand. Feelings clashed in Loren's chest, but need won over dignity. He needed this. Needed to know Felix was still corporeal, wasn't yet a ghost. Loren wound their fingers together.

They ran, hand in hand, into the smothering dark.

CHAPTER XXVII

FELIX

Since he was a little boy, Felix had admired hands.

The measure of their strength. Their variety, some old and some new. Wrinkled or smooth. Frail or rugged. Their capacity for cruelty or kindness, sometimes by the same set of hands in moments back-to-back. Hands told a story that didn't depend on the words Felix couldn't read.

He'd loved his da's hands most. Just the right size for holding his own. Quick as lightning striking, Da' could make anything vanish then reappear before the eye blinked. Never callused or clumsy because, as he often reminded Felix, a fumble for a thief was as good as a death sentence. And he never fumbled, so neither did Felix.

But his father never predicted Felix's clever fingers would one day get him into this much trouble.

He raced down the ruined Via Stabiana, dragging Loren along. Loren's hand slid with sweat where Felix clutched it with a desperation he'd never known. It threatened to slip free. He tightened his grip into an impossible vise. Gods help him, he wouldn't lose Loren now, not the only thing he'd found worth holding on to.

The only *good* thing. Felix also held something far more damning.

Mercury's helmet had hummed to his touch in Servius's courtyard, but now it vibrated, charged with sparking, furious power. Loren had been right, it ought to have been left behind. But it belonged to Felix. In a world that had given him nothing of his own, not his body, not his memories, the helmet responded to him alone. He would carry it to world's end.

Energy crackled. Memories rose to trip him, scenes triggered by Servius's searching thumb. *Twin snakes curling up his father's arm, forked tongues darting. Bells laughing bright. A festival day.* Felix wrestled the flood down, fighting to stay present. He didn't—*sleight of hand, a hundred coins in little pockets, and he pulled them out in a scatter and the others clapped and his da's eyes crinkled and*—

Felix willed his feet faster, feathery flames licking his heels.

Burning rock sprayed from above, rain of hellfire. Sticky smoke wrapped around him, thick and hot on his skin. The cries of those still trapped shredded Felix's soul.

The market street stretched forever, a road with no terminus. If he squinted through the haze, he could barely make out the gate in the distance.

Too far.

Felix didn't need visions to know that Pompeii was about to be swallowed alive. It had reached its end. The last gasp. The final page. Death suffocated the city, agitated, wordless pleas only he could hear. He recognized the ghosts begging for rest, a familiar hum he could never put from his mind. Incorporeal hands grabbed his ankles, his clothes, willing him to reach back.

Felix wanted to. He wanted to slip a coin in every mouth, coax death to its long sleep.

He wanted more time.

"Felix, I can't," Loren wheezed, the grind of his lagging pace slowing them both.

"You have to." Felix clenched his teeth against clouds of stinging ash. He kept moving. Moving was all he was good at. Running from his problems. Never facing them head-on.

Head-on meant danger, and Felix had never been brave.

"My leg—"

"—won't matter if you die." His lungs tightened, bursting with poisoned air. Ash burned inside to out. Every movement tore his muscles past what he could tolerate.

Lantern light glinted off Mercury's winged feet in the temple. Felix waited alone, legs dangling off the altar block. Lately all he knew was alone. He missed watching his father's magic tricks, hearing his ghost stories. He missed the time before cups of sticky wine were pressed into his small hand by the priest. He missed when being here didn't leave him with a hurt he couldn't name.

Smoke bit the corners of Felix's eyes. A fiery boulder hit an awning to the right and it shattered. Flaming fragments of wood and rock exploded outward. Felix ducked to avoid a blow from a piece sailing past. On his left, a building shuddered and collapsed in a plume of dust.

Loren twisted his wrist. Terror seized Felix, and he dug his nails in, a last-ditch effort.

"Let me go." Loren's other hand clawed. "I won't make it, let me—"

Felix snarled, the least human he'd ever felt. It ripped through his chest, splitting him in two angry pieces. He said no words. He had none. His brain ceased thinking in language, only noise and sound and chaos. Primal. Horrifying, but he let the ferality rock through him, the only defense he had.

Loren let out a muffled sob and stopped resisting, and Felix's eyes burned and blistered as he dragged him along, useless as a doll.

Laughter surrounded him, until the laughter stopped, replaced by quiet poppy. Little Felix had no words, then, either. Not beneath the priest's wandering, hurtful hands. Not when the stark temple chilled Felix's skin, bare before the hollow, impassive stare of Mercury's statue.

Watching, and doing nothing.

Felix bit his tongue and learned what silence meant.

The horse was a surprise.

It announced itself with a terrified whinny, hooves stomping on cobblestones. Some monstrous owner had cruelly tied it to a stake beneath a roof to burn with the rest of the city. Felix darted for it. He could do it. He could save all three of them: himself, Loren, this unlucky bastard of a horse.

At least, that was Felix's plan.

And it fell to shit so gracefully.

Felix scrambled to untie the reins. It wasn't until he reached back that he realized Loren wasn't there.

The world stopped.

Felix turned.

Loren had his palms against the ground.

Another of his visions, striking at a bad time as always. That, Felix could have handled. He could've slung Loren's semiconscious body over the horse and ridden far and free. Loren would come around miles from this wretched place. They'd be together. They would heal.

But the truth came ugly when Felix dropped to Loren's side. Because he wasn't drifting, lost somewhere in the urgent future. He was wide-eyed. Shivering.

"Go!" he shouted, shoving Felix away. "Forget me, I can't—"

Felix dropped the helmet. It chattered against stone, an angry thing. He gripped Loren under the arms, tried dragging him, but Loren gave a sharp gasp.

The truth came uglier.

His ankle was crooked, bent in a way that made Felix's own bones ache. Loren must have slipped in the blood pooled in his sandal.

Yesterday, Felix had teased Loren about this, on the road to Vesuvius.

If you twist an ankle, I'm not carrying you back.

This was more than a twist.

"Let's get you up now," Felix muttered.

"Just leave me," Loren begged. Tears streaked through soot, clean tracks on dirty cheeks.

"I can lift you."

"You can't. It's over. I did this. I did this to you. It's my fault. It's over."

"Don't say that." Hours ago, when sky still existed beyond storm, Felix had thought the same, that his road had ended. It seemed fine to think then, but hearing Loren say it stung, vinegar over a fresh cut. "Never say that."

Loren shook his head, frantic. "I met *you* on the mountain. A ghost of you who held your memories, and he told me everything, that if you put the helmet on—but I stopped you. I lied. We were supposed to do this together. I thought—protecting you—"

He broke off in a coughing fit. Felix shut his eyes briefly, letting the truth sink in. He already knew Loren was keeping the answers he'd learned secret, but the confirmation ached. Felix needed to force this down, separate himself from his emotions as he'd done so many times before, his hurt and anger.

Later, he promised himself.

For once—if they survived this—Felix would let himself feel it all.

"Felix," Loren whispered. He cupped Felix's face, and Felix's heart thudded a dull rhythm, beating bruises into his chest. "I'm sorry."

The storm broke.

Felix saw it first in flashes, then in waves.

With any weather event, there's a moment between the break and the fall, when, suspended in time, the world below waits for the blow. The first patter of rain. The first knock of hail or gust of wind. Felix always liked that period of anticipation, knowing what would happen before it hit home; he could sense the change in the air. He'd tip his chin to the sky and wait to feel cool, clean droplets.

This wasn't the same.

What started as a distant rumble crashed into an earsplitting roar, no beginning and no end. Clouds of ash convulsed above. The thread of the moment wound tighter. Tighter still.

Then the sky, held by Atlas's quaking shoulders, fell.

A black curtain dropped, rolling across the horizon, churning and boiling in a great endless wave. It swept forward to seek and devour, never to be sated. Thousands of crawling hands. Reaching.

Toward them.

"Don't look," Felix breathed, even as he kept his eyes trained forward.

Loren's lips were cracked. Felix wanted to press against them still. Press against all of Loren. Their last moments before the darkness hit, tangled together, limb to limb, body to body. Not a terrible way to go.

But Felix was divorced from his flesh, soul torn in two. One half was numb, incapable of thinking past Loren's harsh breath and hot skin. The other half knew what needed to be done.

The helmet is but a conduit. Felix is the untapped vessel.

He curled a hand around the helmet. This choice still belonged to him.

Loren's eyes went impossibly wider. "Felix, no, don't—"

Felix held the helmet out. "Mercury, help me."

Then he slammed it over Loren's head.

His hands had never fumbled. Not once. He suspected there'd be a cost to this stunt. He only hoped he'd live long enough to see it through.

In the instant before the wave crashed, Felix was sure he'd misjudged. Misinterpreted what Servius had said, misunderstood what he'd already known himself—that Felix himself—not the helmet—was the true power. And after all, if this was his helmet by birthright, he'd use it as he saw fit.

Felix couldn't help the city. But he'd burn himself up to save Loren.

At first, nothing.

Then the helmet was down, and Loren's mouth opened in a silent scream, and the metal against Felix's palms lit like a gods-damned sacrificial fire. He bared his teeth through the sear, bracing the helmet as it shook and sang and came to life.

Power shot through his body, a crystal strike. Light brimmed in his chest. Power he'd never known, power that was his alone, power he'd—he could—he could—

Felix could tear the world apart, and he had half a mind to.

But he stared at Loren's face, familiar and dear, seized in agony and framed by silver wings. Felix felt how Loren's soul feathered, detached, fell into a plane no one living could cross. The ghost of fingers brushed the pads of Felix's. A farewell, slipping soft away.

All this power, but Loren was still going to die.

Felix's entire life, he'd run. From bad turns of luck, from those who dared get too close. From belief and from himself. Choosing flight was his long exercise in ensuring no one hurt him again. Choosing flight was all Felix *could* choose in a life that had made him a pawn. Every lesson he'd ever learned had been at the hands of fear.

Until now. Until Loren.

This last lesson was from love.

"Not you," Felix whispered. He reached into the murky space between life and death. He grabbed Loren's hand. And he let the power go in one charged rush.

Thunder rolled.

His vision washed black.

A splitting white sting.

Clarity engulfed him, followed by—

Pain like nothing else.

"You're glowing," Loren breathed before his eyes rolled back into his head.

Felix trembled.

He was certain he could see his father now.

This time when Felix ran, there was no field of poppies. His bloody feet beat against barren land. Scorched earth, rancid and bitter and black.

CHAPTER XXVIII
LOREN

All was white in the aftermath.

Loren came back to himself in pieces: a phantom touch along his shoulder blades. Gravel in his knees, tacky blood drying down his leg, suffocating dust thick on his skin. Silence, and the acrid stench of seared flesh.

He opened his eyes to a dead city.

Ash still flurried like tufts of poplar seed, drifting slow and settling in mounds on the empty street. Loren knew this street. Via Stabiana, the city's pulsing artery. Four days ago, Nonna slipped him a date roll here. Honey coated his tongue, a sour sense-memory.

"We have to go," a scratchy voice said. "Please."

Hands dragged him upright. Pain radiated from his foot, and—oh. Yes. His ankle had snapped. The thought occurred that perhaps he shouldn't put weight on it, but then again, it was a little late for that. It was a little late for anything.

Loren moved forward in a drunk daze, though he could have sworn he was sober before.

Before.

"Be still. I'll lift you. That's it."

Then, unexpectedly, he was on a horse. And Felix—*Felix*—slid on behind him. Arms wrapped around Loren's waist, and Felix smelled like burning skin, and the world slid backward.

They galloped hard and fast from Pompeii.

Loren didn't look back. He didn't look forward, either.

Hours blurred, and their pace didn't slow. Time passed jagged. The ground trembled. Vesuvius billowed. At the crest of a hill, Loren choked on bile as another black surge swept the valley. All cruel, all cold. What he had witnessed in his dreams was child's play next to this reality. The smell of it, taste of it, that he inhaled remnants of a life he'd played a hand in ruining. An ungodly disconnect.

Grief hit not in rolling waves, but individual doses, stinging like poison-tipped arrows. But grief was no good when accompanied by equal measures of guilt. Loren had no right to mourn the dead. Not when he should be numbered among them.

They shouldn't have survived. Loren shouldn't have survived.

His heart thumped slow and methodic, his body convincing itself it still lived. *Blood still flows here*, it announced. *We beat, we breathe, we bleed.* He wished he could tune out the reminder.

On the far side of the hills south of Pompeii, where the wake of destruction was reduced to a sprinkling of ash, it all became too much. He shivered, slumped forward against the horse's neck, and prayed to slip into fever and not resurface at all.

Clumsy stars greeted him when next he woke, and he wondered who had paid his passage to the Underworld.

Had Felix pressed a coin into Loren's mouth, over his eyes? Anointed his body, then let him burn? Or had Felix held his hand, escorted him to Pluto personally? Fitting, given how Felix flitted between this world and the other, stepped between planes with wings at his ankles, half of himself made ghost.

But Loren recognized these stars, even at night through thin candlelight. He spent a winter painting that ceiling, smearing purple as the backdrop, then attacking with imprecise white points and a cupped moon. If he squinted through the fog crowding his brain, he almost remembered the constellations, and that tipped him over the edge.

He vomited nothing onto his childhood bedsheets.

He needed air. He needed to see sky beyond ceiling, proof that anything still existed past this room. That Vesuvius hadn't devoured the world, that he wasn't trapped in a nightmare, condemned deep in Tartarus for the hurt he'd caused.

Loren fell out of bed in a graceless heap. Plastered bandages knocked against tile where his ankle had been set. Wrapped. It hurt like a bastard, and the stitched wound on his thigh burned as he hauled himself upright. His mind tilted precariously until he realized, no, that was his body at a slant, seconds from toppling again. Leaning between his old writing easel and a trunk was the sheathed sword of Aurelia's father. Livia's last gift.

He hoped she wouldn't mind him using it as a walking stick.

His lungs tightened, light sparking at the corners of his vision, as he hobbled from his room. He dragged his useless leg down the empty, low-lit hall, and burst out a side door that opened onto the Lassius estate.

If this was a nightmare, it was the cruelest yet. But the scents were too vivid—remnants of grapes from the harvest decaying in the vineyard to the back, manure from the stables nearby, autumn pome-granates and pears from the orchard across. In none of his dreams had Loren felt so vibrantly *here*, and he hated it. He hated that his bones had led him right back into the cage he thought he'd flown.

VESUVIUS

Gasping, Loren made for the trees and the water trough he knew to be within. Distantly, he registered footsteps, a voice, a familiar presence nearing, but he couldn't focus. He needed proof, to see—to see—

At the water's edge, he collapsed. Unsheathed the sword. His faint reflection, distorted by water, snarled at him.

"What are you doing?"

Loren raised the sword to his neck.

On the downward stoke, Felix caught his wrist and halted the blade's trajectory. Loren grappled to regain control, but Felix was stronger. The sword clattered into the trough. When Loren lunged for it, water soaking the nightclothes he'd been changed into, Felix kicked the hilt, and it disappeared into a perfectly manicured bush.

"Fuck, Felix, I was only cutting my hair." Cursing was cathartic. Really damned soothing. If only Lucius Lassius could hear him. "Please."

"Use this." Felix handed him a pocketknife. The wood-and-iron one that he kept losing and that kept coming back. A sore Loren couldn't be rid of.

Bunching what remained of his braid, Loren sawed. Locks of burnt hair fell away and floated, lifeless. With that, his final shield crumbled. The act stripped him bare, left him with nothing more to hide behind. When he spoke to others now, he would have no choice but to be honest.

"It looks good." Felix sounded hoarse. Too much smoke.

Loren didn't trust himself to respond. A face he didn't recognize stared from the water, a boy with hair shorn in an ugly, chin-length bob, and who existed worlds away from where he knelt.

"Elias," Loren whispered, name a quiet prayer. "Camilia. Nonna."

"What?"

"The Priest. Sera. Shani. Castor and Pollux."

"Counting the dead won't help."

"Celsi. Julia." Loren's voice cracked. *"Julia."*

334

"Screw Julia."

"Don't say that."

Felix let out a single, incredulous laugh. "Are you defending her? Still? She used you. Once you were her heir, the target moved from her back to yours."

Loren shut his eyes tight against his reflection. Acid rose in his throat. Damned if he didn't know that. Damned that he'd been so foolish, had, in one stylus stroke, lived up to every accusation of ignorance and impulsivity his father ever leveled at him. Julia gave Loren hope of change, then snatched it away, and he was too empty to care.

"There at the end, she became desperate. Servius was closing in. After Umbrius . . ." Felix ran his fingers through tangled curls. "What did she say to win you back over? And leaving the contract where she knew he would look the instant she fled town—all of it was a setup. What she didn't predict is that you left too."

"That you sent me away."

Felix swallowed. "To save your life."

Dragging his gaze up, Loren stared at Felix in the dark. He looked ragged, paper-thin, and an instant from collapse. Yet, somehow, still unfairly golden.

Loren wanted to sob because he knew, *he knew* Felix was holding himself together at his own expense. Felix had fought to keep control for hours—days—so he could play his part perfectly, get Loren to safety. He'd wrestled back his own grief to give Loren space for his.

All Loren felt was a sharp hook of anger. Not at Felix. At his own ugly, rotting heart.

"You brought me here," Loren croaked. He stuck the dagger point-down in the dirt. "You brought me here, you saved me, and I want to hate you for it."

"You can. I would understand. I couldn't think where else to go."

"Stop it. Stop being so damned good. I can't stand to hear it."

"I know it hurts."

"How? How would you know anything about what I feel right now? Pompeii was my home. You've never had—" Loren broke off, but the damage was done. Felix's face hardened.

"A home? No. But you still have this one, and that's more than me." He tore from Loren's side. Footsteps crunched away, then came the sound of metal clanking as he resumed whatever task Loren had interrupted.

Ankle screaming, he followed the noise deeper into the orchard. Felix knelt at the base of a pomegranate shrub, back to Loren, hands sunk in the earth. Digging for something, but Loren couldn't fathom what.

"Felix, I didn't mean that."

For a long while, Felix was quiet. When he spoke, his words were tight and angry and carefully controlled. "The closest I had was Mercury's temple in Rome, where my father left me for long weeks while running errands for Servius. Until he learned what the priest was doing to me. How the priest dosed me with wine and poppy sap and—sorry, should I spare you the details?" Felix bit when Loren made a pained noise. "He assaulted me, Loren. Let me say it. No one else ever has."

Sickness hit Loren in such a sudden wave that he flinched. "I'm—listening."

"My father thought I couldn't handle my own past. He"—Felix wrenched a rock from the ground, hurled it over his shoulder, where it hit the trough with a hollow clang—"locked it away. But I never forgot the effects, reactions I couldn't explain, hurts I couldn't name. My father just stole my words to understand them."

"I'm listening," Loren repeated, because it was all he could say.

"The block isn't gone now, but whatever Servius did to my mind—I could feel him prodding around. Trying to show me . . ." Felix took a shaky breath, fists curled against his thighs. "Some scenes slipped through, and I don't know how to hold them. The rest stay gone."

Crickets chirped. Loren ached to reach out. Instead, he kept his distance and watched. Eventually, Felix returned to his task, clawing the earth. Tarnished silver glinted dully, half concealed in the shadow of a nearby garden statue.

On a hunch, Loren lifted Mercury's helmet, now halved, cracked down the bridge of the nose. When the lightning struck, it struck home. The metal was cold and empty. Whatever power it once held had dissipated, burned in Felix's last stand against Vesuvius. He traced the edge of a wing, remembering how the ghost begged him to not let Servius be the one to release the memories. That Servius had an agenda. That only the helmet could be neutral.

"You're burying it," Loren said quietly. "Oh, Felix. You shouldn't."

"You think I want this connection to Mercury? That he, what, led me to the helmet somehow, dangled a chance at remembering, because he felt sorry for what his priest did to me? It's shitty. This"—Felix bared his teeth and nodded to the split helmet—"is shit."

"That isn't why you were called to Pompeii, and you know it. You said it yourself. You were drawn there for a task. Mercury wanted—"

"I don't care," Felix spat. "If Mercury wanted me to believe in him, he wouldn't have let his priest hurt me in his own temple. I don't give a damn if the gods are real, or if I'm Mercury's descendent. If the point of my life is to do his bidding, I don't want it."

"It wasn't by his bidding that you saved me. You channeled your own divinity. You made that choice. Not Mercury."

The scorched imprint of where two hands had held the helmet down framed the eyes. Loren would recognize their shape and size anywhere, in life or death, light or dark. Those hands had pulled him back to the living when he should have been made ash.

Setting aside the fractured metal, Loren reached into the ground and grasped Felix's wrists. Felix attempted to pull free, but Loren held tight, coaxing Felix's fingers to unfurl, revealing his palms. Blazed white. Blistered skin. A fresh throb beat through Loren's dead heart.

"You're hurting yourself doing this."

"Funny," Felix said flatly. "I can't feel a thing."

Fistful by fistful, he cleared out the grave, and he didn't speak again.

Loren sat apart, worse than useless, as a chill crept over the night. He was no medical expert, but his little training confirmed what neither he nor Felix needed to say out loud: Felix's clever hands were wasted. If he were lucky, he might regain sensitivity in his fingers. Might. But they would forever be clumsy.

For a thief, a fumble was a death sentence.

At last, Felix lowered the helmet into the hole. So much for Rome's great gift to Pompeii. Once the earth swallowed the helmet, he hauled a boulder over it to prevent anyone from digging it up again. Then he scrubbed his poor hands in the trough, and that was that.

What a pair they made. Loren with his messed-up leg, and Felix with his messed-up hands. Felix the psychopomp, Loren the boy who should have been left dead.

"You should go inside," Felix said when it was done, not looking over. "You need to rest."

"Will you come with me?" Loren hardly dared ask it.

Jaw tight, Felix shook his head. "Go inside."

"Felix—"

"*Please*. What Servius said, what my father did, what you knew but didn't tell me . . ." His voice cracked. He wrapped his arms around his midsection, keeping himself together by force. "We can speak once you've healed, I promise that. If you care for me at all, you'll let me have this space."

Loren couldn't deny him that. The best he could ever offer anyone was his absence. He had never bettered a situation by making himself *more* present. He collected the sword and hobbled halfway back to the estate. A lantern had flicked on in the servants' quarters. His escape would be noticed soon, and if he didn't return, Loren would be forced to find out if he was worth his parents getting out of bed for.

Still, he lingered just beyond the orchard, waiting for what would never come. His thigh burned. His ankle throbbed. His chest was carved empty. He stared at the sky, cluttered with real stars. Precise stars. A waxing moon teased the night, but for once, her return brought no comfort. Whatever rebirth meant to Isis, Loren didn't want it.

Not now that he knew how it felt.

A measure away but still so achingly close, Loren caught the soft sound of Felix's ragged breathing and knew he, too, watched the sky through the canopy of evenly spaced trees. But he said nothing. No approach came. Part of Loren was glad for it.

Two boys, each alone in the desperate dark.

A chasm of uncrossable distance.

CHAPTER XXIX

FELIX

Lucius Lassius's chief mistake was making himself such a satisfying target to steal from.

When Felix had stolen his expensive reserve wine a month ago, he had already disliked the man on principle for making oversweet wine, but they had never met. Now that Felix had given the estate three days of his life, dislike morphed into loathing. Lassius had hardly spared a glance for Felix, but Felix picked out enough details by watching—how the man stalked his own halls, nose shoved in a letter, expecting those in his path to move first. He reeked of careless entitlement and excused it as business.

Three days in, he hadn't visited his son since the night Felix dragged Loren home.

This time last week, Felix would have brushed these details off as unimportant, but he'd since learned that distracting details were often the most vital. And he began to plan.

Late on his final afternoon at the estate, Felix picked the lock on the study door and pushed it open, ready to put that plan in motion.

Lucius Lassius glanced up, irritation creasing his brow. "I could have sworn I latched that."

"I hoped for a word," Felix said. "Is this a bad time? Loren told me you're adept at handling contracts."

Loren, of course, had said no such thing, and in fact had said nothing at all since the orchard. But the mention of him served its purpose in stroking Lassius's ego.

"So you thought to barge in." The scroll occupying Lassius's attention sprung back to a coil. "I lost a significant swath of land this week. Half of Campania is wiped out. My contracts in Herculaneum and Pompeii are forfeit. I haven't the time for this. I'll entertain you only as payment for bringing Lorenus back. Speak quickly."

Felix's eyes fell onto a folded, dirty sheaf of parchment on the corner of the desk. Target identified. He wet his lips, averting his gaze before it grew obvious. Servants had recovered those papers while undressing a delirious Loren the evening they arrived, pulled from his pocket, and Felix recognized them—though the last time he saw them they were scattered on the floor of Servius's office, Celsi scrambling to shuffle the sheets together.

How Loren came to have them, Felix didn't know, but irritation twinged at seeing the contract here, clearly untouched by Lassius even days later. Any decent father, upon receiving his child bloodied and unconscious after years of separation, would show the slightest bit of interest in the circumstances that put his son in such a state.

Subtly, Felix edged toward the stack. "Generous of you, sir."

"I'm capable of detecting sarcasm," Lassius said. "What did you give your name as?"

"Felix."

"Family name?"

Felix nearly admitted he had none. Then an idea struck him. He wouldn't be able to read the contract on his own to learn exactly what it promised its heir. But maybe he didn't need to. Not when the man before him would be all too willing to boast how much more he knew than Felix.

"Fortunatus," said Felix. "That's what I came to ask after. My father died years ago, and my, ah, older sister, well . . . I lost her in the same explosion that destroyed your northern vineyard."

"Julius Fortunatus, you say? I did business with him years ago, though I don't recall hearing the news of his passing. Nor him having a son."

"Adopted," Felix lied. "I'm afraid I have nowhere to go. Our estate was lost too."

He tried to make himself sound pitiful to sell the story—not that he thought Lassius the type to let pity sway him. True to Felix's prediction, Lassius didn't soften so much as his mouth turned smug, a man who couldn't resist letting others know when they had erred.

"Estates," Lassius corrected, drawing out the plural. "And unless the fire spread much farther than reported, I assume you haven't lost all of them."

"I don't understand." Felix plastered on the sweetest smile he could muster.

The magic phrase.

Lassius's mouth curled, twice as smug, and turned to face the window. "Take your pick of Julius's holiday homes. Amalfi, Rome. For Jupiter's sake, the old man might have expanded to Londinium for all I know, if anything remains of it after the disaster that conquest turned out to be. Go there."

"Rome," Felix said, and with Lassius's back still turned, he swiped the contract, slipping it neatly into his pocket. "Rome could be a nice change."

A dove sang against the dying day when Felix found Loren standing lonely in the courtyard.

Felix once thought Loren would look nice carved in marble, but such stillness now unsettled him. Loren was made for big gestures, sunny smiles, stumbling over his own feet in his perpetual quest to prove a point. Stone didn't become him, but stone greeted Felix as he crossed the grass.

"The moon is out." Loren frowned at the sky.

"It does that," Felix agreed.

"During daylight. I've always found that odd. I can't place what it means, an omen of good or bad fortune." The frown deepened, and Felix hated it. "Perhaps it means nothing at all."

Felix studied him. They hadn't spoken for days, though he'd kept watch at a distance. Listened at doors. Tracked Loren drifting lifeless through the property, ankle plastered, leaning heavily on a cane. Saw how he reached to grab a braid that no longer existed.

"You should be resting," Felix said. "I'll help you back to bed."

Finally, a reaction. Loren bristled, glaring hot. "I'm capable on my own."

He stalked toward the portico, cane indenting the grass, and Felix followed him into the halls, empty but for a pair of servants who averted their eyes and scurried off.

"You came to say goodbye," Loren said, voice laced tight. "I can see it on your face."

Felix wanted to protest that he hadn't yet looked at his face, but the argument would be in vain. Loren was too good at reading him. "I want to. I should."

"Will you?"

"Depends."

Loren paused a moment before pushing into his room. There he tossed his cane onto the window seat and followed, curling in the corner, arms folded. "You remind me of Elias."

"You have a type," Felix said.

"He's dead," Loren said flatly. "So I hope not. And no. He also made a pastime of telling me what I didn't want to hear. Even when I needed to hear it."

Felix kept his distance, idling by the door, scanning the room for the dozenth time, like it might reveal fresh secrets. But the drapes on the walls stayed up, masking Loren's childhood frescoes—so what if he'd peeked? The bed stood neatly made. Gauzy curtains drifted in the breeze of the open shutters, the same draft stirring Loren's chin-length hair.

So much had been lost. So much sacrificed for nothing. Anger at it all ate Felix alive, but when he spoke, he found he could barely muster more than a hard edge.

"You warned me," Felix said at last. "You stopped me from putting the helmet on. Then you stopped Servius from undoing the mind block. You believed if my memories were triggered, it would make me dangerous."

Time dragged as Loren stared hard at his knees, clothed in the white fall of his sleeping tunic. "I met a version of you. The ghost who haunted my dreams, who showed me Pompeii's fate. He held your memories."

"Held my power, you mean."

"Felix. It was more than that. He held—" Loren swallowed. "He held your anger, and he wanted you to take a turn carrying it. When you told me you feared what lay behind the wall of your memory, I couldn't be the one to give him back to you."

"Jupiter." Felix scrubbed a ruined hand across his weary face, then sank onto the edge of the bed when his knees weakened. "You were right about one thing. You're selfish. But in a way that's so selfless it's hard to recognize."

"I drew the wrong conclusion. I thought you and the helmet would wreck the city, when truly you were drawn to Pompeii to help its dead find rest afterward. That the mountain ... I was wrong. All I wanted was to protect you from what the ghost knew."

"But don't you see? That's exactly it. You go into every situation thinking you can solve it, because you were never taught that some problems can't be both solved and survived. Your whole life, you've never had to question your selfishness. From the day we met, you didn't hesitate to take from me too, same as everyone else. My body. My memories. My choice." Felix's voice trembled. He flexed his scarred fingers, testing his reflexes. "Is your opinion of my character so low? That if I remembered, I'd use that power to take in turn? I'm not defined by what Mercury's priest did to me."

"I believe you," Loren whispered. "Felix, I'm sorry."

"I know you are, and that's the worst part. I know you thought you were protecting me, same as my father when he took my memories away. But it should have been *my* decision. Mine, to learn my heritage on my terms." Desperation burned his throat. He slid from the bed and knelt beside the window seat, grabbing Loren's hand and pressing it to his cheek. Felix closed his eyes. "If Servius could reach into my mind, can't you as well? Couldn't you—"

Fingers trembled cold against Felix's face. Loren's voice turned fear-thick. "Felix, I don't—"

"*Couldn't you?*"

"No." Loren wrenched his hand away as though bitten and scooted as far back as the window allowed. Tears wet his cheeks, reddened his eyes. "I don't trust myself not to have an agenda, even if it was protecting you. But I could learn. I would spend the rest of my life studying how. I'd meet with every augur, every priest, in every city until I could do it without hurting you. If that's what you ask of me, I will."

Felix rocked back from his knees to his heels and took a steadying breath. Grief, pain, anger swirled in a concoction bitter as poppy sap in his belly. Too much to handle. When he stood, his stomach lurched. "I won't ask that. I don't want you knowing how to do that to me. But can I not be angry? With the helmet's magic burned up, I might never know, not fully. My power might never be mine."

"You never wanted power," Loren whispered. "You said so."

"It's never been an option. Everyone—my father, Servius, *you*—made sure of that." Felix cast Loren one last, tracing look, committing him to memory. "Should have been my choice."

He left before his resolve could break.

Caesar—the poor horse Felix had inexplicably included in his radius of protection in Pompeii, who he then felt obligated to name with the highest title of all—lifted her head when he burst into the stables. Three days' recovery wasn't long enough for the hell he'd put her through, but Felix swallowed his guilt as he saddled her and swung onto her back. At least she didn't seem to mind. She tossed her brushed mane as he brought her to a trot on the paved lane leading away from the estate, then worked her to a gallop on the main road, startling a burst of starlings from their autumn branches.

It should have felt good, the breeze, the sun, the flex of Caesar's muscles. The freedom.

But Felix couldn't breathe out here, either. Black closed around his vision, throwing him back to the swallow of the pitch-dark wave. That was what he kept returning to. Over and over, a waking nightmare: He never intended to survive.

He didn't mean that in some grand, self-sacrificing way. Heroism wasn't his style. It was more—it'd be easier. Cleaner, if Felix never left Pompeii. If the truth died with him.

But the world moved in messy arcs, and he'd startled awake, still in his body, clutching fragments of the only power he'd ever known. Mercury had saved both, when Felix only meant for him to save one. There was an implication there, but he still didn't have the head—or heart—to interrogate it.

So he'd done the only thing his stunned bones knew. Move. Same as he did now. Anything to escape being forced to think.

The road from the estate wound around the curve of a shallow valley, then over a rocky hillside. Felix clutched Caesar's reins with numb fingers, ruined fingers, and fought the sting in his eyes. Blame that on the wind. Caesar picked up speed, kicking road dust, but at the crest of the hill, Felix cracked.

Yanking the horse to a stop, he did something he swore he wouldn't do. He looked back.

Back at the sprawling vineyard, acres and acres of it, trellises blushing orange in the sunset. The orchard where he laid the helmet to rest. Felix had buried himself on this estate, too, and now he was leaving behind the only boy who'd brought out the best in him. The boy who saw him, even as he slipped through life unseen.

Felix wondered if Loren was watching his flight, dead-eyed from his bedroom window. He wondered how Loren would grieve him. If the grief would fade like a bruise over time, or ache for the rest of his life, a bone fracture healed wrong.

He touched the contract in his pocket. He could take on Julia Fortunata's family name, have a house, a life, a future in Rome. Forget Loren. But that was the catch to letting someone past your walls. Once they were part of your home, their absence echoed.

Felix was sick to death of letting ghosts decide his fate.

The next time he ran, it would be toward something. Not away.

"Damn it all," he muttered.

He turned the horse around.

CHAPTER XXX
LOREN

When Loren slept, his dreams were empty.
He preferred the nightmares.

He began stretching his waking hours, first to midnight, and when that offered little respite, beyond. He paced. Up the halls of the estate, long after servants turned in. Through the orchard, past the helmet's grave. Down the straight, narrow rows of the vineyard. Fatigue tugged him, his ankle begged for rest, but exhaustion and pain were temporary troubles. He endured both.

Only when Felix caught him did Loren allow himself to be coaxed to bed. Felix rarely said a word, even as the routine wore him down, strain apparent in tired eyes and tight shoulders. Another source of guilt. Felix had come back. Chosen Loren as he'd wanted him to. Loren should feel lucky when Felix sat at the foot of his bed, waiting for him to drift off. So lucky. But it was hard to feel anything when he barely felt alive.

He slept. And woke again in his dreams. Gone were blood and daggers, billowing smoke and ragged whispers, as if those, too, were left cinders in the rubble. Instead Loren faced endless nights in an empty temple, its worshippers long since fled. No statue to mark its devotion. Frescoes stripped from the walls. Loren wandered and wandered but never found an exit. Sometimes he heard footsteps, but they flitted away when he sought the source.

He knew the source. He recognized the pattern of stealth and sandal as the same steps that followed him during his waking hours, watching him close.

But Ghost-Felix had nothing more to say, and Loren, despite his efforts, dreamed alone.

If his dreams were empty, they balanced out the way he burst when awake. Rot flooded him to the brim, a constant sickness of festering numbness that little could stir him from. Days slipped and spilled into each other. The moon came and went. Loren didn't care. He stopped tracking.

"You did so much damage to this leg," announced the family physician one morning, "you should thank Apollo we do not need to amputate."

He sounded disappointed that amputation was not, in fact, on the table. Loren felt his eyes glaze over as the man launched into a lecture about the necessity of letting bones come together at their leisure, and not disturbing the process.

"Lorenus gets plenty of rest," his mother, Hemetra, cut in. Loren had nearly forgotten she was in his bedroom, too, so silent by the door. "Convincing him to attend to his responsibilities is Sisyphean. The last thing he needs is more incentive to laze about."

He knew her well enough to pick out an attempt at teasing, but it only stretched the edges of old wounds, same as the physician poking the stitches on Loren's thigh.

The physician's face pinched. "These fresh scratches on his legs suggest otherwise. What did you do, boy, lose a fight with a thornbush?"

Loren bit his tongue. If his mother didn't yet know of his night-time excursions, it wouldn't do to incite a scolding now. The physician wrapped his tools, still shaking his head, and hobbled out, leaving Loren alone with his mother. He studied her, trying to spot the woman who raised him beneath her brittle exterior. She'd aged, certainly, but hadn't they all? Her hair, once the same dark brown as his, now sported gray streaks. New lines creased her lips, held pursed as she perched on the edge of his bed.

When Loren was a child, he thought her aloof as an olive tree, strong-boughed and stern against storms howling from the sea. Something sturdy to cling to, but not made for comfort. Now he wondered what, precisely, she'd been protecting. If it had ever been him at all.

"Has it really been four years? The number of times your father wanted to bring you home, why, I stopped him, of course. I knew you would come around once you worked it from your system." She smoothed his choppy hair back from his face. "This is getting long. Won't you let me cut it?"

Loren reached for his braid and clutched air. "I'd rather not."

"We'll discuss it as a family later," she said, like it was the *family* hair.

Irritation prickled Loren's nerves, their constant state these days. He was tired of being on edge. He was tired of feeling seconds from boiling over. He fiddled with a hole in his sleeping tunic until she batted his fingers away with a sigh.

"I can't help but feel distance between us," she said. "What changed? You were contrary as a child, but now you're obstinate."

Laughter rose, but the kind closer to crying. He wanted to howl at her that if she wanted an answer, she should reflect on each time she'd sided with his father over him, each dismissal of his fears as madness. There she might uncover what dug the chasm.

He couldn't muster the energy. "Father found his success through being headstrong, so you taught me to act the same. Now you punish me for it."

"When have I ever punished you?" From anyone else, it would have been a snap, but proper ladies didn't snap. "The one lesson that clearly didn't stick was humility. Perhaps I indulged you too much. Paints, instruments, tutors, scrolls."

"Don't grow sentimental on me now, Mamma."

She glanced at her lap. "You haven't called me that since you were young."

"Father told me it wasn't proper to use diminutives once I outgrew boyhood."

"Well, I suppose he's right." His mother looked at Loren straight on, and for a moment, he saw her as she'd been before Lucius Lassius stomped the laughter from them both. Their same brown eyes, same pinch of their identical mouth. "I'll leave you to rest."

She smoothed the rumpled bedding that proved she'd been there at all, but at the door, she lingered. "Your friend. How long does he expect to stay?"

Loren tensed. "Is his presence a problem?"

As far as he knew, Felix was a model guest. Sparse, nonintrusive, practiced at staying out of sight. If Felix wasn't trailing Loren around the estate, he spent hours in the orchard on his own. Or he tucked himself away here, while Loren curled at the window seat. Sometimes Felix brought a scroll stolen from Lassius's collection, asked Loren to read it aloud. Mostly they sat in silence.

"He spends an awful lot of time with you," said his mother.

"He's my friend."

"Careful with your tone, Lorenus." She regarded him coolly. "I'm considering your best interests, and you know better than to dwell on a fantasy. Whoever this boy is, put him from your mind. This is your life. This is your family. Resentment will do you no favors, believe me."

Sharp footsteps retreated down the hall.

☙

Grapes undergo an interesting change when turned to wine, a point where rot morphs into fermentation, and later, a prized drink. Loren felt the rot within him, chest packed with sickly-sweet pulp. He felt bubbling fermentation, stretching his patience and splitting his seams. But he was a spoiled batch. When merchants would crack him open in years to come, they'd find a jug gone off. Pour him into the latrine.

Wasteful.

Lucius Lassius strode in without warning after lunch, bread and figs Loren had listlessly picked over. In his haste to scramble off his bed, he nearly snapped his other ankle. But his father didn't spare a glance, crossing instead to gaze out at the vineyard. His favorite hobby, staring at what he owned.

"Still in bed?" Lassius said, clipped as ever. "All this land to call your own, and you waste away in here. In our last conversation before you ran off, you called my home a cage, but have you considered you imprison yourself?"

"My leg hurts," Loren said.

Lassius tsk-ed. "As does my back, but there is work to be done More still with the destruction of our northern vineyards to sort out."

Silence. That was all Loren could muster. His father, with his status and investments, had known about Pompeii's ruination even before Felix dragged Loren home. Had Lassius spared a thought for his son living in Vesuvius's shadow? Had he grieved, organized a search party, considered a body-less funeral?

Lassius faced him, arms clasped behind his back. "We have much to discuss. I need an estimate on your recovery. Gaius Lucretius wants this over with as soon as possible."

"Sorry," Loren said slowly. "Who?"

"Did your mother not tell you? The engagement."

The world tilted sideways. He gripped the headboard to stay upright. "Engagement?"

"Surely this isn't a surprise." Lassius met Loren's horror with a measured stare. "You will be seventeen soon, long past the age I was when I married your mother. The contract is drawn. Gaius Lucretius's daughter is suitable."

It was too much. Fury swelled. He tried to hold it back, but he blurted, "Suitable? A girl I've never met and would have no interest in, besides? Then what? Have a baby, name him Lucius Lassius, and carry on the family tradition of misery?"

"Finding a match for you was difficult enough. Do not sink our family name lower."

Loren breathed heavily. His father's eyes tracked his every move, searching for an opening to strike. When Loren finally spoke, he gritted his teeth to keep his voice steady. "I'm sorry to be an inconvenience. I thought many men would be eager to marry a daughter into your family."

"They should. If you stayed here rather than gallivanting off, they would. The physician suspects you'll walk with a limp the remainder of your life. As it is, you struggle to keep up mentally, not to mention your fits. The next time someone outsmarts you, how will you run away with a mangled leg?"

Under Loren's splint, his ankle throbbed. "Felix keeps pace with me. Wherever we go."

"Where will you turn when he tires of you?"

Humiliation crept up Loren's spine. "Contrary to what you and Mother think, I'm not entirely unlovable."

"You will like Lucretia, if only because she won't challenge you when you demand your way."

"Did her father stamp that out of her, too?" Loren snapped. "Void the contract. I will be your heir and remain here, but I will do so unmarried. That is my condition."

"You're in no position to negotiate."

"See what happens if you decline." He settled in the glare he learned from Lassius himself. "You'll find I can negotiate my own fate just fine."

A beat of thick, sticky silence passed. Lucius Lassius said, "It's high time you start going by your true name. I'll hear nothing more of this *Loren* nonsense."

After his father swept from the room, Loren lay on the floor, staring again at his painted ceiling. He wouldn't cry; that demanded energy he couldn't summon. The fight drained from him as quick as it came. It didn't matter if he married or not. He would still be stuck here. He had no other options, and fleeing the first time had caused all the grief that followed. All his ambitions, politics and priesthood and a love he felt true about, were a dead bird before him.

Somehow, he understood the plight of Elias in a way he hadn't before. Elias had wanted freedom, and to leave nothing behind when he got it, so he could build a life with intention. On his terms. Loren thought of the ache living in his eyes, and their last conversation, and how without a proper burial and an escort to the world of the dead, Elias would never leave Pompeii now.

Slanted light shifted across tile as time dragged on. Pinned under ceiling stars felt safe, like something he could control. His parents could plot away his future. The sky could break and shatter around him. Beneath the weight of familiar paint, Loren almost imagined he was small again.

What he wouldn't give to dream of something besides a vacant temple. To not see white ash behind his lids while awake. To breathe and know he deserved it.

Footsteps drew near the door, quiet padding.

"Comfortable?" Felix asked.

His shadow split the shuttered light, falling over Loren like a blanket. "Plato the philosopher had an allegory about people in a cave, watching shadow figures move across the wall, and letting that be their life instead of—"

Loren cut off with a sigh, pressing the heels of his hands into his eyes. Staring at his ceiling of childhood stars was not Plato's allegory in the same way he wasn't Icarus flying too close to the sun. He was Loren, and he was responsible for himself.

Weight dropped beside him, Felix stretching out on the tile. Their arms brushed, and Loren swallowed, the simple touch so nothing, so everything.

"I've heard that story before, but it never made sense to me. A cave isn't a cage. The people could have left." Felix tilted his head, staring. "Loren, you could leave."

"I don't think I can," Loren whispered. "Leaving was what got me into this mess."

"So what's the alternative? Staying here? You look horrible."

"Way to make a boy feel wanted in his own bedroom."

"That's not—I brought you here because you needed time to rest your body. But what about this?" Felix tapped Loren's forehead, then frowned at his scarred fingers. "I miss when that felt like anything. I asked the physician who wanders around, and he said the damage to my hands is likely permanent. Seemed happy to break the news."

Loren could imagine. "He was dismayed I wouldn't need an amputation."

"Numbness isn't all bad, I suppose. Bet it'll feel like someone else's hand when I—"

"Still vile as ever."

Snorting, Felix rolled onto his stomach, and the effect that had on Loren was impossible. Too big to understand, too fast to escape. Tears burned his eyes, and he blinked rapidly. "I miss you."

Felix smiled sadly. "I see you daily."

"Do you? Do we see each other at all?" He hadn't meant to say it, but the words spilled out. "I'm not myself anymore, and I wonder how much of the old me you knew to begin with."

"But I see you now," Felix said. "When you read to me. When we sit together, and you give me space. Sometimes I'm angry still. But I found that being apart aches from a deeper place."

"People aren't meant to die and return. You brought back a ghost."

"Then that makes us even," Felix said. "Neither of us is whole. So what? I'm not lacking for it, and I don't regret what I did. Damn the rules."

Loren took him all in, his tired eyes and rumpled clothes. His ruined hands and scarred body. Felix was still there, despite the pain Loren inflicted on him, over and over, starting the moment they met. Before that, even, when Loren left the ghost hanging cold in his visions.

"I don't deserve you," Loren said in a ragged gasp. "I failed. All I ever wanted was to help, but I've dreamed of you for years, and I knew—I saw when we were on the mountain that it was Vesuvius all along. The ghost told me how to stop it, and I was too selfish to listen."

"No. No." Felix pushed to his elbows. "It wasn't your fault. Stopping it was never in my power. Nor yours."

Loren was splintering, drawing air into lungs marred by a thousand hairline fractures, a vase about to shatter. "My dreams stopped, Felix. You should have left me to die in the city. What use am I if the only thing that set me apart meant nothing in the end?"

Shock flitted across Felix's face, followed by fury. "Don't say that. Never say that. I'll tell you the alternative. You survive and heal and stop blaming yourself for what you didn't understand."

"It isn't that easy."

"You think I don't know? I watched my father die and did nothing because sometimes there's nothing you can do except run. It's awful.

But it doesn't make you a coward. It means you're too strong to let yourself be torn apart. You keep moving."

A dam burst in Loren's chest, and the sea of grief drowning him spilled out at once. He cried, body-shaking sobs. Wordlessly, Felix flopped onto his back again and leaned his head on Loren's shoulder, that point of contact a lifeline.

Felix was solid and present and there, fixed as the moon, but far, far more reachable.

"How can you still want me," Loren choked, dragging an arm across his wet cheeks, "after everything I've done?"

A scarred hand worked between the gap of their bodies, caught Loren's fingers.

Felix looked over, gray eyes sparkling. "I like a challenge."

CHAPTER XXXI

FELIX

One afternoon in the orchard, Felix sensed a call in the rustling leaves of a changing season.

Time to go.

Not that he needed the trees to tell him. This was the longest he'd stayed in one place since escaping Rome all those years ago, and he'd worn his welcome thin. He was more resilient than most, but there were only so many sidelong glances from Lucius Lassius anyone could endure before taking the hint.

The afternoon was mellow for late autumn, the bare hint of a breeze whistling through the foliage overhanging the stone bench Felix sat on. Pomegranate juice dribbled down his wrist and splattered in the dirt.

"If you splash that on my parchment," Loren warned from beside him, "my father will have a stroke."

"All the more reason for me not to touch it," Felix said.

"These are meant to be your lessons."

A scroll lay unfurled between them, Loren's cane serving as a paperweight. Narrow sunlight tinted his chin-length hair bronze, and he wore a leather band across his crown to tame flyaways. Dressed in a wine-colored tunic that drew out the warm tones of his skin, Loren looked healthy. Proper. Patrician. So different from the wraith in a white sleeping shirt Felix had spent many nights trailing through the vineyard.

He didn't realize he was staring until he squeezed the pomegranate too hard and red seeds burst across his numb fingers. Droplets sprayed.

"Felix!" Loren glared, but not for long. His lips twitched and then he snorted, and Felix snorted, and they devolved into giggles.

"Sorry," Felix said, not feeling sorry at all. He gave up on the pomegranate, tossed it aside, and wiped clean his pocketknife.

The laughter died in Loren's mouth. His eyes had snagged on the knife.

"I think about him," he said unexpectedly. "The ghost I met in my dreams. The one who . . ."

"Remembered," finished Felix.

"I haven't seen him since." Loren ducked his head, and the day frosted over. "I have more to say to him. Apologies. Questions. I walk laps around an empty temple for hours, searching in vain. I wonder if he found closure, now that you recall some of what happened, but that seems naive to hope."

Felix frowned, unsure how to carry on. They'd grown back together in a quiet way, stealing bits of time, frail and fleeting as a petal. But this they hardly addressed. Loren's guilt split them in an ugly gash, divided down the middle with no bridge Felix could find to cross.

Loren wasn't the same boy Felix had met in Pompeii. Unlike Felix, Loren had no frame of reference for this type of loss, no experience to work from. Small noises startled him. Smiles were rare, laughter rarer still. Most days, Felix didn't know if his being near Loren hurt or helped. Because for all the good spending time together did, Loren's irritability tolerance was near-nonexistent. He'd snap, then withdraw, and Felix could do little else besides sit with him until the episode passed.

Good thing Felix now had fresh practice sitting still.

He put the knife away. "If I ask you a question, will you answer honestly?"

Familiar words from that first night at the brothel.

Loren's mouth pinched. "Go on."

"I never understood fully—why me? Your visions, that is. Why us?"

"I don't know. Surely there's no simple answer, but . . . I have a theory."

"Of course you do." Felix hovered a hand over the cane until Loren nodded permission for him to move it aside. Then he lay back, rumpling the parchment, and pillowed his head on Loren's thigh. "Tell me."

Hesitant fingers began to card through his hair. Felix's eyes drifted shut.

"In Greece, they say we're born with our soul split," Loren began, uncertain. "With half placed in someone else. Life's point, then, is to make oneself whole again. I don't know that I agree. Each time I try to make sense of something through myth, I only worsen it. Besides, I think we're born complete on our own. But hearts are built to resonate, and it's a matter of finding one who beats in tune with yours. By coincidence, the ghost found my mind open."

"Since when do you believe in coincidence?"

"Since you started believing in anything. We're proof people change." Whatever wry smile had built on his face faded. "You have godly blood, Felix. You were always meant to be a hero, and whatever curse or blessing granted me my visions tied a string between us. I was to guide you. But no one could have predicted what Mercury's priest did, nor the lengths your father would go to. The version of you in my nightmares was angry. Hurt and alone. And I misunderstood what he needed."

The hand buried in Felix's curls stilled. Cool distance washed over Loren again.

"I don't blame you," Felix said. "You didn't know what the dreams meant. You thought you were protecting me. What could you have done?"

"I could have listened."

"You do. You make your touch a question. And if my answer was no, I trust you would hear me."

Loren paused, a stillness that dragged until Felix cracked his lids open again. Above him, cast against a sky of pale blue, Loren pinned him with his softest look yet. Despite the sweetness of pomegranate lingering on his tongue, Felix's mouth dried. He caught Loren's fingers and pressed his lips to his palm.

"Read to me." Felix tilted his head, kissed the pad of his thumb. "My turn to listen. I like the way you speak."

For another long moment, he wondered if he'd finally broken Loren, the way he fell so silent. Finally, Loren cleared his throat. "Latin or Greek?'

"What?"

Pink washed over Loren's cheeks as he fumbled for his tube of scrolls. "*The Iliad.* I brought pages of each. The translation by Italicus is far inferior to the original, even if the language is easier to digest, but my Greek is rusty, so—"

"Loren? Just read."

"Right." Parchment shuffled. Loren cleared his throat a second time. His fingers returned to Felix's hair. Quietly, he began, *"Sing, O Goddess, the anger of Achilles . . ."*

Felix leaned into it, the touch and sound and smell of this boy. Clouds drifted overhead, and dappled shadows played in the breeze—warm, but with the promise of cooler days to come. Apricots and pomegranates hung swollen ripe. Somewhere, a honeybee made its rounds.

And Felix sat with Loren. And that was all.

"Your arrogance baffles me," Lucius Lassius said before dawn the next morning, the household still hushed. He'd intercepted Felix in the courtyard as he crossed to Loren's wing of the estate. "To masquerade as a dead man's son is obscene, particularly where Julius Fortunatus was my dear friend."

"Some friend," said Felix coolly. "You were surprised to hear of his passing."

"*Felix Fortunatus*. 'Lucky Fortune.' That alone should have tipped me off, but I extended you the benefit of the doubt and let you stay while I waited to have records delivered. Tell me, Felix, how you respected my generosity. Or shall I tell you? By creeping into my son's bedroom night after night?"

"He's teaching me to read."

Lassius jabbed a finger in Felix's face, but no spike of fear accompanied it. "Don't take me for a fool, boy. Lorenus might be simple enough to take advantage of, but I'm not so easily swayed. Do you think yourself worth even a scrap of his attention?"

"I didn't realize you thought so highly of him."

"He's a Lassius. It matters not how I regard him, but how the world sees him. There is nothing you can offer him." Lassius's mouth curled. "Because you have nothing. You are nothing."

If only Lassius knew, but Felix thought of Servius's hand twisted sharp in his hair. *Never let the man holding the chips know what you care about.* Lassius was the same sort as Servius: men only dangerous if you let them open their mouth, let them twist your words into a weapon. The worst blow Felix could deal was to say nothing at all.

He sidestepped, adjusting his packed bag on his shoulder, relishing the way Lassius's jaw clenched, and carried on. Lassius might hold the chips, but Felix still had dice left to throw.

He started by saying goodbye.

Felix was practiced in leaving. Slipping by nightfall from a town he'd never see again. Parting ways with someone he knew only long enough to dip a hand into their pocket. Leaving behind identities, memories, possibilities. Staying in the moment, history discarded, future disregarded. Running to live another day.

For the first time in his life, Felix had something to run toward. The idea of it set his nerves on fire. Went against everything he'd learned.

He couldn't wait to break his own rules.

Loren's bedroom was empty, curtains trailing wispy in the night breeze from open shutters, but Felix had a hunch when he spotted the glow of a lantern cutting through the dark outside. He slipped through the servants' exit and followed the light to the stables. The grassy, musty smell of horses met him, animals stirring from their slumber, but Felix had eyes only for the stall at the end. Caesar gave a soft whinny at his approach.

Loren didn't look over. His cane leaned against the wall, and he smoothed a boar-bristle brush down Caesar's flank in methodic strokes.

"Caesar is a silly name," he said, voice strained. "She's a mare, and I doubt the emperor would be impressed."

"She's a horse," Felix corrected, "and if Titus wants a word, he'll have a chance soon enough."

Loren fiddled with the saddle strap. "I should ask where you plan to go from here, but with the dream I keep having, I think I can guess."

"Mercury's temple," Felix said. "I want to know the truth."

"And you don't want—" With a shaky breath, Loren screwed his eyes tight. "No. I told myself I wouldn't say that. I knew this was coming, I've known all along. My duty is to stay here, and I can't hold you back."

"Loren," Felix said, and when Loren looked over at last, Felix cupped his face and closed the gap.

Kissing Loren was like coming home. No—creating home. Loren's lips were salty, and had Felix not lost sensation in his palms, he would feel that Loren's cheeks were damp. Hot. He clung to the memory of the last time he'd felt Loren's skin, back in the grove. Not the same as touching him now, but better than enough. Felix poured everything he had learned of love into the press of mouths, the exchange of breath: He wanted Loren, wanted him still.

Loren's breathing hitched, and he pushed hard into Felix, desperate, begging, their noses knocking. When he pulled back, he looked brittle as a fallen leaf.

"I'm going to Rome," Felix murmured, "because I know what I'm running to. When you figure out the same for you, meet me there."

He moved Loren's hand to rest on Caesar's saddlebag and hoped—prayed—he'd understand. Not goodbye forever. Just for now.

The sun hadn't yet risen when Felix turned by foot onto the main road, but the streak of red on the horizon announced it wouldn't stay dark long. Stolen wine clanked in the satchel he had nabbed from Loren's wardrobe—an old trick, but one that'd fetch enough profit for passage on a merchant's wagon headed north. This all felt full circle in a way Felix hadn't anticipated. He thought this chapter of his life had begun in the Temple of Apollo, when the helmet snared his attention, but perhaps it had truly started the night he first stole from Lucius Lassius.

By degrees, the sky brightened, shades shifting from red and navy to a hazy pink and lavender dawn. Felix took the path that circled broad around the valley before snaking into the mountains. Gradually, the flat road switched to an incline, and he kept his pace slow.

Savoring.

A clatter of hooves disrupted the still morning.

"Wait!"

Felix turned, heart stuttering with hope he hadn't dared allow. Caesar charged toward him up the hill, kicking up a cloud, her rider's glare furious and beautiful. She skidded, slowed, then clomped in a circle until still.

"I made a mistake," Loren called, swinging from the saddle as gracefully as his plastered ankle allowed. His face was streaky, eyes red but bright. "As a boy, I was fixated on finding an Achilles, a man I'd follow to the ends of the earth, into death. But I was wrong. You're no Achilles, Felix."

A shocked laugh escaped Felix's chest. "Did you run after me just for an insult?"

Loren's chest heaved. "Achilles wouldn't sneak off, leaving only a chance clue behind."

In his hand, he clutched the contract, and Felix's delight grew. "Whether you found it today or months from now, I knew eventually you would. And you'd know. All Julia's properties still belong to you, but I needed you to make the choice to leave on your own."

But Loren wasn't smiling. His glare deepened, and finally it dawned on Felix that perhaps he'd erred. That he'd only managed to stir fresh guilt. His first "easy" gesture gone very, very wrong.

"I thought I dropped this during our escape. Celsi gave it to me." Loren shook the pages. "In the courtyard. I didn't realize what it was. What he tried to do, even after I treated him so poorly. He resented me from the moment I took his position in the temple. But I resented him, too, for being what I wasn't."

"Celsi was a child," Felix said, choosing his words carefully, "but so were you when you met. Servius hurt him, same as he hurt you."

"And you." He wiped his nose with the arm of his tunic. "So you found the contract, then hid it in the saddlebag. Why not keep it for yourself? Without Julia around to say otherwise, her property could have been yours."

"I might not have much to offer you, but I wouldn't leave you with nothing. A contract and a horse to get you there when you were ready. When you knew what you wanted." *When you chose me back,* Felix didn't say.

Loren sobered further, gaze dropping as his anger drained. He bundled the papers back together before returning them to the saddlebag. Then he slipped free his cane from a loop of Caesar's reins,

VESUVIUS

beside which a familiar sheathed sword hung. Time passed before he gathered words to say, so different from his old style of blurting whatever crossed his mind.

"You're no Achilles, but neither am I," Loren said at last. "It seems so silly, but I used to picture being a hero like that. Glory in battle, fighting for honor, all of it. Now I can only imagine the stink of death and ash."

"There's a reason heroes die young. The grief never leaves. They bow out early to avoid what they can." Felix studied him. "Maybe you could try being just Loren."

"Just Loren." He rolled the words, testing their weight on his tongue. He smiled. Small, but genuine. Small, but hopeful. "I think I'd like that, Just Felix."

Felix may well have swallowed the sun, the way his chest warmed. He could practice easy gestures later. For now, he had his most complicated heist yet to carry out.

"Convenient that you're headed to Rome," Loren continued. "If I'm ever to break into politics as Loren Fortunatus, it won't be done stuck in my father's vineyard. You can go with me."

Felix laughed. "Shouldn't it be the other way around?"

"I'm not following you." Loren grabbed the reins and guided Caesar onto the road, but paused, glancing back. "I told you, I made a mistake trying to find an Achilles. But, for what it's worth, I'd rather walk *with* you."

Felix's mouth tugged into a smile, even as Loren took off, cane in one hand, extending his other back for Felix to take. Dust swirled around Loren's ankles, reflecting in the golden streak of light spilling over the horizon.

Until, at last, it settled.

And Felix did what he'd always done, what his bones and blood ached for. He oriented himself to the rising sun, and just—started moving.

ACKNOWLEDGMENTS

Vesuvius was born from a lifelong special interest in historical disasters and the stories we tell about them. It's only fitting I first thank my parents for indulging my earliest hyperfixation and showing me *Titanic* (1997)—drawing scene and all—at the formative age of five years old. More than that, thank you for never restricting my reading. Queer books have always been my lifeline; I hope this one can offer a sliver of comfort to even a single reader out there.

Felix's story came from a place of hurt, but with the care and love of the hands this book has passed through, it transformed into one of healing. Annalise Errico, my agent, believed in it (and me) when it was still a mess in the query trenches. Everything I write with her on my side helps me understand myself better. Zoie Janelle Konneker, my beloved editor (and cat encyclopedia), guided me to a version of this book I never thought I'd reach. She challenged me in all the ways I needed to grow—not just as a writer, but as a person. To her and the entire Peachtree Teen team, thank you for giving Felix and Loren a home.

Across the ocean, my UK editor Tig Wallace's insight and vision offered the push I needed to let the heart of the story beat stronger. To him and the Atom Books/Little, Brown UK team, thank you for helping me get this story to readers around the world.

My cover artist, Chris Sack (they are holding hands <3), and cover designer, Lily Steele, brought the world of *Vesuvius* to life at a level I never could have predicted. I'm forever in awe at the sheer talent I'm blessed to be surrounded by. Thank you also to Niko Espera for the stunning preorder piece of my ghost boy. And I'm so lucky to have such a beautiful international cover, too—artist Devin Elle Kurtz and designer Ella captured the atmosphere perfectly.

Is it really an acknowledgments section without a little sap? Kae— we met through cosplay, but your kindness, creativity, and passion made you family. When I came to you with my weird idea to write a weird gay Pompeii book inspired by a Sufjan Stevens song, you said go for it, and I wouldn't be here without you. Antonia—you made me believe in fate from our first meeting in Fferm Penglais. Even with an ocean separating us, you'll always be my land. You're the truest person I know. Declan—you were a surprise, but I'm thankful for it.

To every early reader, beta, and friend: Your influence, time, and friendship is stitched into the seams of this book. To my street team especially, thank you for rising to help me get Felix and Loren out there.

To Alicia Armeli, my colleague, creative partner, and friend— thank you for your mentorship over the years. Your work ethic and passion shines through in everything you do. I'm so grateful to work with you.

To Zeba Shahnaz, my mentor from Author Mentor Match, I can never thank you enough for your honesty. To the rest of my AMM Round 9 family, I'm grateful for the community we formed, and I'm honored to be in such company.

To my professors at SLCC, Weber State University, and Aberystwyth University—notably Christy Call, Ryan Ridge, Anoush Simon, and Elisa Stone—thank you for the opportunities you've provided to help me succeed. I wouldn't be the writer I am without your encouragement.

To the online communities I'm part of—I'm looking at you, capritwt, writingtwt, and Sufjan Stevens Feelsposting—thank you for cheering me on (or offering a distraction when I needed it).

I owe many hours and many words to the lovely folks at Salt Lake Coffee Break and Bottle & Barrel in Aberystwyth. And to Orion, Raelle, and the team at The Legendarium, I'll never be able to thank you enough for the sincerity, hope, and community you've offered.

To Edith, my niece: Yes, we can dance and lie in the grass together. I hope you never stop asking that.

To my dogs, past and present: I look to the stars, and there you are.

Finally—and most vitally—to Michelle Smith, who told me as a lonely, hopeless sixteen-year-old with feelings and dreams too big to hold to "be my best"—I'm trying. Every day.

RESOURCES

If you or someone you know is in need of support,
resources are available to help.

The Trevor Project
thetrevorproject.org
1-866-488-7386

RAINN National Sexual Assault Hotline
online.rainn.org
1-800-656-4673

National Sexual Violence Resource Center
nsvrc.org/survivors

National Safe Place, TXT 4 HELP
nationalsafeplace.org/txt-4-help

These resources are provided for
informational purposes only.

ABOUT THE AUTHOR

CASS BIEHN (they/them) writes messy queer characters in messier situations—and always with angsty kissing. They hold a Master of Library Science from Aberystwyth University in rainy Wales, and currently live in the Utah desert, where they split their time between cosplaying and wrangling their dogs. Learn more about them at CassBiehn.com or @CassBeeWrites on Instagram, X, and Bluesky.